MEDICAL

Pulse-racing passion

Winning Back His Runaway Wife

Louisa George

A Marriage Healed In Hawaii

Becky Wicks

MILLS & BOON

WINNING BACK HIS RUNAWAY WIFE
© 2024 by Louisa George
Philippine Copyright 2024
Australian Copyright 2024
New Zealand Copyright 2024
First Published 2024
First Australian Paperback Edition 2024
ISBN 978 1 038 91038 7

A MARRIAGE HEALED IN HAWAII
© 2024 by Becky Wicks
Philippine Copyright 2024
Australian Copyright 2024
New Zealand Copyright 2024
First Published 2024
First Australian Paperback Edition 2024
ISBN 978 1 038 91038 7

Published by
Harlequin Mills & Boon
An imprint of Harlequin Enterprises (Australia) Pty Limited
(ABN 47 001 180 918), a subsidiary of HarperCollins Publishers Australia Pty Limited
(ABN 36 009 913 517)
Level 19, 201 Elizabeth Street
SYDNEY NSW 2000 AUSTRALIA

Printed and bound in Australia by McPherson's Printing Group

Winning Back His Runaway Wife

Louisa George

MILLS & BOON

Award-winning author **Louisa George** has been an avid reader her whole life. In between chapters, she's managed to train as a nurse, marry her doctor hero and have two sons. Now she writes chapters of her own in the medical romance, contemporary romance and women's fiction genres. Louisa's books have variously been nominated for the coveted RITA® Award and the New Zealand Koru Award and have been translated into twelve languages. She lives in Auckland, New Zealand.

Visit the Author Profile page
at millsandboon.com.au for more titles.

Dear Reader,

I do love a reunion story. What's better than to watch the love and attraction our couple originally had grow and develop...but not without some stumbling blocks along the way! (Oh, the evil mind of a romance writer!)

When Lewis and Charlotte's marriage tragically broke up five years ago, neither of them could see a way through the sadness of it all or ever imagine being in another relationship again. But when an accident brings them together, they are forced to confront all the reasons for their breakup and are shocked to find themselves unable to deny their sizzling attraction.

But are the embers of their love enough for them to try again? Well, that depends on trust, and when one person has already walked away once, what are the chances they might do it again? Oh, poor Charlie and Lewis. I loved writing their Auckland-set story and seeing them fight hard against their attraction and then learn to fight for themselves and each other.

I hope you enjoy *Winning Back His Runaway Wife*. Thank you for taking a chance on one of my books. Catch up with my news at www.louisageorge.com.

Happy reading!

Louisa xxx

DEDICATION

To Flo Nicoll, the best editor any writer could ask for. Thank you for taking a chance on me and for encouraging and supporting my writing dreams. And to the Harlequin Medical Romance team, thank you so much for bringing me into your family and making my writing dreams come true!

CHAPTER ONE

FIVE YEARS AGO Charlotte Rose would have cherished this moment.

This...exact...moment: clipping the most adorable, smiling baby into her car seat after a night of nine hours' sleep—nine whole hours! And she was only six months old. Baby Stella was a veritable miracle of cuteness overload. Climbing into the driver's seat and heading across the city she loved to a job she adored: part-time emergency doctor at busy Auckland Central hospital. And enjoying the whole Auckland summer vibe of sunshine, sparkling waterfront views and, today, surprisingly little traffic.

Five years ago, Charlotte would have thought this scenario would make her life utterly complete: a baby; the perfect job with hours to suit; being back in her beloved hometown. But here she was, wishing everything could be different.

From the back seat baby Stella made a little hiccupping noise. Charlotte's heart jolted, knowing that specific sound was a precursor to... Oh, yes: here it came, loud and heart-wrenching, not just a cry but a full-on bawl.

Smiling, Charlotte glanced in her mirror and cooed, 'Stella, Stella, sweetie. Please don't cry. Hush. Hush.'

The baby had been fed, nappy-changed and had a toy to play with for the short drive. Maybe she'd dropped it. Ah, well, it would have to wait.

Charlotte switched the talkback radio station to something with upbeat music, hoping that would soothe her precious cargo. Sure enough, Stella blinked, mouth open. A pause…? A reprieve…? Yes…? Yes…?

Then she inhaled deeply and started with that heart-breaking sound again.

No.

'Stella, darling. Please don't cry. It's all going to be okay.'

Please let it all be okay.

Charlotte sighed, wondering whether she should pull over, find the dropped toy and give Stella a quick cuddle because, yes, she was a softie who would rather cradle a baby than let it cry. And why not? Babies didn't understand timetables and deadlines. Didn't know about having to go to work. One quick smooch wouldn't hurt. Maybe Stella needed a drink or a snack.

She spied a good parking spot across the other side of the traffic lights. She cooed some more as they sat idling at the front of the car line, waiting at the intersection until the lights turned green. Then she headed across…

A shadow whooshed across her line of vision. Her neck and upper body jerked as she felt an impact, as if she were a rag doll being shaken. Then her car was shunted from the side, across the road, out of control.

What the hell?

Panic made her hands shake, made her limbs weak and her heart race. She managed to turn her head to work out what the hell was going on. The front of a huge truck was glued to her door. There was a screech of tires. The stench of burning rubber. The crunch of metal on concrete. A looming lamp post.

And a very quiet baby.

CHAPTER TWO

'MATE, MIA'S FRIENDS *loved* you. She said to tell you that any time you fancy coming over again for a break we can organise a double date…'

'Thanks, but no.' Lewis Parry laughed but jumped in to shut his colleague up. Being on holiday for two weeks with Brin and his family on Rāwhiti Island had been amazing. They'd gone fishing, swimming and diving. They'd eaten what they'd caught from the ocean and drunk the local craft beer. 'I had a great holiday and I've come back to work feeling refreshed and relaxed. In my experience, a relationship would put a swift end to that kind of vibe.'

'Just saying…' Brin put up his hands. 'I thought the same, but find the right woman and it all clicks into place.'

Been there. Done that. And it all fell apart.

'I'm thinking you got lucky.' Lewis finished up his electronic notes from their last call out and slipped the tablet into the glove box. Sometimes he wished he worked in wide open spaces rather than the confines of an ambulance with a newly ordained and far too enthusiastic matchmaker as sidekick.

'You have to make your own luck, mate.' Brin grinned. 'Hey, maybe you'll make some luck at the fundraiser on Saturday night. Lots of hospital staff will be there…' He winked and nudged Lewis's arm.

Great. Brin's happily settled so he thinks we all have to be.

The radio crackled.

'Code Red. R Four. MVA. Female driver. Baby passenger. Ponsonby Road and Picton Street intersection.'

Lewis was immediately grateful for the spotlight shifting from his woeful love life to their jobs.

'Ten-two. Unit Four responding. Over,' he radioed back to control. Then he turned to Brin. 'A baby? Damn. Let's get a move on.'

As they approached the accident scene, it was obvious that a truck had ploughed into the side of an old blue sedan which had then been shunted into a lamp post. The car's rear driver's side door had been totalled and the driver's door buckled and dented enough to impede opening. The passenger-side doors rear and front were dented but openable. He assessed the area for safety as he jumped from the van: no evidence of spilt petrol or oil.

The truck driver was sitting on the side of the road, head in hands.

Lewis called out, 'You okay? Do you need help?'

Face pale and wan, the man shook his head. 'Help the others. I'm… I'm okay. My brakes… I kept pressing on them but they didn't…'

'Thanks, man. We'll come back to you and check you over.' The man was walking and talking: he could wait. Lewis turned to Brin. 'I'll check the driver, you check the baby.'

'On it.' Brin nodded and peeled off to the far side of the car.

The driver's window was smashed and Lewis had a partial view of the person in the driving seat as he tried to tug open the distorted door. She had her head turned away, looking into the back seat. Her shoulders were shaking, and she was saying something he couldn't quite hear. Her hair—a beautiful shade of russet red—was tied into a low ponytail.

Red…

Charlie?

A long-forgotten ache slammed into his gut, mingling with memories he'd tried to keep at bay for five years. Memories that flashed through his mind: red hair entwined with flowers and a gossamer veil; red hair splayed on a pillow as they'd made love. A tight ponytail, shoulders shuddering as she'd walked away, suitcase in hand—the last image of her as she'd left him.

No, it couldn't be Charlie. He shook himself. She lived in London. But funny-weird how, even though she lived on the opposite side of the world, he sometimes thought he saw her at the beach, in a crowded street or in a shopping mall.

It was never her.

Focus, man.

Her screams were becoming clearer now. 'The baby! Is the baby okay? *Please.* Please get the baby.'

Definitely not Charlie. There were no babies in her life; there couldn't be. But as she turned to look at him, her blue eyes red-rimmed and imploring, cheeks streaked with running mascara, his gut folded in on itself. It felt as if the world had stopped turning. It was her, with her mesmerising eyes and perfect mouth.

His wife.

Ex-wife.

'Charlie?'

'Lewis?' Her chest caved forward then, and her face crumpled. 'Oh, my God, Lewis, thank God it's you. You've got to help me. Please, get the baby. She's too quiet.'

Damn. Was it her baby? He pushed the spike of hurt away. 'It's okay, Charlie. My colleague's opening the door now. He'll check your baby. What's her name?'

'St… Stella,' Charlie stuttered through gulps of air. 'Is she okay? Please make sure she's okay.'

'It's okay, it's okay, I can hear her fussing,' He lowered his voice and crouched to talk to her. Charlie was his patient now. Their past had nothing to do with this. He needed to be the paramedic, despite his shaking hands. *Damn.* She'd always had this effect on him: taking his breath away, tipping his world sideways. 'She doesn't look hurt at all. The car seat kept her safe. My colleague Brin will look after Stella. I'm here for you. Tell me, where do *you* hurt?'

The front airbag hadn't activated. It was an old car, and probably didn't even have side bags.

'I don't know.' She looked down at her trembling hands and his eyes followed: no wedding ring. There was no ring at all where her platinum bands used to be. 'I think… I'm okay. My chest hurts a little. And my shoulder…it's not bad. Probably from the seatbelt.'

'I bet. You want me to take a look?'

She edged sideways away from him and for a moment he thought she was recoiling at his suggestion, but in fact she was making room in the tight space. 'I think it's just bruised. Yes, look—check.'

Her gaze caught his and for a moment his need to look after her almost overwhelmed him, even after all these years apart. Even after she'd walked away.

He drew his gaze from hers. Just looking at her made his heart sore. He couldn't bear to see her hurting too, and he reached in and moved the soft fabric of her blouse away from her shoulder. Her familiar perfume of rose and sweet citrus hung in the air, spinning him back in time. 'Ouch. Yes, it's red raw. You're going to have a nasty bruise there. Do your ribs hurt?' He quickly moved his hand away and closed down more memories that assaulted his brain.

She blinked up at him and something flickered across her eyes: gratitude? He wasn't sure. She gave him a shoddy attempt at a smile. 'Only if I move.'

'So, stay still. What about your feet? Legs?' He could see bent metal close to her knees but not around her feet. It was a miracle she hadn't been badly hurt.

'They're okay, not hurt. I'm just wedged in by the door. Oh, Lewis, I need to get to work. But I need… I can't leave Stella. I can't take her to nursery. Not now after this.'

Work? She lived here now?

'Oh, no, you don't.' He peered into the car and tried to get a better view of her body so he could assess for any more injuries. 'We need to get you out of this vehicle and checked out at the hospital. You're in shock. You could be hurt and not even realise—whiplash, for example.'

'Hey.' Brin came round to this side of the car, a baby cradled in his arms. 'Someone needs their mama.'

Charlie's face filled with love and panic. 'Is she…?'

Brin grinned. 'She seems fine, love. A little bewildered by all the drama, but absolutely fine. I'll give her a proper check in a minute, but thought you'd want to see her first.'

'Thank God.' Relief flooded Charlie's face as she reached through the cracked window and stroked little Stella's head. 'I'm sorry, baby. I love you. You're okay. You're okay.'

The baby gurgled and giggled, her arms stretched out to be held by her mother. But Charlie smiled through her tears and shook her head. Lewis recognised the brave face she'd spent a good eighteen months out of their four-year marriage trying to put on as she cooed, 'Hey, hey, baby. I'm a bit stuck. I'll hold you when I can get out of here.'

Lewis's gut hollowed out.

Charlie and a baby: all they'd ever wanted.

But how? It didn't matter, right? She'd got the baby she'd so desperately wanted…just with another guy.

He tugged again at the door and breathed out in relief at the sound of a siren. 'Sounds like help is on its way. We'll get you out in no time.'

'The car is wrecked.' She shook her head.

'Thank God it was just the car, right?'

She put her head on the steering wheel. 'Ugh. Lucy's going to kill me.'

'It's Lucy's car?'

'Yes. I haven't had time to find one for me yet.' She slowly sat up and rubbed her shoulder. 'And I don't even know what happened. How the hell am I going to explain this?'

So she hadn't been back long enough to buy herself a car. Why was she back? And why did he care? Why did it matter? They were ancient history. She'd been so unhappy back then she'd fled to the other side of the world without him. What mattered now was that she and her baby were safe and unhurt.

'Truck driver said his brakes failed.'

'Oh. I guess it could have been much worse.' She closed her eyes and swallowed, as if imaging what worse would look like.

'Do you want me to call her—Lucy? Your parents? Call…someone else?' She'd moved on, right? Was Stella's father still in the picture?

'No!' Her eyes flashed pure panic for a brief moment, then she relaxed. 'No, it's fine. I'll call Lucy when I'm done at the hospital.'

'Okay…' He thought about asking her more about some significant other she might need to call, but thought better of it. It wasn't his business.

But she was still looking at him. 'Look, Lewis, I need to explain…'

'Like I said, the truck driver seems to be taking responsibility.' He got the feeling she wasn't referring to the accident, but he didn't want to get into anything deeper here. She had a family now; she'd moved on. Just as he had…*kind of.* Sure, he'd thought he had, but the ache at seeing her again had blindsided him. 'Honestly. We just need to get you safe. The firies are almost here; I can hear the sirens. They'll lever the door open, then we can take you and your baby to Central.'

She put her hand to her head. 'Ugh. A patient at my own workplace. That sucks.'

'You're working there?'

'Yes. I came back a few weeks ago. It's a long—'

'Hey, Lewis. Missy's getting a bit antsy.' Brin handed him the baby who was now wriggling and fretting—not quite crying but it was a definite overture before the big crescendo. 'Can you have a go at soothing her? She might like your face better than mine.'

'Damn right she will,' Lewis quipped with a smile that he didn't feel as he took baby Stella into his arms. She was a good weight, about six months old, maybe seven. Same shock of red hair as her mother. She was healthy; cute as a damned button.

He cleared his throat as it had become surprisingly raw all of a sudden. 'Um…hey, you. Look who's here. She's right here. And she wants to give you a cuddle, but she's stuck in the car. So you're stuck with me.'

Little Stella gazed up at him and tapped his nose with her little fist. She had huge navy eyes which were swimming with tears. Lewis's heart contracted. *No.* He did not want to feel anything. Not the hurt he'd felt at Charlotte leaving. Not the tug towards her that was as natural as breathing. Not the softening, or the care. He did not want those things again—ever.

This was not Charlie's and his baby, but his chest hurt, his throat burning as he held her. Panicked, he turned to hand her back to Brin, but he was over checking on the truck driver.

So, there he was, holding his ex-wife's much-wanted baby with feet feeling like clay and his chest like a vice around his heart. A weird and unexpected start to a Monday morning.

''Scuse me, mate.' A fire fighter in full yellow uniform was standing behind him holding the metal 'jaws of life' hydraulic rescue tool. 'Give us some room, yeah?'

'Sure.' Lewis swallowed back all the emotion rattling through him and rocked the baby up and down, pulling faces at her to try make her laugh. Maybe she was scared at seeing her mummy stuck in the car. Maybe this kind of thing traumatised a kid. Or maybe she was too young for it to make a difference.

He only knew of his own experiences—that what adults did and said, or neglected to do and neglected to say, had a lasting effect. So he turned away from the car and showed Stella the seagull sitting on top of the damaged lamp post, the flowers on the grass verge and an aeroplane high in the sky.

'You're a natural.'

What?

He whirled round to see Charlotte standing in front of him. Her face was damp from tears, her expression soul-deep sad and her cheeks now red with a blush. 'Um… I said, you're a natural. With the baby, I mean.'

He didn't know what to say; he did not want to go over old history. Talking about the past didn't change what had happened. Better to hold his guard and keep schtum.

And…there was the root of all their problems. He'd spent the last five years mentally unravelling their unravelling. Perhaps…*maybe*…he could have said more back then instead of keeping it all balled up inside him instead of trying to bolster her up to his own detriment and feeding her… not lies, exactly, but little wishes he'd wanted to be true. He should have ditched the stoicism and just been outright, totally, unequivocally honest.

But he'd thought he was doing the right thing. He'd done what he'd learnt to do: biting back his own truths, because no one wanted to hear your problems. No one wanted to hear how you feel.

She held out her hands for her baby, which he gave her gladly. Her eyes roamed her daughter's face, then her body, as if checking for signs of injury. 'There you are. You're okay, you're just perfect.' Then she smooched the little girl's face with kisses. When she seemed satisfied all was okay, she turned back to Lewis. 'Brin says we have to go to hospital, and I think I should get Stella checked out. I mean, I'm okay, but I want to be sure about her.'

'Of course. Very wise. Get your neck and shoulder checked too.'

'Are you…in the back of the ambulance? Will you be there…with us?' Worry nipped at her features.

He shook his head. 'I'm driver today.'

Her eyebrows rose. 'Oh.'

He couldn't identify the emotion behind that word. Relief that they wouldn't be in an enclosed space together or disappointment? Why did he hope it was the latter? Oh, poor, pathetic heart.

She left you, mate. Reel it in.

Brin, oblivious to *everything*, laughed and opened the back doors of the ambulance. 'He thinks I'm too Perez to be a paramedic.'

She frowned as she climbed into the back of the van. 'Perez?'

'He's a Formula One racing-car driver.' Lewis found a smile. 'Trust me, it's safer this way.'

Trust me.

Another knife to his heart.

Trust me to listen, to support. To grow with you. To be flexible. To change as we change.

Yet he'd done none of those things, although

he'd tried damned hard. It just hadn't been enough, apparently.

It was all too late now anyway.

He turned and walked to the front of his van, readying himself to take her to the hospital, her place of work. The place he visited on a very regular basis. The place where he was going to see her daily, probably more than that, handing over patients, sharing the lunchroom space, the café and the corridors.

Up until today he hadn't realised how easier his life had been, knowing she was at the other side of the world and that he wouldn't bump into her here in Auckland. Or how much effect she would still have on him even after five years apart.

But Charlotte Rose was back and she was going to haunt his working days now, as well as his nights.

CHAPTER THREE

TELLING LUCY ABOUT the accident was one of the worst things Charlie had ever done, even though they were both just fine—apart from Charlie's chest and shoulder bruising. But she'd broken the news gently and reassured her sister that they were both okay.

Lucy shrugged the blankets off her knee and slowly sat up from her prone position on the couch, taking Stella in her arms. 'Poor baby. A car crash? What an adventure.'

'An adventure? I wish I had your slant on things. I'm supposed to be here to help you, not cause even more stress.' But, when she looked at her sister, Charlie saw the pain she was hiding. The worry lines that made her look older than her thirty-eight years: the dark rings under her eyes; the slack skin from her weight loss—a direct result of the disease inside her—and the medication that was poisoning her and curing her in equal measure.

Lucy sighed. 'You're being a massive help. You know I couldn't have gone through this on my own. I'm so grateful you came back. Hell, you gave up your whole London life for me and Stella. Come sit down, Charlie. You look terrible, so pale and shocked. I'll get the kettle on.'

'No, I'm fine, really. Just a bit bruised and heart sore. I'd hate anything to happen to Stella, especially if it was on my watch. Sit.' She mock-glared at her sister, who was supposed to be resting. 'You stay here, and I'll get the kettle on. Maybe we can go sit outside in the sun for a while.'

'Oh, yes please. And let's have the ginger biscuits. I'm starving.'

'That's great. The nausea has settled, then?'

'I'm trying to ignore it.' Lucy shook her head and smiled wanly. 'I need to keep my strength up for this little one.'

'That's why I'm here to help.' Charlie sat down next to her sister.

Lucy's eyes glistened with tears, showing a rare chink in her 'I'll be fine' armour. 'I love you. Thank you.'

'I love you too.' Charlie circled her arms round her older sister and hugged her gently, so glad she'd come back to help her.

She'd been away too long, licking her own wounds after her infertility diagnosis and failed marriage, and had only barely acknowledged her family's attempts to connect. But getting that call from a terrified Lucy had been the shake-up Charlie had needed. Lucy hadn't wanted to spoil their parents' overseas charity-work trip of a lifetime, as they'd no doubt have rushed back to help out, so the first person she'd called was her sister. Charlie had jumped at the chance to walk this cancer journey with her.

And she was not going to lambast Lucy's ex-boyfriend for not stepping up to help look after his child. It was none of her business, and his loss. But the way Lucy was handling things now was impressive.

'I don't understand how you can be so upbeat when you must be knackered after the chemo.' One round down, six more to go…. maybe…hopefully…and a long road to recovery.

'Hey, I feel like crap, yes. But I choose to be positive. Look, I still have my hair. And my sense of humour.' Lucy pulled a funny face, although they both knew that the hair would be gone soon. Charlie just hoped Lucy could maintain her sunny outlook through the gruelling treatment. Lucy sighed and snuggled her daughter. 'It could all have been worse.'

'That's what I said to Lewis—'

'Oh my God, you saw Lewis?' Lucy's eyes widened. 'You kept that quiet.'

'I thought it was more important that I told you about the accident than the attending paramedic.'

'But, wow, imagine that. You have an accident and the paramedic is your ex-husband. Thank God you parted agreeably.'

'Yeah. Imagine.' She hadn't gone into a lot of

detail with her family about the reasons for her marriage break-up, although they knew it had been to do with her infertility.

But she hadn't been aware her sister thought it had been an agreeable split. In truth, they'd barely been speaking. Communication had dwindled over months until they'd been more like distant flatmates than married partners. But there hadn't been any raging arguments or outward bitterness, just sadness that they hadn't been able to make it as a couple. Sadness that Charlie had taken a long time to shake off.

In truth, she hadn't known what to say about seeing Lewis. Their meeting was inevitable, given where she now worked, and she'd thought she'd prepared herself for seeing him in the flesh. But nothing could have equipped her for the onslaught of emotions—happiness and bone-deep sadness—that had accompanied the panic of being in an MVA and the relief at having him, of all people, help her.

'How did it go? What was he like?'

Still gorgeous.

Through the haze of panic, fear and, yes, some pain, she hadn't been immune to his beautiful, soulful brown eyes and dazzling smile. He'd always taken her breath away with that smile. And the way he'd gently examined her shoulder, the look in his eyes filled with emotion, had made her heart squeeze. She remembered the way he used to look at her, with such affection and love, then… disappointment. Although he'd never admit it.

'I was just glad he was there. He's very good at his job and made me feel a lot better—very professional. He checked Stella over. Distracted her from anything that might have scared her.'

'Did you talk? You know, about what happened?'

'We didn't talk about anything, Luce. I was his patient, then I was taken to hospital and he left to go to his next call-out.'

Lucy frowned. 'Not even a brief conversation?'

'About what? How? He was busy and working. You'd never have known we even knew each other, never mind been married.'

'Still tight-lipped about his feelings, then.' Lucy laughed hollowly.

'Yeah. Strong and silent and infuriating. And I'm feeling a bit…battered.' Not just physically, but emotionally, even though she had no right to feel that at all.

But he'd never told her his true feelings about their break-up or her infertility. He'd always been an enigma. His expressions had betrayed his emotions, but he would refuse to talk about the way he felt. Oh, he'd told her he loved her and cherished her; about how much he'd cared; that he believed in her, that she was amazing… But getting him to talk about raw things, core-deep things? He'd rather have stuck pins in his eyes. He'd thought it was stoicism to keep quiet about difficult issues but in the end it was just intractability.

Was he married now? Had he a family of his own? Had he made it work with someone else? That thought hurt her too much for her to dwell on.

She looked at her little niece, fast asleep in her mother's arms, and her heart twinged.

'He held her, Lucy. He looked so right with a baby in his arms. It clarified everything—I did the right thing by leaving him so he could have that in his future. Even though he would never admit I did us both a favour.' It had almost broken her to see him hold Stella and remind her of the dreams they'd once shared. And she'd told him he was a natural parent. Oh, God, why had she said that? But she'd been so wrong-footed at seeing him, and him cooing over the baby, the words had tumbled out of her.

Lucy patted Charlie's arm. 'Oh, honey. I can imagine how it must have felt seeing him with a baby in his arms.'

'I think… I don't know if I managed to set him straight or not, it's all a bit blurry. But I think he believes Stella is *my* baby.'

'Yikes.' Her sister pulled a face. 'Awkward.'

'Very. It all seemed too much to explain all at once—why I'm here, who Stella belongs to and why she was in my car…your car. Your very wrecked car.' Charlie winced at the thought of dealing with all of the insurance stuff now. 'See?

It's a lot. Plus, I didn't want to tell him about your illness without checking in with you first. I know you're still coming to terms with it all and it's not common knowledge.'

'Tell whoever you like. It's not a secret. Except Mum and Dad, obviously. I'm not ready for their reaction yet. I need to be stronger for their panic than I feel right now.'

Their parents would drop everything if they knew Lucy was sick, even their dream trip. 'Okay, well, if it comes up I'll set Lewis straight about why I'm back.' To look after Lucy and Stella—not…repeat, *not*…to pine after the man she'd left. Or pine about what they'd once had before the sex on schedule, the failed pregnancy tests and the medical tests and scans.

Okay, enough now.

Time to put thought into action. She stood up and headed towards the kitchen. 'Right, then, let's get that tea made.'

'Thanks, hun.' Lucy grimaced. 'It's so weird, having you look after me.'

Charlie hovered in the kitchen doorway. 'Why?'

'Because I'm the older sister. I'm supposed to look after you.'

'You always have. Very well.' Too much, if she was being honest. There was eight years between Lucy and her, so she'd had a big sister to look out for her from day one. A very devoted big sister.

Born to older parents, Charlie had always felt

she might have been a 'Band-Aid' baby to help heal a possible rift between her mother and father. A child to make everyone happy again, another focus. And, given that Lucy had never wanted to follow in the family footsteps as a doctor, there'd been a lot of pressure on Charlie to fulfil her parents' expectations, and a lot of attending to Charlie's every need.

By the time she'd graduated from medical school, and then married and moved in with Lewis, she hadn't had a day living on her own or fighting her own battles—being herself. She'd always been Lucy's kid sister, the formidable Dr Rose's daughter, Lewis's wife. She'd been well taken care of but smothered too. It hadn't been until she'd settled on her own in London that she'd realised just how much she'd leaned into that.

Not any more. 'Sit back and rest; it's my turn to look after you.'

She'd deal with the Lewis problem later. *If* she could get him out of her head. But, after seeing him up close, having him touch her with such tenderness and care, getting him out of her head was proving a lot more difficult than she'd thought.

'Eighty-two-year-old gentleman: Henry Gerald Woods. Slipped on wet lino in the kitchen at home last night. Couldn't get himself back up and had to wait for his carers to come in this morning. Complaining of severe pain in his right hip.

Blood pressure eighty over fifty at presentation, now ninety-four over sixty-seven. Slightly hypothermic at thirty-four point nine degrees when found, rising steadily now. IV zero point nine percent normal saline in situ. Pain score eight out of ten initially, but has come down to five after morphine administration. We brought his medications in. Takes daily fluid tablets and beta blockers.' Lewis handed his patient's tablets over to the A and E triage nurse.

'Thanks, we'll take over from here,' she said, and smiled at Henry as they lifted him from the portable trolley onto the hospital gurney. 'Hello, Henry. Back again so soon? What on earth have you been up to this time?'

'See you, mate.' Lewis nodded at Henry, one of their 'frequent flyers' who insisted on independent living whilst also refusing to wear the alert necklace that would bring help quickly when needed. 'Don't go giving these lovely nurses any of your cheek, okay?'

'You're just jealous of my charisma,' Henry joked, just audible around the confines of his oxygen mask.

'To be fair, our man Lewis here has plenty of charisma. He just keeps it well hidden.' Brin laughed and opened the cubicle curtain for Lewis to step into the hustle and bustle of the A and E logistics area.

Lewis's heart immediately started its staccato

rhythm of anxiety and, unexpectedly, excitement. Was Charlie here? He glanced around the large open space. She was not at the work stations in the centre of the room; not obviously in the corridor. He couldn't hear her voice coming from one of the cubicles. Couldn't see her giveaway red locks.

Hot damn, he'd never been on the lookout for a glimpse of her and her gorgeous hair in here before. In fact, because she'd been doing her medical rotations when they'd been married, they'd never worked in the same department until now—today.

Yesterday, to be factually correct, but he'd earlier overheard one of the nurses saying that the new emergency doctor had been involved in a car crash and that she was mostly unharmed and had come back this morning. So far, he'd managed three visits here over his shift and he hadn't seen anything of her. Now he was clocking off, he could breathe again. The chances of seeing her now were slim to nil.

Until tomorrow. When he'd be on high alert all over again.

'Lewis?' Brin's tone was brisk and he was frowning. 'I said, do you want to go sort the van out and I'll grab us some takeaway coffees?'

'Sure.' The sooner he got out of here, the sooner he'd stop looking for her.

Brin's frown deepened. 'You seem a bit distracted today. You okay?'

'Never better.' Lewis nodded, determined to

stay focused on the job. He hadn't thought it necessary to tell Brin about his relationship status with the new emergency doctor, but no doubt he'd have to soon enough. 'Cheers, yes. Trim flat white, please, and one of those giant chocolate-chip cookies. Meet you at the van.'

Once in the ambulance bay, he took a deep breath of the fresh, sea-salted air and was just about to climb into the back of the van to tidy up when he caught a flash of red hair. A figure was walking towards the hospital entry, moving stiffly with her head down, right next to where he was standing.

She lifted her head. Their gazes tangled. *Damn.* Now she'd seen him, neither of them could avoid the inevitable, awkward small talk.

'Um… Hi, Lewis.' She inhaled as she approached, a hesitant smile hovering on her lips.

And, damn it, if he couldn't help thinking about the way she tasted. *Don't. Just don't.*

Now there was no urgency of injury assessment or need to rescue, as there had been yesterday, he was able to take a longer look at her. She was still achingly beautiful with her huge blue eyes, pale Celtic skin, that gorgeous kissable mouth and blush-pink lips. But she was thinner, her cheekbones more pronounced, and there were little lines around her eyes when she smiled. She hadn't done a lot of that with him in the later years of their marriage, but he'd seen them there yesterday when she'd hugged her baby. He swallowed. 'Hey, Charlotte.'

'*Charlotte?* Not Charlie?' A pause. Clearly, she was finding this as difficult as he was. 'Okay, yes. I guess we're at that point, right?'

Which point, exactly? They'd breached breaking point a long time ago. His gut clenched as he cleared his throat. 'I was just being polite.'

In truth, 'Charlie' was the woman he'd adored. Using her formal, full name 'Charlotte' gave him emotional space.

'I know…exactly. It's just, you never called me Charlotte.' She shook her head and her eyes darkened, as if she was carrying the world on her shoulders. 'Okay, so, while I have the chance, I want to thank you for what you did for me yesterday.'

'No problem. I was just doing my job. How are you?'

She shrugged her right shoulder and winced. 'Sore, as expected, and bruised. But I'll live.'

His innate immediate response was to put his arms round her and tell her to rest up, that he'd look after her, but they weren't in that space any more. Things between them had broken. Instead, he found what he hoped was a benign smile and said, 'So take it easy, okay? No heavy lifting.'

She nodded, her expression difficult to read. 'Okay. Thank you.'

He was just about to turn away but then had

another thought. 'And your baby—Stella? She's okay?'

Her features softened at the mention of Stella. She clearly loved her daughter very much. 'Yes, she's fine. No issues at all. In fact, I've just been to check on her at the hospital creche.'

Oh, God, this was all too painful. He needed not to be here with her. 'Good to hear. Right, well, I've got to get on, you know…'

'Wait, Lewis. I need to explain.' Her hand touched his wrist, stopping him from turning away. He felt warmth on his skin from a gesture that was almost too intimate. Her skin was soft, her grip light with delicate bones, beautiful hands. But he didn't, couldn't, draw attention to the gesture because that would make things even more awkward.

'No, look, you don't have to explain anything. It's not my business.' Nevertheless, the ache to know everything was surprising and deep. That Charlie had a family was a shock, and it wasn't just the 'who with?', but the *'how?'*.

She looked at her fingers on his and her eyes widened. Grimacing, she lifted her hand and shoved it into her scrubs pocket. 'Um… Stella isn't my baby. She's my niece—Lucy's daughter.'

'Ah.' *Okay*...he'd jumped to conclusions. Something in his chest shifted and eased a little. 'Okay…. Lucy. Of course, Lucy's baby. I see.'

Charlie shook her head. 'No, I don't think you

do. I've come home because Lucy is sick.' Her eyes flickered closed briefly as if she was finding it hard to say the words. 'Breast cancer.'

His gut knotted. 'God, I'm sorry. And with a young baby too. That's terrible. Is she…is she going to be okay?'

'It's early days with the chemo, but the odds are good. I'm helping her look after Stella, and of course I'm trying my best to look after Lucy too, but you might remember that that's not always easy.'

Of course; he remembered that the two sisters had had a difficult dynamic at times. Lucy had always been slightly domineering, a bit meddlesome but well intentioned. Charlie used to complain that her family was trying to be the third spoke in her marriage, in her life.

The Roses were a tight unit: a doting sister and helicopter parents. They'd always been in each other's business, with entangled lives…in a good way, mostly. He'd kind of envied them that closeness which was so very, very different from his own family. His parents had never lived in the same town, never mind the same house. He hadn't heard from his dad…ever. And he wasn't exactly sure where his nomad mother was; last time he'd heard, she was in Invercargill but planning to leave there because it was too cold. That was, what, six months ago? She wasn't great at keeping in touch, regardless of how many times he texted or called.

But at least he had a good bond with his twin brother, Logan. If Logan had been ill, Lewis would have done the same as Charlie and given up his life to look after his sibling. 'Of course I remember. You were joined at the hip growing up. Maybe she'll let you look after her, for a change. *Maybe?*'

'I wish.' Charlie seemed to relax a little, knowing he understood her dilemma. 'She's hellbent on doing everything, but she's so tired. Looking after a baby is knackering enough without cancer treatment too. But that's why I took a part-time job here—so I can fit my work around my life for a change. To be honest, I'd prefer not to be working at all while I look after her, but someone needs to pay the bills, right?'

'Right, of course. I hope she has a speedy recovery.' So Charlie hadn't had a sudden change of heart about her ex and rushed back for him. Not that he'd thought that but...maybe his pathetic heart had hoped? Yeah, he didn't want to admit to a fleeting hope. 'And your parents? Are they okay too?'

He had to ask, right? He couldn't exactly have a half-conversation about her family. But this was just about the most awkward he'd ever felt: asking guarded, polite questions about people he'd known, loved and spent many happy times with of the woman he'd rocked into; whose hair he'd held when she'd vomited after a fun night out and too many drinks; with whom he'd laughed; with whom he'd planned his whole life. Now she was like a stranger, with a completely different life.

'They're fine. Retired now, but doing charity work in Uganda. We haven't told them about Lucy's diagnosis because they'd rush back. You know what they're like; they need to be in the thick of our lives and it's a bit stifling. I can't tell you how relieved we were when they decided to travel, just doing things for themselves, you know? Lucy didn't want them to cut their time in Uganda short so I just told them I'd decided to come home for a while to spend time with my sister.'

She suddenly looked flustered, shaking her head and rolling her eyes. 'God, I don't know why I'm telling you all this. You're busy; you should probably go. What am I saying? I'm busy too. And I'm going to be late back to work. I'm sorry, Lewis.'

'Don't, Charlotte. Don't apologise.' He was amused by her fluster, glad she'd been able to let off some steam and talk about her sister's illness. 'Give my regards to Lucy.'

'I will. Thanks.' She looked a little relieved and smiled. Had she been worried about how this whole interaction would go? Had she thought he might bring up their past? Because, hell, there was a lot to unpick there. But maybe it was best to keep it firmly in the past.

He found himself smiling too, despite the weirdness of everything. 'Take care, Charlotte…um… Charlie. See you around.'

'Yes. Undoubtedly.' She smiled properly then, a full-blown mega-watt smile that did something to his chest. He hadn't realised just how much he'd been looking forward to seeing that smile again. How much the ache for her was still embedded in his DNA.

Then he watched her walk away.

The story of my life.

There was no way he'd let himself fall for her again. She'd broken his heart once and, if he wasn't careful, she could do it again.

CHAPTER FOUR

CHARLIE TOOK A seat at the empty round table in the fundraiser venue, not entirely happy to be here when she should have been at home looking after her sister and her niece. But Lucy had made her come, waving her off with a big smile, a sigh and a promise to call if she felt poorly.

'You need to get out more,' Lucy had said. 'You can't spend your whole life stuck within these four walls with me. You need some friends, Charlie.'

'I go out to work and to the supermarket,' Charlie had replied, as if grocery shopping was the most exciting thing in the world. 'I want to be here.'

'And I need you to go out. You're making me feel guilty, hogging you all the time when you should be building a social life now that you've come home. You're too young to be spending all your waking hours around sick people.' Lucy had smiled her wan smile and sighed. 'Go to that comedy night you were talking about the other day, have fun then come home and tell me all about it. I want to live a normal Saturday night vicariously.'

I need you to go out. Just like that, Charlie had read between the lines. Lucy was grateful to have

Charlie here to help, but spending all this time together was as stifling as their home had been growing up. Lucy wanted things to feel normal instead of staring down the barrel of sickness and uncertainty. So here Charlie was, hoping the comedy part of the night would give her something to laugh about so she could retell it all to Lucy and make her giggle too.

A chatting, laughing group of people entered the large events centre and scanned the room for their table. Charlie recognised them: Patience and Arno, two staff nurses from work, followed by a couple of junior doctors who had recently joined the team, Seung and Mei. Charlie stood up and waved. 'Here! We're over here.'

Patience waved back and started to make her way over with the doctors, while Arno nodded, then turned to speak to people behind him: a woman she didn't know, who was holding hands with one of the paramedics that seemed to spend their life in the A and E department, and behind them…

Lewis.

No. Her belly tightened.

No.

Charlie slid down in her seat. Did the Emergency department have so few people keen to make up a table of eight that they'd had to invite the visiting paramedics too? The last thing she wanted to do was spend the evening with him.

That had been her normal once upon a time but it wasn't now. Hadn't been for five years and, judging by the way her body prickled at the sight of him, her instinctive reaction at seeing him was one of excitement and anticipation.

No. Please, no. She was supposed to be building a new life. Despite him being nice to her, he was probably just being polite. He probably hated her. He probably had a wife and kids.

How to act with him in the company of colleagues and friends? Did they acknowledge they knew each other more than people thought they did, or pretend they were strangers?

She patted the space next to her and indicated to Patience to come and sit down. But she wasn't quick enough, embroiled as she was in air kisses with her colleagues, to see that all the seats were being taken except for the one on the other side of her. And there was only one person left still standing.

'Lewis, hi.' She gave him a tight smile. 'Looks like this is your seat.'

'This is awkward,' he whispered, as if feeling her embarrassment. 'Sorry. There isn't anywhere else.'

So he was approaching this head-on. She nodded, her throat tight. 'It's okay. I'm sure we can get through one evening.'

'Of course. I don't think anyone here knows about our past so let's just keep it that way, right?

Let's just forget about everything and try have a good time.' He caught her gaze and...*oh, dear...* those brown eyes had her all tangled up inside.

Forget everything? What was he saying? She could never forget being married to Lewis: their courtship, the wedding, the dreamy honeymoon, the laughter, the fun...the sex. *Oh*, the sex.

But it wasn't meant to be. They'd tried to make it work and failed. She'd walked away in the end, desperate for some space from the sadness of it all. She'd left him, taken a job on the other side of the world, and the guilt of doing that still stung. Should she have stayed and tried harder? Could they have worn the difficulties they'd faced if they'd stuck it through? He probably did hate her, but how would she know? He'd agreed they separate, but he hadn't told her how he felt about any of it.

So what could she do now but agree to keep everything civil? Just civil, as if they were mere colleagues. She nodded. 'Sure. I don't want to bring the mood down either. Deal.'

'Drink?' He reached for one of the bottles of wine on the table and hovered it over her glass.

'Absolutely. Thanks.'

Lewis poured their drinks and sat down, his knee knocking against hers. He grimaced and shifted away but she was left with his scent lingering in the air: his favourite cologne and something that was uniquely Lewis. It was as familiar to her as her morning coffee aroma.

But she needn't have worried about any further awkwardness because he was immediately embroiled in a conversation with Dr Mei beside him. And Patience engaged Charlie in a conversation about the emergency department politics then introduced her to the other paramedic, Brin—of whom she'd seen lots but didn't know—and his girlfriend Mia.

Apparently Mia was a nurse practitioner at a local GP practice. She told Charlie that Brin was Irish but had settled here now. They had a little girl called Harper. They spent half their lives on Rāwhiti Island and they'd recently been there with the guy sitting next to her—Lewis. Did Charlie know him?

Remembering their deal, Charlie simply nodded at that and redirected her conversation to their holiday with him. *Had he been there with a significant other—a wife, girlfriend?* Of course she didn't ask that, even though she was suddenly very keen to know the answer. Had he found someone else? She tried to read between the conversation lines…she was getting good at that these days… but it was just *Lewis this, Lewis that…*

He was such good fun, apparently: a talented fisherman; a good friend; a dab hand at the barbecue; great with kids. He babysat their daughter sometimes. He was a real good guy.

Her heart felt raw. She knew that, of course,

more than any of them. A good guy with a heart of gold…

Eventually Lewis rolled his eyes at Brin and told him to stop with the ego massaging but Brin just grinned. 'Ah, man. I'm just telling Charlie here how it is.' Brin turned back to her. 'I see you're here on your own tonight, Charlie. Do you have a partner? Family?'

They all looked at her then and her mouth felt as dry as a husk. 'Um… No to both—'

'What is this?' Lewis interrupted, jumping to her aid like he used to, his voice imbued with humour, but Charlie knew him better. Knew it was forced. 'I'm sure Charlie doesn't need an interrogation.'

Brin shrugged and shot his friend a curious look. 'Being friendly, is all. Getting to know the new doc in town.'

Charlie didn't need Lewis's help any more. She'd grown up a lot while she'd been in London and could fight her own battles. She smiled at them both. 'No worries at all. I've no partner, no kids. I'm from Auckland but I've been away for a few years. Now I'm back.'

'And we're glad to have you.' Brin raised his glass and looked at Lewis. He made some sort of face, pigging his eyes at him as if to encourage him to say something.

Lewis shook his head tightly… There was something going on between these two—some in joke or something. In the end, Lewis cleared his throat and said almost robotically, 'Hey. Yes. We're glad you're here.'

Yet she didn't think he was glad at all. He didn't want anyone to know about their shared past. He'd physically shifted away from her when he'd sat down. He'd glared at any suggestion of being too friendly towards her.

The lights dimmed and the comedienne took to the stage. She was funny, and told some great stories that almost distracted Charlie from the fact she was sitting here in the dark next to her ex-husband who clearly wanted to be anywhere but next to her. But they were all crammed in round the table. He was so close, and she was acutely aware of him. Once upon a time they'd have held hands at an event like this, played footsie under the table. He'd have slid his arm around the back of her chair, absentmindedly playing with her hair or massaging her shoulder. She'd have leant into him and he'd have kissed the top of her head.

Even now his leg kept pressing against hers as they shifted position in their seats, but that was more because they'd been shunted together than by desire. But she was wrapped in his scent, mesmerised by his hands as they played with the stem of his wine glass. She'd always loved his hands and his long, slender fingers.

Her gaze roamed the place where his wedding band had once sat. They'd bought their rings from a high street chain because they hadn't been able to afford anything too swanky. But they'd loved their choices—a simple band for him and stacked engagement and wedding rings for her. There wasn't even a white line on his finger any more. Time and the sun had filled in the place where his ring used to be.

She looked at her own hands then. Her wedding-ring finger was empty too; there were no tan lines around where the platinum ring had been. It was all so long ago. She'd kept the rings, though, at the bottom of her jewellery box. There'd been something so desperately sad about getting rid of them. Even after the divorce had come through, she kept them as a reminder that once she'd been in love and been loved. That she'd planned an idyllic future…until the dream had fallen apart due to her damned useless uterus.

It was a great relief when, during the interval, they were all encouraged to bid on items in a silent auction. Charlie jumped up and took some well-needed breathing space, walking down the side of the room, reading the details of the silent-auction items. She wrote her name and her bid on a few of them, then made her way back to her seat. The table was empty and she could see most of her colleagues standing in a queue to bid in the auction too.

But where was…? 'Hey.'

Ah. Lewis was here, taking his seat next to her

again. His tone was flat, as if he was pushing himself to talk to her and fill in the yawning conversational gap.

'Hi.' She turned to speak to him and smiled to try and soften the atmosphere. 'I managed to bid on a few things—a couple of spa packages for Lucy for when she's feeling up to having some nice treatments, and the paddling pool for Stella. You?'

'I'm sure Lucy would love to be pampered when she's up to it.' He shrugged. 'There's not much there for guys, to be honest, but I'm bidding on the dinner at that fancy restaurant, Marcel's.'

'Is it good? I'm a bit out of the loop when it comes to restaurants here.'

'I don't know.' He gave another shrug. 'I've been wanting to try it for a while.'

'Oh.' Fleetingly she wondered whether he was planning to take a date there. And then her competitive streak got the better of her. 'Well, I was the last one to bid on that, so don't you dare outbid me.'

His eyebrows rose. And there…just there…she saw a glimpse of the old Lewis in the glimmer of a smile playing across his lips and the spark of tease. 'Or…what?'

'Or…' She jumped up, throwing him a gauntlet she thought he might not refuse, because he never could resist a dare. 'I'll just have to bid higher than you.'

'Not likely.' He jumped up too and started towards the table that held the restaurant auction. And just like that they were back seven years playing, competing, laughing.

'Don't you dare, Lewis Parry!' She dashed ahead of him but he scooted in front of her as they both arrived at the table at the same time. They reached out, their hands entwining as their fingers curled round the pen. For the briefest moment, she felt a skitter of electricity through her skin, arrowing towards her heart. But she wasn't going to let go of the pen for love nor money.

'Mine!' He looked at her, pulling a face and laughing. 'Mine. Mine.'

Back in the halcyon days of their relationship, they'd watched *Finding Nemo* and had laughed so hard at the seagull scene where the birds fought for fish shouting, 'Mine, mine, mine!' Every time they'd seen a seagull after that, they'd mimicked the word over and over, dissolving into fits of laughter.

Her heart flooded with something… Nostalgia, or just muscle memory? She laughed at his victorious expression: *I win*. 'I think not, Mr Parry. *Mine.* I was here first.'

'Hey hey, children. Now, now.' A voice behind them made them jump apart.

They turned to see Brin grinning at them both. 'This is for charity, it's not WWE wrestling. Truce?'

They looked at each other and she saw Lewis trying to stifle more laughter as much as she was. In the end, she couldn't hold it in, and chuckled. 'We were a bit petty, weren't we?'

'Nothing like a bit of healthy competition.' Lewis grinned back. 'I'm still going to beat you.'

'Not a chance, Lewis. Not a chance.'

Brin looked from one to the other, frowning at first, but the frown slowly dissolved as the moments ticked by. He was clearly cooking up something. 'I have an idea—hear me out. It's not guaranteed that either of you will win, cos there are plenty of others bidding on this auction too, but if one of you does win…why don't you share the prize?'

'What?' Charlie and Lewis said to Brin at the same time, both wide-eyed.

'Genius, yes?' Brin laughed.

Charlie could think of other words to describe the suggestion: meddlesome, idiotic, dangerous. If she was spending this evening looking at Lewis's wedding-ring finger, and trying to prise information out of him when he clearly wasn't interested, then she needed to spend less time with him, not more.

Hell, she wasn't interested in her ex-husband… was she?

No. Working with him was just a new dynamic she had to get used to. She'd need to work out a new normal. Besides, someone else could easily outbid them. She looked at Brin, then at Lewis, and they both stared back expectantly. And now she couldn't exactly say no, could she? That would just seem rude. 'Okay…maybe.'

'Oh.' Lewis scrunched his nose as he thought—playful Lewis replaced again with the earlier, more detached one. 'Well. Um… I guess…maybe too.'

Huh. Don't hold back on the enthusiasm, matey. His reluctance bit deep.

Brin nodded. 'Nice. Good. I'll take that as two yesses.'

Now was her chance to find out Lewis's relationship status. She looked up at him. 'Shouldn't you check with your partner first?'

Lewis frowned, confused, then he shook his head and threw Brin a wry look. 'This is all your fault, *partner.* So, I'm not asking permission. I may well kill you later, though.'

Yikes. But he was at least smiling a little. So perhaps he didn't find the prospect of dinner with her so odious. And…was that Lewis's way of telling her he was single? Okay, dinner might be a good idea—maybe they could clear the air and stop all this awkwardness around them whenever they met.

They wandered back to their table and the evening continued, but Charlie was a little blindsided about what she'd just agreed to. She couldn't get it out of her head: dinner with Lewis?

Dinner with Lewis...after everything they'd

been through? After their divorce? What in the actual hell had she been thinking when she'd said yes?

The comedienne finally started going through the silent auction and announcing the winners. Charlie stood and waved at the applause for her generous bid on one of the spa packages. She also won the paddling pool for Stella.

Then came the announcement for dinner at Marcel's. The comedienne cleared her throat. 'Now for the last auction item of the night. We're very lucky to have Marcel, the restaurant owner, here with us tonight. His father was an in-patient at the hospital a couple of weeks ago, and Marcel was so impressed with the care given that he has decided to add an extra-special treat for the person who wins the bid for dinner at his restaurant…'

'Ooh? Wonder what it is?' Brin gave Lewis and Charlie a thumbs-up. 'Maybe a bottle of champagne too?'

She shook her head. 'Won't be me. I'm never that lucky.'

Lewis laughed. 'Well, I'm always up for a free bottle of champagne.'

'Not just dinner…but also a night for two in the luxury of the Quay Hotel. Time for some rest and relaxation or…' the comedienne winked suggestively '…whatever you fancy doing in a very swanky hotel for the night. I know I wouldn't want to just sleep between those eight-hundred-thread-count sheets…'

Charlie glanced at Lewis. He was looking right at her.

A night in a hotel…together…between the sheets. Something inside her flickered to life. And something in his eyes told her he was thinking the same thing. His gaze softened yet heated at the same time. She knew that look. She had basked in it many, many times. His eyes were molten and, in return, her insides melted. Heat shot through her. Her body thrummed.

One night with him…

He was so close. Close enough to touch, to kiss. And she'd seen the old Lewis a few moments ago, laughing and playing, uninhibited by disappointment or sadness. She had a sudden ache to run her fingers across his jaw, to press her mouth against his.

Whoa. Really? But then, the physical side of their relationship had never been the problem. Their desire for each other had been insatiable.

Did he feel the same need?

No. No. No.

He looked away and shook his head, as if giving himself a good telling off. *So maybe, yes, yes, yes?* He had been thinking the same thing!

The ache inside her intensified. She ran her fingers round the stem of her wine glass, hoping the cool condensation would bring her some relief. Hoping like hell that neither of them won that prize.

'And the winner of this amazing prize is… Drum roll, please…' The whole room erupted with people banging the tables. 'Lewis Parry!'

'Oh?' His chest inflated as he sucked in air. His eyebrows rose and then he nodded at her. 'Okay. Okay, looks like we're doing this.'

She watched him walk across the room with his long legs and confident stride. The years had been good to him; he looked fitter, stronger, even more gorgeous.

And so off-limits.

She'd broken everything. It had been her fault, in the end. Doing the right thing by him had meant breaking her own heart too. But she cheered as he stepped onto the stage and shook hands with the famous Marcel.

He collected the vouchers, chatted with some other members of the audience then returned to the table as everyone was starting to put on coats to leave. The night was over.

He helped her with her denim jacket and then handed her the hotel information. 'Hey, you can have the hotel room, I don't want it.'

She looked down at the pamphlet. It was indeed a very fine-looking place and, oh, so tempting.

'No thanks. I'll need to be back for Lucy, in case she needs me. You take it.'

'No, Charlie. You should take it. You're doing a lot for your sister; you deserve a good night's sleep.'

'If you don't take it, I'll give it away.' She laughed. 'Maybe to your partner in crime?'

His gaze flicked to Brin, ahead of them in the crowd milling towards the exit, and he laughed. 'Not a chance. He doesn't know about our past. I think he was trying to…you know…'

'Get us together?' She watched Lewis's reaction. 'Bit of a stirrer?'

He shook his head, a little guarded, and rolled his eyes. 'He's got a good sense of humour, for sure. One of these days it's going to get him into trouble. Right, I'll book the restaurant. Friday? Saturday? I can do either. I'm on early shifts this week.'

With a roll of his eyes, he showed he was clearly still reluctant. And yet they were planning a dinner out. 'Feel free to take someone else, Lewis.'

'Oh, no, you don't. You had a deal,' chipped in Brin, who had obviously overheard bits of their conversation. 'Both of you go, or I'll take Mia. I do love a free dinner, and a hotel room. You can babysit instead of a lovely meal. Yes, please.'

'Funny guy.' Lewis flicked his thumb towards Brin and shook his head. Then he leaned closer to Charlie and lowered his voice. 'Truth is, I only bid one cent more than you anyway.'

'What? You little…' She laughed and gasped at the whisper of his breath across her skin. 'Anything to win, right?'

'You know me.' His eyebrows rose and he stopped walking.

'I certainly do.' Her gaze landed on his mouth and joy fizzed through her as she watched him laugh. It was so refreshing, so damned lovely to see. She'd missed it, missed him. Missed *them*. Oh, God. She hadn't realised how confusing seeing him again, being with him, would be.

Maybe they needed this dinner to clear the air. *Yes—excellent idea.* 'I'm on call Friday night but Saturday works. Then you can have a nice lie-in on Sunday morning in your swanky hotel room—not that I'd be jealous at all.'

Sunday morning—their favourite time for sex. Long, lazy mornings in bed on the rare occasions they'd both had Sundays off. It was a ritual they'd enjoyed almost until the end—uncomplicated, leisurely, exploring each other. She remembered the touch of his fingers and the press of his body on her, over her, inside her…the way he'd tasted. Her body tingled in awareness. He was still so damned close.

His breath hitched and he cleared his throat, and she was fairly sure he was remembering all their Sunday mornings too.

'Cool,' he said. 'Saturday it is.'

Which meant she had precisely one week to stop thinking about Lewis in bed. And to start thinking of him as purely and only her colleague.

CHAPTER FIVE

SO OUT OF NOWHERE, and after five years apart, he was going out to dinner with his ex-wife—*tomorrow.*

If anyone had told him last week, last month or even last year he'd be doing this, he'd have laughed in their face. But, yeah, dinner.

He was finishing up a few days on early shift so hadn't seen much of Charlie, except in passing in the corridor and twice at a patient handover surrounded by the team—certainly not long enough for a chat.

It had given him enough time to put some well-needed space and perspective on the whole thing. Dinner was a good idea. A chance to catch up on everything and smooth the transition from not seeing each other for a very long time to working together a few times a week. To work out how to be, with her back in his life. It wasn't as if he could avoid it, so he needed a plan to get through it.

He wandered across the hospital ambulance shared car park towards his car, planning a quick ride home, a speedy shower and then heading to his niece's birthday party.

'Lewis!' A female voice behind him had him turning round.

He spotted luscious red curls coming towards him, bobbing between the cars: *Charlie*, her hand raised in a wave.

His heart did a weird leap as all the perspective faded away and he was back to the other night, imagining her in bed. In his bed, for Sunday morning sex—his favourite time of the week.

He couldn't have stopped the smile if he'd tried. 'Hey, we have to stop meeting like this.' *Yeah. Corny as hell.*

'I know, right? Who would have thought the work car park would be our new rendezvous place?' She laughed, but her smile was sad and her eyes were red-rimmed.

His gut knotted the way it always did when Charlie was anything other than happy, as if it was his own personal mission to put a smile back on her face.

But that had been before. Now, he needed to keep some emotional distance before he got all bent out of shape with trying to make her happy. That wasn't his job any more. She'd walked away, but not before telling him he needed to focus on himself and not on her. That she didn't want or need his platitudes.

But, still, she looked upset and he couldn't ignore that. 'You okay?'

She shrugged, her eyes weary. 'Sure.'

She didn't look okay at all. He nodded towards the creche. 'Just been to see Stella?'

'Actually, just on my way to pick her up. I'm done working for the day.'

'And she's okay?' At her nod, he frowned. 'So, what's up? You look upset.'

'Oh, I'm just tired.' She waved her hand wearily in front of her face. 'Lucy had a bad night with pain and vomiting. She refuses to let me get up if Stella wakes, but she's so weak after her chemo, so I make sure to get up too. For some reason, Stella was agitated just after midnight, and around two-thirty, and then again at four-eighteen precisely. Not that I was clock-watching.' She rolled her eyes.

'Could be teething. Is she drooling more than usual? Pink cheeks?' Then he smacked his head with his palm. 'Duh. You're talking to a doctor, Lewis.'

She laughed. 'Always happy for advice. What do you know about teething?'

'Logan had hellish sleepless nights with both Lily and Lola, remember?'

'Oh, yes, of course. I'd forgotten about your brother's kids. We babysat them that time and couldn't calm Lily down at all. I thought she didn't like me.'

'She loved you.'

We all did.

His heart twinged. When Charlie had fled to London, she'd left a hole in his family. She'd not just been his wife, but an auntie and sister-in-law too. He hadn't told Logan she was back...that was going to be an interesting conversation. 'Teething—a whole new dynamic to test you, just when you think you're getting into a routine.'

Charlie chuckled. 'Yes, it's probably just her teeth coming through. She's definitely unsettled. I hope she's not feeding off our worries over Lucy's diagnosis. Kids are funny like that.'

'Sure are. Logan used to cool teething rings and let them suck on them. Said it worked a treat.' It made him sad to think they could talk about other people's child-rearing woes but not their own. And he knew damned well just how much a parent's anxiety, worry or neglect could have an effect. He'd lived it, breathed it. His mother had barely hidden her struggles with her twin sons.

You ruined my life. I could have been something if you two hadn't come along.

Of course, looking back, he knew it had been more her struggles with her own mental health than anything to do with their behaviour, but at the time it had been devastating. 'I'm sure you're doing all the right things to shield her from any upset.'

Charlie sighed. 'Oh, I hope so. But it's a vicious circle sometimes. If Lucy's upset, then Stella seems more grizzly. And of course if Stella's awake, then so is Lucy. And so am I. I've come to work for the rest.' She laughed wryly.

'It's a lot.'

'It certainly is. I'm never going to admit it to Lucy, because she needs my help, not my gripes, but I didn't realise babies were such hard work.' She pressed her lips together, wincing. 'Oh… sorry.'

Her eyes caught his and their shared past flickered into view.

He recalled the doctor's gentle words. *I'm so sorry, but it is impossible for you to carry a child. There may be other options you could explore…*

It embarrassed Lewis to admit it now, but he hadn't wanted to consider other options back then. His whole focus had been to try to stop Charlie from hurting, hiding his own grief at losing his dream of being a father and helping her get through: throwing the bundle of unused pregnancy tests away when she wasn't looking; deleting the ovulation app from her phone; helping her in the way he'd *thought* she'd needed to be helped and giving no attention to the fact he needed help too. Of course, she'd noticed these things missing and had called him out, saying he needed to face his own grief and not try to protect her from hers.

And, in hindsight, he wondered whether this had tipped her over the edge, pushed her into her decision to leave.

He shook his head. 'It's fine, honestly. But, yes, I've heard the first six months are the worst. Until the second six months.' He chuckled.

She groaned. 'Gee, you're filling me with confidence.'

'Hey, you'll cope. Just like when you did your medical rotations and had those horrific weekends on call.' He winked, knowing how she'd managed to work but had been too exhausted to do anything else at the end of the weekends. He'd been the cook, the cleaner and the cheerleader. Hell, he'd always been her cheerleader…until it hadn't worked for her any more. She hadn't wanted to hear how much he loved her, how things were going to be okay, because they'd both known they weren't. 'But with a new job, a sick sister plus a grizzly baby: that's a triple whammy.'

'All the while you just fake it till you make it, right?' She flashed a fake smile, then a real one. Her eyes lit up and she just glowed. Or it could have been the way the setting sun lit up her face and hair in golden hues.

Either way, she was still so beautiful—older now but no less stunning. Just looking at her made his heart swell and his body prickle. He swallowed, trying to dampen the tingles firing across his skin and the tightening in his groin. 'And we are champion fakers, right? You remember Matt and Claire's wedding?'

'Oh, hell, yes. The traffic down to Tauranga was terrible. We were so late for the wedding that we met the bride and groom as they were coming out of the chapel…married.' She pulled a face: *woops.*

'And we pretended we'd watched the whole ceremony.' He laughed at the memory, parroting the way they'd greeted the new Mr and Mrs Sinclair. *'Congratulations, lovely service.'*

'Lovely service…' She laughed, putting on a cute, posh English accent. *'Just lovely.* They never knew we hadn't seen any of it and were just throwing confetti like we'd been there the whole time.'

'Faking pros, see? You can do it. You've got this.' Words he'd said over and over to her, from when they'd first started dating in the final year of school until that very last day when she'd told him she absolutely couldn't do it any more. That she *hadn't* got this. She didn't have a functioning uterus. She didn't have a child-filled future. She had no answers. That he was blinkered and no amount of positivity would get them through.

But he'd always believed in her. She believed she could do anything. And when her belief in herself had withered, he'd soldiered on, bolstering her up, thinking that was the way to show his love. Because that was what had always been missing in his life: no one had ever the hell said it to him. Not his mother, not the many random relatives they'd been sent to stay with in the school holidays and not even his brother.

But Charlie…yeah. She'd never actually said it when they'd been together but he'd always *felt* her belief in him: bone-deep; soul-deep.

Until she'd left.

He shook his head, coming back to reality with a bump. Because if thoughts about what she'd done to him weren't a warning call, he didn't know what was. He should have left then. He could have made an excuse and gone—hell, he was going to be late for Lola's birthday tea and that would not go down well with his brother.

But Charlie was still laughing and, he now realised, he was still acutely drawn to her, circling her like she was the goddamned sun.

'So don't be surprised if I fall asleep in my soup tomorrow night,' she quipped.

'Charming.' He fake-coughed. 'I hope my conversation is a little more riveting than that.'

'Well, I didn't want to say, but…' she joked, one eyebrow raised, her mouth all cocky and impudent as she fake-yawned.

And did she step closer? She was fingertip-distance away. He could see the flecks of silver in her eyes. The freckles she hated and he'd always loved. The laughter on her mouth and at the corners of her eyes. His first love—right here.

'You called me a lot of things over the years, Charlie Jade Rose.' He grinned and his gaze connected with hers. 'But boring was never one of them.'

'No.' She squared up to him, capturing his gaze, her pupils dilating and softening. Something white-hot fired there, igniting something scalding inside him. 'Definitely not boring.'

She was looking at him the way she had last week at the comedy night, eyes misted, body tilting towards him, all turned on and trembling. He *knew* that look. He knew her, and what she wanted.

Did she want him? Was he imagining it?

Did she want…?

He took a breath, but couldn't get enough oxygen into his lungs and drew his eyes away from hers. Everything was getting tangled up inside him. He looked away, then back. This time his gaze landed on her mouth. He wanted to kiss her. How the hell could he want to kiss her, after everything? But…he did. It was like an ache that had never really abated, only now rekindled, a hundred times more intense.

He took a step back before he did something stupid, like reach out and slide his mouth over hers. 'Look, I should go…'

'Sure.' But she didn't move.

How did a person greet and leave an ex-wife? Especially when there was this atmosphere of heat. There had been so much intimacy shared before, and now there was this five-year fissure. But they'd straddled it a little and were forging something like a collegial relationship at worst, a friendship at best.

Okay, he was freaking turned on as all hell. Should he give her a hug or an air-kiss goodbye?

A nod didn't seem enough. A hug would be too much…for him.

He leaned to kiss her cheek, trying to be platonic when platonic was not the way he felt.

The touch of his mouth on her skin sent his pulse into orbit. She smelt insanely delicious, and it felt as if her cheek was pressing against his mouth rather than the other way round. Maintaining skin contact, she turned her cheek until her mouth was centimetres from his.

His whole body buzzed. He should have moved back, away from her touch, but he couldn't.

'Lewis…' It was more of a tremble than a word and it connected with his gut, his groin, his skin, throbbing and beating inside him until the world around them faded to nothing and all he could see was her face—so compassionate, so beautiful, so familiar. *Charlie…*

And he couldn't have stopped it if he'd tried. He slid his fingers into her silken hair, cupped the back of her neck and slid his mouth softly over hers.

She shivered and moaned, her body trembling under his touch. Her eyes flickered closed. Her breath stuttered.

'Lewis…' she whispered against his mouth. 'I missed you.'

'*God,* Charlie. I never stopped missing you.' That was the truth of it.

He pulled her against him, relishing the press of

her body against his. Two pieces of a jigsaw slotting neatly and perfectly together. She raised her arms and framed his face with her hands, deepening the kiss. She tasted of fresh air and salty tears. Of Charlie from five years ago and something new…something intoxicating and exciting. There was no re-learning; it was as if they'd never stopped kissing. Had never had those five years apart.

His tongue slid into her mouth and she whimpered, which set him aflame. He wanted her, right here in the damned car park. But she pulled away and looked at him, her chest heaving. She just stared at him, her face a mix of sadness, surprise and heat. In those dark-blue eyes, he saw need and desire and he thought of all the things he wanted to do to her, with her, right now.

She opened her mouth to speak but his phone beeped.

He jumped and checked his phone: Logan. Could Lewis pick up some ice on the way over to the tea party?

Man, he loved his brother, but his timing was diabolical.

Although, also very wise.

Charlie was now studying her phone too as if she couldn't quite look him in the eye. Hell. What were they doing? The kiss was one road they should not have gone down. But then she shoved her phone into her bag and put her hand on his chest, looking up at him as if she was as confused as he was, and aching to be kissed again.

He shook his head and stepped well away. 'No. No. Just no, Charlie. We can't do this. *I* can't do this.'

Because he had to save them both here. They'd broken the good thing they'd once had. It could not be fixed back together with a kiss or a wish. It had taken him years to come to terms with his part in it all, get over her and move on.

She stepped back too, her expression half-regret and half-relief, but she was trembling as much as he was. 'Right. Yes. Okay. I've got to get Stella.'

He nodded, torn between wanting a repeat kiss and stopping this craving dead.

In the end, self-preservation won out. Once upon a time, she'd told him he had to stop putting her needs before his.

She was damned right.

And this time it was he who walked away and didn't look back.

CHAPTER SIX

DO NOT KISS HIM. Do not kiss him.

Lewis had made it very clear yesterday that kissing was not on his agenda and, while it stung… because it had been the most amazing kiss…he was right. Kissing was not a good idea.

But, hell, it had been inevitable. From the moment Charlie had seen him again after five years, she'd been assaulted by conflicting emotions—some sad, some funny, most hot—all about him and what they'd once had and lost. But the attraction was very much still there, simmering between them the way it always had.

But that was yesterday. Today, she'd convinced herself that they'd both needed some closure for the old part of their lives and the kiss had been the final full-stop on that.

So why they were still meeting up at Marcel's, she didn't know, but neither of them had cancelled so it appeared it was all still on. Well, he had paid an arm and a leg for it, so she guessed he didn't want to lose his money. As for her, well, it would be rude not to turn up after she'd agreed to accompany him as a friend. Besides, they really did need to get their relationship into civil territory, for a more congenial working environment as much as anything else.

And, of course, it was raining, with the promise of worse to come. Her umbrella had blown inside out twice since she'd climbed out of the taxi so now she was just holding it all limp and dripping above her head in a feeble attempt to keep maybe one strand of hair dry. But, as she approached the restaurant and caught her reflection in the window, she knew even that hadn't worked. Her trench coat was not, in fact, as advertised, waterproof. Her hair, which had been expertly and beautifully clipped up into a loose bun by her sister, was a flattened soggy mess, and her eyeliner and mascara were probably running down her face.

Lewis was standing in the restaurant doorway, hands shoved deeply into his jacket pockets, collar turned up, looking immaculate and, somehow, dry. He met her gaze with a little warmth—probably because he was resigned to coming tonight, so was making an effort to be cordial. 'Hey, Charlie. Quick, come inside; this weather is nuts.'

There was no kiss this time, not even an air-kiss. But he held the door open, she stepped inside the warm restaurant and was immediately assailed by the aroma of garlic, anise and something else exotic and delicious.

She shook her cold, wet hands and grimaced as water pooled at her feet. 'Ugh, sorry. Okay, I'm just heading to the bathroom to dry off. I must look a wreck.'

'No. You look amaz…' He swallowed and shook his head, taking her umbrella from her and putting it in a receptacle at the door. 'Okay, sure, of course. I'll find the table.'

Glumly, she stared at herself in the bathroom mirror. She'd been right: her hair needed drying and redoing and her mascara was now just two black smudges beneath her eyes—pretty much exactly the way she'd looked the day she'd left him. She'd been down and out, bedraggled, beaten up by elements out of her control. At least, that was how she'd felt back then.

But for some reason she wanted to show him, and show herself, that she'd put those days behind her. She was a different person from the one who'd gone to London. She was independent, capable and well put together…usually. She'd come to terms with her infertility and divorce, even though both stung when she dwelt on them too much. So she didn't dwell on them. There was no point looking back.

And yet here she was, looking back, going back. Wasn't it a sign of madness, repeating the same thing and expecting a different result? But this was just two friends catching up. That was all. No kissing allowed.

She quickly dried her hair under the hand drier, reapplied her make-up and slicked on her favourite lip gloss: *his* favourite lip gloss. *Whatever.* She just hadn't got round to finding one she liked better. *Honestly.* Well, you kept some things out of habit, right? And others purely for nostalgia.

She found him at a table overlooking the road and, beyond, the harbour. Water ran down the outside of the windows, distorting the reflections of people rushing through the early evening, car lights were fuzzy and the occasional blare of a car horn reminded her that driving in an Auckland downpour was dangerous.

As if she needed reminding about the dangers of cars. She rubbed her shoulder where the bruising was starting to fade from purple to yellow. Relaxing was difficult: not because she was in pain, but because she didn't know what to say or how to act. This felt intimate and yet disparate. They'd never been short on conversation before and now she was racking her mind, trying to think of the right things to say.

Trying not to think of that kiss.

Lewis frowned as he watched her movements. 'Does your shoulder hurt? Are you okay?'

'Oh, I'm fine, honestly. It's not so bad.' She rotated her shoulder forward and back to show him her range of movement. 'I was just thinking how nice and cosy it is in here, compared to outside.'

'There's flash-flooding forecast.' He laughed and then grimaced. 'I bet that's not easy to say after a couple of wines.'

'Flash flooding forecast,' she repeated, grateful that he'd broken the atmosphere with a joke. 'Maybe we should have some wine and see?'

As if on cue, Marcel appeared and shook their hands. 'Thank you, thank you, for bidding so much on the auction for the degustation dinner for two...'

What did he mean, *so much*? She glanced at Lewis for clarification. But Lewis just bugged his eyes at her to be quiet.

Marcel continued, 'I will throw in the wine match as a token of thanks.'

Lewis shook his head and smiled at the restaurant owner. 'Not necessary, honestly.'

'I insist.' Marcel reached for a bottle in an ice-bucket he'd brought with him and poured them a glass each of champagne. 'Bubbles to start. Are we celebrating anything tonight?'

They stared at each other.

Awkward.

How did they label this?

'Not really. Just—just two...um...old *friends*,' Lewis stammered, echoing the sudden panic inside her.

Old friends who happened to have been married and divorced. Old friends who had shared a searing hot kiss yesterday.

Marcel beamed. 'Well, old friends, have an excellent evening.'

Once he'd gone, Charlie leaned forward and whispered to Lewis, 'You said you'd paid one cent more than me. But I know I probably didn't bid enough to cover the cost of the meal.'

'Well, I may have embroidered the truth a little. All in a good cause—it's for the hospital cancer unit, right?' He sat back and regarded her, his arms casually crossed. His sultry gaze reached into her soul and something inside her flipped and danced. He'd always had a knack of disarming her just by looking at her. 'How are you doing, Charlie? I mean, *really*—how are you?'

She inhaled and thought about everything she was juggling at the moment and how it all seemed far away from here and now. 'I'm okay, I think. Yes, I'm good.'

'Good. Because I know you're under a lot of pressure.'

'It's nothing I can't handle.' She flashed him a wry smile because only yesterday she'd been bleating on about how it was all so difficult. But today she felt as if she could manage her way through being a decent sister, a good auntie and an efficient and compassionate doctor.

He smiled. 'You had a better sleep last night?'

'After we gave Stella the cooled teething ring, which worked like magic—thanks for the tip—we slept all night.' Apart from replaying that mind-warping kiss over and over before she'd fallen asleep, and immediately on waking.

His eyes flitted to her mouth and she wondered if he was remembering their kiss too or whether he'd put it to the back of his mind. She'd tried, but it was here now at the front, and she couldn't stop thinking about it.

He cleared his throat. 'Do we…um…need to talk about yesterday?'

Ah, so he had been thinking about it. And, even though she'd agreed they wouldn't do it again, her cheeks heated at the memory. 'No. No, we don't. I agree with you—we can't go back, Lewis. It's all done and gone.'

He nodded. 'And we don't want any awkwardness tipping over into our work, do we?'

Of course. This was just two people catching up after a long five years, trying to be normal. Trying to clear the air because they were colleagues. But here was the thing: Lewis never dealt with things like this head-on. He always shied away from conflict or difficult conversations but they were facing this awkward moment and he was totally in control. Maybe she wasn't the only one who'd changed, at least a little. 'No. No, we don't. I'd hate for anything to affect how we work together.'

'Okay, then. It's good that we agree.' He held up his glass, those soft, dark eyes capturing her gaze. God, he was so good to look at. He tipped his glass to hers. 'So…to friends and the future.'

'And flash-flooding forecasts.' She clinked his glass and laughed. 'Okay, tell me, what the heck have you been doing these last five years?'

'Not a lot, you know; just plodding along.'

He'd been promoted three times, apparently, but she wasn't surprised. He was damned good at his job.

He'd bought a house. Travelled to Laos, Cambodia and Singapore and had hiked in Australia. Been on three stag weekends and attended four of their mutual friends' weddings, which she'd decided not to come home for, because of so many reasons…mainly, Lewis.

He'd become an uncle to another girl, now three in total: Lola, Lily and Luna. Luna had been a surprise, but also a joy. Logan had said it was their last, but Lewis wasn't so sure. He'd spent yesterday afternoon at Lola's eighth birthday party, a tie-dye party, but he'd chosen not to wear his pink-and-orange T-shirt tonight. Then they'd cooked pizzas in Logan's outdoor pizza oven for the birthday tea.

All that, straight after the hotter than hot kiss.

How had he managed to function in public after that? She'd been a trembling wreck and had needed a lie down before being able to look her sister in the eye, while keeping the kiss a secret, close to her chest. Because why tell her something that might worry her, or excite her, when it had been a mistake?

She shook her head and tried to put thoughts of Lewis's mouth to the back of her mind. 'What is it with your family and names starting with L? I'm sure this wasn't a thing a few years ago.'

He laughed and shrugged. 'Don't ask me. Neither of our parents have L names, it's just something Logan's decided to do with his kids.'

'You obviously married the wrong sister, then. Should have been Lucy. She'd have fit right in.' She laughed, but stopped short when she saw his expression suddenly change from light to dark. His gaze dipped to his glass, then back to her. He paused a beat, then two.

She wished she could take it back but it was too late.

'I definitely married the right sister, Charlie.' He held her gaze and it felt simultaneously like a knife lancing her chest and her heart weakening. He'd thought he'd chosen well, but she'd left him. Would he have been better off with Lucy, with someone else? Would he have been happy?

She couldn't bear to think of him married to another woman, and yet, she'd been the one who'd filed for divorce. Torn apart by grief for her future, she'd wanted to make a positive move for a fresh start, for both of them. Perhaps if she'd stood on her own two feet from an earlier age, had made that stand for herself instead of letting everyone else take care of her, she might have been stronger at fighting for her marriage too.

She didn't know how to answer him, so scrambled around to change the subject. 'So, you bought a house? That's impressive, especially with house prices these days.'

'Yes.' Pride glittered in his eyes now. 'I finally

managed to get a mortgage. All grown-up, right? It's a do-up, but it's all mine. It's in Grey Lynn.'

All mine.

They'd been saving to buy their own house and had almost made enough for a deposit when everything had fallen apart. She shook herself and ignored the hurt slicing through her. They weren't going back that far, just covering the last five years. 'Oh! Lucy lives in Ponsonby. We must be almost neighbours.'

They shared address details; they were close but not quite neighbours.

'Walking distance, though. That's funny—I thought Lucy lived in Titirangi.' His eyebrows rose. 'It's weird, isn't it, that when a relationship breaks up you lose touch with people you were once close with?'

'I know. It's like a part of you is shirred off. I often wondered about Logan and your friends and, well…' *You.* Her throat felt scratchy—too much nostalgia. 'Anyway, after her split with Tony, Lucy moved to Grey Lynn.'

'They're not together any more? I didn't want to ask…you know…' He grimaced and shrugged again.

'Because *I'm* here looking after her, not him?'

'And because it's none of my business.'

It was once.

'Lucy wouldn't care if I told you; she's very open about it. Basically, he didn't want kids and bolted when Lucy fell pregnant.'

'What a guy.' He shook his head and took another drink of wine. There'd never been a big friendship between Lewis and Tony but they had met up at family gatherings. She tried not to think about the gaps that existed now, the empty places at the table whenever, if ever, the Rose family got together. Conversely, she'd also lost Lewis's twin brother and the cosy friendships they'd once all shared.

'Yes, well, Mum and Dad moved in with Lucy to help her for the first four weeks of Stella's life until Lucy pushed them to go to Uganda.'

Marcel arrived with the *amuse bouche*, which was a divine nibble of goat's cheese panna cotta and gone in one delicious mouthful. But she took the brief conversation hiatus to settle her emotions. Splitting with him had been the right decision at the time, so there was no point reliving the pain of getting used to life without him.

He looked up from his plate and smiled, much more relaxed than she was, especially now they'd agreed not to kiss again. 'What about you, Charlie? How have the five years been for you?'

'Oh. Work, mainly. Yes, work with a few weekend city breaks to places in Europe. I went to the Edinburgh Fringe a couple of times. Spent a fortnight in France. But, yeah, work… I couldn't afford to buy a flat in London on a single doctor's salary, so I rented. But that did make it easier for me to leave.'

'You enjoyed it over there?'

'Oh, yes. London is amazing. There's always something to do, new things popping up all the time. There's a real buzz—' She was interrupted by the drum of heavy rain on the window. It sounded like rapid gunfire: *rata-tata-rata*. Then it became louder and harder—hail now too. The cars in the street had slowed and somehow the night sky had got even darker. 'Looks like the flash-flooding forecast was right.'

'Got to love Auckland summer weather.' He shook his head, smiling. 'Do you think you'd ever have come home if it hadn't been for Lucy's illness?'

'Um…well… I have been back a couple of times, actually. Just briefly, for Christmas.' But she hadn't contacted him because she'd thought it would hurt too much, for herself and for him.

'Oh.' His eyes widened with a flash of disappointment. 'Yes, Christmas. Of course.'

'You don't think Mum and Dad would have let me get away with not being here for five years?'

'No. That is very true. Your parents would have hated not seeing you at Christmas.' He cleared his throat, not very good at hiding his emotion. Did he miss her at Christmas, on every birthday? Did he remember their anniversary and light a candle in memory of what they'd once had, the way she did?

He shook his head. 'Right. I wonder where that next course is?'

He turned and nodded at Marcel who came running over, took away their plates and poured them a small glass of Riesling to pair with their starter of prosciutto and pickles, accompanied by the most divine olive and rosemary focaccia she'd ever tasted.

Soon enough, Marcel was back with their fish course, then slow-roasted lamb plus a half-glass of Sangiovese, while she chatted with Lewis about the differences in hospital emergency rooms between London and Auckland, about baby girls, seeing as they had those in common, and about recent movies they'd seen.

They didn't talk about whether either of them had had any other relationships or about their feelings or their shared past. And, while it was a good catch-up, the shared past was glaringly the elephant in the room, there in every look and every word. Because they couldn't escape it, could they? But at some point they needed to face it, even if only to put it to rest.

They were both distracted momentarily by the blare of a car horn outside. The rain still hammered against the window, making them raise their voices to be heard.

'And now you're back.' He smiled and she thought he might actually be okay with her being here. At least, now they'd had this chance to talk.

She found herself smiling too. Who would have thought she'd be sitting here doing this with Lewis? 'Yes, I'm back.'

He turned his warm gaze back to her. 'In a high-level job you must have worked hard to get. Well done. You always were a high flyer.'

'Thanks.' He'd always been her cheerleader, and she'd always let him be. Until the end, when she'd realised he was using his support of her to abnegate his own emotional needs. 'Well, I had to negotiate hard for the part-time bit, but I've promised to increase my hours once Lucy feels better. I'm not that desperate mess I was back then; I can manage full time just fine under normal circumstances. I just want to be able to give Stella and Lucy my time and attention.'

Um...like you are right now?

She pushed away her guilt at leaving them at home. Lucy had all but shoved her out of the door anyway.

'You were never a mess, Charlie, just messed up by grief and disappointment. There's a difference.' He paused for a beat, his eyes roving over her face, her mouth. 'I hope I've changed too. I'd have done things differently.'

What did he mean? 'You would...?'

Her words were stolen by another blare of a horn, so long and so loud, they could hear it from their table.

CHAPTER SEVEN

'WHAT THE HELL? Did you hear that?' Lewis tore his eyes away from Charlie's exquisite features and tried to listen to the street noises, trying to zone out the restaurant chatter.

The horn sounded again, then there was shouting.

He glanced at Charlie and she nodded, clearly reading his mind. Something bad had happened and they were duty-bound, and *needed*, to go and help. He jumped up and rushed to the door, pausing only for a moment to hold it open for her.

'Over there!' He pointed to a small crowd at the other side of the road. The traffic had come to a standstill so they quickly jogged across.

'Excuse me. 'Scuse me. I'm a paramedic and Charlie is a doctor. Can someone tell us what's happened?' He gently squeezed through the huddle of strangers to find a young woman, soaked through with rain, kneeling in the road and talking to an elderly gentleman, who was lying on the ground, pale, shocked and obviously in pain.

The young woman looked up at him and blinked through the rain. 'This is Graham. He was running across the road, trying to dodge the traffic, and suddenly collapsed. I don't know if he tripped or what, but he hit the ground with a real bump. And now he tells me he's got back and arm pain.'

'Okay, thanks.' Charlie turned to the crowd as Lewis knelt to assess the man. Had it been a trip or a collapse? 'Has anyone called an ambulance?'

The woman nodded. 'Yes, I did.'

'Great, thank you. We've got this now.'

'Brilliant.' She turned to Graham. 'Graham? Graham, this is a paramedic. He's going to help you.'

'And, lucky for us all, we've a doctor here too,' Lewis said to Graham as Charlie knelt in a puddle to start her examination. He turned to the crowd as he stripped off his jacket and laid it over the man in an attempt to keep him warm.

'Can someone ask in the restaurants for a blanket? We need to keep our friend here as warm and dry as possible. And can someone please redirect the traffic? Otherwise we'll be snarled up from here to Hamilton. You...perfect.' He pointed to a guy who was filming everything on his mobile phone; best to keep him occupied with something else. 'Please put that away. I'm sure our friend here doesn't want this all over the Internet. And can someone else please keep an eye out for the ambulance and direct them here? Right...' He turned back to Charlie. 'How are we doing?'

'Graham's got a blinding headache, but is managing to tell me where else he's got pain. He's trying not to move and I think that's a very good idea.' She looked up at Lewis and nodded, water dripping off her nose, and she blinked more rain out of her eyes. But she focused and he read between the lines. Graham had a possible head and neck injury but was conscious and responsive, all of which were good signs. 'Pain in his right wrist. Swelling and accompanying grazes on his elbow, palm and forehead. What was that…?' She looked back at their patient. 'What's that? Chest pain.'

He watched her fingers go instinctively to Graham's radial pulse point. She looked up warily. 'Thready. Weak. Irregular.'

Not good. Did he have a history of heart problems? 'Anyone here with Graham?' Lewis asked the now-diminishing crowd.

No one answered. The poor guy was on his own. And that meant there was no information.

'Graham? Graham, can you hear me? Damn. Graham?' Charlie's voice grew louder. 'Graham.' She put her hands to the man's carotid artery and shook her head. Then she put her face close to the man's lips and shook her head again. 'Lewis, cardiac arrest…'

After checking his airway, she tipped Graham's head back, lifted his chin, pinched his nose and put her mouth over his, then blew twice.

Lewis watched for Graham's chest to rise and fall with Charlie's breaths then he knelt alongside

Graham, placed the heel of his hand over the centre of the man's chest and started compressions, counting quickly. 'One, two, three…'

'Hey! Can you go look for an AED…defibrillator…please?' Charlie called to a passer-by. 'Ask in a shop. The museum. Any public space.'

'Twenty-nine, thirty…' Lewis called and she blew again twice.

Lewis nodded and started compressions again. 'One, two, three…'

'Where's that ambulance?' Charlie stood and peered down the car-blocked road. 'Can someone please provide some privacy? Stand here and here…' She directed three people, totally in command. But then, this was her turf.

And it was his. He huffed out, 'Twenty-nine, thirty.'

He leant back as she did mouth-to-mouth again. 'I can hear a distant siren but it's probably stuck in this snarled traffic.'

'Then we don't give up.'

'We don't give up.' Lewis nodded as he took her in. Her face was set and determined, her tone positive but guarded. Her hair was stuck to her cheeks, her clothes completely saturated. But her eyes blazed with a resolve bordering on stubbornness. She would not give up.

And she was quite possibly the most beautiful he'd ever seen her.

They did not give up. Not when the crowd began

to disperse. Not when the hail started again, hitting them like pellets of ice on their faces and hands. Not when the paramedics finally arrived—Emma and Raj, Lewis's colleagues. Not until Graham had pads attached to his chest and had been shocked twice then bundled into the ambulance and taken away.

Lewis watched the ambulance drive away, wishing he could be in there, giving the drugs and doing the hard yards to keep Graham alive. But he was also glad he was here, with Charlie, sharing this most profound experience.

She was talking to someone in the crowd, thanking them for their help. As she said goodbye, she turned, caught his eye and walked over to him, the friendly smile she'd put on for the bystander slipping to reveal her real thoughts. She inhaled deeply then blew out slowly. 'We did our best, right?'

He grimaced. 'We did.'

They both knew the odds of Graham being alive when he arrived at the emergency department were slim to none. And, even though they lived and breathed this kind of scenario every day, and had both learnt to deal with loss and the fragile human condition, he wanted to put his arms round her and hold her close. Because this was different. This was them against the odds and the elements.

It seemed they could work in perfect harmony even if they couldn't live in it.

Couldn't: past tense. Could never again, he reminded himself. Their chance was over. They were different people now, and still bruised from what had happened before. It would be madness to try get any of it back.

We don't give up.

You stay.

But they had given up on themselves. They'd stopped talking, stopped kissing, stopped being *them*. They'd become disparate people living under the same roof.

He'd stayed. But staying hadn't helped, had it? He'd thrown all his energy into making her feel better and had ignored his own needs. He'd pushed them aside and refused to talk about how he felt.

And it had all been for nothing, because how could she have stayed with someone who'd refused to acknowledge there was a problem, especially when the problem ended up being him?

He should have been open to talking about adoption or surrogacy, but he hadn't been able to see past her pain, and had thought talking about alternatives to her carrying a child would be even more painful.

God, he didn't know, even now, whether she'd thought about those options since, once the rawness had faded. Maybe in time, if they'd stuck it out, they'd have reached a place where they could have talked about that. The thought made his heart ache. So many missed opportunities because they'd been enmeshed in so much grief.

She shook her head and then her arms, and laughed as water sprayed and sluiced onto the ground. 'Ugh. I am completely soaked.'

'So I see.' He laughed and his gaze grazed her wet top which showed the outline of her bra.

Lace...

Something deep inside him flared. *Stop.* But how could he help it? She was freaking beautiful. Not just because she looked amazing, all dishevelled and undone, but because she didn't care about getting wet and cold for the sake of someone who needed her skills.

'Ah.' She tugged her jacket around her breasts and then put her palm on his chest. Even though they were both cold, her touch was warm and steady, unlike his heart. 'You didn't even have a jacket on. Wow, your heart is beating very fast, Lewis.'

'Cardiac compressions can do that to a guy.' As could the tender touch of a beautiful woman. And the thought of what was beneath her lacy bra.

'Mr Parry!' It was Marcel calling from across the road, outside the restaurant. He ducked between the now slow-moving cars making his way towards them. 'Thought you might be still here.'

Lewis glanced at the restaurant. The closed sign hung in the window. 'Hi. Yes, sorry we had to dash off like that. There was a medical emergency and we had to help.'

'Not a problem. How is he?'

Lewis sighed. 'Touch and go, to be honest.'

'Well, thank you for being there for him, especially on a night like this.' Marcel held up a brown paper carrier bag. 'You missed your dessert but I've packed it up for you. Plus some sticky wine to go with it.'

'Sticky?' Charlie frowned. He could feel her shivering next to him.

The restaurant owner laughed. 'Dessert wine—thick and sweet and delicious. You'll like it.'

'You know, I've never tried dessert wine.' Charlie beamed at Marcel. 'Thank you.'

'Yes, thank you, Marcel. That's very kind.' Lewis took the paper bag and thought if it got any more soggy it might not last the trip back to the hotel, only a couple of streets away.

Once Marcel had returned to his restaurant, Charlie looked at her phone. 'I'm freezing. I'm going to call a cab and go home.'

No. Lewis's gut contracted. He wasn't ready to let her go, because they hadn't really talked, had they? They'd only just started to unpack things before Graham's emergency had interrupted everything. But they were both soaked and cold. It was probably a good idea to end the night now, before he read too much into the warmth of her palm on his chest and the way she sometimes looked at him with regret, sadness and…desire. 'Sounds good.'

But a frown formed as she looked at the car-hire app, her teeth chattering now. 'Is there something else going on tonight—a gig or big sports game? Because I can't seem to get any take-up on my ride home. *Oh...* It's not even responding now. I've just got the swirl of doom on my screen. Maybe the app's down, or my phone's drowned.'

'I'll give it a go.' He pulled out his phone, trying to keep his own shivering under control. 'Nope, nothing. Look, my hotel is literally two streets away. Why don't you come up to my room, dry off and wait until the app's working again? Or wait until the alcohol's worn off enough for me to be safe to drive you.'

'Go to your hotel?' Her gaze tangled with his and, despite the shivering and teeth chattering, her eyes misted the way they'd always used to when she'd been all turned on. 'I… I don't know, Lewis.'

But he knew it wasn't just a question of whether they should go together, it was a question of what might happen. Because the warmth of her palm was good. The desire in her eyes was better.

The flare of need inside him threatened to overwhelm him. But they'd agreed, nothing was going to happen.

Nothing could happen.

CHAPTER EIGHT

GO TO HIS HOTEL?

Charlotte's head filled with all the things that could happen in a hotel room with Lewis. They had form, right? Back when they'd been married, a hotel room had always meant sex. They had a relationship history of many hotel rooms and lots of good times. History that should not be repeated.

And yet, that kiss yesterday had been…hot. And needed, and like some kind of switch that had flipped her world upside down. Because she couldn't deny that she wanted to do it again…and again…and again. So going to his hotel would be dangerous. 'I… I don't know, Lewis.'

He blinked as rain ran in rivulets down his cheeks, then he pulled her into a doorway out of the rain. 'Because what? You think I'll make a move? No way, Charlie. We agreed, right?'

'Yes, we agreed.' Although, up close with him in a doorway, she was currently regretting that agreement.

Stop it.

His eyes widened. 'So, where's the harm? We are both completely soaked and shivering. That is not good. What if you're waiting for half an hour for a cab? I don't want you getting hypothermia on my watch.'

The harm was, she didn't think she could keep her promise if she was in a hotel room with him. But she *was* freezing and completely drenched and he was holding up the soggy restaurant takeaway bag saying, 'There's pudding too.'

And she'd always been a sucker for dessert. 'Oh, okay. Just until I'm dry and warm.'

'Come on, then.' He stretched out his hand and she grabbed it and ran with him through the Auckland streets to his hotel. She was holding Lewis's hand. And it felt so instinctively right and good.

But when they entered the hotel and he had to retrieve his room key from his wallet, he let go, pausing for a moment as he looked at her, then at their hands. 'Sorry. Habit, I guess.'

'It's okay. It helped us get here quicker, that's all. I'm not sure I'd have kept up with you otherwise. You're very fit, Lewis.'

'I try.' He grinned and she followed him into the lift, her heart sagging, but knowing he was right. Kissing and hand-holding were not on the agenda. The question she had to ask herself, then, was… what was really on the agenda here? Because she could have waited for a cab, or even got a bus. She could have taken her share of the dessert home and given half to Lucy.

But all questions were forgotten when she

walked into the penthouse suite he'd been given. The walls were dark slatted wood, the furnishings made of the softest cream leather and the curtains were a lovely, soft taupe linen. It was all very top-end and luxurious. 'Wow. This is seriously expensive and very, very swanky. I bet it's a great view on a fine day.'

'When I checked in this afternoon, I could see right out over the harbour bridge and up to the North Shore,' he said. But all they could see now was the rain lashing against the floor-to-ceiling windows. 'It's also got an outside fire pit, but that's a bit redundant tonight. Go hop in the shower; I'll plate this up. You want a hot drink too?' He pulled out a drawer in a console. 'There's a kettle and coffee and tea here.'

She was so cold, her body had gone from shivering to bone-rattling and her fingers were numb. 'Can you see if they've got hot chocolate?'

He grinned and his eyes grew wide and wicked. 'Hot chocolate, dessert wine *and* pudding—now you're talking. I'll see what I can do. Go—shower.'

The shower was glorious, with high-end shower gel, shampoo and conditioner and a rain shower-head. *This* rain was going to be hot and healing. Although she probably should have a cold shower if she was going to get through dessert with Lewis.

She scrubbed and shampooed herself and then wrapped her hair in a thick towel and drew a fluffy white robe round her naked body. When she went back into the bedroom, she found him standing by the console, stirring a cup of something that smelt delicious. He'd changed out of his wet clothes and was now in a dry pair of shorts and T-shirt. He glanced up as she approached, his eyes warm and soft as he smiled. 'Feel better?'

That smile was so good, it made her insides tingle. 'Oh, yes. I've stopped shivering, and these towels are *so* fluffy. Your turn.'

He shook his head. 'It's okay. I'll just finish making the hot drinks.'

'Lewis, please. You must be freezing.'

'No. You…' He looked as if he was about to say something more but closed his mouth. 'As it happens, I am cold, actually. Can you finish off stirring these? I won't be long.'

*You…*what? Had he been about to put her needs above his again? But he hadn't, had he? He'd stopped himself. *Interesting.* It was a small thing, but the second time she'd noticed he'd put his needs first. That was good; he needed to do that.

She could hear him singing in the bathroom like he used to at home. Always the same tune, Rihanna's *Umbrella.* Which was pretty appropriate right now.

But…*home.* Her gut tightened in sadness. They'd loved that little rented cottage in Parnell. they'd made it theirs with the pieces of furniture they'd carefully chosen from second-hand shops.

It had been hard leaving that place too, hard leaving him.

She heard the water running and imagined him in there, and wondered how the last five years had changed his body. She'd met him at high school and had watched with delight as he'd grown from lanky, sporty teenager to a man. She'd encouraged him to follow his dream of being a paramedic and celebrated when he got accepted on the course and when he'd graduated top of the class.

He'd kept himself fit for his job by running, swimming and gym work. She'd always loved the hard ridges of his muscles, the way she'd felt so safe and wanted in his arms. The way he'd looked at her as they'd made love.

She recalled the words he'd whispered to her on their wedding night: *I promise I'll always love you, Charlie. Whatever happens. I don't want a life without you. Ever.*

But, even so, she'd forced him to have one. Tears threatened, prickling the back of her eyes. Her heart hurt.

God, Lewis...

The door lock clicked and she swallowed back her regret and sadness. She must not show him how she felt. Which was...what exactly? Mixed up. *Turned on.* More... All the feelings, all the things.

Was she just hankering for what they'd once had? She didn't know. But something new beat inside her and she couldn't ignore it. She also didn't know what the hell to do with it, because it seemed to be beating louder and harder every second she spent with him.

He came out of the bathroom in a cloud of steam, dressed again in his shorts and T shirt and, disappointingly, not just with a small towel at his waist.

Had she really been hoping for that?

Yes, she had. She'd been secretly hoping to see him half-naked.

All naked, actually.

Oh, God, she had it bad. Why hadn't she stayed, tried harder?

She settled on the comfortable chair next to the little coffee table in the middle of the room, tucked her feet up under her bottom and cradled her mug, relishing the scent and taking little sips just for something to take her focus away from Lewis. 'This is delicious.'

'Excellent.' He grabbed his cup and drank, leaning against the console. His eyes widened. 'Wow. It really is. Everything in here is next level.'

'I wanted to say, you did good before, Lewis—with the CPR. In all our years together, I never actually saw you working. You're very professional. Amazing.'

'That's high praise from an emergency doctor; thanks. You too.' He rubbed his hair dry with a hand towel. 'It wasn't easy kneeling on wet tarmac trying to save someone's life. But you didn't hesitate.'

'Of course not. And neither did you. But I think I've got gravel burns on my knees.' She examined them: just a little bruising. She looked up and caught him looking at her legs too. 'Do you still love your job?'

'Absolutely. There is nothing I'd rather do for work.' His gaze moved to her face. 'You? Emergency medicine was always on your radar. Are you glad you chose it?'

'Hell, yes. I love the urgency and the adrenalin rush. And I love helping people.'

'You always did.' He thought for a moment. 'I wonder how Graham's doing.'

'I don't have great hopes, I'm afraid.'

Lewis's eyebrows rose as he sat down opposite her. 'I'll ask at work tomorrow.'

'Or I could.' She bugged her eyes at him and chuckled.

He laughed and scrubbed a hand through his tousled hair. 'This is so weird. Who would have thought I'd be working with you? And be *here* in a hotel room with you?'

She glanced down at her towelling robe. Half-naked in a hotel room; once upon a time, he'd have slipped his hands in between the robe folds and made some sexy comment.

She tightened the tie at her waist. 'Well, who else would you like to be in a hotel room with?

Please don't tell me you still have a crush on Amanda Seyfried?'

'Oh, *Mamma Mia*.' He made a 'chef's kiss' gesture, bringing his thumb and two fingers to his mouth and flaring them out. 'There's just something about her I can't let go of. She was in the best movies of my youth.'

'Um...you were late teens when *Mamma Mia* came out.' She laughed. She'd always ribbed him about his love for the actress who'd played the starring role in the movie. She knew him so well—*had* known him so well—and suddenly she wanted to fill the important gaps in her knowledge of him, even though some of his answers might hurt her. 'Have you...um...dated anyone since... you know...? Is it okay to ask?'

'Sure.' He blinked, obviously a little taken aback. 'I guess we were bound to get round to this conversation at some point. I've been out with a couple of women, yes.'

Why had she asked him that when any answer other than *no* would stab her heart? 'Oh? And...?'

He shrugged and sat back. 'Didn't work out. You?'

'A couple of dinner dates, nothing more. When I got to London I decided to throw myself into my job. Seemed a lot easier than getting into another relationship.'

'So nothing serious?' He drained his hot chocolate, his expression one that said, 'seriously, you haven't had sex for five years?'

'Nothing much at all. It took a long time to come to terms with everything. I didn't feel I had a lot to offer someone.'

He put his cup down and frowned at her. 'Please, Charlie. For God's sake. You've got so much to offer anyone.'

'Oh, I'm not saying it to get sympathy. Just, most guys our age are looking to settle down and I couldn't commit to anything. Not after...you.'

He inhaled sharply, took a moment, then leaned forward and touched her hand. 'Charlie, I'm sorry I broke it. I didn't give you what you needed. I thought I was saying and doing the right things but in hindsight...' His voice trailed off but he kept on looking at her. Kept his hand on hers.

'Hell, even I didn't know what I needed, so don't beat yourself up about that.' She shook her head. So here they were, suddenly in the thick of it. There was so much they needed to unpack, and yet at the same time she wondered if they should venture into their past at all. Because it might only drum up the old arguments and they'd be no further on, except five years older. '*I* left, Lewis. I broke it. Me and my stupid uterus.'

'Don't ever say that. Nothing about you is stupid, Charlie. Nothing at all.' His jaw set as he looked at her. And in his expression she saw so many tangled emotions that mirrored hers: confusion, desire, affection. Fear…yes, fear, because they were treading new territory here. Forging something out of the ashes of their marriage…. *friendship?*

Everything was loaded with the weight of their break-up and there needed to be some honesty before anything, including their fledging friendship, could grow. And here tonight, after they'd shared something so momentous as trying to save a life, it felt right to do a deep dive.

She rested her cup on her knee and tried to explain her version of what had happened after she'd left. 'I had some counselling, you know. Talked myself silly going round and round. But eventually I came to terms with why I was so devastated by it all.'

She didn't know why she'd suddenly blurted out that particular thing but it felt right to say something, to show him and herself that she'd tried to understand everything.

He frowned. 'Because the infertility was a shock. Because it was cruel, Charlie.'

'Yes.' *The* infertility—not *your* infertility. Lewis generally chose his words carefully. Maybe he still didn't see it as just *her* problem. She didn't know how to feel about that. 'And because I felt as if I let everyone down.'

'Whoa. No way.' He raised his palm. 'That wasn't it at all. I didn't feel let down. I hurt for you—with you.'

'I know, but I could see in your eyes how you pretended you were okay about it but, deep down, you weren't. You couldn't have been okay with it. You had this idea of what a perfect family looked like...'

'Sure. I always wanted a family, you know that. Especially after my crappy childhood, being shunted from pillar to post because my mum didn't actually want or like children, and my dad never, ever being in the picture. I missed not having a dad like other kids. I missed my mum a lot too.'

He hauled in a breath. 'In my head, I had this blueprint of a family: two kids, two parents; probably something I'd seen on TV. But if I ever did it I wanted to get it right. I wanted to have what Logan and I never had, what Logan is creating with Alice and the girls. Is that such a bad thing—to want to love your own child? To have a tight bond? To be *present*?'

'Not at all. You deserve to have that, Lewis.' She took a breath, her chest constricting. 'But when I couldn't do that you still said everything would be okay, everything was fine. It was like you weren't listening or understanding the situation.' She watched his expression, hoping she wasn't hurting him all over again. Because they were actually talking about this—really *talking*—for the first time.

But he just smiled sadly. 'I wanted you to believe in yourself the way I believed in you.'

Her heart squeezed. 'And I just felt trapped by impossible dreams I couldn't fulfil.'

His expression hollowed out to one of shock and uncertainty. '*Trapped* by me?'

She drew her gaze away from him, swallowing down the raw lump in her throat. 'By you, by my parents, by other people's expectations: to carry on the family doctoring tradition; bear the grand-children my parents desperately wanted; provide the family you so desperately deserved to have. Your mother wasn't there for you when you grew up, Lewis. You scratched a family out of distant relatives. You and Logan clung to each other and you both deserved to grow something good for yourselves. Logan has done that; you need that too. But I couldn't…can't…do that for you. And no amount of you telling me everything was going to be fine was going to magically make things what they weren't.'

He swallowed as he digested her words. 'You were struggling; I was trying to make it better for you.'

'I know. And you did. *You did.*' She ached to soothe away the hurt they'd both endured during that rocky time. 'But rightly or wrongly I felt as if there was a sheen of facade, a brave face rather than an honest one. You never told me how you *felt* about it all. It was like trying to talk to a rock.'

'I was trying to *be* a rock for you—staunch and solid. If I said it was all okay, it would be. If

I said we'd get through it, we would. I was trying to be a support. Have you any idea how hard it is to see someone you love cry every day for eighteen months? To endure endless painful tests and investigations? And to have nothing…*nothing*… you can do to help them? To see them closed off, hibernating under the duvet, refusing to come out, to *live*? Then to see the anger rip through them, to come home to broken plates and slashed cushions? To not know which Charlotte I was actually coming home to? Depressed Charlotte, angry Charlotte, numb Charlotte…'

He shook his head, eyes sad. 'I tried; God help me I did. I knew you were hurting so badly but I didn't know what else to do, other than try make you believe things would be okay.'

Her lips trembled and she pressed them together. Because she had been that person—she wasn't now, but she had been. Torn apart by despair, she'd allowed her emotions to engulf her. 'I was devastated and I took it out on you. But I could see you were broken too. You just wanted to hide that from me.'

His dark-brown eyes blazed then. 'Damn right I did. I was protecting you. I didn't want to make you feel worse by adding my feelings to the mix.'

'And that…right there. That's why I had to go, Lewis. We'd always talked openly about having kids. You were thrilled when Logan had his. You were, and I'm sure still are, an amazing uncle.

But, when it came to us, you couldn't admit how disappointed you were. You clammed up. You refused to talk about your feelings.

'But I saw it. I tried to get through to you. I pushed you because I didn't want you to resent me further down the track. But the more I pushed, the more distant you became. Then I got angry…with you and the unfairness of having our plans taken away. And then I stopped trying. In the end, it felt like were living separate lives. We both deserved more than that.'

He shook his head, his eyes flickering closed for a beat. When he looked up at her again, he saw fathomless sadness there. 'I'm so sorry. I thought saying that everything would be okay was what you wanted to hear. And I realise I was wrong; I see that now. I've thought about it so much over the years and I get it. But back then I loved you so much, Charlie. I just wanted you to stop hurting.'

Loved: past tense. But, hell, what else could she expect? That he'd held a torch for her these last few years? That he'd put his life on hold until she decided to come back? No. But the loss of it reverberated through her, core-deep.

She reached out and stroked her fingertips across his jaw, because this was so profound, so damned deep, she couldn't sit there and not touch him. She needed to feel the physical connection as well as the emotional one. 'You know what? I don't even know what I wanted to hear back then except for, *I'm sorry, Mrs Parry, we made a mistake. Of course you can have a baby.*'

'I wish that had happened, Charlie. I really do. More than anything.' His eyes glistened. 'And I'm sorry I got it so wrong.'

She moved her hand from his cheek and knitted her fingers with his. 'Oh, we were so young, Lewis. And blindsided at the news. I'd always had everything given to me on a plate. I had you, my doting parents and a loving sister, and you all conspired to keep me happy and boost my ego and soothe my journey through life. God knows why.'

'Because we loved you, Charlie. Plain and simple.'

Loved: there it was again. 'And I'd had it so easy up until then. I'd never failed at anything before and didn't know how to cope with it all.'

'And I refused to discuss some things. I refused to acknowledge how I felt.'

'Which was?' She waited, wondering if he had enough personal growth and faith in her to be honest. 'How did you feel about what *you'd* lost?'

'You want me to say those things? That I was broken up that I couldn't be a dad? That it hurt whenever I saw pregnant women, or when I held little Lola? It hurt that I'd never have that; I'd never get to watch my son play football.'

'Or do ballet?' She smiled, because it was never going to happen for her, but if it did for Lewis...if someone was lucky enough to find him and keep him…then he needed to be open to all opportunities for his kids.

'Or ballet. I didn't say those things because I didn't want you to hurt more.' He exhaled a long breath, then looked her full in the eyes. He hesitated and closed his eyes briefly. When he opened them, he nodded sadly. 'I was gutted, if I'm honest. Absolutely broken.'

Finally.

She let go of the breath she felt she'd been holding for nearly six and a half years, since that day at the doctor when they'd got the terrible news. Finally, he was being honest. *Finally.* She felt hollowed out, as broken as he was describing, but also felt relief too. This was a breakthrough for them.

Tears sprang in her eyes and she fisted them away. 'I'm sorry, Lewis. So sorry we couldn't fulfil your dream. But thank you for telling me the truth.'

'I should have done it a long time ago.'

The dream hadn't fallen apart because of her uterus. The dream had fallen apart because they'd been unable to deal with that. 'Were we too young? Was that it? Too disconnected from each other or too immature to deal with such big personal issues?'

Her parents had never wanted them to get married so young. It had almost been a case of 'told you so' when she'd left him. *You should have listened to us; we know what's best for you.*

'We did the best we could at the time. Two hurting people who didn't know what to do.' He brought her hand to his mouth, kissing it gently, the way he used to back when things between them had been a whole lot better. She shivered at the touch of his lips on her skin. There was something so intimate in such a small gesture, it almost overpowered her.

She needed some space before she crawled into his lap and kissed him properly again, long and hard. She took a deep breath, then another, trying to find her equilibrium again. She slipped her hand from his, found a smile and made it real… for Lewis. 'Hey, you know what's going to make us both feel better?'

'I'm all ears.' He smiled, the glistening eyes dry now.

'Marcel's pudding. And what about that wine? It would be a shame not to have it.'

You were supposed to be leaving, Charlie.

But she needed some light relief before going home and facing Lucy's questions.

One little taste...*of the wine.*

'Excellent idea, Dr Rose.' He looked relieved to be chartering less difficult territory as he jumped up to find plates, arrange the dessert items on a large one and then pull a piece of card out of the bag. 'There's a copy of the menu here. Looks like these are mini almond-and-espresso cannoli, and chocolate-and-salted-caramel bom…boloni… bomboloni.' He stumbled over the Italian word, then brought the plate to the little coffee table. 'That must be these little doughnut-shaped things. And…mini cheesecake.'

'Oh, *yes*!' Charlie fist-pumped the air. 'I'm going to go for the chee—'

'Cheesecake first? Your favourite, right?' He laughed and handed her a glass of the wine he'd just opened. 'Try it with some of this.'

There was a new ease to the atmosphere now—breathing space, an understanding. Things felt brighter inside her, as if the weight of nearly seven years…the difficult last two of their marriage and five apart…was lifting.

She bit into the cheesecake, which was light and yet rich, followed by a mouthful of the wine. 'Oh, okay, it's sweet, all right. Oh. Wow.' She blinked and swallowed. 'Okay. There's a lot going on there. That's…different.'

He grinned. 'Yes, but what do you think?'

'It's like drinking jam. Winey jam. Jammy wine.' She laughed. 'Is it strong?'

He examined the bottle. 'Only fourteen and a half percent.'

'Hmm. Strong enough.' She had another mouthful. 'Okay, I'm getting used to it. It's nice—yummy, actually.

'Let me try again then, ahem: flash-flooding

forecast. Flash flooding florecast.' She giggled. 'Imagine me after more than one glass.'

'Lightweight.' He leaned forward across the little table to pick up a mini cannoli at the same time she did. Their noses almost touched. He inhaled sharply as he captured her gaze. '*God.*'

'What?' Her forehead brushed against his. He smelt of expensive shampoo. He smelt good. She was acutely aware of him so close, so here, so… Lewis.

'Your laugh. Your smile…' He ran the back of his fingertips down her cheek. 'Jeez, Charlie.'

She closed her eyes and tried to swallow away the rush of desire but found herself curling towards his fingers and his heat.

'Lewis,' she whispered, every cell in her body straining for his touch.

No. They'd agreed. But he was so damned irresistible.

She drew away, picked up a *bombol…* doughnutty thing…and held it to his mouth. He took a bite and sighed. 'Oh, my God. You have got to try this.' He took the leftover half from her fingers and held it to her lips. 'Try it, Charlie. Bomboloni is "the bomb". This is the best thing you'll taste all night.'

I hope not.

She opened her mouth and bit into the bomboloni. Salted caramel and chocolate cream burst onto her tongue, sweet, salty and delicious. 'Oh, God, that is heaven.'

He edged away slightly and looked at her, cupping her cheek with his palm. 'No, darling. You are.'

The world stopped turning right then and shrank to that room, that night, that man. She swallowed then cleared her throat. 'But, Lewis… We said…' She didn't have the fight in her to say any more. She wanted it—wanted him.

He shrugged. 'Hey, I'm trying here, I promise. But you are so damned gorgeous. I tried to not be attracted to you. I tried not to notice how amazing you looked when you arrived at the restaurant. I tried not to look at your gorgeous nipples through your wet top. I'm trying to be platonic but I'm failing…badly.'

She gasped at his words, her body tingling with the rush of need rippling through her, and laughed as she remembered her restaurant entrance: dripping wet with a useless umbrella held over her soggy hair. 'I was drenched.'

'You looked beautiful to me.'

She curled her fingers round his wrist. His pulse beat fast and furious against her fingers. 'Please, Lewis. Don't try bolster me up. I know I looked a mess.'

'I'm telling you the truth, Charlie. I like you all undone.' His eyes flickered closed briefly, as if he was wrestling with his self-control. Clearly he failed, as he whispered, ‘I particularly like the way you’re looking at me right now.’

She swallowed, her grip on her own self-control weakening with every word he said. ‘Like how?’

‘Like you want to kiss me.’

CHAPTER NINE

He didn't wait for her answer. He knew his Charlie—knew when she was turned on, knew how to make her so. Knew when she needed to be kissed, and right now she needed it as much as he did.

He stood up and strode towards her, framing her cheek with his palm as he bent and slid his lips over hers. She gripped his shoulder and moaned, whispering his name like a sacred psalm. 'Lewis. Lewis. *Lewis...*'

She closed her eyes and sank into the kiss, sliding her tongue into his mouth and deepening their connection even more.

His pulse sky-rocketed. Need heated him. *She* heated him. This evening had been so intense, the embers of what they'd once had crashing back into full, incandescent life. The raw honesty was something only they could share. No one else had experienced the things they'd been through, and there was a new and deeper connection, so much swelling emotion between them—he and his amazing wife.

Ex-wife... The thought fleetingly assailed him and threatened to douse the desire coursing through him. But he pushed away all the pain and hurt from the past. She was here, she wanted him and, right now, he wanted this new version of her. She was sexier, more beautiful, more fun than he remembered and the way she was looking at him stoked the fire prickling over his skin, under his skin and deep in his belly.

There was only one way this could go. The kiss started soft and slow, achingly familiar and yet different too. He felt a new, heightened thrum of desire between them, the frank honesty lacing their connection and tightening it. He'd never wanted a woman as damned much as he did right now.

She tasted of jammy wine and chocolate; of the past and the now—this moment, this woman.

Charlie. The first woman he'd ever loved. The only woman he'd ever loved.

He needed to explore her, to feel her tight against him, so he broke the kiss and offered his hand. She took it, standing up and stroking her palm across his chest. He kissed the top of her head, her forehead, her nose. He imprinted the new things he noticed into his memory banks: the scent of high-end shower gel; little laughter lines at the corners of her eyes. 'I can't get enough of you, Charlie. Stay the night?'

Her teeth worried at her bottom lip as she stared up at him, those beautiful blue eyes glittering with need but also concern. 'Lucy… She might be worried.'

Not a refusal, just hesitation.

'Call her, then—see if she's okay. Then stay.' His lips were on her throat and he murmured the words against her skin. 'I want you so much. I need this, Charlie, and I think you do too.'

'I do. But…' She kissed him again, long and slow. Then she pulled away, picked up her bag from the floor and rummaged for her phone. 'Hang on a second.'

She wrote a text and showed it to him, smiling, before sending it.

Luce, hey. Just checking in. Got stuck in rain downpour and now drying off at Lewis's hotel. Car hire apps are down. Might not be back until morning.

'Excellent. Might as well keep busy while we wait for her reply.' He tipped her chin so he could kiss her again. This time it was a slow burn kiss, backlit with a lightning show from the midnight sky. They were literally on top of the world, the forces of nature outside amplifying the potency of their passion in the penthouse.

Her hands slid down his back and pulled him tightly against her. She pressed against him and, when he slid his leg between hers, she moaned and rubbed her core against it. Her eyes flashed pure sex as she looked at him. 'God, Lewis, I want you so much.'

'You drive me crazy.' His body flooded with a deep, long-forgotten hunger as he slid his hand into the folds of her robe, finding her nipple and stroking until the tight bud peaked. Then he cupped her breast, relishing the soft silk of her skin and the misting of her eyes as he stroked and caressed.

Her phone beeped.

'Damn.' She reached for it, tutted then giggled. Then she showed him her sister's response:

You should change professions, sis. Novelist would be good. Fiction is your strong suit. You could just have told me you were having sex. Lucky thing. I would say be careful but you're a grown adult and you never listen to me anyway. See you in the morning. Have a good night.

He guffawed. 'Your sister has the measure of you.'

'Of you, more like.' She shook her head.

'Me? How? I'm just looking after you until the car hire app works.' He made to look all innocent, when he actually felt the complete opposite: desperate for her; carnal, base.

'Sure you are. Come here.' Laughing, she tugged at the neck of his T-shirt and brought him closer. Her hands were trembling.

He stilled and tilted her chin, looking deep into her eyes. 'You're shaking. Are you sure about this, Charlie?'

'I'm more sure about this than anything ever in my life.' She frowned. 'You have to ask?'

'Yes, I do. This…it's a lot.'

'It is. And I don't know what it means. I just know that I want it now. I want *you* now. Tonight.' She kissed his throat. 'I have no idea what it'll mean tomorrow, though.'

'That we're two grown adults who make rash decisions based on intense sexual craving and a deep sense of nostalgia, fuelled by adrenalin from a recent intense CPR situation?' Laughing, he slid his hand down to her thigh and whispered, 'Basically, I want to be deep inside you, Charlie. And damned quickly.'

'You've got such a way with words.' She giggled then put her arms round his neck and kissed his throat. 'Intense sexual craving…huh? I like the sound of that. Now, where were we?'

'I think…we were about here…' Her towelling robe had slipped down one shoulder, revealing her breast, and he slid his hand across the naked nipple and watched desire and delight heat her face. But when he looked back at her body he was jolted by the yellow-black bruising across her shoulder. He shuddered. 'I hate to see you so bruised, Charlie. I don't want to hurt you. Tell me to stop any time.'

'I'm not made of paper, Lewis. I'm a tough old cookie these days.' She kissed his jaw, then his mouth. By the time she pulled away, he was fairly sure she was sure. But he very gently kissed the bruising, making sure not to hurt her.

She smiled. 'You're just a softie at heart, aren't you?'

He growled as his erection pressed against her core. 'Soft?'

'Hard. So hard.' Her body tensed as she moaned and writhed against him, her hands sliding into his hair. 'God, that's so…good.'

'Yes. It is. But actually…' He slipped his hands behind her knees and picked her up.

She screeched. 'Lewis Parry, what the actual hell?'

'Got to do this properly.' It wasn't exactly far. Three strides and he was laying her down on the plush, soft comforter, her hair splayed on his pillow, copper against white. Just as he remembered. Just as he'd dreamt of so many times.

He lay next to her, propped his head up on his hand and cupped her face for more kisses. He untied the robe and let the fabric fall open. Emotion caught in his throat. 'You are so beautiful, Charlie.'

She smiled at him. 'I want to see you too. All of you.'

He knelt and reached for the hem of his T-shirt but she stopped him. 'Wait. I want to undress you.'

'Be my guest.' He laughed, but then stopped as he watched her still trembling hands tug at the hem.

'You sure you're okay, Charlie?'

'I'm better than okay. I'm just… I don't know. Nervous. Excited.'

'It's me—no need to be nervous.'

'But we've both changed so much over five years. Oh, Lewis, when I think about how much we've missed out on—'

'Don't.' He interrupted her. 'Don't over-think. Just go with this.'

'Intense sexual craving, right?' She knelt up, tugged his T-shirt over his head then ran her fingertips across his chest. 'Wow. You've kept up the gym work, then?'

Pride punched his gut. Okay, yes, he shouldn't care how he looked, but he liked that she still found his hard-worked-for body sexy. She traced over his nipples and giggled when he winced. 'Still ticklish?'

'I guess so.' But his throat was dry and he wasn't laughing any more. The atmosphere was too thick with need, their scent and…anticipation. As her fingers explored his pecs, making her way south towards his erection, he hauled in a stuttering breath, trying hard to rein in the overwhelm of pure lust. He wanted her so much that, if those fingers went anywhere near his groin, he'd explode. So he gently pushed her back on the bed and kissed her again, tracing his own fingertip path down her belly.

He slid his fingers between her legs and she gasped. 'Yes. Yes.'

He slipped his fingers inside her, revelling in her pleasure as she rocked against his hand. A few thrusts had her arching her back, guttural moans filling the room. He found her nub and rubbed slowly.

'Oh. Oh, please, Lewis. I need you. Now...' she managed through snatched, breathless kisses. He felt her tighten, stroking her to a wonderful hot, slick mess of moaning.

'Whoa. You really do want it.'

'Yes. Now.' But then she was pulsing around his fingers and kissing him greedily. 'Please.'

He held her as her orgasm rocked through her, waiting until she rode the crescendo. He kissed her long and hard. But she reached for him and stroked his length, and he held his breath, garnering whatever flimsy thread of control he had left.

'Condom....wallet....' He shook his head then smacked the bed with his palm. 'Damn. They've probably expired.' He grimaced and explained, 'It's been a while.'

But she beamed up at him and stroked his cheek. 'Hey, have you forgotten? There's zero chance of pregnancy. And I haven't had sex with anyone for a long time. Not...since you. I'm good.'

Not since him... His heart squeezed. And *God,* yes—no babies. That had been the core of their problem. But this was now, this was new. 'It's been a long while for me too.'

She pulled him closer and rubbed her wet heat against his erection. 'I want you inside me. I want you, Lewis.'

And he couldn't hold back any longer. He rolled on top of her and gently pushed her legs apart, positioning himself at her entrance. Then he nudged inside her.

God. She was so ready for him. So...*much*. He inhaled sharply and withdrew because it was too much, too fast.

'No! Don't stop.' She moaned. 'Please.'

He thrust into her again, deeper, harder.

'Yes. Please.' She wrapped her legs around his backside, ramping up the rhythm with the rock of her hips. 'This is so good.'

He brushed her damp hair from her face and kissed her. Their gazes locked and he slowed the rhythm. He couldn't take his eyes from her. She was achingly beautiful and here in his arms. She stared up at him as if he was a freaking god or something—the way she used to, back when they'd had so much future to look forward to.

When they could make each other feel this good, how had it all gone so wrong?

Tears slipped down her cheek.

'Hey.' He kissed them away one by one. 'Don't cry. This is...perfect. You are perfect, Charlie.

You're beautiful. *Man*, you are so beautiful, it makes my heart hurt.'

'Oh, Lewis.' She gripped him and hiccupped out a sob, then laughed…all of which mirrored the same confused emotions whirling round his body. She fisted the tears away. 'I'm sorry, I can't help it. It's just, I never thought this could happen. It's so good. I love the way you feel inside me. But it's all just so much.'

'I know. I know. I know.' He pressed his lips to her cheek, then captured her mouth in a searing hot kiss as he thrust into her, faster and harder. Bright light flashed in front of his eyes, in his brain, in his body.

'Lewis.'

He'd never thought he'd hear his name on her lips again.

'Lewis. Yes… *Yes…*' Her tears were coming thick and fast now as he felt her clench and contract around him, then shudder her release in a cry. And his world balled tight into this moment, this woman—this beautiful, amazing woman taking him over the edge too.

For a few long minutes he lay there, cradling her in his arms, dazed, satisfied and happy for the first time in a very long time. It wasn't that they'd rewound, but that they'd built something new out of intense sorrow and confusion.

'Lewis, I'm sorry.' She kept her arms around him, holding him tightly against her. 'I'm sorry.'

He didn't know what she meant. Sorry that she was crying? Sorry that she'd left? Sorry that she'd come back and tipped his world upside down?

But he held her tight and stroked her hair, feeling her heat, feeling her chest heave against him, the wet of her tears on his arm. Then slowly… slowly…she settled. But he kept on holding her closely, not wanting to let her go. *Again.*

She was back and somehow he'd allowed her to creep under his skin, to make him want her, to hope for things they couldn't have—impossible dreams. A future? That was crazy talk, after everything they'd been through before.

And yet…his heart couldn't separate this feeling from the feeling he'd had before it had all started going wrong.

Hope.

He knew then without a doubt that he was going to lose his heart to her all over again.

If he didn't do something about it…fast.

CHAPTER TEN

*H*OTEL ROOMS HAD *always meant sex.*

It hadn't felt like *just* sex, though. It had felt consequential in some way: meaningful.

She'd cried, for God's sake. It had all been too much for her poor heart to take. It seemed unreal, as if their problems, their divorce, had somehow magically fallen away.

And yet she couldn't allow any wishful thinking here. She couldn't let this be more than two people having a good time for one night. She couldn't pretend that the last five years hadn't happened—she had left him and broken both their hearts. She'd sent him papers to sign. She'd cried her heart out every night for eighteen months.

It was six-forty-two in the morning and the summer sun was already peeping through the blinds. Charlie had fallen asleep snuggled into the crook of Lewis's arm—fitting exactly the way she'd fitted before—a deep, satisfying sleep that she hadn't experienced for a long time. Then she'd woken suddenly, not quite sure where she was.

When reality hit, guilt did too. She should be with Lucy, not there. She'd got carried away with her own needs and wants instead of putting her sister first.

Should she sneak out and leave him sleeping? His eyes were closed, his long, dark lashes something any woman would be envious of. His hair was tousled. Would he be as confused as she was? She could leave now and avoid what could be an embarrassing conversation trawling through regret and recrimination about being here together. Although she'd had the best time, and would not regret that one night with Lewis.

'Morning,' he whispered against her throat as his warm hand snaked across her naked belly. He tugged her closer to him, her back tight against his chest, spooning her. 'You slept.'

She relaxed back against the pillows. There was no sneaking out now. 'I did.'

'You also snored.' He laughed.

She pushed back gently against his shoulder. 'I did not.'

'Okay, more a purr than a snore. But you were out like a light.'

She turned over, about to say she was going to grab a shower and head off, but he smiled, and her belly quivered and tingled in response. She would not regret last night. And she could not resist him now. 'I need to go…soon.'

'I know.' His nose wrinkled as he pulled a face.

It made good sense to leave now; it would alleviate some of her guilt if she got home this early in the morning, and hopefully found her sister and niece still sleeping, and it would give her much-needed emotional space to work out exactly what she felt about making love with Lewis.

But she did not want to leave. 'Maybe in five minutes?'

He edged away a little. 'Look, if you need to go, that's fine.'

'Whoa. Are you trying to get rid of me?' *God*, he regretted this. He regretted her staying.

But he frowned and shook his head. 'Of course not. I just know you want to get back to Lucy.' He raised himself up on his elbow, threading his fingers through her hair and rubbing a strand against his cheek. 'You know, I always loved your hair. I'm glad you didn't change it or dye it some random colour.'

Was he remembering their wedding night too, when he'd unclipped her hair, let it fall over her shoulders, nuzzled his face into it and told her how much he loved her? She'd forgotten how much he'd adored her hair back then. 'I've been sorely tempted to change it over the years. This colour runs in the family. Stella's got it too.' She grimaced. 'Poor kid.'

'Why? It's the most beautiful colour I've ever seen.'

'Not when you're in primary school and everyone calls you Carrot Top and other less nice nicknames. It's the kind of colour you grow into and only appreciate when you're older.'

'Tell me who they were and I'll… I'll sort them out for calling you names.' He flexed his biceps. 'I have a certain set of skills.'

'Sort them out? No need, Mr Bodyguard. Stand down.' She stroked his arm, laughing. 'I love it now and I don't care what anyone thinks.'

But with the thought of Stella her chest constricted and she wriggled out from under his arm. 'Look, I do really need to get back. Lucy… She pretends she's okay…'

Like you always did.

When would people start to treat her as if she was a grown adult and start being honest with her? When would they stop protecting her and let her protect them for a change? 'But I want to take the burden off her.'

'Sure.' He jumped out of bed and slipped on the robe she'd been wearing last night. 'Coffee first; I know you don't like to function without it.'

'You remember! I *can't* function without it.' She laughed. 'I need it IV'd in the mornings.'

He fiddled with the chrome coffee machine, then peered at the selection of purple, silver and gold coffee pods. 'Coming up. Hop in the shower and it'll be ready when you're done. You want me to give you a ride home?'

'That would be great. Thanks.'

Was he in a hurry to get rid of her—just being

polite about the coffee and the shower when he really wanted her gone?

She went through to the bathroom and turned on the shower. Two minutes on her own, and she was immediately hit with all the questions she'd wilfully ignored last night.

A ride home…and then what? What did this mean? Were they back together? No. That would be…difficult, given what they'd been through before. The warm water didn't help soothe her confusion. Did it have to mean anything? It could just be two consenting adults having fun.

But then what?

Last night the answer to that question hadn't seemed important, but today she needed certainty. Oh, she was no good at this. How could she pretend it had just been casual sex when…well…when her heart's reaction was far from casual?

She dried and dressed in yesterday's clothes, used the hotel's freebie toothbrush and paste then went back into the main room. He was sitting at the coffee table, looking at his phone.

Her heart danced just to look at him. What was he thinking?

He looked up and pointed at two steaming cups of coffee. 'There you go. Ambrosia from the gods.'

'Thanks.' She grabbed a cup and had a sip. 'What have you got planned today? Anything fun?'

He glanced back at his phone. 'Just messaging Logan. I'm going to the beach with him and the family, then lunch at their place in Meadowbank. It's a sort of tradition now, whenever I get the weekend off—which isn't often. We hang out, and sometimes I even babysit.'

'It sounds lovely. It's good that you two are so close.' He had made his brother's family, his own family. Made up for the lack of his own kids. Which, despite him being at odds to tell her it wasn't her fault, it was. And all of a sudden she felt a little *lost*….robbed, even…because she couldn't pretend they didn't have a break-up history mired in her infertility. Or that he still wanted a family she couldn't give him.

She needed to go.

'Okay, do you mind if we make tracks now? I really need to give Lucy a break from parenting duties. She needs to get her rest.' To add to the emotional rollercoaster, guilt shimmied down her spine. Being with Lewis, amazing as he was, wasn't what she was supposed to be doing. Lucy would forgive her, right? 'I feel bad about staying out overnight.'

He fleetingly frowned. 'Don't. She would have said if she needed you, right?'

'I'm not so sure. You're not the only one who hides their feelings, Lewis.'

'Hey, I'm trying here. You're not the only one who's done a lot of thinking over the last few years, Charlie. And some growing up too.' He ran his hand through his hair and then smiled. But there was something about it that was almost sad, as if he was contemplating something coming to an end. Maybe he was. 'I had a great night, Charlie. I'm glad you're back.'

Okay... This new honest and open Lewis, the Lewis who told her what he wanted and needed, was someone else—interesting and refreshing and so not what he used to be like. And yet she was waiting for the 'but', which should be a relief and would make things less difficult. But... at the same time...she liked him. Last night had been amazing.

Oh, she was all kinds of confused. 'I'm not sure you were very glad when you found me in that smashed-up car.'

'Okay, I'll admit I was shocked.' He laughed. 'And I understand about Lucy. She's the big sister, right? She feels responsible—like Logan does with me. Only thirty minutes' difference but sometimes he acts like it's thirty years.'

'She's always looked out for me, and has been one of my fiercest supporters. I think I took it for granted, *expected* the support even. It was too easy for me not to stand on my own two feet because I had my parents, Lucy and you to do the hard yards for me.'

'Hey, you got the brilliant exam results, not us.' He drained his cup.

'But you made sure I had nothing else to worry

about. You made food or my parents brought us food parcels. My mother paid a cleaner every week to come spruce the house. I was a spoilt princess.'

'You weren't.' He cleared the empty coffee cups onto a little tray and carried them to the console. 'You were studying and learning your new job. It's not easy being a junior doctor.'

'Oh, I was spoilt, Lewis. I was also selfish and a little bit lazy. I didn't like being pampered by everyone but I couldn't bring myself to take control either. Then, when I moved to London, I... Well, I pushed *everyone* away—not just you. I only came back twice in five years and even then only briefly. I wouldn't even let my family visit me in London.' And she'd felt so very alone, but hadn't had any energy to give to anyone else, to answer their questions or even have a conversation about what was going on inside her head and her heart.

He leaned back against the console, legs crossed at the ankles. 'I had no idea. Why?'

'I don't know for sure. I think I needed some distance from everyone. Some space from everything I knew—a new direction. A new life with no pain in it. No reminder of what I couldn't do or who I was.' Until she'd realised she couldn't run away from herself or her feelings. She'd had to face them. 'But, again selfishly, didn't think how that might have affected my mum and dad. And Lucy.'

'You're being very hard on yourself. You'd been through a very difficult time; you were all over the place emotionally. I'm sure they understood.'

'I didn't give them a choice. But I can imagine how hurt they must have felt and worried about my mental wellbeing. I only stayed in cursory contact when necessary for the first couple of years. When Lucy called to tell me about her pregnancy, I didn't rush home to be with her for the birth; I just sent flowers and cooed over video calls. I missed some of Stella's firsts, and didn't help in those difficult early days. I wasn't here when Lucy found the lump. She didn't tell anyone until after Mum and Dad went away to do their charity work. She was facing all that on her own. There was a chasm between us and it was my fault.' Now it was time for her to give back. 'I'm trying to make amends for that.'

'I'm sure you don't need to. I am absolutely sure Lucy understands you just needed some alone time.' He smiled. 'But, what are you waiting for? Get your bag. I'll take you.'

'I can get a bus if you need to get to Logan's.'

He frowned. 'We're neighbours, remember? I won't let you get the bus when I practically drive past your house. I have to change and grab Lola's present anyway.'

'Oh, okay. If you insist.' She grabbed her bag, not ready for this intimate time with him to end, because she had no idea how they would navigate the 'what next?'

Twenty minutes later, they pulled up outside Lucy's home and Lewis twisted in his seat to talk to Charlie. The conversation from the hotel had been sparse and the atmosphere a little loaded, as if they both knew they needed to say something but didn't know what.

'Right, here you go.' He rubbed the back of his neck. 'Um… What do we do now?'

Awkward.

'I don't know. I came here to look after Lucy and Stella and then somehow here I am, doing the drive of shame.' She looked down at yesterday's clothes, and felt a belt of contrition tightening around her chest, but smiled nonetheless.

He stroked her hair, then palmed her cheek. 'Hey. There's absolutely nothing to be ashamed of. We're consenting adults. We were married once.' What had he said last night about grown adults and sexual craving? But there was something in his expression that gave her pause before he added, 'How about we catch up when we're both ready?'

What? When? Wasn't he ready either? Did he feel the same discombobulation?

Suddenly she felt a little out of her depth. They'd spent an intense few hours getting to the core of what had split them up, but they certainly weren't healed enough to lay their hearts wide open yet.

And she shouldn't be doing this when she had so little time to give. It wasn't fair on him or on Lucy.

And it wasn't fair on her own heart. She didn't want to fall for him again and then lose him. She'd barely recovered from that before. 'Sure. Yes. I'm in a difficult space at the moment.'

'I get it: Lucy; Stella; the job… It's a lot. No problem. You know where I am and you have my phone number if you need me. But, in the meantime, no doubt I'll see you at work.' He nodded.

And she'd have the tease and temptation of seeing him…probably on every shift, trying to ignore the ache, the want and the need. But neither of them was in a position to make more of this. She sighed as her chest constricted. 'So, you're okay with this? You know…not making plans? Please—tell me the truth.'

He smiled wryly. 'Hey, don't stress. I have to get my head straight too. I did not expect any of last night to ever happen, so I'm just sort of…working through it. But, for the record, I had a good time—*great* time. And I'd like us to be friends, if that works for you.'

'Friends. Sure, I can do that.'

And wow: *just sort of working through it*. His honesty about his feelings was coming thick and fast. She squeezed his hand, but when he leaned in to kiss her cheek she turned her mouth to meet his. She couldn't resist kissing him again.

He hesitated, then groaned as their lips met.

And, oh, how her body heated and responded to his kiss.

It was a while before they came up for air.

She chuckled, more in embarrassment at her lack of restraint than anything else. 'Okay, sorry. That was a very un-friend thing to do. But I couldn't resist just one last kiss. Right; friends from now?'

He chuckled, his eyes still filled with heat. 'Yeah. Friends from now. You want to synchronise watches or something?'

'No need; I think I'm good now. Right, I should go.' She opened the door and climbed out, but leaned back in through the window to add, 'I'll see you…some time. Thanks for a great night.'

'Yeah. Back at ya, Charlie.' He leaned across the passenger seat and smiled up at her.

Oh, those eyes. That mouth. That man.

Last night.

This kiss.

Oh, hell…the friend thing wasn't working very well at all.

CHAPTER ELEVEN

It was a great night, Lewis thought as he jogged down the path to the beach. *Pinch me.*

Had it really happened—Charlie back in his arms? After their deep and raw conversation, so many emotions had been swimming through his veins. He hadn't been so honest or felt so close to anyone for a long time. Sex had been the natural conclusion—inevitable after that first stolen kiss.

And now what?

He wasn't sure how to navigate casual sex with his ex, or just being friends, or how to protect himself from falling for her again. Because, even though they'd straddled some of the niggly reasons why they'd split, some issues were still there, right? Big issues too. Besides, she'd made it clear she didn't want anything deep or involved.

So why the hell had he allowed last night to happen?

He spotted the girls in bright-pink bathers paddling in the shallows, with Logan helicoptering over them. Lewis watched them splash each other for a moment with a sting in his chest. Lucky Logan; he'd got it all: a lovely wife and three gorgeous kids. Lewis was thrilled for him; he was. After what they'd been through growing up, his brother deserved every scrap of happiness, every moment of family life with his precious girls.

But it didn't stop him craving that for himself, even now.

His brother met him with a bro hug of hand-slap and back-clap. 'Hey, you look bright-eyed and bushy-tailed. Early night?'

'Hmm.' Far from it, but he wasn't sure what to say. As far as Logan was concerned, Charlie had abandoned her husband…just like everyone else had over their early years. Logan was a stickler for staying and trying to work things through, just like Lewis. And Lewis hadn't yet found the head space or opportunity to tell Logan that Charlotte Rose was back.

Logan frowned at Lewis's non-committal response. 'What did you do, watch the game? Shame about the result, eh? It was a lousy night to be out anyway. There was flash-flooding on Tamaki Drive. You wouldn't think so now, though. It's a beaut of a day.'

Flash-flooding florecast.

God, she was beautiful. And his head was a mess. Images from last night kept flashing through his brain: her mouth; her smile; the tight press of her body. 'Actually, I went out with Charlie.'

Logan stepped back, almost falling over a sand castle, then stepped down into a deep hole. He staggered, then fell backwards onto the sand. 'Charlie? Your Charlie? Dr Charlie? Your wife?'

'Ex-wife.' Lewis held out his hand and hauled Logan upright.

Logan brushed the sand from his shorts. 'How? Why?'

'She's moved back to Auckland and we bumped into each other at work.'

Logan's eyes roamed Lewis face, assessing. 'And…?'

Siblings—they always wanted a piece of you. 'We had dinner.'

'So you're getting back together? Just like that?'

'We had dinner, Logan.' And great sex. 'No one said anything about getting back together.'

'Okay.' Logan's eyebrows rose and he blew out a slow breath. 'How was she? How are you?'

He thought of her underneath him—the way she'd looked at him as he'd entered her; the way she'd clung to him. The way tears had slipped down her cheeks, emotion spilling over. 'She's great, actually. Really good.'

'And you?' Logan peered closer at him. 'You look too happy about it and that gives me the hee-bie-jeebies.'

Lewis inhaled deeply. Happy? Confused, more like. 'Yeah. I'm not gonna lie. It was a shock to see her at first but we talked and…well… I'm okay… I think. We agreed to try be friends, seeing as we're likely going to be working together on occasion.'

'Friends?' His brother's eyes widened in shock. 'Be careful, bro. I remember how you were after she'd gone. I don't ever want to see you like that again.'

Lewis remembered too and no way was he going back to that darkness again. 'Don't worry, I can handle it. I'm in a good space now.'

'Yes. And it's good to see.' Logan shook his head and put his hand on Lewis's shoulder. 'But, with Charlie back, how long is that going to last?'

He had a point. Lewis had been broken into a million pieces when she'd left. 'I'm being careful. We're both older and wiser.' *Liar.* Last night he'd felt like a giddy teenager again, carried away with wild need.

'Do you…you know…?' Logan inhaled as his question trailed off.

'Know what?' Lewis frowned at his brother. Where was this going?

'Still love her?'

'Whoa. Get straight to the point, why don't you?' But Logan had always talked about how he was feeling. He didn't hold back. He was open and honest; Lewis had got the other side of that coin. He preferred to keep everything inside so he could work it through. And, anyway, no one had ever cared what he thought about stuff. If he'd had a problem and wanted help from an adult, he might as well have shouted into the wind.

Except for Charlie… She'd pushed him to say

things. And he was trying. He just wasn't sure if he trusted himself, or her…although after last night he wasn't sure. She hadn't given him false hope or led him on. They'd both consented and parted in agreement.

It had been a good night. He wanted to do it again.

But did he still *love* her? Absolutely not. She'd thrashed his heart. He couldn't do that to himself, never again.

Logan was still looking at him, waiting for a response. Lewis shook his head. 'Come on, man. It was one night.'

'Night?' His brother glared at him. 'You said dinner.'

Great. There was no getting out of this. 'We got caught in the rain doing a resus on some poor bloke who got run over in the middle of Quay Street, and then she couldn't get a taxi, and I had that hotel room booked…' He shrugged. Yeah, it did sound a likely story, now he thought about it, but he wasn't going to lie. 'So she spent the night, okay? It was probably closure for both of us. One night, then we can both properly move on.'

Because, in reality, it looked as if he hadn't fully moved on at all, no matter how much he told himself he had. He was healed, yes, but he hadn't been able to find happiness with anyone else.

Logan shot him a blunt look and was about to

say something when Lily hurtled towards them. 'Uncle Lewis, piggy-back ride?'

'Please,' admonished Logan.

Lily beamed her toothy smile. '*Please,* Uncle Lewis?'

How could he resist? This could be the only chance at a family he ever got, these little poppets in pink. Plus, maybe it'd get him back in the good books with his brother. He bent down onto all fours. 'Okay, hop on, both of you. And be nice to each other.'

The little girls giggled and screeched as they scrambled onto his back with Lily in front and Lola at the back, complaining about being behind her little sister and giggling at the same time.

He crawled across the sand, ignoring the burn in his knees and palms…and in his heart. This was everything he'd dreamt of happening with Charlie: two little copper-headed kids, squirming and wriggling and laughing. Then Sunday lunch all together, maybe with Logan and his brood too—family time.

Charlie had thought that impossible and he'd been too distraught to argue. But there were options, right? Why hadn't they talked about adoption or surrogacy? Why had he been so closed to that idea five years ago?

But how could they talk about that now? They weren't in that space. She'd drawn her boundary and he had to respect that. Hell, he needed that line in the sand too.

So why the hell was he imagining happy families when nothing could be further from reality?

'Hey, there,' Charlie whispered as she opened the door to Lucy's bedroom to find her niece asleep on her sister's chest. Lucy's eyes were closed as she lay on the bed, her chest steadily rising and falling. She looked peaceful, which was lovely, given the stress she was under right now.

Charlie's heart squeezed. These two here were what was important. *But, oops…*

Charlie tiptoed backwards and closed the door as quietly as she could.

'Charlie? Charlotte, is that you?' came a strained whisper.

Charlie opened the door again and popped her head round. 'Hey, yes. Sorry, I didn't mean to disturb you.'

'Oh, don't worry. She's been napping for an hour now so it's probably time she woke up.' Lucy looked down at her daughter and smiled that soft mamma smile filled with adoration. 'She had a restless night.'

Charlie's chest ached with guilt. 'Oh, I'm sorry, I should have been here.'

'No, you should not. I told you to go. The least I can do is let you have a night out every now and then.'

Which did not erase the guilt at all. 'How are you feeling?'

'Yuck.' Lucy sat up, leaning back against the pillows, and hoisted a fast-asleep Stella higher on her chest. She looked worn out, but she smiled. 'But I don't want to talk about me. I want every little detail about your illicit night.'

To be honest, Charlie didn't know what to say, or how to feel. 'Oh, you know? It was nice.'

Lucy guffawed. 'You stay at a fabulous hotel with a gorgeous man and it's *nice*?'

'Well, we did have a medical emergency to deal with as well.' Her sex-induced tachycardia, as well as poor Graham.

Lucy rolled her eyes. 'Yeah, yeah. And it was raining and all the apps were down and there was absolutely nothing you could do except go to his hotel.' Lucy smiled softly. 'So what happened?'

Charlie shook her head and glanced down at her sleeping niece. 'No can do. Stella is far too young to hear this.'

'Oh? That good?'

Charlie plopped down on the bed next to her sister. 'Yes. *That* good.'

Lucy peered more closely at Charlie's face. 'And yet, you don't seem your usually happy self.'

Charlie pressed her lips together, because she was smiling inside; she really was. It had been un-freaking-believable but tinged now with 'what next?' and guilt at not being here. 'I'm not sure where we're at.'

'You're seeing him again?' Lucy frowned at Charlie's shrug. 'You're not seeing him again?'

'Undoubtedly I'll see him again. He brings in my patients. Our paths will cross many, many times.' The enormity of the potential emotional and personal fallout from last night finally hit her. Making love had muddied everything: distracted her from her commitment to looking after her family members; intruded into her work space and bruised her heart. 'We're friends, apparently. He's working things through.'

Lucy's eyes widened. 'He said that?'

'Yeah. But anyway…it doesn't matter. It's not a good time for me.'

Lucy's frown deepened. 'Because of me? Please don't let me stop you having fun. Watching you living a great life might be the only good thing I have left, after this little one, of course.' She kissed the top of her daughter's head.

'No.' Tears pricked Charlie's eyes. 'Don't say that.'

'It's true. We have to face up to it. My life is crappy and horrible and I'm scared to death. Let's just hope the medicine is working, okay?'

Charlie nodded and squeezed her sister's hand. 'Absolutely. It will. It *will*.'

'And I don't want to talk about it any more. It's all I ever seem to think about and it's not good for me. I need a distraction and, unfortunately for you, you're it.'

Lucy cupped Charlie's face with her Stella-free hand and sighed. 'I know this thing with Lewis is complicated; you have so much history. And I do not want you hurting like you did before or scurrying away overseas again. I should be telling you to be careful. To take your time. To figure out what *you* want. If it's just that one night, then great, you can tick that box. If it's more, then, you'll have to talk to him about it. Tell him what you want. Find out what he wants.'

'The same as he always did—kids.' Charlie exhaled slowly.

'So you talked about it?'

'No. But he's so close with Logan's girls. It's obvious.'

I was gutted, if I'm honest. Absolutely broken. His words rubbed a bruise in her chest wall.

'I don't suppose you talked about other options? Adoption? Fostering?'

'It wasn't that kind of conversation, Luce.'

Lucy brushed Charlotte's hair back from her forehead and smiled softly. 'Oh, sweetheart, I'm sorry.'

'Because, if he doesn't want that, we'd still have

the same issues as before and I'm not ready to be rejected. Anyway, it was one night, Lucy. You are my number one focus.' She wrapped Lucy and Stella in a warm hug. 'Other than to see you get better, I have no idea what I want.'

How about a carefree, problem-free, happy, committed relationship with a gorgeous man? Lots of kids. *Love.*

'I don't want a life without you,' he'd said on their wedding night.

Yet he'd managed just fine—was thriving, in fact.

While her heart, it seemed, was still a fractured mess.

CHAPTER TWELVE

'THIS IS TIA, a twenty-seven-year-old woman who fell off her horse when she was trying to do a jump at speed. She fell forward over the horse's head; face and head took the brunt of the impact, as you can see by the grazing and swelling on her forehead and bruising around the eyes. Luckily, she was wearing a helmet, but a witness said she was possibly unconscious for a few minutes. Glasgow coma scale was thirteen on initial assessment but fifteen now.' Lewis glanced up at the group of medics he was handing over to and momentarily froze.

He hadn't seen Charlie come in. He certainly hadn't realised she was standing right in front of him, her startling blue eyes watching him as she listened intently. Her hair was piled on top of her head in a gorgeously messy bun with stray, loose tendrils framing her pretty face. Lip gloss highlighted her perfect Cupid's bow. His brain immediately rewound to the night in the hotel: the heat, the touch, the intensity of it all; the honesty.

No.

He shook himself. He was not going there. He

was doing his job. Charlie was a friend, that was all. 'She also has swelling and pain in her upper right arm, right hip and right knee. She's had ketorolac for pain relief, which is working well.'

'Hi, Tia. My name is Charlie. I'm one of the doctors here. Good to hear Lewis's magic medicine is working.' Charlie flashed him a smile that reached deep into his heart and tugged it in a way not so much friendly, more sexy, then fixed back on their patient. 'I'll need to ask you a few more questions and examine you again, so I'm sorry if it seems as if we're repeating ourselves.'

He stepped back and let her do her stuff. He couldn't begin to count how many handovers he'd given over the course of his career, but he'd felt like a blathering idiot every time he'd done one in front of Charlie in the past few days.

He was so aware of her. Aware of her eyes on him and of the memories from years ago bolstered by the memories of Saturday night. Memories of the mind-blowing kisses, and her beautiful naked body. Of him finally opening up, as if a pressure valve had been released inside him, giving him hope and making him…what? *Exposed.* All of these messy emotions didn't stop him doing his job—he'd never let anything get in the way of that—but they didn't make it easy.

He stepped away out of the cubicle, eager to put distance between himself and his ex-wife. Maybe one day he would come to work and feel platonic vibes about her.

Today was not that day.

Keen to leave, Lewis found Brin at the nurses' station, chatting to some of the medical team. 'Hey, Brin, ready to go?'

Brin nodded. 'Sure. But I'm parched and it's my turn for coffees again. So, I'll go grab them and meet you in the van.'

'Great.' That would give Lewis some time to breathe and get his head straight after seeing Charlie. He turned to leave but came face to face with her as she stepped out from behind the cubicle curtain.

She looked surprised and a little embarrassed now it was just the two of them. She gave him a half-smile. She was guarded, unsure. 'Hey… um…friend.'

'Hey, Charlie. How's things?' Was it his imagination or had there been extra emphasis on the word 'friend', as if she was feeling the same discombobulation he was? The memory of their night together filled the air, unacknowledged, loaded.

'Good.' She nodded. 'Yes. I'm good.'

He waited for her to ask him how he was, but nothing came, so he said, 'And Lucy? Stella?'

'They're okay.'

'Right. Good.' He wasn't sure what to say next. She wasn't exactly encouraging conversation but she wasn't making moves to leave either. They'd shared a very intimate night together… hell, a marriage of four years and longer than that in a relationship… but friends? It seemed it didn't come naturally. Maybe they couldn't have a relationship that didn't involve the emotional and physical. *Ouch.* That didn't bode well for their future professional relationship.

Because what he wanted was to whip her into his arms and kiss her right here in the emergency room. Take her to his bed and make long, slow, sweet love to her. Wake up with her in the morning, lots of mornings…. *Every* morning…

Hot damn. He couldn't let these emotions take hold. He shoved his hands into his pockets and rocked back on his heels, trying to be nonchalant when his body felt the opposite. 'Cool. Well, I should be going.'

'Yeah. Me too.' But she paused, a smile flickering as something seemed to occur to her. 'Oh, I almost forgot. Did you hear about Graham?'

'Graham?' For a moment he was confused, then he realised. 'Oh, yes, our CPR man. No, I haven't had the chance to ask after him.'

'He's actually hanging in there. In Intensive Care, but improving. Apparently, it was touch and go for a while, but he pulled through. We did good, Lewis.'

And, with that, the tension between them seemed to diminish. Maybe it was because they were in safe territory talking about work. Or maybe because they'd been reminded of how good they could be together. 'That's great news. I'm so pleased. I might pop up to see him if I get a chance.'

'Yeah.' She nodded, her eyes brighter now. 'Just goes to show that things don't always end up the way you think they might.'

Tell that to my pathetic, hopeful heart.

'Go us.' He raised his palm and she high-fived it.

'The dream team.' Her smile was worth all the awkward tension.

'Hey, you two.' Brin was striding towards them carrying two takeaway cups. 'I've just had Mia on the phone and she wondered if you'd like to come for a barbecue at the weekend?'

Lewis wasn't sure whether Brin meant the two of them generally or *together*. His meddling was getting a little out of control. He glanced at Charlie, and she looked as uncomfortable as he felt at the invitation, so before he replied Lewis narrowed his eyes in a question to his colleague. 'What's the occasion?'

Brin rolled his eyes. 'Sorry, should have been clearer—house warming. It's a little overdue, but Mia's sister-in-law and family are coming over for the weekend, so we thought it'd be a good opportunity to throw a party.'

Which meant there'd be others there, it wouldn't be just a double date kind of thing. Lewis exhaled and agreed to come, because refusing the invitation would be out of character and would probably engender more questions from his co-worker, not fewer. 'Sure thing, sounds good. Let me know what to bring.'

But Charlie shook her head. 'No, sorry. Thanks, anyway, but I need to look after Lucy.'

Brin frowned. 'Your daughter?'

'Sister.' She smiled tightly. At the mention of Lucy, her body language had become guarded and taut. Looking after her family was taking a toll and Lewis wondered how he could ease that burden. Then he remembered he was not getting involved.

Brin smiled. 'No worries. Bring her too.'

'Okay, I'll ask her. Thanks.' Charlie's gaze darted to Lewis. It seemed she was checking if that was okay by him. He nodded. He could hardly refuse, could he? She looked back at Brin. 'She's got a baby, six months old: is it okay to bring her too?'

Brin grinned. 'That's no problem. Mia loves babies. We've got a little one too. Bring them all. The more the merrier. Stay an hour, stay all evening, whatever works.' Brin nodded at Lewis and handed him a warm takeaway cup. 'Okay, boss. I'll be in the van clearing up. Take your time.'

As they watched him walk away, Lewis heaved a sigh. 'Geez, I am so sorry about him.'

She laughed. 'It's fine. He's just being friendly.'

'Or meddling. Looks like we're not going to be let out of this. You good with it?'

'Yes. I guess. It's actually nice to be invited out somewhere and hopefully make some friends. I haven't had much of a chance to meet many people or catch up with my old Auckland mates.' Her eyebrows rose and he wondered if she was alluding to *their* old Auckland mates, joint school friends with whom she'd lost touch with living so far away, while he'd done his best to stay in contact. She shrugged. 'I'll ask Lucy to come, because she could use cheering up. With the chemo, she's not keen on going out and mingling too much. Her immune system's not great.'

'I could pick you all up…' The words were out of his mouth before he realised what he was saying. Not only would he be up close with Charlie in a car, but he'd have to see Lucy again after the messy divorce from her little sister. How would he navigate that? But he couldn't sit by and see them worry or struggle when he might be able to help somehow. 'It would save you driving your little broken car or using public transport, which is a greater risk for catching infections. And if it's all too much for her then I can run her home any time, no worries.'

Her smile widened. 'That would be lovely.'

'That's what friends are for, right?' This time he made himself *feel* the emphasis on the word 'friend'.

'Yeah. I guess.' She put her hand on his arm, sending sparks of need firing across his skin, arrowing to his chest and lower...way lower. He thought about the way she tasted, and the soft sounds she'd made when he'd slid inside her, and the sparks in his belly threatened to burst into flame. 'Thanks, Lewis.'

He tried to push back all sexy thoughts of her. 'No worries. I just have to put on my big boy pants to face your older sister. Otherwise, everything is golden.'

'She won't bite.' She chuckled. 'She always liked you. She knows I was the one who left.'

'Hmm. The jury's still out on that. You were heartbroken and I couldn't fix it. That was my job, right?' He imagined what Logan might say whenever—*if ever*—he got to see Charlie again.

'Oh, Lewis, it was never your job to fix my broken heart. I'm responsible for my own emotions.' She patted his arm and he realised just how much she'd changed in the intervening years since their break-up. Back then, she'd have allowed him to wade in and try to fix everything. Now she was self-determined and fiercely autonomous. It suited her, a lot. She grinned. 'Don't worry. If I say you're generously being our taxi driver, she'll be fine with it. She just wants me to be happy.'

'And are you?' It was the million-dollar question. It was probably unfair to ask, really, given what she was going through.

She closed her eyes briefly, then exhaled long and slowly. 'That's too big a question for work time. I'm loving spending time with my family. I have a great job and…ahem…*interesting* friends and colleagues.' She shot him a knowing smile. 'But ask me again in a few months, when Lucy's treatment's finished. That's all I can think of at the moment. When she gets the all-clear, I'll be deliriously happy.'

If ever there was a sign they needed to be platonic more than ever, this was it. Because he realised he wanted her to say, yes, she was happy they'd spent the night together. That they'd found each other again. That there was still something between them. Which was pathetic wishful thinking on his part, and also very selfish. Charlie was conflicted and busy and had other people she needed to put ahead of herself, and therefore ahead of him. He nodded. 'Sure. I get it.'

'And I mean thanks for understanding, Lewis. For sticking to the plan. You know…being friends. Not asking for more. And, on the other hand, for not ghosting me. I'm not sure which would be harder to deal with.' Her hand was still on his arm and the way she was looking at him, as if she was truly grateful, made him want to wrap his arms round her and hold her close. To soothe her worries and make her feel better. But that wasn't his job any more.

'I would never ghost you, Charlie. We're too old and wise to play those kinds of games.' He couldn't help smiling. 'Thank God you're not a mind-reader, is all.'

She blinked, then her smile grew into a grin, sexy and loaded. 'Lewis! Not you too?'

'Me what?' He was all mock-innocence.

She leaned closer so no one else could hear. 'Struggling with the aftermath of the other night?'

'I can't get it out of my head.' This close, he could see deep into her eyes. He saw the tease she was fighting, the need for affection. He was struggling with his need to protect her too, to be the one to solve all her problems and to have the answers. She hadn't wanted them five years ago and she certainly wouldn't want them now. But he couldn't help wanting to erase all her pain.

He needed to keep this growing connection between them under control if he was going to get out whole.

He took a sip of coffee and remembered that Brin was waiting for him. 'Look, I'd better go. Let me know if you want me to pick you all up. Otherwise, I'll see you at Brin's. I'll message you his address.'

Then he flashed her a quick smile and left, balling up his emotions and stuffing them deep inside, exactly where they should have stayed the moment he knew she was back.

* * *

It was silly to be nervous. It was a barbecue—friends from work—that was all.

But, the moment Lewis's car pulled up outside, her heart jumped into a very weird tachycardic rhythm she was fairly sure no cardiologist had ever seen on a heart trace.

Stop it.

As he crunched up the gravel path, she started to feel a little dizzy due to her jumpy heart rate and anticipatory nerves.

Ridiculous.

The rap on the door made her jump, even though she was expecting it.

'Lucy! We're heading off,' she called up the stairs. And received a muffled grunt in return. Then she took a deep breath and opened the door.

Hell... He looked good today in his untucked white linen shirt and duck-egg-blue shorts. His dark hair was casually tousled as always and there was a smattering of stubble on his jaw. His lovely soulful brown eyes glittered as he smiled. 'Taxi for Dr Rose?'

'Hey. Thanks so much for this.'

After holding off asking him to pick them all up, she'd capitulated at Lucy's urging: 'He has a much bigger car and it'll be so much more comfortable for us all.'

That was before Lucy had decided not to join them after all.

Laughing, Charlie hauled the car seat from the ground and handed it to him. 'Could you take this? You have to put the seat belt through the back.'

'Got it.' He grinned. 'Three nieces; I know the drill.' Then he disappeared down the path and into the car. She was mesmerised by the rhythm of his steps, the way he turned and winked at her, as he'd used to when they'd been happily married, and the cute smile that seemed to reach to her uterus and stroked. Which was damned unfair, given she had a non-functioning uterus and no amount of stroking would make it work.

But, oh, he was lovely. Her body prickled with awareness. Was he more lovely now than five years ago? He seemed more centred, wiser, happier in himself. He seemed confident. He was definitely better in so many ways. It was only when he backed out of the back passenger door that she realised she'd been staring at his backside for far longer than anyone would consider acceptable. If staring at a hunk of man's backside was acceptable at all… *Oops.*

'Come on, lovely,' she cooed at little Stella and picked her up from the travel cot they used as a playpen in the lounge. 'Time to be sociable.'

She was glad they were going to be surrounded by friends new to her, so temptation could stay at bay. And also frustrated that they would be surrounded by friends, so temptation could stay at bay. Oh, life was so complicated these days.

She yelled upstairs again. 'Bye, Luce. Please call me if you need anything.'

She waited for a reply. There came some splashing then a long sigh. 'Have fun, girls.'

'Car seat is in,' Lewis said as he walked back up the path. But he frowned as she pulled the door closed behind her. He ran up to take Stella's change bag out of Charlie's hands. 'Hey, give that to me. Where's Lucy?'

'In the bath. And she's not coming out for anyone or anything, apparently.' Charlie giggled. 'She has a glass of her favourite rosé, scented candles, some chocolate-covered ginger and a new romance novel to devour. She's not up to seeing anyone, but she is up to pampering herself. I told her I'd bring Stella with us so she can relax.'

'Great idea.' After he put the changing bag into the car boot, he took Stella from her arms as naturally as anything, then he beamed at the baby, swinging her high in the air until she giggled. 'Hello, little one. Yes, it's me, Lewis. We have met, but you probably don't remember. Yes, that's my chin. Yes, it's scratchy.' He shot Charlie a smile. 'She's a feisty little thing.'

'She needs to be, for her mum's sake.'

'It's difficult, for sure. But she won't understand what's going on.' His smile flattened a little, his eyes filling with warmth and worry. Then he turned another full-beam grin on Stella. 'Okay, missy. Let's get you plugged in so we can all go party.'

Charlie's breath caught in her throat. Lewis was gorgeous when he was just being himself but, smiling and laughing with a baby in his arms, he was devastating.

She'd tried to keep her distance, had not encouraged anything past polite conversation at work. Yet here she was, about to get into a car with him, go to a party and play. Once upon a time, playing with Lewis had been her most favourite thing.

Maybe it still was…

'Hey!' Brin grinned as he tugged open the front door twenty minutes later. 'Come in! Come in! Glad you could make it. Hello, little one.' He tickled Stella under her chin as he walked them through to a bright, smart-looking kitchen. 'This must be…?'

He glanced at Charlie. She smiled and bounced Stella up and down in her arms. 'Stella, my niece.'

'Something you guys have in common, then. Nieces.' Brin threw Lewis a look of encouragement and nodded towards Charlie with raised eyebrows, as if to say, *get in, lad. Make a move.*

She rolled her eyes at Lewis in solidarity. He smiled and mouthed the word, 'Sorry.' Somehow, their joint reaction at Brin's unsubtle matchmaking attempts was bringing them closer together. *Go figure.*

'Girls, yes, so many girls, including your Harper.'

Lewis shook his head as he put a large bowl of delicious-looking caprese salad, gourmet sausages and halloumi cheese onto the kitchen counter. 'Where's Mia, and Harper?'

Brin gestured towards the back door. 'Outside. Come and look at our new back yard, mate. You're going to love it.'

'Huh?' Lewis frowned again and they all followed Brin outside to a neat back garden with a large wooden deck, built-in pizza oven and huge gas barbecue. Lewis's eyes widened. 'Ah, you got it? Lucky man. Yes, tasty.'

Brin preened in the sunshine. 'Back home in Ireland it's always hit and miss for barbecue weather. But here, it's pretty much always a hit. Thought I'd get the best one I could.'

Lewis lovingly ran his fingers over the chrome and cooed the way he had at Stella. 'She's a beauty. I have serious barbecue envy.'

'Men!' Laughing, Charlie looked round the little crowd of people for some female cavalry and noted Mia walking towards her. 'Hello. Thank goodness you're here. I was starting feel pressured into have a conversation about the benefits of gas barbecues over charcoal and boast about how many burners mine has.' Charlie puffed out her chest and flexed her left bicep.

'Men! Good to see you again, Charlie.' Mia laughed and gave her a hug. 'Let's leave them to their barbecue adoration. My daughter's around here somewhere. She's so excited to be having a party. And who is this?' She stroked Stella's hand.

'This is my niece, Stella. We left Mum relaxing in the bath at home. She needed some time off.'

Mia raised her eyebrows and groaned in delight. 'Oh, lucky lady.'

'Yes.' *Not lucky at all.* 'I was wondering if it would be okay to put Stella down for a nap somewhere in about an hour or so?'

'No problem at all. We've got a travel cot. I can put that up in Harper's room and she can nap in there.'

'I don't want to put you to any trouble.'

'Not at all. There are a few babies and kids coming, so it'll be put to good use.' Mia glanced at the kitchen door and smiled at a couple walking into the garden. 'Excuse me while I go welcome my other guests. I'll be back in a minute. Help yourself to a drink.' Mia pointed to a table with glasses and a large cool box filled with ice, bottles of wine, beer and soft drinks.

'Yes. Sure.' Although, she wasn't sure how she was going to manage that with a baby in her arms. She'd have to wait until Lewis came to her rescue. Her heart crumpled a little. Her knight in shining armour had always been exactly that. Too much. Too long ago.

She didn't have to wait long. While Lewis turned sausages on the barbecue, Brin brought her a glass of wine then steered her towards the newly arrived couple standing with Mia. He introduced her to Carly and Owen, who lived on Rāwhiti Island, and their boy Mason. Owen shook her hand. 'Your name's familiar. Maybe our paths have crossed?'

'I'm working in A and E at Auckland Central at the moment. Emergency registrar.'

'Ah. That must be it. I've probably had a discharge letter from you for some of my patients.' It turned out that Owen was a doctor too. He used to have a practice in the city but now worked full-time on the island. Charlie remembered that Mia was a practice nurse working for a GP partnership just up the road.

'Is there anyone here who isn't a medic?' Charlie laughed, then lost her breath as she saw Lewis heading over towards them. His smile was so warm and friendly, and she thought back to the days when they used to host parties like this. When he'd casually wrap his arm around her waist as they chatted, just the way Brin was doing to Mia now.

Lewis kissed Carly and shook hands with Owen. It seemed they all knew each other very well, leaving Charlie feeling just a little out of the loop.

Owen stood back and looked Lewis up and down. 'Hey, looking sharp, man.'

'All that training,' Brin quipped.

'Oh? Training for what?' Charlie asked. Lewis

hadn't mentioned any training or event, although they had been distracted by other things recently: making love, navigating a fledgling friendship and kissing, mostly.

Her core heated at that thought and she drew her gaze from his sharp-looking body and made faces to entertain Stella, who was getting heavy and restless on her hip.

Brin put his hand on Lewis's shoulder and spoke in an extremely proud fatherly tone. 'This guy is a machine. We did the vertical challenge as a work team and you should have seen him go.'

'What's a vertical challenge?' Charlie asked. 'Sounds painful.'

'Running up fifty-one levels of the Sky Tower, and he left us all for dust. Which was pretty favourable, as it happens, because it meant we made a mint for charity too. He's a bona-fide legend.' Brin's eyes flitted to Charlie and she got the distinct impression he was saying all of this for her benefit.

But, yes, he was indeed a legend. Because not only was he super-fit for work but he used his skills, strength, spare energy and even money to support charities: first the silent auction, now the vertical challenge. *Impressive.*

But then, she knew that already. She caught Lewis's eye and he shook his head, clearly embarrassed at all the praise, but laughing. His gaze locked on hers and he rolled his eyes, as if to say, *this guy, huh?*

It was time to put poor Brin to rights, for the truth to be told at last. She cleared her throat. 'Yes, Lewis has always been devoted to being fit for his job—running, gym work, swimming. I used to call him an exercise junkie.'

Brin frowned and glanced from Lewis to Charlie. '*Always*? How do you…? Did you two know each other before you started working together?'

'You could say that.' She licked her lips and glanced at Lewis to make sure it was okay for her to explain their relationship. He nodded and smiled encouragingly. 'We were married once.'

'What?' Brin's expression turned from interest to shock to a full-on blush. He smacked his forehead with his palm. 'Here I was pushing you two together, thinking you both needed…company.' He coughed. 'I am so sorry.'

'Don't worry. It's okay, honestly.' She looked directly at Lewis and her tummy tumbled in delight and confusion. 'We're friends now.'

'Right. Wow, okay. Well, friends is good at least. Because that could have made for a mighty awkward barbecue otherwise.' Brin inhaled, then turned to Lewis, bugging his eyes at his friend. 'And you were going to tell me when, *partner*?'

'Now seemed like a good time.' Lewis laughed. 'I'm sorry to let you find out this way but you did kind of deserve it.'

'Jeez, mate. I am mortified.' Brin shook his head, but chuckled. *'Mortified.'*

'It'll wear off. Have another beer. Seriously, we're good, aren't we, Charlie?' Lewis looked over at Charlie and his laugh died away as his gaze settled on Stella wriggling. 'Whoa, little one, fancy giving your auntie a break? She's got a sore shoulder and you're probably not helping.'

'Thanks.' Charlie eased out the muscles in her neck as she passed the baby over to him to hold. 'She's getting a bit grizzly.'

He frowned at Stella, as if trying to solve a maths equation. 'Something to eat, maybe?'

'It's not long since she had a snack but we could try another one, I guess.'

He jiggled Stella up and down on his hip, blowing raspberries at her in a vain attempt to make the little girl laugh, to no avail. He grimaced. 'Raspberries usually work with my girls. Maybe she's tired?'

My girls. Her heart melted as he referenced Lily, Lola and Luna. 'Maybe. Mia said I could put her down in Harper's room.'

Lewis nodded. 'Great idea. You take her up and I'll grab her changing bag from the kitchen. We can give her some milk and see if it helps her drop off?'

So they really were the dream team now. 'Sure. Yes, thanks. The powder's in a little pot and you need to heat—'

'The milk carefully. And test the temperature on the back of my hand. I know.' He winked. 'I've got this. Go.'

Oh, Lewis. Her throat was suddenly raw and scratchy. She felt dejected that she couldn't give him the gift of fatherhood that he craved and was perfect for, yet her heart lifted to have him want to share this with her. She was a good auntie and would always hold Stella very close to her heart. She blinked back the stab of tears as she took Stella from him, feeling his heat and strength as he passed the baby over. Then she walked upstairs on wobbly legs, trying to put her attraction and sadness into a metaphorical box and leave it there.

She'd thought she'd got over the sadness years ago. And she could generally deal with it if it raised its head. She'd had therapy; she knew there was no surmounting the facts of her body's limits. There was no point in wishing for impossible things.

But it was the attraction that continually derailed her. She wanted him in so many ways.

And it was dangerous, making her reckless.

Making her forget all her promises to keep away.

CHAPTER THIRTEEN

LEWIS CAREFULLY OPENED the door into the dimly lit bedroom, and then paused, rooted to the spot.

Charlie was sitting in a nursing chair, cradling Stella and singing softly, a nursery lullaby. She was stroking the baby's head, staring lovingly down at her, while Stella's little fist bumped against Charlie's arm as she grizzled and fussed.

His chest hurt at the sight. Charlie was beautiful, that was all, stunning. And he hated that she would never get to hold her own child. He swallowed and tried to clear the lump in his throat.

'Hey,' he whispered, stepping into the room and closing the door against the loud, happy chatter of the party downstairs. 'Here's her bottle.'

'Thanks.' She looked up at him and smiled, taking the warm bottle and offering it to Stella. The baby immediately started to suck greedily. 'Oh, you were hungry, weren't you? I can't keep up with you.'

He watched Stella's breathless sucks. 'Yep, that definitely seems to be the answer.'

'I can't believe how much this baby eats.' She

laughed. 'Hey, go down and talk to your friends. You don't have to stay here with me.'

Leaving them both here would be a wise thing to do, but he couldn't tear himself away. This was so intimate, so exactly what they'd dreamt about. It was too lovely to leave. He would just indulge himself for a few minutes and play that game of 'what if?'; what might have been; pretend they didn't have a million obstacles from their past pressing in on them. Just a few more moments.

'It's okay. I'll wait. You might need something else. How about a glass of wine? A plate of food?'

'No need. I'm fine, thanks.' She glanced at Stella and then back at him with an adorable smile. 'I think we've managed to get her off.'

'Sometimes it's the simplest of things, right? Peace and quiet and a full belly. That certainly works for me.'

'I remember. My mum used to say she'd never met anyone who ate as much as you did.' Charlie laughed. She was looking at him so fondly, the tension of the last few days gone from her face. The tension of their last two heart-breaking years together completely erased. She looked young and bright and ethereal in the orange glow from the night light.

He decided to focus on Stella because there was no good in doing or thinking anything else. And because the obstacles of the present threatened now too. 'There were a lot of new faces for her to take in down there; she might have been a bit overwhelmed.' He bent in front of Charlie and the milk-drunk baby. 'You want me to pop her in the cot?'

'Thanks. Yes. She's little but she's getting heavier every day.'

He slid his hands under the sleeping babe, very gently deposited her onto the cot mattress and covered her with a blanket. This whole scenario felt surreal: the warmth; the baby; Charlie. It was *cosy.*

He turned back to look at her. 'Are you ready to go back down?'

She wrinkled her nose and shook her head. 'Not quite.'

He sighed. 'I get it. Sometimes all those new faces are overwhelming for adults too. I'm sorry you don't know many people here.'

'It's fine. I want to make friends and all yours seem lovely. I just need a minute to catch my breath.' She giggled softly. 'Oh, my God, did you see poor Brin's face? I felt bad that I told him about our connection like that.'

'Poor Brin nothing.' Lewis chuckled. Making sure Stella was fast asleep and their voices wouldn't wake her, he slid down the wall and sat on the floor next to Charlie's chair. 'He's been trying to get us together since he set eyes on you. For some reason he seems to think we're a good fit.'

'For *some* reason?' She laughed hollowly.

'Maybe he sees us the way we used to see each other?'

Oh, the delicious, poignant naivety of youth. No one had ever been in love as much as they had. No one could possibly have known how it felt to be them, falling deeper and deeper, as if they'd been unbeatable for ever. He smiled at the memories bombarding his brain. 'I liked those days, back when we were starting out—dating, our wedding day…'

'Yes. Good times.' Her tone was as wistful as he felt. 'You remember when we were in sixth form and just started seeing each other, how I used to sneak out from home in the middle of the night and climb through your bedroom window?' She laughed. 'Good job you had a bungalow.'

'And when your parents found out and grounded you, I sneaked into your bedroom instead…via a tree-climb and a drain pipe. Almost broke my neck on more than two occasions.'

'We didn't care. It added to the drama of our…' She put her hand to her chest and swayed softly from side to side, then whispered, almost as if she couldn't bring herself to say the word, 'Love'.

Love that had shattered under pressure. He tried for a lighter note. 'You remember when Uncle Paul tripped and almost fell onto our uncut wedding cake?'

'And we all held our breath when his hand flew out as he careened towards the table. Luckily he righted himself before disaster struck.' She laughed. 'And Logan's best man speech. He was so funny.'

Lewis tutted at the memory of his brother spilling too many of Lewis's boyhood antics. 'I could have killed him at times.'

'Oh, everyone thought it was hilarious. Then all the bridesmaids did a flash-mob dance and you...*you* knew all about it and never told me.' She nudged his leg with hers. 'We had the best wedding, Lewis.'

He felt the punch of pride now in his solar plexus as much as he had that day so long ago. The first time he'd seen her as she'd stepped into the little church, the sun haloing her from behind, had taken his breath away. 'I felt like I was the luckiest damned man in the world. I couldn't believe you'd chosen me.'

'Oh, Lewis. I was the lucky one.' Her hand slid down by the side of the chair next to him and he couldn't stop himself from taking her palm and stroking it. Then he slipped his fingers between hers. He heard her breathing hitch, felt a shift in the atmosphere, but she didn't let go.

They sat for a few minutes in silence. He listened to Stella's even breaths and his more staccato ones. He wondered what was going on in Charlie's head.

Then she inhaled and said, 'Lewis, can I ask you something?'

He dared not hope or think what it might be. 'Sure.'

'If it wasn't for me having to look after Lucy would you want a rerun of the other night?'

Yes. God, yes.

'If things weren't complicated? If we had no past? If we'd just met, two strangers?' Maybe here in the dark they could be honest about the way they felt because, in the real world, they couldn't admit that these feelings were growing.

She squeezed his hand. 'Or if none of the bad stuff had happened. Yes.'

'Then, yes. I wouldn't just want a rerun, I'd want more, Charlie.'

'Oh, God.' Silence lingered for a beat, then two. Then she breathed out. 'Me too.'

The baby stirred, a little cry that had him glancing over to the cot. He held his breath, wondering if he needed to go to her, but she seemed to settle on her own. His gaze drifted to a little device above the bed. 'Damn. Check the monitor—make sure it's not on.' The last thing they needed was an audience downstairs listening to their intimate confessions.

'I can't see a light on. We're good.' Charlie sighed and paused. 'Lewis…'

'Yes?'

There came another pause, then, 'The harder I try to keep away from you, the more I struggle.'

'*Charlie*. Please.' He closed his eyes and tried to

control his stuttered exhale. It was too much; too much for him to handle. His heart hammered and his chest felt hollowed out. Because what did 'what if?' matter if they couldn't act on it? Being honest was a mistake. Staying up here was a mistake.

And yet he wanted it. He wanted her, wanted it all, so much that it was a physical ache he could not erase.

He was at risk here—serious risk. He'd tried so hard to make things work before, and then had watched her walk away, and it had left him broken. He couldn't let her do it again, no matter how much he wanted her. So he slipped his fingers out from hers. 'Okay. Well, I'd better go see if Brin needs help with the barbecue.'

Then he forced himself to stand up and walk away.

Because, if he didn't leave right then, he would something they both might regret.

'This is baby Leo Hudson. Eight months old.' Lewis's voice sounded uncharacteristically strained as he lifted the fitting baby onto the trolley in the resus room. Sick babies did that to Charlie too. It didn't matter how long she'd been doing this job, or how many kids she treated, poorly babies tugged hard at every thread of maternal instinct she had.

She looked up into Lewis's eyes and her heart ached and jumped. She had an intense urge to reach for him and soothe away the pain in his eyes, but she refused to allow herself to be derailed from this emergency. This little one needed all their focus so they could fit the diagnosis jigsaw puzzle together. She nodded for him to continue.

'No medical history of note. Normal vaginal delivery at thirty-nine weeks. Generally well, but has been grizzly and snotty the last couple of days. Parents reported seeing some unusual twitching and jerking that has not stopped for a good hour and has worsened. No history of epilepsy or previous seizures. Airway is patent, oxygen administered, blood glucose normal. Temperature a little high at thirty-eight point one. IO Midazolam administered en route with no effect. Mum's just outside. Dad's followed in the car with two older children.'

'Thanks, Lewis. Arno,' she called to one of the senior nurses. 'Page Paeds, please—*urgently.* Tell them we have a status epilepticus. Someone please go talk to Mum and explain that we're doing all we can and I'll come talk to her when I get a chance.'

'I've explained some,' Lewis said. 'I'll go have a word in a minute. She said she'd wait in reception until her husband got here, but she's frantic with worry.'

'Understandable. Thanks. Take one of the nurses too; they'll be able to bring her in to see Leo once we've got him stable.' She knew Lewis would have built some rapport when he had attended the emergency. *Eight months old*—not much older than Stella. She could only imagine the way the mum was feeling, but she'd be in good hands with Lewis.

She grabbed the tiny oxygen mask and held it over the baby's mouth while she started her assessment. 'He's tachycardic with poor peripheral perfusion, pupils unreactive. Can I have a temperature reading please? And let's try another bolus of Midazolam.'

She was aware of Lewis's presence as they worked on the infant. By some miracle in the back of a moving ambulance, he'd managed to get IV access into Leo's tiny veins. He'd explained everything to the little baby, even though Leo wouldn't have a clue what was happening. It was comforting to have an extra pair of hands helping.

Then suddenly he wasn't there any more and she missed his strength and solid steadiness next to her. Was it her imagination that he was avoiding her? Every time he'd been in the department recently he'd barely glanced her way. Sure, he'd done his job professionally and efficiently, just as he was doing now, but there was no friendly chit chat afterwards. Maybe the closeness they'd shared on Saturday night had scared him away. Maybe she was over-thinking, and being a tad too sensitive. He was a busy man after all, and why would he specifically choose to chat to her at work?

Or maybe she was falling harder and quicker than she'd thought. Because, it had been six days since their heart-to-heart in Harper's bedroom and she'd burned every moment since just to see him again.

After she'd handed over to the paediatrics team, she stepped outside to get a breath of fresh air. From the back door of the emergency department she could see the hospital nursery and felt a pull to go and see Stella. Lately she'd been spending quite a lot of her break time with her niece and she realised it wasn't just to keep Stella happy: it fed something inside Charlie too.

She saw Seung walk by and called over, 'Hey, I'm well past due my break. Just popping over to the nursery. I'll be back soon as.'

'No worries.' Seung waved. 'Paeds are sorting Leo out. Arno's with Mum and Dad, and they're having a cup of tea before they all go up to Peter Pan Ward. Everywhere else is quiet.'

'Hush! Do not say that. Don't! You'll jinx us.' She waved back and headed across the car park for some serious snuggles with her favourite six-month-old.

But it wasn't Stella or Leo on her mind right now. It was Lewis. It felt as if she would never get used to working with him. Ever since the barbecue, all her shifts since had coincided with his. Which meant she couldn't get away from her admission in that darkened room: she was struggling to keep away from him and, in an ideal world, she'd want more and take more.

And she would never forget the tender stroke of his hand, the way she'd wanted to sink into another kiss with him or the deep yearning she had to be in his arms, in his bed, in his life.

Yes, back in his life, which would be a one-way ticket to heartbreak.

She'd been both glad and sad when he'd gone back down to the party, because she'd been feeling so mixed up she hadn't known what to do. So she'd stayed upstairs for as long as she could without appearing impolite to her hosts, until Mia had come looking for her and coaxed her down for some food. Of course, somehow she'd ended up sitting next to Lewis, and the rest of the evening had been pure torture.

Every time she'd looked round, he'd been there with his smile, his dark eyes glittering. She'd caught his scent on the air and felt the whisper of his breath as he laughed. And with every second she spent with him the torture had intensified. They both knew the truth of their need but she knew they could not, would not, *should not* act on it—not again.

It had almost been a relief for him to drop her home, her hands mercifully too full of baby and bags to reach for him and tug him close. A relief to close the door behind her and be free of his tempting presence. Yet here he was, every day in her space, at her place of work, tempting and torturing her. And, of course, there he was now, in her direct path, putting something into the boot of his car.

She closed her eyes and took a moment to erase any giveaway facial expressions, trying to act normally instead of jumping into his arms. 'Hey, Lewis.'

'Hey. Finished up for the day?' He was standing right where they'd had their first 'this time round' kiss. Her body flushed at the memory. Since then they'd vowed not to get involved and yet had shared a wonderful night together. They'd admitted feelings for each other, but agreed they couldn't act on them again.

No wonder she was confused.

She found him a smile. 'Not yet. I've got another couple of hours to go. Just going to see Stella in my break time. I feel a need to hug her.' She didn't want to admit to the rest of her work colleagues that she'd been shaken up dealing with a sick baby, but she knew Lewis would understand.

'Yep, I get that. Sometimes a hug works wonders.' He nodded. 'How's the little lad doing?'

It seemed she didn't even need to explain why she had the urge to see her niece. 'We managed to stop the fitting. He's on his way up to the ward now and stabilised, but it'll be a while until we know what's causing the seizures.'

He stepped closer, his expression concerned. 'You okay, though?'

'Yep.' She blew out a breath. 'You know how it is, sick kids are hard to deal with sometimes.'

'Yeah. I dread the day I get a call out for Lola, Lily or Luna.'

She shuddered. 'Here's hoping that will never happen.'

'Indeed. It was bad enough that I had to attend your accident. It's always worse when you know the person involved.'

She hadn't actually given any thought to how he must have felt seeing her potentially injured, only to how he'd felt seeing her in the flesh again. 'Well, I for one am very glad it was you.'

'Don't you dare do that to me again.' He gave her a rueful smile.

'I'll try not to. Once is enough.' Then she remembered something that would make his smile grow. 'Oh, I had a call from the High Dependency Unit this morning. Graham's been transferred out of ICU and has been asking to see us.'

'Really?' It was lovely to see the genuine and huge smile bloom on his face, all trace of worry defused. 'I never get to see patients once they're out of my hands.'

'I was thinking about popping up there after my shift ends. Maybe we could go together?' It made sense, didn't it?

But his expression clouded. 'Oh. I don't know…'

'We're going to see a patient, Lewis. I'm not

going to…' *Oh, hell. How to broach this?* 'Not going to say more of the things I said on Saturday.'

'Oh. Right.' He breathed out, looking a little taken aback and also relieved. 'No, me neither. I guess I could come with you. I'm off for the next couple of days so it would save me coming back into town to visit him. And, to be honest, I do really want to see the guy that survived CPR in the pouring rain.'

Flash-flooding florecast.

'Me too.' Grinning at the memory of what they'd done after saving Graham's life, she checked the time. 'Say, two and a half hours?'

'Sure. I've got paperwork to catch up on anyway so I could do that until you're ready.' He slammed the boot closed. 'I'll meet you outside HDU.'

Despite everything she'd promised herself, her tummy tumbled at the thought of seeing him again so soon. 'Can't wait.'

'Me neither. It'll be good to see him. Enjoy the Stella hugs. Say hi from me. See you soon, Charlie.' He turned and flashed her a look that was filled with the kind of promise that had her knees turning to jelly.

It's not a date, silly woman. He couldn't wait to see Graham, not to see her.

It was the way things were going to be. Had to be—two colleagues doing colleague-type things. Friends doing friend-type things. Because, upstairs at Brin's in that little dark room, she'd found the courage to tell him what she wanted and he'd let go of her hand and walked away, telling her through his actions that he was still too bruised, or hurt, to try again. Or that he was protecting himself...*from her*...and that thought made her heart hurt.

But it didn't stop the wish for the hugs she so badly needed to come from him. Or the senseless hope for the promise of more.

Because she couldn't ignore it any longer: she wanted more. Wanted more chats about their day and the shared patients they saw; more time with him; more kisses, more hugs; more *everything* with Lewis.

And that was going to be her downfall.

CHAPTER FOURTEEN

HIS HEART TRIPPED as he found Charlotte outside HDU. She'd changed out of her scrubs into a pretty pale-pink summer dress and white cardigan. Her hair hung loosely around her shoulders. *God,* he loved her hair. And she was carrying chocolates he recognised from the hospital shop in the lobby downstairs. It was so sweet she'd had the forethought to do that.

She beamed at him, excitement clear in her expression. 'Hey, Lewis.'

'Hey.' His immediate instinct was to reach out his hand for her to hold but he reined it in. So far, since Saturday, his avoidance tactics had been working. The less time he spent with her, the better. But, the moment she'd invited him to see the guy they'd worked on together, he'd folded. He knew he'd have folded at some time. He just couldn't keep away from her. It seemed as though she was a magnetic force he was destined to spin around.

He gestured to the door. 'Should we?'

'Indeed.' Her smile was infectious.

He buzzed the intercom and they were let in

by the ward clerk, who showed them to Graham's bed. He was sitting upright, propped up by pillows. His arm was in a sling, his bruised chest dotted with sticky heart-monitor pads and he had a nasal cannula taped to his cheek delivering oxygen. His frail-looking features lit up as they approached and he raised his good arm in a small wave.

'Graham, hello.' Lewis gently shook the man's hand. 'I'm Lewis and this is Charlie. We're the paramedic and doctor who just happened to be in the right place at the right time a couple of weeks ago. Well, you're certainly looking better than the last time we met.'

'I hope so.' Graham's voice was weak even though he was clearly on the mend. 'Sorry if I don't recognise you, but I can't remember much of it.'

Lewis smiled. 'That's absolutely fine. You were a bit out of it.'

Understatement of the year.

Charlie sat down next to the bed. 'It was a hell of a night. All that rain didn't help. But we're so glad to see that you're out of the woods. Hope you feel up to eating these soon.' She handed Graham the box of chocolates.

'Thank you. I hope so too.' Graham nodded. He looked first at Charlie and then at Lewis, as if committing them to memory. 'They tell me that you two saved my life.'

Lewis glanced over at Charlie. 'Well, we did our best to keep your heart going until we could hand you over to the team. You're obviously one hell of a fighter, Graham.'

'You need to be these days. But I'm glad you two were on my side.' He laughed, which brought on a coughing fit. His monitor started to beep and a nurse came running over. She tutted and frowned, but her tone was jolly. 'Graham, honestly. What do I keep telling you about overdoing things?'

'I'm fine. I'm fine.' He waved her away weakly then looked at Charlie. 'I want you to know how much I appreciate what you both did. I owe you my life.'

'It's our pleasure. We were lucky to be there to help.' She smiled at him and patted his hand. 'Now, we don't want to put you under any more stress or tire you out, so we'll say good bye for now. We'll pop back again soon and, in the meantime, keep getting better, Graham.'

The old man smiled and nodded, exhaustion bruising his eyes. 'What a lovely couple you are. Thank you again.'

Couple. It seemed as though everyone thought they should be or could be a couple…except the couple themselves.

Lewis glanced at Charlie. Her cheeks bloomed red, which was interesting, because she'd handled telling Brin the truth about their relationship so easily the other day. She scrunched up her nose as she smiled. 'Just doing our jobs. Get well soon, Graham.'

Lewis's heart felt lighter as they walked out of the ward and Charlie's smile was wide, her eyes dancing with light as she said, 'That was lovely.'

'Always great to meet a success story,' he agreed. But it was the happy glow in Charlie's eyes that was making his heart thump more quickly, not pride in doing his job well. She looked almost ethereal in that flowing dress. All he wanted to do was capture her mouth and taste that smile.

They wandered through the hospital and out into the car park, chatting about success stories and the weird and unusual cases they'd seen. So far, so collegial.

But once out in the car park she stopped, her expression morphing from animated to cautious. 'Lewis?'

His heart started to hammer against his chest. Where was this going? 'Yes?'

'Look, I just want you to know that you don't have to avoid me at work.'

'What do you mean?' He knew exactly what she meant.

She looked stricken. 'It just feels as if every time we meet on the department, you're very keen to make a quick retreat from my presence.'

Damn right he was keen not to spend any time with her. It was self-preservation, really. The more time he spent with her, the more torture it became. He *wanted* her…always. 'No. That's not it, Charlie…'

'Okay, maybe I'm being sensitive then. Sorry, forget I mentioned it. It's just… Oh, look, never mind.' Her brightness and elation of a few minutes ago now flattened, she turned away.

Now he felt as if he was gaslighting her, just because he wanted to protect his own heart from further damage, and he couldn't do that. He reached out and touched her shoulder. 'Wait, Charlie. I'm sorry. You're right: I have been trying to spend less time in the emergency department, if I can.'

'Oh?' She turned back to him, looking hurt. 'Because of me?'

Ugh. He'd been trying to be honest with her as much as he could. She kept asking him, pushing him to tell her how he was feeling, and she was showing him how, so why couldn't he do it?

He took a breath. 'Um…okay. So, what we said on Saturday… It's been playing on my mind—occupying it, actually.' He smiled but he knew it had a hint of wariness in it. 'I'm confused, if I'm honest. You coming back has thrown me for six. I need some space to get my head round everything. More for my benefit than yours.'

Her frown deepened. 'That makes me feel so many things, Lewis. I'm upset that you feel you have to actively avoid me and I'm so…so sad we can't be friends. Especially after what we said on

Saturday.' She swallowed, her eyes large and soft. 'I thought I was doing okay, you know? But, the truth is, I'm not okay. I miss the closeness we once had. Sometimes, I just want to talk to you.'

As with today; after attending to a sick baby, she'd needed a hug and had had to get it from her niece, not from him.

'Oh, Charlie.' His heart felt as if it were turning inside out. He hated to see her upset, and because of something he'd done. Before he could stop himself, he'd pulled her into his arms. He stroked her hair as she lent her head against his chest. 'I'm here for you. Talk to me any time you want.'

She looked up at him and smiled almost shyly. Then she turned her head away, holding him tight, hugging him to her. As they stood there in that desolate car park, he felt the rise and fall of her chest and heard the soft sound of her breath. Awareness prickled through him. Something changed in the atmosphere around them, like a buzz of electricity sparking through him. His skin tingled at each pressure point where his body touched hers.

Her head nuzzled against his chin. He closed his eyes, trying to force away the urge to kiss her again, trying to wish away the growing erection between them. But she made a little sound in her throat and in the next moment all his fight was snapped into a thousand pieces, leaving just desire and heat winding through him.

'Sometimes I want more, Lewis. Sometimes

I don't want to talk at all.' Her mouth was close to his ear, her warm breath tickling his skin. He turned his face to hers and she was so close, so very close. 'Just touch. And… I know that's not fair, because I can't give you what you want…the family you want.'

Right now, *she* was all he wanted. All he'd ever wanted. Her pupils were huge and her breathing fast. Her eyelids fluttered closed as her fingers stroked his back. Her hot body pressed against him in all the right places, her breasts against his chest, her core against his growing erection.

Then he couldn't control anything any longer. He walked her back towards his car and pressed her against it, capturing her mouth in his. 'Charlie. God, Charlie…'

Next he was kissing, kissing and kissing her, telling her in his kisses exactly what he wanted: that he couldn't bear to see her confused or upset; that he couldn't keep holding back; that he'd rather die than not be able to slide inside her, to hold her, to drown in her kisses.

'I had to avoid you because all I want to do is this.' He dragged his lips from hers, framing her face with his palms. 'You are the only woman I've ever wanted, Charlie. My Charlie Rose.'

He kissed her again, long, slowly and sensuously, and she whimpered…or was it him?

'I love the way you kiss me. I love…' She suddenly pulled back, shaking and breathless. 'Shoot. I…um… I have to go pick up Stella from nursery.'

I love... You...? Was that what she'd been about to say?

No. No. No. That was not where they were heading. He couldn't allow it full-stop. She'd loved him last time, but not enough to stay. Not enough to try and make things work. She loved his kisses, that was all.

'Yeah. I should go too.' His voice was gravelly as reality hit him hard. Firstly, they were kissing in the staff car park where anyone could see them. And secondly, and far more importantly, they'd stepped right over that line again. Blurred everything into a kiss, into hot need, into something from which he didn't know he could disentangle himself.

She swallowed, her hand on her chest as if trying to calm down her racing heart. 'And I need to check on Lucy too. She had another dose of chemo last week, so this week is where she starts to feel yuck again.'

'Of course. Of course.' He watched her walk away, feeling the pull to walk with her, to stay by her side. To talk whenever she needed him to, to listen, to soothe and to kiss.

But he couldn't ask where this was going or what this blurring of boundaries might mean. Couldn't put her in that situation to make rational choices when she was so involved with caring for her family. And he had no idea himself what could happen next, only that with every new moment spent with her…every kiss, every touch and with every *I love*...he was drawn back under her spell.

And he didn't know if he could fight it any more. Even though he had to, if he was going to get out sane.

She tried to keep away. She spent about thirty-two solid hours tending to Lucy's and Stella's every need when she wasn't at work. She focused on helping them get through this difficult week and tried to put Lewis to the back of her mind.

It was a futile exercise, of course. Because when she wasn't holding Lucy's hair back as she vomited, or changing Stella's nappy, cooing her to sleep, cajoling her to eat or reading her a picture book, the only thing she thought about was Lewis.

She still wanted him.

She wanted him right now, standing outside his house, wondering if she had actually gone mad with need, desire or…whatever it was that she refused to put a name to. Because if she acknowledged the depth of her feelings she'd have to walk away. So she told herself it was lust and possibly loneliness. That both those things could be easily remedied by sex, by friendship, maybe a combination of the two.

Friends with benefits—would he agree to that?

She pressed the doorbell and heard the echoing

ring inside. She waited. Her heart thudded as she craned to hear thumping footsteps.

Nothing.

She pressed the bell again and waited. Maybe he wasn't here after all. Maybe he was fast asleep and couldn't hear the bell. Maybe he knew it was her and was choosing to ignore her, like a sensible person, not lust-drunk, would.

Eventually she turned away and started to walk down the path.

'Charlie?'

She whipped round, her breath stalling in her chest as the sight of him, in an old grey T-shirt and tight black boxer shorts made her feel dizzy with need. Could he look any sexier?

'Charlie?' His face crumpled as he reached out his hand, immediately worried. 'What's wrong?'

Her courage started to fail her. But she had to say something. 'Can I come in?'

'Sure.' He opened the door wider and let her walk in front of him into his lounge, switching on the wall lights, bringing a warm, soft glow. 'What's happened? Is everything all right?'

She turned to look at him, her heart pounding in her ears. 'Everything is fine. Don't worry.'

'Is Lucy okay? Stella?'

'Yes.' She smiled at his concern. 'Calm down, Lewis. They're fine. They're fast asleep.'

He shook his head. 'So, why are you here?'

Such a bad idea after all. She sighed and chuckled. 'It never used to be this difficult. For God's sake, do I have to spell it out? This is the adult woman version of sneaking out of my house in the middle of the night.'

He gasped, then laughed…more of a groan. 'Charlie Jade Rose—this is a booty call? What the hell?'

'What can I say? I wanted to see you. I couldn't sleep and wondered if you couldn't either.'

'As it happens, I was wide awake.' He met her gaze, suddenly heated. 'Thinking about you, actually.'

Thinking about what, exactly? 'You took your time answering the door.'

He ran his hand through his hair, eyes wide. 'I didn't think for a minute that it could be you. I thought it was kids messing about.'

She took a breath, thinking about what they used to get up to in his bedroom, in *their* bedroom, back when things had been fun. 'Maybe we could be.'

He swallowed and grinned. Clearly he remembered too. 'Charlie…' His voice was guttural, base.

It was probably meant to be a warning. A reminder of everything they'd agreed. But it sounded like the sexiest growl she'd ever heard.

'So, tell me to go if you're not…up for it…' She stepped towards him, or he stepped towards her; she wasn't sure. But suddenly he was up close, his forehead against hers, his hand snaking round her waist.

'How did you know my address?'

'Is it very lame to say I remembered from way back when we were checking to see if we were neighbours?' She chuckled. 'Plus, your car is parked in the drive.'

'Ah.' He nodded, swallowing hard as he looked her up and down, his gaze landing on her mouth. 'Doesn't take a genius, then.'

'And you're worrying about details and I'm standing here wanting you. Does my seduction technique need work?' She raised her eyebrows in question as she snaked her arms around his waist. 'It never used to fail me. You used to welcome me with a kiss and take me straight to bed.'

The cloud of hesitation that seemed to have been hovering over him dissipated. He laughed, his fingers trailing over her cheek. 'You have a seduction technique?'

'Hey, you.' She giggled. 'I can seduce.'

'Really? Interesting. Tell me when you're starting.' Tongue in cheek, he grinned, pretending to be immune to her advances when the tent in his boxer shorts told her he very much wasn't immune at all.

But he did have a point: she actually had to do or say something. Shrugging off her coat, she revealed her matching black lace bra and panties. God, she'd taken such a risk coming here in the middle of the night dressed like this. But it could be worth every threaded breath, every second-guess, every kiss, every touch, every stroke of his fingertips against her skin. Every second spent in his arms. 'You're telling me you hadn't thought about Sunday morning sex?'

'It's still…' His eyes darted to the wall clock. 'Oh, wait. Yes, Sunday morning. *Charlie…*'

Then his mouth found hers in a greedy, desperate kiss. He palmed her breast and she reached for his pants, each of them stripping each other in a haze of clumsy, desperate hunger.

Still kissing her as if he never wanted to let go, he tugged her to the bedroom and laid her on the bed. She reached for him, stroking her fingers down his length. He was so hard….for her.

After this, she would go.

Sunday morning sex—just sex. Just friends and sex, and that was all.

She swallowed back the rawness in her throat. Whatever label they put on it, it was hot and irresistible. She put aside their promises, ignoring the beat of anxiety at the back of her mind, and sank into this, with him—with Lewis.

He shuddered at her touch and groaned again. 'Jeez, Charlie. What you do to me…'

She whispered into his ear, 'Is what?'

'You turn me on so much.'

'Aha.' She slicked kisses across his throat. 'How?'

'You're supposed to be seducing me, right? Not the other way round.' He laughed and whispered, 'What do you want, Charlotte?'

'Oh, it's Charlotte now?' She laughed, then the laughter died in her throat as she thought about what she wanted.

I want you to hold me, to hug me. To be with me. I want you inside me. I want you to... I want you, *Lewis. I want* you, *so much I can't breathe.*

'I want to kiss you, Lewis. I want you to fill me. I want to ride you.'

'Jeez…' His breath stuttered on the inhale.

'Do you want that too?' She kissed his jaw, his bottom lip and his top lip, stroking him gently up and down, up and down… 'Tell me what you want.'

'I want to slide deep inside you. I want to feel you around me.' He turned onto his side and slid his hand between her legs, arrowing for her core and rubbing the sensitive spot right…*there*.

He stroked her, then slid his fingers inside her, making her squirm, contract and writhe against him. He was telling her what he needed. *Hell…* Sex had always been great with Lewis, but he'd never actually told her what he wanted. They'd just gone by feel and instinct before. It had been enough back then. She'd loved the way they'd made love. But this was next-level sexy. She was breathing so fast, she could barely get enough air into her lungs.

Her grip on him tightened and he groaned in delight. She was so dizzy with need she could barely form words. 'I want…'

'What else do you want, Charlie?'

'Everything.' She wanted this, wanted him. Wanted what they'd had years ago, before it had all gone wrong. Wanted this new thing they had going, this honesty, this need.

She'd only ever wanted him.

He lay back and lifted her onto his lap. '*God*, Charlie. I need to be inside you.'

Hot, electric need coursed through her and she knew she was hanging on the edge. One move, one thrust of him inside her, and she'd be undone.

'Now. Please. *Now.*' She straddled his thighs, his erection hard against her core. She positioned herself over him and lowered herself with a moan. And he was inside her again, rocking slowly, and it was so intense and perfect; perfectly intense.

She closed her eyes as their rhythm quickened, catching her breath in stuttered gasps. The pressure rising at her core sent flashes of sparks and light flickering across her skin, over her, inside her, deep and white-hot. She felt him ripple, heard him grind out her name and she clung on and rode with him until they were both crying out, mouths welded together in a messy, needy, hungry kiss.

Together. First and last.

Her Lewis. Her love. Her always.

CHAPTER FIFTEEN

IT TOOK SOME time for her breathing to steady and for her to feel emotionally anchored enough to climb off his thighs and snuggle against him. He wrapped his arms around her, hugging her the way she needed. If she was honest, that was what she'd come for, after all. Making love had been an accumulation of her need for him, all of him, but she'd needed to be with him because she'd simply been unable to keep away. She'd wanted *his* hug. Wanted his arms around her. She missed him.

'Sunday morning sex. The best ever.' He stroked her shoulder, his tone soft. 'Lucy didn't mind you coming out?'

'I didn't ask. It was the middle of the night, Lewis. They were both fine and well and fast asleep, and I'm not planning on staying long. No harm done. They won't even know I'm gone.'

'Oh. You're not staying?'

Feeling his frown against her neck, she turned round to look at him. 'Don't frown, Lewis. You know I have to go. It's just like old times, right? I have to be back in my bed before everyone wakes up. We have maybe another hour.'

'Makes it even more foolish to waste more time, then.' He pushed her hair back from her face and kissed her again. This time it was slow and tender and filled with so much emotion, it made her heart ache.

How could they be just friends when there was this much emotion between them, this much connection? Was it too early to talk about what next? Yes, it was too early. She couldn't push him into a corner. Better to enjoy this silly, fun sex.

She broke the kiss and snuggled into the crook of his arm, closing her eyes, her head on his chest. He wrapped his other arm round her and she felt the strong, steady beat of his heart against her ribcage.

None of this felt silly. It felt consequential. Her heart had opened to him again. She stroked his forearm and closed her eyes. Being held like this made her feel as if nothing in the world could hurt her. She felt safe and secure. Nothing bad could happen in this haven of his strength, of their… their what? Their craving? Their need? Their love?

Love?

What?

Her eyes flickered open. Had she fallen in love with him again?

Had she ever stopped loving him?

Had she? She'd tried. She'd moved to the other side of the world to stop loving him but it hadn't worked. So the simple answer was no. And the most difficult, heart-wrenching answer was still… no. She'd always loved him and, instead of dimming, it was growing, glowing brighter and stronger. And she couldn't help it, she couldn't stop it.

And so what if…what if he didn't feel the same? What if…? She knew the 'what if?' Her stomach went into freefall.

Stupid, stupid, stupid Charlie.

He wanted kids and she couldn't have them—end of. That was the brutal truth. He would tell her it didn't matter. And she'd have to watch him coo at other people's babies and keep on pretending.

And her heart would break.

Oblivious to the sudden crisis in her heart, he lazily drew circles over her hip as he said, 'One thing I regret…well, I regret a lot of things about how we broke up…but we should have talked more…'

He didn't finish the sentence.

Completely alert now, she propped herself up on her elbow to look at him. 'What do you mean?'

His eyes were closed, but his breathing hitched. 'I was too closed off. But…' His voice trailed off again, as if he was rethinking the sentence or the whole conversation.

'But *what*, Lewis?'

He looked at her, eyes dark, haunted almost. Then he shook his head, as if shaking away his thoughts. 'It's… Ah, look, nothing. It's…too heavy for this time of night. You have to go soon, and that's okay.' He smiled but it was kind of sad. 'You have other commitments now.'

But…what?

Should we adopt? What about surrogacy? How about fostering? How about moving back in together? How about my giving up all my hopes and dreams for you? How about falling deeper in love? Were those the things he meant, those things he wasn't actually going to say again? The things he didn't want to talk about.

All the emotions were tangling up inside her and the only respite she ever seemed to have was when they were making love. For a few amazing minutes she could forget the past, but then it would barrel into her, along with all the reasons why they couldn't do this. 'Please, Lewis, I want to hear what you have to say.'

He rolled onto his back and stared up at the ceiling.

She waited, barely breathing.

He looked at her briefly, then away. 'We can't have kids.'

'*I* can't have kids, Lewis. You? You could probably have a whole football team of mini-mes if you wanted to.'

His eyes flashed at her words and that hurt her the most. He had options. He had a chance and he still wanted that; he could not refute the obvious minute flicker of hope at her words. But he shook his head. 'There are other ways to be happy, right?'

'Like what? Please don't say you'll give up your dream for me. Please don't give up your chance for a family, to be a dad. And please don't put that decision on me.'

He frowned. 'What do you mean?'

Okay, so they were going to talk about this. It felt as if a huge weight was crushing her chest. 'I don't want you to promise me something and then regret it down the line. Give me up for a woman who can give you children. I couldn't bear that.'

'Charlie. Please don't think like that. That's not what I'm saying. I'm saying you must never give up that hope.'

'Oh, the hope thing again?' She sighed, her heart hurting. They'd been down this road before. *Keep believing, Charlie. Everything's going to be okay.* Things had not been okay.

His jaw tightened. 'There are other things we could do.'

'Like get a dog?'

'Yes, if you want. But there's also adoption or surrogacy.'

Oh. Okay.

Breathing out, she ventured, 'In New Zealand? The odds are very much against us. There aren't enough babies up for adoption and surrogacy has to be altruistic; it's not like we can pay someone to have a baby for us.'

But there was a chance. It wasn't impossible. A tiny flicker of hope fluttered in her chest. They were talking about this. *We*: he was talking about them as a couple. He was considering options.

Which meant things had gone too far already. Because no amount of wanting him to say that he loved her, that nothing could come between them or that they had options, would change the facts. The same facts that had influenced their break-up. He still wanted a child of his own, regardless of what he said. She could see the longing every time he looked at a child or held a baby. And she couldn't give him one.

More than that...so much more...she wouldn't be able to bear seeing his realisation that he'd chosen the wrong woman. She couldn't risk him leaving her. That was something she'd never recover from. She was scared of the strength of her feelings for him and the vulnerability that instilled in her.

Because she loved him. She'd never stopped loving him. Hell, she'd adored him since sixth form and that love still burned strong inside her. But it was one thing to love him from a distance, another to love him up close...and wait for the truth to dawn on him that she would not be enough.

Her phone from downstairs intruded into the weighted silence. She held her breath and listened. 'Did you hear that?'

'Your phone?' He sat up.

'It's the early hours; everyone should be asleep. It's either Lucy or our parents.' Neither of them phoning at this time would be good news. 'I've got to go see who it is. It could be important.'

Throwing on his T-shirt, she ran down to the lounge, grabbed her phone from her bag and her heart constricted.

'It's Lucy,' she shouted up to Lewis. 'There must be something wrong. She never rings me.' She pressed the answer buttons and heard her sister's terrified cries. 'Charlie, please, where are you? I need you. Please come home. Please.'

'Wh-what's happened?' Charlie could only imagine something terrible.

A sob came, then another. 'Please just come home.'

'Of course. I'm on my way.' Her heart drummed against her ribcage as she turned to Lewis who was now standing in front of her, dressed in T-shirt and shorts. 'I've got to go.'

Face set in determination, he nodded. 'I'll grab your clothes. I'm coming with you.'

But she put her hand on his chest, shaking her head.

This was all her fault. She'd sneaked out instead of staying where she would have been all along. She'd given in to temptation, put her own needs first again. Her needs before those of Lewis…who would have been asleep still if she hadn't come booty calling. Her needs before those of her her sister and her niece.

Lewis's dark eyes bored into her. She knew him well enough to know he wanted to help and didn't like not being able to. Feeling helpless was something she'd experienced for a while; she knew exactly how it felt.

'No. No, Lewis. You can't come with me. I'm sorry.' She needed to be with her sister. Just the two of them, not with Lewis.

Not Lewis. Stark reality hit her hard: not Lewis…

They couldn't keep doing this and pretending everything would work out well. She couldn't keep bruising her heart. She had to, finally, put a stop to this. She shook her head again, not wanting to say things she knew she had to say. She'd said them all once before then she'd walked away.

He looked at her and a dozen questions ran across his gaze. She shook her head.

Don't make me say anything else. They'd got carried away.

But he squeezed her hand; either he didn't realise what she was trying to say or he didn't want to acknowledge it. 'Okay, you know where I am if you need me.'

'Thanks. But this is something I need to do on my own.'

Words she'd said before. She walked to the door and closed it behind her, heart aching, all on repeat.

It wasn't any easier the second time around.

* * *

She found Lucy bent over the toilet bowl, her eyes red-rimmed, her pale, too-thin body shaking inside her winter pyjamas. Fleecy pyjamas in the height of summer—poor Lucy was always cold these days. Charlie gasped, ran across the cold tiles and wrapped her arms round her sister's shoulders. 'Hey, girl. Lucy, what's wrong, darling?'

Her sister groaned. 'I've been attached to this loo for the last hour and I feel like absolute crap. But…' She held up a fistful of her beautiful Titian hair and her face crumpled. 'Worse than anything else, my hair's falling out, in clumps.'

The Rose crowning glory, the hair they'd hated and loved in equal measure growing up. They'd been warned it would happen after the chemo but it wasn't something they'd really talked about, maybe hoping they'd never have to face it. Charlie felt tears pricking her eyes but she forced them back. She would be her sister's tower of strength here. She would not cry. 'Oh, honey, I'm so sorry.'

Lucy sat back looking defeated and dejected. 'I wasn't ready for this to happen. I pretended I was going to be different to everyone else. I know I shouldn't care about how I look, but I do. I don't want to be bald. I don't want…any of this.'

Charlie's heart felt as if it were breaking from leaving Lewis amidst such confusion, and now seeing her sister in pieces. 'It's cruel, Lucy.'

'Yes, it is. I don't want this. I just want to be able to spend happy, lovely time with my daughter and my sister. Bloody cancer. And I'm ranting now too.' She gave a sniff and the faintest hint of a rueful smile. 'Sorry about that too.'

'You can rant and shout and scream all you need. None of this is fair, none of it. Not the lump or the cancer or the surgery or the chemo that makes you sick. And definitely not your beautiful hair. But if your hair's falling out, it means the medicine is working, right?'

'I suppose.' Lucy wiped her eyes with the back of her hand. 'I'm sorry if I gave you a fright. Were you at Lewis's house?'

Oh, Lewis... They hadn't finished their conversation and everything was up in the air. Neither of them had been brave enough to face the truth and say it. They'd grasped at one more chance to be together, to sink into each other's arms. 'Yes. I was only gone a couple of hours. I was about to head home anyway.'

'I'm sorry I interrupted your night.'

Charlie squeezed her sister in a warm hug. 'Never say sorry for what you're going through, Luce. I love you. *I'm* sorry I wasn't here when you needed me.'

'You are, hun. You're here all of the time. You work, sleep and look after me. I know that.'

She wiped her sister's forehead with a damp

flannel then helped her to stand. 'I won't leave you again, I promise.'

But Lucy chuckled and put her head on Charlie's shoulder, leaning heavily on her as they walked slowly to her bedroom. 'Hey, don't make promises you can't keep.'

Charlie had tried to tell Lewis that, hadn't she? That good intentions were just that: good intentions. They weren't fixed in stone. Not that she'd ever leave her sister again to cope with this on her own, but she could. Just like Lewis could promise to stay with her and then leave when someone or something else came along. That was the risk, wasn't it, the risk with love? You put all your dreams into one person and hoped they'd stick with you. Hoped they'd stay.

Lucy slumped heavily on to her bed. Charlie lifted her sister's legs under the sheets and surreptitiously disposed of the fallen copper strands on her pillow. Her mind was made up. 'Well, obviously I'll be at work some of the time, but I'll be here for you, Lucy. Always. Lewis… Well, Lewis is only going to be a friend from now on. A proper friend, nothing more.'

'Don't put yourself second. Live your life, Charlie. You have so much to give.'

Not the right things for Lewis, though.

'I'm here. I'm not going anywhere.'

But he'd broached the subject of options, something they'd never managed to do five years ago. He'd brought it up. He'd been thinking about it.

I'm not going anywhere.

Why did she believe herself and not Lewis?

Because she knew that vows and promises could be broken by hardship and struggle. She knew, because she'd broken them herself.

So how could she trust anyone else to stay when she hadn't?

CHAPTER SIXTEEN

HE'D HANDLED IT BADLY. He'd clammed up right at the time when he should have been more open. But he hadn't known where they stood, especially after agreeing it had just been a friend thing, a booty call. Had it just been fun or was it more? Now it couldn't be anything, he realised that, because she'd be terrified of leaving her sister again.

He knocked on the front door, wondering whether this was a mistake. Charlie opened the door and peered out with wary, tired eyes. She was wearing cute shortie pyjamas, her hair was messy and, given that it was four o'clock in the afternoon, that was unusual. But she gave him a small smile. 'Hey. This is a surprise.'

'You left your purse. Thought I'd drop it by in case you needed it.' He held it out to her.

She opened the door a little further and took her purse from him. 'Thanks. It must have fallen out of my bag when I was in such a hurry to get back here.'

'Not surprising. You left in a whirl of panic. I thought I might see you at work to give it back to you, but they tell me you've been off for a few days.'

'Yes. I've taken a couple of carer's days.'

He should have known that, if they'd been involved in any way. But she hadn't answered his messages and hadn't sent any of her own. What was he meant to do with that—just walk away? Pretend that they hadn't made love or that they hadn't reconnected deeper and harder than before? 'I wanted to make sure you're okay. I don't want to come in, I just wanted to let you know I'm here for you. How's Lucy?'

Charlie's voice softened and she smiled sadly. 'She's trying to get some sleep. The chemo makes her sick and now her hair's falling out too.'

He looked at Charlie's messy beautiful hair and his gut lurched. 'Damn. I'm so sorry. You know there are charities that can help her feel better about the way she looks?'

'Yeah. I grabbed some leaflets from work last week. I just haven't got round to reading any of them yet.'

He watched as guilt flitted across her face. 'It's not a sin to want some relief for yourself too.'

'You mean sneaking out in the middle of the night?' Her eyebrows rose. 'Like a teenager?'

'Yeah. Time out.'

'Well, I'm not a teenager, Lewis. And nothing you can say will make me feel better about not being here when my sister needed me.' She shook her head and he knew that that conversation was dead in the water before it began.

A little cry came from inside the house.

'Ugh. Stella needs entertaining and we're both exhausted. Bless her.' She looked distraught, torn, sad and guilty all rolled into one. She turned round and called out, 'Hush, sweetie. It's okay, Stella baby, I'm coming.'

Here was something he could help with, at least. 'Do you want me to take her out for an hour, so you can get some rest?'

'Oh.' She blinked and looked sorely tempted but shook her head, raising her voice over the increasingly loud cries. 'Oh, well…no. No, thanks all the same.'

'You could do with some rest too, right? The carers need to be cared for.'

She pressed her lips together. The connection they'd had on Sunday morning was hanging by a thread. He could see she'd closed herself off. She was barely coping with her responsibilities here. Did she feel he was a responsibility too?

Finally, she nodded. 'Okay, yes. Thanks, Lewis. I owe you.'

'You owe me nothing. It's okay, I've got plenty of time. I'm on earlies this week.' Although he'd have moved heaven and earth to help her, taken carer's days off too if she'd needed him to, phoned in sick or given up his damned job. Because, regardless of what she told him, or how much he tried to convince himself otherwise, he was hard-wired to be her champion, her cheerleader and her supporter.

She opened the door wide and let him in. Stella was sitting in the play pen in the lounge, bawling her eyes out, so he picked her up and soothed her, rocking her against his chest. 'Hey, hey. Look at you, clever girl. You were sitting up all by yourself. What's the matter? Was no one here? Auntie Charlie was just talking to me. So much noise from one so little! What is it? There's no need to cry.'

As if by some miracle the little girl stopped crying and stared at him. She patted his cheek with her hand as she inhaled shuddering breaths, then she smiled.

He grinned back. 'That's better. Now, should we go for a walk, see what we can find at the park? Shall we go? Oh, butter wouldn't melt now, right?'

From behind him he heard a sharp intake of breath; or was it a strained, throaty cry…?

He turned to see Charlie striding towards him, arms outstretched for the baby. 'Actually, it's time for her nap. I'll take her for a quick walk round the block later.'

'I can do that. You look bushed.'

'No, Lewis.' Her tone was sharp enough to make him stop in his tracks.

Okay. She's tired and stressed.

He kissed Stella on the cheek and put her back

into the playpen. Then he walked towards Charlie, his gut tightening in a knot. Her mouth was set in a line and he knew, just knew, that her tone wasn't just because she was tired and stressed; it was far more than that. He knew, soul-deep, this was the end.

Not again. Don't do this again.

He shook his head, not wanting her to say the words, not wanting to hear them. 'Before you say anything final, hear me out. I can wait… I will wait for you, Charlie. I'll wait as long as I have to until you're freed up a little.'

She walked to the front door, then outside, and he couldn't do anything but follow. She stopped on the path and turned to him. 'No, Lewis. You cannot wait for me. I don't know how long this will take. Lucy needs me and I need to take care of her. This isn't something you can fix for me.'

But I want to.

'No, I get that. But I can be here for you. I can help, or just be at the end of the phone.'

They'd never finished their important conversation.

She shook her head, resolute. 'I don't think that's a good idea. I'm not sure we can even stay friends, not the way things are between us.'

'You mean the way we're good together? The way we make each other feel? The way we keep coming back to each other even after everything that happened? We're divorced, Charlie. We've lived apart for five years and missed so much of each other's lives and yet none of that matters, none of it, because I believe in us.'

Her hand flew to her mouth. 'Please. Don't.'

'So you're going to walk way *again*?' His heart felt cleaved in two.

It wasn't supposed to have got this intense. He hadn't wanted to feel this much. He was meant to have protected himself from this very scenario. And yet here he was, trying to make her see sense again. Because he knew that they could have something very special, could be happy together, if they gave it a shot. If she did.

She swallowed, looking as hurt as he felt. 'Last time I had to go for *me*. I needed space to lick my wounds and come to terms with my infertility. This time it's for you.'

'For me? That's bull, Charlie.' He knew his tone was becoming sharp too and he tried to soften it. 'You haven't even asked what I want.'

'Because I already know. We were just about to talk about it, the other morning, right? Really talk about what we might do as a...couple. How you're willing to put your wants and needs second to mine. But we don't know if we can adopt, or find a surrogate. We don't know if we'd be lucky enough to be chosen to be parents. That's a very uncertain future for someone who's desperate to be a daddy.

'I don't want to wake up one morning and see

regret in your eyes, Lewis. Regret that you made the wrong choice, and a realisation that you could have what you want with someone else. So we can't be a couple, Lewis. I won't let it happen. I won't let either of us take that risk. I don't want to have my heart broken again and I imagine you don't want that either.'

It was already breaking; couldn't she see that? She was breaking him, breaking this amazing thing they could have together. 'We don't walk away when things get tough, Charlie. We stay. We stay and we fight. I would never walk away.'

'I know. I know you'd try to stay to the bitter end. You'd fight and fight and fight.' She put her palm up. 'So please don't make this harder than it has to be. We both knew coming into it that there were huge barriers. Nothing can change facts, Lewis. I am not the right person for you.

'I'm okay with what life has thrown at me. I know I can be fulfilled and happy without having kids. I've come to terms with a child-free future. I am a fantastic auntie and godmother and a great doctor. I have so many amazing plans for travel, and for my life. I am whole and I am thriving. But, every time I see you with Stella, I see that longing ripple through you. I can't trust that you won't decide to leave me. And I couldn't live every day waiting for it to happen.'

'You don't believe it when I tell you I'll wait? That I'll stay? I'll be here for you, Charlie, always. But, hell you can't *trust* me?' That was the lowest blow. Even after everything he'd said and done, she didn't think he had staying power. 'You walked away last time, Charlie, not me.'

He knew he should be walking away now, relieved that she'd set him free. But his feet were lead, his limbs too heavy to move. He didn't feel free, he felt broken.

She put her hand on his arm. 'I know, more than anyone, how sometimes you have to escape for your own sanity. And I couldn't bear to see you do the same. I'm sorry, Lewis.'

'So am I.' He shook his arm and got her to take her hand away. If she touched him again, he'd fold. 'But I'm not sure how you can say you want to leave when you were talking about love only the other day.'

She blinked, shock flashing across her expression. 'When?'

'In the car park. When we were making out.' His heart had swollen in panic but also comfort and relief.

Her eyes widened as the memory hit her. 'Oh, Lewis. I said "I love the way you kiss me". I love your smile, yes. I love lots of things about you—'

'But you don't love me enough to stay.'

She looked up at him, her eyes swimming with tears. Her mouth trembled and he could see she was trying hard not to cry. 'No, Lewis. That's the problem, don't you see? I love you too much to stay.'

Then she walked up the path and closed the door.

She was gone—again.

He stared at the red paint.

She did love him.

He rubbed his forehead with the heel of his hand then stalked up to the door to hammer on it. To tell her to come back out and that they'd sort it all. Make her believe that he'd stay. Make her understand.

But Lucy... Stella... He couldn't disturb them and add to her problems.

He heard the baby start to cry again and heard someone cooing in a cracked voice, then an adult sob.

Charlie. Come back.

He walked down the path then back up again.

How the hell could he convince her that this time they could work it through?

He kicked the doorstep and slumped down on it.

'Charlie,' he whispered. 'For God's sake.'

How would he survive seeing her every day at work? How would she survive seeing him? How would he cope hearing her voice, her laughter? How would he be able to hand over a patient when there was this chasm between them?

He put his head in his hands.

Oh, Charlie, why the hell are you doing this to us?

How would he ever get over her second time round?

'Who was at the door?' Lucy croaked as she sat down at the kitchen table. 'Did I hear someone?'

'It was Lewis.' Charlie put a bowl of home-made chicken soup in front of her sister, then sat down in front of her own food, but she had no appetite.

Lucy frowned. 'He didn't want to come in?'

'Oh, he did.' Charlie tried to control herself. She'd been stuffing back the tears the whole time she'd been playing with Stella, putting on that false happy voice as she'd read to her from the little cloth book, trying to get her to go to sleep. She'd pretended she was okay when she'd chopped the carrots and onions. She'd forced herself to hold back when she'd called Lucy down for dinner. 'I ended it.'

'What?' Lucy's sunken eyes fizzed with shock as she reached over the table for Charlie's hand. 'Why?'

Charlie put up her palm. 'Don't. Please don't. If you touch me or say one single nice thing, I'll cry.'

Lucy scraped her chair back, went over and wrapped her arms around Charlie. 'Cry all you want, sis. I'm here.'

But Charlie squeezed her eyelids closed, pressing back the threatening tears. 'I'm okay. It's for the best. It is.'

She had to keep telling herself that. She had to believe it. She needed to forget him.

Her gaze fell on the leaflets scattered on the console. Leaflets about a charity that ran programmes to support women going through chemotherapy and hair loss. About another one that did free counselling, one that provided wigs, another that accepted hair donations and another that raised money for cancer charities by running head shaves. There was help for everything Lucy was going through and more. Charlie determined to put all her focus on her sister to help her reach out for this available support.

Maybe then she might forget Lewis.

Fat chance, when she'd see him most days.

Maybe then things wouldn't hurt so much.

Fat chance, because real, honest, true love didn't fade, did it? She knew that already. She'd been there, trying to forget her marriage and Lewis for five years, and had learnt that she would not, could not, forget him. She loved him more now than ever before.

She cleared her throat and picked up the leaflets, unable to meet her sister's piercing and enquiring gaze. 'Hey, why don't we take a look through these? Maybe we can contact a couple of these places tomorrow?'

'Charlie, look at me. *Look at me.* Stop deflecting.' Lucy stepped back and peered at her. 'Oh, honey. You are so not okay.'

Charlie's throat felt raw and thick. She couldn't pretend to her sister that she was all right when she was actually falling to pieces. She was trying not to say the words again, because they were barbs in her heart, but they were stuck in her gullet and she couldn't say or swallow anything unless she set them free. 'I love him, Lucy.'

Lucy stroked Charlie's hair. 'I know you do. So I don't understand why you ended it. And, God, please don't say you did it because you're looking after me.'

'No. Not for you, for me. I wish we'd never started up again.' She shook her head. 'No. That's not true. It's been lovely, really lovely. I just wish it didn't all hurt this much.' It was twice as bad as last time because he'd changed, and so had she. They'd become wiser, bolder and more willing to share their feelings. He'd changed so much for the better.

Truth was, there was no better man than Lewis Parry. And she'd lost him again. The hurt and sadness swelled through her until it threatened to overpower her. She stood up on wobbly legs. 'Sorry. I'll be back in a minute.'

She flung back her chair, not wanting her sister to see her in such a state. Then she ran up to her room and flopped on her bed.

And finally gave in to the tears and grief.

CHAPTER SEVENTEEN

'COME ON, MATE, it's for charity.' Brin steered the van into the beach-side car park and pulled on the hand brake. 'The team are relying on you.'

Lewis shrugged, the lethargy that had been dogging him for the last two weeks feeling worse, not better. He stared at the ocean, choppy and churning today, kind of how he felt too: roiling, swirling, out of sorts. 'I don't feel like going out.'

'Which means you need to.' Brin nudged him, about to take a bite out of his chicken and cranberry pie. 'You can't keep moping around like this. To be brutally honest, you're becoming a bit of a tragic.'

'I'm not moping. Or tragic.' Lewis shook his head and stared at the soggy sandwich he'd brought with him for lunch. He missed her. He hated seeing her at work and feeling the awkwardness between them. Hated the short, patient-focused conversations, the sadness in her eyes, the pain. Hated hearing her laughter and not being part of the joke or the fun. 'I don't feel like being sociable.'

Brin turned to him. 'Well, you have to. You're

Mr Charity. You run up buildings…you bid too much in auctions… You have to come with us.'

'I don't, actually.'

'No, mate. You don't have to do anything. You can just never go out again. Sit around all day like a bear with a sore head. Actually, I'd prefer it if you did actually snap or growl. I'm not a huge fan of this sullen apathy.' Brin took a mouthful of pie and they sat in a loaded silence.

Lewis put his uneaten sandwich back in the container. 'I'm not apathetic. I come to work, do my job.'

'Then go home again and do nothing. You know, I haven't heard you talking about your running or training recently. You haven't been to any of the team nights out. You just…exist.' Brin's expression softened. 'I'm worried about you.'

'No need.' But Brin was right. Ever since Charlie had closed that doo, Lewis had lost his sense of fun and humour. Not wanting to ruin the vibe, he'd skipped Lily's ballet concert and had got a rap from his brother for his absence.

Bad Uncle Lewis.

Bad colleague Lewis.

Bad friend Lewis.

Yeah, okay, so maybe he was feeling sorry for himself.

Brin fixed him with his gaze. 'You know you're going to have to try to forget her…or win her back.'

'Who?' He hadn't discussed Charlie with Brin, apart from telling him to back off with his matchmaking.

Brin chortled. 'You know who.'

'I can't win her back if she doesn't want me.'

'I saw the way she looked at you, mate. I heard…' Brin shook his head and winced. 'Oh, never mind.'

'Heard what?' Lewis's gut tightened.

'I heard you talking in Harper's room. The baby monitor was on.' Brin screwed up his face. 'Sorry.'

'What exactly did you hear?' Lewis cringed. They'd thought the monitor was off. They hadn't seen a light on it.

'Something about wanting more… Struggling to keep away from you…' Brin's face bloomed red. 'As soon as I realised you were in there I turned the app off, honest.'

Lewis swore. 'Oh, God. Embarrassing.'

'Or witness to how much you care about each other.'

'Well, forget whatever you heard. She's broken it off. We're done.'

'And you're just going to take it? Not fight?' Brin frowned. 'Surely if you got back together so quickly there's something worth fighting for? Remember what I did when I fell love with Mia and decided to fight for her, for us?'

'Gave me notice on your job. Yeah, I remember.

And also asked for the job back when you both admitted your feelings for each other.'

Charlie had told him she loved him. He hadn't done that. He hadn't told her the depth of his feelings. Maybe he should have. 'I don't think admitting anything is going to help.'

But there was a kernel of something bright and hopeful in his chest. She wanted him to open up, didn't she?

'Well, anything's worth a try, right?'

'I don't know.' Lewis checked the time. 'We need to head off.'

'Okay.' His colleague sighed heavily and handed him a leaflet that had been stuffed in the glove compartment with other detritus. 'Look, I don't want to sound like I'm nagging, but this is the biggest charity event of the season. Some of our team are having their heads shaved to support the cancer patients. It's the biggest money-raiser they have all year. You've got to come support us.'

'You're going to get your head shaved?' How had he missed that? But then, he'd not been focusing on anything except getting through work so he could go home and…okay…mope a bit.

'Yes, I told you.' Brin tutted and shook his head. 'Me and Emma and Raj.'

Lucy. Charlie had been distraught about Lucy losing her hair.

Charlie. He couldn't help them in person but

he could do this—give money to the people that helped them.

For the first time in the last couple of weeks he felt the fog in his brain start to shift. He had a purpose. 'Okay.'

She did care for him. She loved him. And where there was love there was hope.

He'd go to the event then he'd go round and see her, try to get her to understand things from his point of view.

He'd let her go last time. This time he was going to fight a damned sight harder.

Charlie watched from the side of the stage as the compere announced the final event of the fund-raising evening. She'd kept a low profile backstage, because she hadn't felt like talking to anyone, but she kind of wished she'd had a couple of drinks, because what she was about to do scared her to death. But if Lucy was going through it then the least Charlie could do was show her support by doing it too.

She took a deep breath and headed to the back of the small queue of people waiting to go on stage.

'Charlie?'

She turned to the sound of a male voice, her heart jumping, then diving. 'Brin! Hi. Are you going for the big shave too?'

Brin was standing in front of her with a couple of other paramedics she recognised from work.

He ran his fingers over his short hair. 'Not that it'll make much difference to my head, but I've got quite a few sponsors, so hopefully it'll raise a bit of cash.'

'Good on you.' She tugged her hair out of the ponytail and ran her fingers through the strands, easing out any knots. It would make a massive difference to her, and the money she was going to raise would help the charity.

The compere called for the first three people to come up to the stage. She stood with Brin and watched them go. She heard the chatter and the audience clapping, the buzz of the razor.

Her heart quickened. Her stomach lurched. Was this a good idea? What would Lucy say? Or Lewis, when he saw her at work?

Oh, Lewis. She missed him so much.

The next three went. She closed her eyes and tried to steady her nerves.

There was more talking, and cheering this time. There was snipping and buzzing. Everyone's motivation and story was similar to hers. People were shaving their heads for loved ones who were going through treatments, in memory of people who had passed or for those who had got through and were living their full lives. People just wanting to help somehow.

'Good luck,' Brin called to her as he stepped on to the stage.

'You too.'

I'm going to need it. I also need a hug.

A Lewis hug in particular. She knew without a doubt that he'd hate her shaving off her hair, but would also support her one hundred percent. Because he was her supporter, her cheerleader. Always had been.

There wasn't a single minute of her day when she didn't miss him. For five long years she'd learnt to get along without him, but now—after only a few weeks back in his presence, in his arms and in his bed—she could not get him out of her mind. It was as if her body couldn't function without him but needed him to fully live, to breathe.

But it was for the best.

It was—for his best, not hers.

Then it was her turn. She stepped on to the stage, her legs shaking just a little. *Be brave.* This was only a shave; she wasn't going to endure anything like Lucy was.

She'd devoted every spare minute to looking after her sister and niece. Last week they'd got word that Lucy was responding better than expected to the treatment. There were still long days ahead but the news had given them all a lift. For the first time since she'd closed the door on any kind of relationship with Lewis, she'd felt positive.

But hell, she'd ached to call him and tell him the good news. To share their milestones with him. To share her life.

She sat down and looked out at the crowd. There

must have been five hundred people in the auditorium but in the sea of faces only one stood out.

Lewis.

Her heart hammered. Lewis was here; of course he was. He was supporting his colleagues, as he always did. He was that kind of guy—good, kind and compassionate.

He was sexy, fun, gorgeous and lovable. So loved…

The microphone was thrust into her hands and she was asked about her motivation for doing this. She cleared her throat and her eyes locked with his. He hadn't known she'd be here, that was obvious. She shifted her gaze away from his shocked one to somewhere in the middle of the crowd, because she couldn't look at him without crying.

'I'm doing this to raise money for cancer care. My sister's going through a hard time with chemotherapy at the moment and I wanted to show her she wasn't on her own. To show her that she is loved and that no one going through cancer treatment need be alone. Believe that you are loved and that we will walk this journey with you. Whatever it takes, we'll stay by your side.'

We'll stay.

She hadn't. She'd left him when things had got tough, and had chosen to walk away instead of staying and fighting. Because she was scared of being left on her own—something she'd never been allowed to do—she'd made it happen. She'd got in there first. She'd chosen that path because staying and hoping *he* wouldn't leave her had been worse. She hadn't been able to bear watching him realise he'd made the wrong choice. Hadn't been able to bear seeing the disappointment on her parents' faces or on Lewis's.

There came a round of applause, then the hairdresser walked forward.

Heart thumping, Charlie looked over at the place where Lewis had been sitting, but he wasn't there. Had he walked out? He'd always loved her hair. Was he angry that she was shaving her hair off? Her throat filled with the swell of tears. She felt sure he'd somehow have managed to convince her not to do this.

Oh, Lewis.

'I want to donate my hair for wigs, please. It's not dyed and in good condition.'

'Great. It's lovely and long. I'll tie it back, because it's easier to cut off all in one go.' The hairdresser nodded and gathered Charlie's hair into ponytail. 'Are you ready?'

Was she? She took a deep breath, sad to her core that Lewis hadn't been able to sit and watch. 'Sure am.'

She listened to the *snip-snip* of the scissors close to her head, then the hairdresser held up her cut ponytail to the cheers and applause of the crowd. Then all she could hear was the thud-thud of her heart in her ears. Then the buzzing, first up the back.

'It's a bit cold.' She laughed nervously.

The hairdresser didn't answer. The crowd gasped.

'Do I look that bad?' Charlie asked.

'No. You look beautiful. You're always beautiful to me, Charlie.'

That voice. That tone. That man. *Lewis.*

She closed her eyes as she felt his fingers run over the tufts of hair she had left. Lewis was shaving her head. Her hands curled into fists as she tried to stop herself from crying. 'No. You can't do this. Stop. You love my hair.'

'I love you, Charlie Jade Rose. I love *you.* Your hair is icing.' He came to stand in front of her, crouched and looked her in the eyes. 'I'm not going anywhere. If you want to do this, then I want to help and support you. I love you. And if you love someone, you stay. You stay for the good and the bad. You stay.'

'You love me?'

No. No. No. No. That would make everything ten times worse.

'Of course, Charlie. I've never stopped. If it's possible, I love you more now than ever.'

'Then you have to leave now. Go. Please.' She grabbed his arm. 'Please. Don't make this any worse for me.'

'I'm not going anywhere.' He flicked the razor on and shaved one side, then the next. Then he took the microphone from the compere and said, 'Charlotte Rose, you are incredible. You have donated your lovely hair to be made into a wig so someone else can feel more like themselves when they're going through challenging times. And then you've allowed me to shave your hair completely off. You look…' he inhaled and shook his head, staring at her as if she was a model '…truly the most beautiful I have ever seen you.'

The audience gasped as one.

'How much have you raised?' he asked her.

He loves me. He thinks I'm beautiful. He's told me in front of all these people.

She couldn't believe what she was hearing. 'Um…for the charity? I think about fifteen hundred.'

'Brilliant.' He nodded. 'If you shave my hair, I'll double it.'

The crowd erupted in cheers, stamping their feet and clapping. The compere handed round orange buckets for donations and there was nothing she could do but change places.

She held the razor and took a breath. Because she couldn't allow herself to get all carried away like the audience. There were still insurmountable obstacles here. 'I love you, Lewis. I love you so much and I miss you. But there is no future for us. I've seen you with Stella. You need to be a dad.'

Not wanting to hear his answer, she set about shaving his head, starting at the back then the sides and then the top. In a few minutes she was done. And, hell, he looked beautiful too.

Just as she thought he'd given up on an answer, he took her razor-free hand. 'I love you, Charlie. Any way you are. With or without hair. With or without a baby, or a family. Nothing else matters. I love everything about you. I will always love you as you are, wholly, fully.'

She looked at the floor, at his hair mingling with hers and the drops of her tears. 'But…'

He put the microphone down and spoke directly to her. 'Listen to me, Charlie. You always told me I should put my needs first. Well, here I am, knowing what I need, standing up for what I need, telling you what I need.

'It's *you*, Charlie. *I need you.* If you want to explore surrogacy or adoption or any other options, then we can do exactly that. Whatever you want—whatever *we* want. We can talk about it; we can investigate it together. Because we do have options, being a parent isn't about blood ties, I know that from experience. And if children don't happen, then that will be absolutely fine too. We have four little girls who want our love. We can be the most doting auntie and uncle in the world. I have everything I need right here with you. I promise that *you* are all I need, Charlie. You *are* my family.'

She thought about Lucy, Stella and their little family of two. That was enough for her sister.

She thought about how she'd stayed with Lucy,

not out of obligation but out of pure love. 'Don't put yourself second,' she'd told him and he'd promised her that nothing else mattered because he loved her so much. The same way she'd promised those things to Lucy because she loved her. She'd do anything for her, willingly and happily.

Was that how he felt—that selfless love for someone else, for *her*? No expectations, no conditions, just love.

She saw him now, doing this—shaving her head, having his head shaved. An act of true love, love that was inspiring and deep. He'd told her he loved her since high school and she'd loved him right back, even when she'd tried hard not to. That love had coddled her, fuelled her and now filled her with absolute joy. Their love was enduring and ever-lasting.

And, finally, she allowed herself to believe him. He would stay. Whatever happened, he would stay. And so would she. 'Oh, Lewis. I love you so, so much.'

But he bent down on one knee. 'So, Charlie Jade Rose…'

'Oh! What are you doing?' She blinked at him and then at the audience.

The crowd whistled and cheered. She heard the *thunk-thunk-thunk* of coins being thrown into the buckets. Whatever else happened, they'd raised a lot more money for the charity than she'd hoped for. She smiled as she looked down at her beautiful man.

He took her hand. 'I thought, given that our wedding was the best ever, we might have a rerun. What do you think? Will you marry me, Charlie Rose, all over again?'

'Oh, yes. Of course. Yes!' She pulled him up and he took her into his arms—exactly where she was meant to be.

The crowd went wild.

One year later...

'Trying to co-ordinate four little bridesmaids and an eighteen-month-old flower girl is like herding cats.' Lucy grinned as she picked up Stella and smacked a kiss on her chubby cheek. 'Now, go with Lily. Let her help you throw the petals on to the path while Mummy walks in front of Auntie Charlie.'

'You are the best flower girl I could ask for.' Charlie kissed Stella goodbye and watched Lily take the toddler to their places in preparation for the wedding procession. Then she gave her sister a hug, her beautiful, happy and very healthy sister. 'Thank you.'

'No, thank you for asking her to be flower girl. She doesn't quite understand but she loves twirling in her pretty dress.' Lucy grinned. 'I love what you've done with your hair.'

Charlie patted the cornflowers entwined in her

short pixie cut. 'Thanks. I'm going to keep it short, I think. It's a lot easier for work.'

'It suits you. And now we're all matchy-matchy.' She ran her fingertips over her short cut. The music began to play, the same tune they'd chosen for their first wedding. 'Now, where's Dad? Time to make your big entrance.'

Their parents had dashed back from Uganda two weeks after Charlie's head shave—and the moment Lucy had finally told them about her cancer—as both Lucy and Charlie had known they would. But they'd had their long-hoped-for overseas charity experience before moving in with Lucy and Stella and helping out. Somehow, they seemed to have mellowed a little, and only wanted to help, not domineer or take over.

And it had seemed an appropriate time then for a now homeless Charlie to move in with Lewis, and those empty seats at the dinner tables and social gatherings were filled again.

Their wedding was even better second time round. It was smaller, at the beach, with just family and a few close friends. Co-ordinating Lily, Lola, Luna, Harper and Stella all to stand still for the photos was the biggest and funniest challenge. Lewis wrapped his arms around Charlie's waist as they watched the girls skipping, jumping and wriggling and she leaned back against him.

'Five girls.' She laughed. 'Maybe one of our

siblings will have a boy some time. You must be getting over all the pink.'

'What? I've got my football team all sorted. Lily's my star attacker, Lola's in goals and Luna's showing great potential in midfield. Harper's more thoughtful and watchful, plus she's tall…probably good at centre back.' They watched as Stella waddled towards her mum then plopped down on the sand. 'Stella might need a little more training.'

'Aw. She's only been walking a few months.'

'Got to get them when they're young.' He laughed, then squeezed Charlie tightly and kissed her cheek. His love for his girls shone and made her heart sing with love—even more love, if that were possible.

They'd applied to the adoption agency and had advertised for surrogates but no luck so far. That didn't matter; if it happened, it happened. If not, then…they had each other, the four blood-tied nieces plus Harper who, they'd all decided, must become an honorary niece. Their lives were full of babysitting and school concerts, loud and chaotic lunches and laughter. They were one big family.

'Are you happy?' Lewis whispered against her throat.

He'd asked her that not long after they'd reconnected and she'd told him to ask her again when Lucy had finished her treatment. 'More than I thought I ever could be. I'm married to my best husband. I can say that because I've had two now.' She grinned up at him. 'My sister's improving every day. We have the most amazing friends and family.'

As if on cue, best-man-again Logan ambled over. 'Hey, I'm sorry, but the weather forecast isn't great for the evening. We'll have to bring the chairs and tables inside the venue. It's going to rain.'

They'd planned an early-evening dinner outside at a long table under the trees. But Lewis grinned as he turned to Charlie. 'You know what that means?'

She laughed. 'Flash flooding?'

'I damned well hope so.' His eyes twinkled as they both remembered their night in the fancy hotel.

'Me too. I love you, Lewis Parry.'

'I love you too, Charlie. Always have and always will.'

And now she believed him, with all her heart.

* * * * *

A Marriage Healed In Hawaii

Becky Wicks

MILLS & BOON

Born in the UK, **Becky Wicks** has suffered interminable wanderlust from an early age. She's lived and worked all over the world, from London to Dubai, Sydney, Bali, New York City and Amsterdam. She's written for the likes of *GQ*, *Hello!*, *Fabulous* and *Time Out*, and has written a host of YA romance, plus three travel memoirs—*Burqalicious*, *Balilicious* and *Latinalicious* (HarperCollins, Australia). Now she blends travel with romance for Harlequin and loves every minute! Tweet her @bex_wicks and subscribe at beckywicks.com.

Visit the Author Profile page
at millsandboon.com.au for more titles.

Dear Reader,

I started writing this romance before the devastating wildfires in Hawaii, and my thoughts are still with all the people who lost their homes and livelihoods. While I've never been to Hawaii in person, it's a place I've always wanted to visit, and still do. Here's to the infallible aloha spirit, and I hope a little time with our feisty marine vet heroes and their dolphin friends will make you smile.

Becky

DEDICATION

For Hawaii, with love for all who are still rebuilding after the 2023 wildfires.

CHAPTER ONE

LANI KEKOA STEPPED onto the decking of Mermaid Cove Marine Sanctuary, and sucked in a lungful of fresh, salty air. The midday sun kissed the surface of the ocean in sparkles and high in the palms, two myna birds trilled in conversation. Crossing to Pua's tank, she ran her hand softly over the turtle's lumpy brown shell. "How are you, buddy?"

Pua wriggled his wrinkly legs in reply, and she leaned against the rail of the dock, letting the warm breeze tickle her skin. Her eyes scanned the bay, searching for the dolphins playing around the early-morning boats, but something else caught her eye. What was that in the water, floating in the white surf? A long white object, but not driftwood, and not an abandoned water toy either, she was sure. Lani stared at it for a few moments, trying to make out what it was. Then…

Oh, no.

Quick as a flash she was on her feet, racing down the steps and across the sand for the Jet Ski. Revving the engine to life, she tore across the waves toward the object, her heart pounding with dread as the shape became clearer. Cutting the engine, she drifted closer to the baby dolphin, so still and lifeless. "Oh, poor baby."

Taking a deep breath, she cast her eyes to the Hawaiian sky, trying to calm herself. Not an easy task, as her emotions were bubbling like lava inside her. They should have been able to stop this by now!

A flash of silver caught her eye. The pod of dolphins was leaping and playing in the waves, except for one. The mother of this calf no doubt. The creature swam up close, put her silver head up inches from the Jet Ski, and nudged the baby. The action brought tears to Lani's eyes; she knew what it was like to be a mother in distress, the gut-wrenching, soul-shattering pain of realizing you've lost something irreplaceable, forever.

"I'm so sorry," she whispered. "I'll figure out what's happening, what's causing this, I promise."

The dolphin met her eyes in a moment of what she swore was understanding, and Lani again felt the urge to cry. It was her duty to protect them, to always look after the ocean for them, but this felt out of her control. Why were the dolphins dying?

Reaching the shore with the lifeless calf on the back of the Jet Ski, she saw Mahina. Her assistant was walking from the back room onto the dock, carrying a white storage container full of fish.

She took one look at Lani's face and dropped the container. "No!" she wailed, speeding down the steps, dropping to her knees beside the poor, dead creature.

Lani's shoulders tensed, noting the marks on the dolphin's skin. Blemishes, almost like burns, just like the one they'd discovered just a few days ago. That one hadn't died, thank goodness, but it had been badly injured and carried the same marks.

"What is going on?" Lani whispered, forcing her emotions to stay buried as Arnie and Mo, from the conservation management program, arrived to take the calf away for an autopsy. She'd join them later—she often worked with the scientists on necropsies of marine mammals. But it was going to be beyond frustrating having to wait four to six weeks for the finalized reports.

Mahina hung her head, her face hidden behind her mass of wavy brown hair.

"We need to find out what's causing this," she said to the guys, flashing her eyes to Lani, who nodded slowly. Lani had been working with the dolphins for years and something had definitely changed recently. They were suffering some kind of skin disease—that much was clear—but even as senior vet at the marine sanctuary with over twenty years of experience dealing with every oceanic creature around Oahu, she was out of ideas as to what might be causing the strange marks to appear.

Later, as they did their rounds with the mammals in the tanks at the back of the sanctuary,

Mahina shoved her hair back, looking at her with some trepidation. "Maybe you should call…you know."

Lani bristled. "Mika? No."

Mahina sighed, like she'd been storing this question up all day, and expecting this very reply, too. "But he deals with stuff like this all the time. He was the one who figured out why the sharks were getting sick in the Red Triangle, he linked it to that shipping route…"

"We don't need my ex-husband getting involved, Mahina. Just…no."

Lani huffed out a sigh as Mahina held her hands up. She didn't mean to snap, but her assistant vet nurse had struck a nerve. The last time she'd heard anything about Mika had been about a year ago, when she'd run into his mother and learned he had a serious girlfriend.

Hayley was some perky blonde thing, no more than thirty, probably, judging by the photo she'd been shown later after Mahina had stalked him online. Older than *they* had been when they'd walked down the aisle, her own pregnant belly bulging from her white gown, her hand gripping her father's…seeing Mika, at twenty-four, two years her senior and impossibly, devastatingly handsome, waiting for her *I do* in his tux.

Catching a glimpse of herself in the window to the storage room, she puffed up her hair. At forty-seven, people said she hardly looked a day older than thirty-five, but they were probably just being kind. Her thighs weren't as firm, her belly wasn't so quick to fit so snugly into the band of her jeans, her hair was losing its luster and at times she missed the old her—the one who'd grown complacent in her smooth, taut skin, and her uniform of Daisy Dukes and bikini tops. But then, it wasn't like she was out to look sexy these days, or even lure another man! What could she have to offer a man, anyway? Her whole life was the sanctuary these days, and her foster daughter, Anela, just eight years old and already the biggest challenge she'd ever taken on, she thought, picturing Anela's mother suddenly—her good friend Sharie. Had it really been nearly a year since she'd taken on the new foster duties, after Sharie had unexpectedly passed away?

Life is just a series of challenges I'm not equipped to handle, she thought briefly, before she could bite back the surge of self-loathing.

Every bit of self-deprecation boiled down to what had happened to Iolana; she knew this, but it didn't stop her dwelling on her misgivings anyway. Or on her baby daughter, who'd be an adult by now, if she'd lived.

Did Mika still think about it all, too? Maybe he did, but he'd moved on in other ways. At least, over twenty years spent in the US, away from the island and *her*, had proved enough time for him to get the full replacement package in Hayley. Good for him, she thought. If that made him happy, good. God knows they'd only brought each other misery before he'd packed up and left for California.

You know why he left, the voice inside her head chided.

And she closed her eyes as the image of their beautiful, perfect daughter flashed into her mind's eye, faster than she could block the rush of stomach-twisting pain that followed.

No. Focus.

There was work to do, and anyway, Mika probably wouldn't come here even if she called him. He was always busy. And there were too many memories here, waiting to bite them both.

Lani was still battling with what to do as she lay in the hammock on the house porch later, listening to Anela giggling at the new batch of kittens who'd already clawed their way into their hearts. Was she being silly, not calling him? Mika knew the ocean around here better than anyone. He'd grown up in it; the waters around Oahu used to be his playground. Him and his sharks. No one could believe the way he'd actually befriended a tiger shark!

A small frown creased her brow as she looked at Anela bopping her nose to a kitten's. Anela's mother, Sharie, had lost her life just over a year ago as a result of her own too-close encounter with a great white shark. Hence Lani had put her own maternal inadequacies aside and stepped up. Sharie was her friend, so of course she'd taken Anela in; the kid had no one else! What Mika did would scare the child silly if she knew about his job, but maybe Mahina was right and he *was* the only one who could help the dolphins. If there was even the slightest glimmer of a chance he could help, it would be worth a few bad trips down memory lane.

She picked up her phone.

After a few rings, a gruff voice answered, "This is Mika."

Oh... God, he sounds the same, only more... distant.

"Hi," she said, clearing her throat. "It's Lani."

A spark ignited in his voice then. "What's wrong?"

What? Just three words from me and he knows something's wrong?

"It's the dolphins," she said, clutching the phone tight. "We found a dead calf today, and we've noticed some kind of skin disease on several others but the tests we've run so far haven't shown anything conclusive. I mean, we'll know more after this necropsy but it'll take weeks for that to happen and... I thought maybe..."

"Lani. Breathe."

She shut her mouth. His command cut straight through her rambling monologue like a knife blade, and she swallowed a giant lump from her throat that felt an awful lot like a sob being stamped out. Closing her eyes, she breathed long and hard. *In. Out.* He knew how passionate she was about the dolphins.

"They're dying, Mika," she managed to say. She was gripping the phone so hard now her palms were sweating.

"Okay," he said, after a pause. "I can probably make the 10:00 a.m. from LAX."

She sprang up in the hammock and stared at Anela, stunned.

"Tomorrow? Oh…okay."

"See you tomorrow. Keep breathing, Lani." He clicked the phone off.

Lani sat back, letting out all the air she'd been storing in her lungs. Ten a.m. tomorrow? Was he serious?

Anela's head was cocked in interest now. "Who was that?"

Lani blinked. What to say…what to say. Who was Mika now? She shrugged, fighting a smile. Mika wasn't just her ex-husband, she thought, glancing at her wrist. The tattooed turtle with its geometric shell was still a jet-black inky reminder that he'd been her Honu longer than her ex. The Honu, or turtle, was a Hawaiian cultural symbol of longevity, safety, and mana, the spiritual energy that coursed through everyone's blood here. Maybe Mika thought of her, too, every time he looked at his matching tattoo. He'd had his inked on his upper arm, hers on her inner wrist.

"Someone who used to be very important to me," she replied, noting how the words *used to* from her own mouth sent her stomach into a knot. What had she just gone and done, inviting him back into her life?

CHAPTER TWO

MIKA STEPPED OFF the plane onto the sun-kissed tarmac at Daniel K. Inouye International Airport. Dragging his small case, he felt the warm Hawaiian breeze sweep over him, carrying with it the familiar earthy scent of salt water and plumeria. In arrivals, judging by the bustle of locals and tourists already draped in leis made from sweet-smelling frangipanis, Oahu was no different from his last visit several years ago. But everything *felt* different. Because last time he'd only seen family and friends, not Lani. And now, no one else knew he was even coming.

He'd taken a much-needed vacation over the month of July in order to come here, but he hadn't even told Manu yet. His brother, aka Sparky-Man—the renowned island electrician—would give him no end of stick over that, no doubt, never mind his mother, but he'd only thought of Lani when he'd packed his bags. She was here. Less than twenty miles away. And she needed him.

It made him more apprehensive than it should, seeing as he'd known the woman most of his life. What on earth had propelled him to offer to fly here, mere seconds after answering the phone? He could only blame the fact that he was tired, a little bored and emotionally drained after the breakup with Hayley.

Despite it being an almost incomprehensible twenty-two years now since his and Lani's divorce, something about hearing his ex-wife upset had always spoken to his heart. Part of that, he had to admit, was definitely due to the guilt. It weighed heavily on him like an anchor: guilt for not taking a step back from his work when it had mattered, when being there for Lani and Iolana had been more important than anything. Guilt for not realizing how badly Lani had wanted to get back to her veterinary studies and qualify, for not picking up some of the slack with the baby sooner. Guilt for not knowing the early signs of meningitis, for brushing off his daughter's cold hands and feet and sniffles as a mild cold before calling the sitter and heading out with Lani out on the dive boat that day after her dive partner had canceled at the last minute. He'd wanted to support her getting back into her research, finally, but hours later, when Iolana had been lying in hospital, surrounded by strangers, attached to tubes and drips, they'd still been out on the dive boat, making up for being so distracted in the first place. That guilt, for letting down his daughter and his wife, would follow him until the day he died.

Mika bundled his case into the rental car. No

need for GPS. Driving down the island's winding roads, verdant foliage hugged every curve, and glimpses of turquoise water winked at him through the gaps in towering palm trees. He was certainly not in Pasadena anymore. He was… home?

He sniffed at himself. Oahu hadn't been his home for years, but his heart told him otherwise as he kept on driving. It was a familiar ache that he'd grown used to ignoring, but now it pulsed like an open wound. The Mermaid Cove Marine Sanctuary Lani had started and built from the ground up was near Kahala, the laid-back part of the island, famed for its tranquil solitude, limited fanfare and next to no nightlife. The best part. Far from the world-renowned surf breaks and the craziness of Waikiki, it was where they'd grown up and fallen in love, and then fallen to pieces, he thought grimly, stopping at a light and rubbing at his temples. He wasn't here to dredge up the past.

Oahu was a magical place, the perfect blend of island paradise and urban energy—something he'd never quite managed to find in California. Vibrant flowers painted a rainbow of colors at every turn in the road. With each passing mile, the rhythmic sound of waves washing gently against the shore felt intoxicating and invigorating, waking him up despite his tiredness. How had he forgotten the way this place always made him feel? There was never any reason to be bored here; he'd never once turned to the TV for comfort at the end of a long day like he'd been doing these last few weeks, without Hayley around. The ocean was all he'd needed, living on the brink of it, immersing himself in its depths. This island had been his forever home. Before they'd lost Iolana. Before he'd also lost Lani, and part of himself, too.

A message popped up on his phone, on the dash. Hayley.

I miss you babe :-(

She's used the sad face, he thought, suddenly irritated.

Emojis were so devoid of the characteristics they were supposed to embody; they were the lazy person's language. He'd been with her for two years, delighting at first in her busy, fulfilled life; her carefree attitude. The age gap had been an issue for a while, though, at least for him. He was happy winding down the day with a book or a sunset from the veranda. She was in her thirties, and wasn't happy unless her diary was full, morning to night—bands, parties, launches, lunches, most of which she now wanted him to attend with her. "It's a couple's thing," she would say, which had eventually forced him to admit to himself that he wasn't in the right couple after all.

He still felt bad about the way he'd called it off, right before she'd left for her girls' vacation to Milan. But between his senior vet duties at the aquarium and the talk he was set to deliver at the upcoming event for global maritime professionals on the treatment he'd played a major role in implementing for gray reef sharks under threat in the Red Sea, he hadn't found time for that difficult discussion. Sure enough, he'd put his work first again.

And then you came here to another ex, he reminded himself, feeling his jaw twist. *You came the second Lani asked you to.*

Even Hayley knew he and Lani had shared something huge. Lani Kekoa had been a part of so much in his life: childhood dreams, the loss of their little one, his first and only marriage, and the end of it. They'd agreed to stop counseling just two months after Iolana had died; Lani hadn't wanted any of it, instead hiding in her shell like a hermit crab. And in truth, he'd had no interest in its merits back then either, no faith that anything could help either of them. The overpowering grief that they'd never actually addressed properly together still formed the backbone of his existence.

A man carrying a crate of pineapples waved at him from the roadside, and he waved back, wondering if he knew him, deciding he didn't. Hawaiians were just so friendly and welcoming, always willing to drop everything if it meant sharing the aloha spirit that defined their culture. A jolt of pride struck him like a lion. His people, his home.

Nowhere else compared. If he was honest, he'd never stopped wondering if someday he would find the strength to move back.

He shrugged off the thought immediately. Of course, he never would. It would be too painful. Lani might need his expertise right now but she would never forget the way he'd put his new family second, back when Iolana was a newborn, or how he'd been so intent on being the breadwinner, becoming a success, that he'd missed vital moments with his daughter he would never get back.

Being two years older and already a qualified vet, even when Lani did stop being a stay-at-home mom to go back to her studies, he'd continued to work just as hard, often calling the sitter when he should have been with his daughter himself. He could still hear the tears in Lani's voice when they'd argued about his tunnel vision. Months before Iolana died she'd begged him not to do that course in disease ecology off the island, said she'd needed him with her. He'd been so sure he was doing the right thing for them all, but all he'd done was deny her the family time she'd wanted. All he'd done was prove he was a terrible husband and father.

Mika scowled. Ending things with Hayley was right, he reminded himself. And not just because she never did quite understand why, after two years together, he wasn't interested in having another child—not with her, not with anyone. He could still hardly believe Lani was fostering a kid now, either. Manu had told him. At first he'd been shocked; how could she do it? How could she put her heart out there again after what she'd been through? But that was Lani all over, forging ahead, onward and upward, offering all that room in her big heart to those who needed it. Still, it was going to be strange, seeing her caring for a child again. Everything they'd planned to do together, she'd gone and done without him.

By the time he had passed the Welcome to Kahala sign and pulled up outside the marine sanctuary, thoughts of seeing Lani again—with all of her beauty and all of their history, and all of their arguments still as fresh as the day they'd happened—made him feel far too hot and bothered. He kind of hoped she'd spare him the agony of looking into her eyes, seeing all that pain, and that a member of her staff would give him the paper file on the dolphins he'd been promised before he drove on to Mama Pip's guesthouse.

But trust his luck to run out now. The door swung open before he reached the porch, and suddenly there she was—looking a picture in denim overalls, holding a bird in her arms.

The lump rose like a stone in Lani's throat as Mika walked toward her, the morning sunlight shining like a halo behind him as he took the steps two at a time up to the porch.

“Hi,” she said, her voice sounding small.

“Hi,” he replied. “It’s good to see you.”

She stared at him as her mind spun. He was saying it, but was it true? Was he really thinking it was good to see her, when all they’d done toward the end of their marriage was argue and then avoid each other? This was awkward as hell. There was nothing good about it, she realized now.

The gray, brown and white Hawaiian petrel fidgeted in her arms, and she crossed to the cages, gently placed it inside and closed the door. Mika followed and stood behind her. His presence consumed every single one of her senses, until she forced herself to turn around, and her throat went bone-dry.

Mika was handsome as ever, sturdy and fit. The same strong jaw set in a square frame, the same wide smile that spoke of a thousand boyish secrets. It took her breath away, right before the silent acknowledgment of their shared tragic past stole his expression clean from his face. She saw it then: the deep sorrow that would always unite them, clouding his eyes. He looked like he was about to say something profoundly serious.

“This place looks great. So do you,” he said instead, stepping backward, leaning on the railing with his elbow and running his eyes from hers down to the leather sandals she was wearing, then across to the beach.

“You, too,” she replied, for lack of anything else

to say, instantly self-conscious. "I'm not sure about that bandanna, though. You're more Californian than even I expected."

Mika smirked, touching a hand to the red bandanna tied around his forehead. It was *way* too young for him, she thought with a trace of disdain she knew instantly was just her brain's way of fighting the fact that he looked sexy as hell. Forty-nine years old, and he didn't look a day older than forty, if that.

"Well, I guess that's where I live now," he said, scuffing a boot to the decking. He wore a safari shirt, too. The collar was open and she ran her eyes along the dark hair on his chest beneath it, down to his jeans, really taking in his chunky boots. The boots were made for walking city streets, not Hawaiian beaches. He used to live in sandals, like her.

"Well, thank you for coming." She busied her hands with moving a box of fish toward the rehabilitation tanks. He moved beside her to help as she started tossing tiny fish into the tank with a recovering sea lion in it, stealing glances at him. "I wasn't sure if you would come, Mika. All things considered."

Her words hung in the salty air and he glanced at her sideways, resting both arms on the tank. Would he bring up Iolana?

Please don't... Please don't.

"You sounded like you needed me," was his tactful reply.

"I do… We do," she corrected herself. So he *wasn't* going to bring up Iolana. Why did that worry her just as much now? Everything they'd gone through together, had it really faded so fast for him?

They fed the other animals together, her conscious of his every movement, while she explained in more detail what had happened with the dolphins. His brow furrowed as he listened and she committed this new version of her ex-husband to memory. He looked different, but better, in the way gorgeous men always did when they aged. Did Hayley know he was here? What did she think about it all? Had he ever told her about their daughter?

His hair was tight to his skull now under the bandanna, the color of a river fish, she thought: black, speckled with silver. It looked good. His years gave it a sheen that only nature's palette could create. She'd stopped the years creeping into her own hair the only way she knew how: with regular trips to the salon. What used to be long tendrils of honeyed blond was now a crop of silver-white, streaked with mahogany, which she usually wore scraped back from her face. Everyone said the color in it made her look younger. In truth she wished she could let it all go gray and be done with it. What was so wrong with ageing anyway? So many people never got the chance. Like their daughter.

Did he think she looked old? she wondered, suddenly self-conscious all over again.

Mika was tanned in the way most Californians were, like the sunshine ran through his blood and up through his skin. She'd felt the muscles underneath his clothes for the first time that day when her shoes had washed away on the tide, back when she'd first realized she had feelings for him. Big feelings. She had crushed so hard watching the then-fifteen-year-old Mika Mahoe on his surfboard, she hadn't even noticed the disappearance of her shoes. He'd given her a piggyback to the road after that, like a knight in shining armor, and she'd wished the moment could've lasted forever.

"Who's this, Lani?"

Anela's voice yanked her from her thoughts. She'd appeared with Mele from the main building, both dressed in denim shorts, colored T-shirts and baseball hats. Seventeen-year-old Mele was her neighbor's daughter. She often collected young Anela from school when Lani was busy at the sanctuary and now the teen was looking at her with a grin on her freckled face.

"Anela, Mele, hi," she said hurriedly. "This is Mika. He's come to see if he can help figure out what's going on with the dolphins."

Little Anela took his outstretched hand with some trepidation, mouthing the name Mika. Mele did the same. Then the penny dropped for the teen, and her brown eyes widened.

"*The* Mika. As in, your ex-husband?"

"The one and only," Mika replied without missing a beat. "I see my reputation precedes me."

Mele looked him up and down, her grin widening. "I never know who is who. Lani has so many male admirers."

Lani flushed at the blatant lie. "Teenage exaggeration," she refuted.

"It's true," Mele laughed, nudging Anela. "What about Mr. Benos the other week? He was practically begging her to let him take her out after she fixed up that injured bird he brought in, right, Anela?"

"Mr. Benos is seventy-two years old," Lani reminded her.

"Yeah, but he knows a thing or two about how to treat a woman. He's been bringing you fresh fruit and flowers from his greenhouse ever since! Not like that last guy you went out with, the tourist who ghosted you after two dates. What was his name?"

"Don't you have a riding lesson to get to?" Lani replied quickly, noting with excruciating embarrassment the way Mika was observing this banter with a slight smile on his lips. She noticed part of a frown, too, as Mele bid them farewell, ruffled Anela's hair and ran down the steps to the beach.

"She's a treat," he quipped when she was gone,

and Lani sighed, picking up the now-empty box of fish. "Quirky. Like you used to be." He took it from her, carrying it back to the refrigerator in the storeroom, and she watched his muscles flex as he lifted it to the top shelf. Maybe it was weird for him, seeing her around kids and teenagers. They'd been younger than Mele when they'd met, and it felt like only five minutes later she'd been pregnant, moving into his parents' annex. Her own parents had been supportive, but had moved to Maui long before that. She'd insisted on staying put, with Mika. Now she saw them twice a month, but they too had drifted from the Mahoes over the years, no thanks to her own emotional retreat after the death of their beloved granddaughter.

She couldn't help remembering the annex now, and the time Mika had bought a ton of roses, stripped them of their petals and used them to spell out Mika Loves Lani on the porch. She'd had to pause her studies for a while after she'd had Iolana, and Mika, being only newly qualified himself, had worked so hard to support them. Sometimes he'd worked so hard she'd barely seen him, which was how she'd gotten so close with his parents. He'd missed a lot, like Iolana's first tooth, but they'd seen it all. They'd loved Iolana so much.

"What's *quirky* mean?" Anela asked him now, following them with a skip in her step, then swirling a finger in the water of the turtle's tank.

"It means interesting," Lani told her, before

Mika could cut in, and he raised his eyebrows at the little girl, which made her giggle and ask to borrow his bandanna. He looked confused for a moment, like he wasn't sure what to do.

"Manu told me you were fostering your friend's child," he said quietly, bobbing his head toward an engrossed Anela.

She swallowed tightly, hearing the slight uncertainty in his voice. He probably wondered what kind of foster mother she'd be, when she'd abandoned her own baby to go out in the name of her studies. She'd been so caught up in getting back on track to qualify that she hadn't seen just *how* sick Iolana really was before getting on that research dive boat...

Of course, Manu would have told Mika she was fostering now. Not that she'd seen her ex-brother-in-law lately. Sharing her grief with anyone had felt impossible for so long that she'd shut everyone out. She also couldn't help fear their judgment for her not wanting to be a stay-at-home mom anymore, for not being there when Iolana had needed her most.

Manu had done the wiring for the sanctuary before she'd opened, but it had been pretty awkward for her to say the least.

"What happened to Anela's parents?" Mika asked now.

"Her dad passed away before she was born, and her mom...died a year ago. She has no other living relatives." Lani held back the rest of the information. She debated telling him about the fatal shark attack that had taken Sharie. Mika lived and breathed sharks, while Anela understandably couldn't even stand to step foot in the ocean.

Mika was nodding at her in thought. Again, he looked like he wanted to say something. But a sudden ruckus behind them took his words away.

CHAPTER THREE

MAHINA WAS A MESS, bloodied and bruised. "I couldn't swerve in time," she managed to explain as Lani ushered her back through to the bench in the operating room. She could barely put any weight on her left leg and her left elbow was bleeding, too.

Anela was staring at the blood. Before she could order the child back outside, Mika stood in front of her, shielding her eyes from it, so Lani rushed for the first aid kit.

"Why didn't you go to the hospital?"

"This was the closest place!"

"What happened?"

"A motorcycle happened, right in front of me! Forced me off the road on my bike, then he sped off!"

Behind her, Mika had walked Anela back to the door and pulled something out of his bag. She couldn't quite make out what it was with his back to them, but thank goodness the girl was distracted. Soon they had Mahina lying flat on her back on the table they usually reserved for sea lions and injured wild birds.

"I was almost here when he hit me, so I came to you," she explained, wincing in pain as Mika rolled up her trouser leg and inspected the wound. The gash looked pretty nasty. It probably needed stitches. "Good to see you, Mika," she managed.

"Good to see you, too, not so much the blood. Last time I used a needle it was on a shark's fin but…" Mika reached for the gauze as Lani swabbed the wound with antiseptic. "I can try, save you another trip to the hospital?"

"I trust you, Mika," Mahina said, gasping for breath, clutching Lani's hand.

Lani tossed her cotton swabs into the trash and stepped between them. Sure, they all knew each other. Mahina had been a teenager when Mika had left the island and she'd always idolized him; didn't everyone around here? But letting him stitch up her leg?

"I think we should get her to St. Paul's," she said, and thankfully he agreed.

"We can take my car."

"I have an appointment arriving in fifteen minutes," Lani explained apologetically, but Mika was already lifting Mahina carefully in his big arms, heading back the way he'd come in, where his rental car was parked on the driveway. Lani rushed to open the door and he laid Mahina out on the back seat, then Lani watched in bewilderment as the vehicle rumbled away in a cloud of sand and dust. What just happened?

"Will she be okay?" Anela asked behind her. She was clutching a book, and seemed as unsure about it as the situation with poor Mahina.

"She'll be all right… I hope," she replied, although, the more she thought about it, it didn't seem like Mahina would be able to put weight on her leg for a while, even after the hospital stitched her up. She'd probably need time off, and rightly so after what had happened, but they were already short-staffed.

"What have you got there?" she asked Anela now, taking the book from her hands distractedly, wondering who she might call to cover. Hilda, their Danish locum, had already left for her annual trip home.

"Mika gave it to me but I don't like it," Anela said, walking to where the injured petrel was resting in the cage at the side of the room. Lani had saved the petrel's wing from the threat of amputation. Anela stuck her finger through the bars and stroked its soft feathers and Lani frowned as she flipped through *Anatomy of a Shark*, written by Mika himself. It was packed with incredible photos he'd taken while diving and conducting his research. Hmmm. So he'd brought it with him. And given it to Anela, without knowing it would freak her out more than seeing Mahina all bloodied and bruised.

It wasn't his fault. She sighed, realizing she was thinking more about how impressive it was, holding a book that Mika had written. After the photo book he'd self-published in his late teens he'd always said he wanted to write and publish a children's book to encourage wildlife conservation. This one wasn't exactly for kids, but then maybe that dream had died with their daughter. There was so much she didn't know about her Honu now.

Between appointments, she found herself flicking through the book on the deck, admiring the colorful photos, and wondering if the tiger shark he'd somehow befriended, Nala, was still around. Would that graceful creature recognize Mika, if the two were to meet again? Sometimes people saw Nala on dives, but it must have been years since Mika met her himself. That relationship had been such a testament to his loving soul; he loved all creatures. These days, she didn't even know if he had a dog! It was sad, not knowing him anymore, she thought despondently.

When her phone sounded out a couple hours later, it wasn't news from the hospital, like she'd been expecting. It was Mika.

Mahina would be fine but being at the hospital had drained Mika, both physically and emotionally. Hospitals for humans were the worst, never mind all those memories of being there with Lani the night they'd lost Iolana rushing back in. Still, he had to admit, there were good memories everywhere on this island, too.

Time hadn't marred Lani's looks one little bit, he thought as he steered the car back toward the sanctuary. In fact, she looked better than ever and just seeing her had his brain on rewind—all the times he'd walked behind her when they were teenagers, admiring her butt in her Daisy Dukes, before he'd even worked up the courage to kiss her.

Despite the years that had passed since they last saw each other, her beauty still took his breath away. He was just wondering about all those men that Mele had said swarmed around her, realizing a scowl had taken his face hostage, when he noticed the line of cars ahead of his had crept to a standstill. People were hurrying from their vehicles and taking the path down to the beach, one after the other. He opened his door.

"It's a humpback whale, she's stranded near the shore. We need to act fast," someone said, and he bolted from the car with his phone to his ear, a surge of adrenaline coursing through his veins. In seconds he was standing on the sand, asking *himself* how on earth a humpback whale got stuck like this.

"Don't touch it. I've just called Lani at the marine sanctuary," he heard himself say, feeling his heart clench at the sight of the majestic creature lying helpless on the damp sand. Its massive body heaved with each labored breath, and fear and pain shone in the whale's dark, gentle eyes.

In minutes, Lani had arrived and was hurrying

from the rescue vehicle, her shirt flapping in the wind, her sandals clacking on the hard sand, Anela at her heels. The crowd parted as she approached, and he helped her move the gawking crowd to a reasonable distance. Anela stopped even farther back, looking on like she was afraid. An island kid, afraid of a whale? Or maybe it was the water she was scared of, he thought, which would be even stranger.

No time to think about how that could even be possible. The whale was slowly being strangled by fishing nets.

"Get some towels and blankets from the truck, keep it wet and cool," Lani instructed him. He didn't miss her eyes roving his body for a moment as his shirt flew open. "I'm going to check its vitals."

"Got it," he answered, racing to the rescue truck, quickly grabbing supplies and hurrying back again.

Mika watched Lani's slender fingers working deftly as she checked the whale's heartbeat, while he instructed two of the bystanders to gently douse the animal with water. Every now and then their eyes would meet, and he knew they were both thinking that this was just like old times. Lani was never sexier to him than when she was calling the shots.

The whale was a grayish color, so beautiful, so soft to the touch. Its fin was bent and its body covered in barnacles and scars from years of fighting off sharks, but still magnificent nonetheless. Outside of an aquarium, he hadn't seen anything quite like this for a long time.

Pulling a knife from the bag, he got to work alongside Lani, cutting and snipping and detangling, all the while noting how Lani never took her eyes off the whale, not unless she was glancing at Anela, making sure she was okay.

It was pretty impressive that she'd taken to fostering; he'd been *more* than shocked when he'd heard about it from his brother, though he'd tried not to show it, of course. It wasn't just that she could put her heart out there again for another little girl. She was risking something going wrong again, something terrible. He'd be terrified of messing up again, if he were to ever take on a role like that. What if he missed another crucial sign, made a selfish move he couldn't undo? No. There was just no way he'd ever do it. He didn't even know how to react around kids now anyway, he thought, cringing as he remembered how he'd just stood there, when Anela had asked to see his bandanna up close.

"Is it going to be okay?" Anela asked now, her voice filled with concern as much as trepidation.

"Yes, honey, don't worry...just stay there, okay?" Lani said.

But then she looked at him and his heart contracted. He knew what she was thinking. It wasn't good. They needed to get this creature back into the water, and soon. He sped up his cutting, and so did Lani, determination written all over her face. Every second counted. Soon enough, the netting fell away, and Lani pulled the last of it to the side while he sprinted back to the rescue truck.

"Hurry," Lani urged through gritted teeth, her voice hoarse from exertion.

Mika quickly grabbed the specially designed net. He shouted to Lani to help throw it over the whale's body, securing it tightly around the gentle giant. Then, as fast as he could, he tied the other end to the winch on the nearby rescue truck. "Ready?" he called to her, his hand hovering over the controls.

"Ready," Lani confirmed, taking a step back and motioning for the anxious crowd to do the same.

"Here we go!" Mika held his breath as the winch whirred to life, pulling the net taut and gently lifting the whale off the sand. The crowd seemed to be holding their breath, too, as the whale was lifted closer to the water. It was a slow process; he had no choice, but with each passing second their humpback came one millimeter closer to freedom.

"Keep going!" Lani instructed, her eyes still fixed on the whale, even as he caught a reporter speeding from the roadside down to the beach with a camera. "We're almost there!"

Mika watched as Lani walked around the whale, guiding his every movement.

"Stop!" Lani yelled suddenly as the whale released a bellowing sound, causing him to release the winch controls. "We need to check her breathing before we move any further, she's probably stressed, poor thing. She might be pregnant."

Lani pressed a stethoscope against the whale's side. After a few tense seconds, she nodded. "Okay, we're good. And she's not pregnant. Keep going."

Relief washed over him as he resumed operating the winch. Inch by inch, the creature moved closer to the water, until finally, he was able to get it submerged in the shallows.

"Well done," Lani said, her voice barely audible to him over the sound of crashing waves. His heart pounded as he watched her wade into the water, the salty sea foaming around her waist, soaking her shirt, which she'd probably been too distracted to remove.

The woman with the camera was wading in after her, but Lani ignored her, focused only on the whale. Soon it was free. He couldn't keep the grin from his face as it swam for the horizon, emitting a mighty gush of water from its blowhole. The crowd erupted into cheers and laughter and whoops of relief.

"Was she just saying thank you?" Anela asked as he met them on the sand.

"I think so," Lani said, and Mika tried not to look at the way her wet shirt was sticking to her skin, showing her bra through the fabric. "I can't believe we did that," Lani exclaimed, her eyes wide with amazement as the reporter hurried up to them. "We actually saved a humpback whale, your first day back on the island. It's almost like it knew you could help it, that you'd be there..."

She met his eyes and he felt a rare surge of pride at the way she was looking at him. It threw him right back to the night she'd told him nervously that she was pregnant. An accident. At first he'd been too stunned to speak; they were both so young. Yes, he'd wanted to be a dad, but not then—they had too much to do! Both of them were on track for successful careers, and Lani would have to postpone her studies...

But the idea of a child, *their* child, had suddenly felt so right, such a blessing, that he'd picked her up and spun her around and asked her to marry him right there and then. He knew he'd do whatever it took to make it work, to keep them safe and stable and provided for.

"Can I get an interview?" the reporter interrupted, pointing the camera at them.

Lani cleared her throat before starting to answer her questions, glancing at him even as he stepped back and let her take the helm. Usually, he was the one answering questions about marine rescues, but this was Lani's territory now, not his.

When the reporter finally left, Lani ushered Anela back toward the rescue vehicle. "We'd better get back. I have an appointment with a frigate bird and it looks like it's going to be just me for a while," he heard her explain to the child.

Mika sprinted after her. "Just you?"

She bundled the scraps of netting into the back, buckling Anela into the back seat. "Yes, just me, I guess, till Mahina gets better. She's my only full-timer at the moment."

She sat in the driver's seat, and shut the door as if she suddenly couldn't wait to put some distance between them again. Mika watched her click her own seat belt into place. For a second, when she turned back to check if Anela was good to go, and told her the whale would be fine, he was moved to silence by the look of pure, maternal affection on her face. The same way she'd looked at Iolana, he thought with a pang of raw emotion.

"Well, how busy are you at the sanctuary?" he said through the window as she turned the key in the ignition. He should get back into his own car and go to Mama Pip's guesthouse before he landed himself in trouble, but already the wheels of thought were keeping him from walking away.

"Very busy," she answered. He could tell the thought was unsettling her as much as his reignited urges to fix her problems were unsettling *him*.

"Let me help you out while she's recovering," he said, before he could think too much about it.

"Thanks, Mika," Lani said with a tired smile.

"But I don't think I can afford another assistant right now."

"Who said anything about paying me? Consider it my penance for being away so long. Besides, I'm pretty good at this stuff, as you know."

"I know," she said and smiled. "You're pretty good at a lot of things, Mr. Author. I saw your book on—" she lowered her voice, glancing back at Anela "—sharks," she whispered.

He felt his eyebrows shoot up. "Why are you whispering?"

"I'll tell you later," she murmured.

He shrugged, resting an arm on the open window. The engine was still running, and she still had her thinking face on.

"Just let me help you, Lani. Being around the sanctuary more might throw some extra light on what's going on with the dolphins. Maybe there's a link with some of the other sick animals..."

"We haven't found one yet." She let out a sigh and he knew he'd put her on the spot. She probably didn't want him around at all except for when he *needed* to be around her, figuring out what was affecting the dolphins, but he was damned if he'd stay here knowing she was suffering in any way. The guilt from taking his eyes off the ball when it came to Iolana still seeped into every one of his actions. The cold hands, her cold feet. His baby girl had been sick and pale, but he'd brushed it off as a minor cold. All babies got the sniffles from time to time, right? He'd chosen to go with Lani after her dive partner had canceled last minute; he'd known the research meant a lot to her. He should have just stayed with his two-year-old daughter instead of leaving her with the sitter. Would he have spotted the signs earlier if he had?

The meningitis had crept up so quickly, the hospital staff had said later. It had been too late, even as they'd rushed through the doors, panting and red-faced, beside themselves with terror and still sticky with seawater. She'd died in Lani's arms.

"Lani..."

"Okay, fine," she said abruptly, and he stepped back from the vehicle. "I guess I could do with a pair of capable hands around the place."

"My hands are your hands, until Mahina's are better," he heard himself say, and he caught a glimmer of a smile on her face as she drove off.

"My hands are your hands," he repeated, cursing himself.

Who even says that?

After all this time, and all that was behind them, here he was, being reduced to mush again as soon as he was around her. Maybe he'd always known it would be this way, he admitted to himself with a sigh. It was probably why he'd avoided her for more than twenty years. So what on earth was he doing here now?

CHAPTER FOUR

MIKA WAS STANDING at the controls of the research boat, navigating the vessel with practiced ease, as if he'd never been away from the island. He looked so good in a loose denim shirt, unbuttoned, with the morning sun dancing across his chest in the ocean spray. A chest she'd rested her head upon a thousand times, Lani reminisced as a fresh surge of attraction threatened to throw her off-balance on the already rocking boat.

She shouldn't have come out here with him; she should have just let him do the first inspection alone, but something had compelled her; the same thing that had led her to accept his offer of standing in for Mahina the other day. The way he'd handled that whale experience had affected her more than she wanted to admit to herself. And now look at him, shirt flapping open, looking as delicious as when he'd taught her to surf all those years ago. She'd been so bad at it, at first, but then, every time she fell off and he "rescued" her it was so enjoyable, she'd kind of failed on purpose a lot of the time.

Despite the beauty of the ocean, a somber atmosphere had settled between them. She had to wonder if he was thinking about the mysterious dolphin deaths now, or was he thinking of the day they'd lost Iolana, while they were out here together on the waves?

Do not even bring that up, not even in your own head, she reminded herself sternly.

She should have been more concerned about the toddler's sniffles, but she'd been obsessed with getting out here again, back to her plants and coral. The sitter was great; she'd always been a blessing, and Lani had spent so much time with Iolana up till then that she'd decided her studies needed a swift revival if she was ever going to qualify as a vet. Little had she known she was leaving her stay-at-home mom role for good that day, and not just because of her career.

No, talking about it would turn her knees to jelly and bring it all back for him, too, how selfish of a mother she'd been.

Better to focus on their shared passion for protecting marine life, for the new hope he'd brought her by being here, she decided. The photo of her in the paper this morning had started tongues wagging all over town, because of course Mika had been captured in the background. Everyone within a fifty-mile radius knew their history and was now talking about them, which unsettled her more than the boat was doing on these waters.

She'd isolated herself from almost everyone

over the years, afraid people would judge her as harshly as she'd always judged herself. Maybe that was one of the reasons she'd agreed to take on Anela, she thought now. A child wouldn't judge her. With a child, she could start afresh, and maybe be a better version of herself than she'd been for Iolana.

"Here," Mika said, turning and handing her a clipboard filled with data sheets. They were out to record any abnormalities they might find, something he intended to do every day that he was here. Apparently, it was crucial that he gather as much information as possible himself; he didn't trust prerecorded data to be accurate.

His eyes scanned the sheets before locking onto Lani's. "What do you think is happening? You mentioned it could be pollution. Or disease. What does your heart say?"

"Hard to know," she admitted, glancing toward the circling gulls on the horizon. "I can't always trust my heart."

"You used to," he reminded her, taking the wheel again.

"That was before..." Lani swallowed back her words, but not before he drew his lips into a thin line. He knew what she meant, surely.

Before they'd lost their daughter.

Before her heart had imploded and left a gaping hole that made her feel like only half of a person, loaded with so much shame and self-blame that some days, if she thought about it too hard, she could barely breathe. She'd never openly admitted how harshly she'd blamed herself for Iolana's death, for fear that someone might agree with her, but she knew full well her own inadequacies as a mother. The shame of leaving her daughter in her hour of need was so profound, she'd never shift it completely, even if she fostered every living, impoverished, broken child in Hawaii.

"It takes up to six weeks to receive the final necropsy reports, even if I personally attend an autopsy," she said instead, hoping he wouldn't bring up anything personal related to their past. Her heart couldn't handle it if she were to hear even a trace of blame in his voice. He was hiding it well, but surely he still felt it. She'd been relieved he'd called the sitter that day so he could go with her; had barely given it a thought.

"There are so many hoops to jump through, I feel like a dolphin myself sometimes," she said distractedly.

"I can help make that go faster," he replied.

Of course he could, she thought—he'd always known how to get things done, had prided himself on it.

Still, as they collected samples and tested hypotheses and kept the focus of their conversation solely on the marine life, the weight of their past hung heavy in the air like a sail that might suddenly get caught in the wind and blow them in another direction. It had been a day just like this, when it had happened.

Finally, it seemed like Mika couldn't bear the silence any longer. "Lani," he began hesitantly, and her heart almost catapulted out of her chest.

He put the clipboard down and studied her eyes, and she braced herself for him to bring it up: all the things he'd never said, like how if she hadn't been so preoccupied with getting her damn career back on track that they might still have a daughter, *oh, God.*

"Why is Anela so afraid of the water?" he asked.

"What?" Lani released the breath she'd been holding, her hands stilling momentarily as she turned to face him.

"Yesterday," he said, adjusting his bandanna. "On the beach, she looked as if she was scared. At first I thought she was afraid of the whale but no kid in Hawaii thinks whales are anything to be afraid of."

"Anela doesn't like anything that comes from the water," she said, realizing her palms were damp. "A great white shark went for her mother just over a year ago. The poor woman didn't even make it back to shore before she bled out."

"I didn't hear about that," Mika said after a moment, his brow furrowing. "I mean, I usually hear about all shark-related incidents around here."

"They were on vacation in Australia," she explained.

"Damn."

"I know. Anela was with friends, so she didn't see it happen, but she still won't go in the water. She's convinced the same thing will happen to her the second she does."

Mika shook his head at the horizon, and before she knew it he was reaching for her hand, squeezing her fingers till the empathy and long-forgotten feel of his flesh and bone entwined with hers made her blood tingle.

"She can't live here, in a place like this, and avoid the water forever," he said.

"I've tried to coax her in so many times. We all have, but she just won't do it," she heard herself say distractedly, looking down at their hands. Why was her heart singing?

Mika's phone pinged and as he pulled his hand back she saw the name Hayley appear on the screen, along with a sad-face emoji. Gosh, what did someone like her have to be sad about? she thought unkindly, before shaking it off. It wasn't Hayley's fault she was younger and beautiful and would soon have *her* ex-husband back in her skinny yoga-toned arms.

She bristled again, imagining them together, Mika and his pretty young thing. If he still found *Lani* attractive, it was probably just muscle memory, him remembering how she *used to* look underneath her clothes. But still, the thought of him sleeping at Mama Pip's guesthouse, less than half a mile away from her house on the hill, had kept sleep beyond her grasp for most of the night. Their sex life had always been off the charts; did he even remember that? The two guys she'd slept with since their divorce had been brief flings, and neither could hold a candle up to the raging fire she and Mika had ignited.

"Maybe I can help her," he said now, breaking into her unwelcome thoughts.

"With Anela?" Lani felt her brow crease above her sunglasses. She was about to counter his words but she thought better of it. He always wanted to help; everyone had always gone to Mika when things needed to be done. Wasn't that why he was here now, for the good of the dolphins? But Anela had suffered as tragic a loss as they had, and she was only eight years old!

"If she keeps delaying going back into the water, it'll scare her her whole life. You know how those things stay with you."

"Hmmm," she replied without meeting his eyes. Then she realized he was waiting for her to agree with him. *Those things.* Those *things* he was talking about had nothing to do with Anela, not really. But they had everything to do with them.

"Maybe she's not ready yet," she said after a moment, and turned her back, refocusing on checking the map of the reef, so he couldn't press her.

"Maybe she isn't. Or maybe you're not?" he said quietly.

Lani ignored him. Her heart was suddenly pounding like high tide against the base of a cliff.

Of course, she'd only cared about the dolphins when she'd called him, but she should have known that Mika's return would bring up everything she'd tried to barricade away. What had happened to Iolana was an invisible force connecting them, even with her mouth shut and her back turned. Lani's tears, long after he'd left, had never *just* been about their daughter, either. They'd been about everything *they* had lost together, every dream they had buried and every promise that had gone unfulfilled.

Still, she would have to do her best to keep things professional, she thought, glancing back at him directing a water sample into a tube. As long as she was careful not to remind him of her misgivings, not to drag up *any* of the emotions and hardships that had no doubt contributed to his departure from the island and their marriage in the first place, maybe they had a chance at coexisting as colleagues for the few short weeks he'd be here.

Mika approached the injured seal with caution, a tranquilizer syringe at the ready. He didn't want to use the tranquilizer unless it was necessary, but the animal was in critical condition. They'd checked its vital signs. Its body was battered and bruised, and red with lacerations they were struggling to stitch back up. It was laboring for breath, but that didn't stop the muscled creature lunging at himself and Lani from the table, pulling at the straps securing it to the metal slab.

"You're just frightened, buddy, come on," he coaxed, lowering the syringe, stepping in front of Lani in concern as she narrowly avoided a heavy swipe by the creature's head.

"I'm okay," she told him breathlessly, and he nodded. His instinct to protect her had never quite gone away.

Someone had been waiting outside the sanctuary with the seal when they'd stepped off the boat. The seal had been caught in the path of a Jet Ski, which sadly, wasn't that uncommon. He and Lani had set to work quickly, lifting it to a stretcher and bringing the heavy mammal straight inside. The operation was touch and go once they'd sedated it, thankfully without the use of the tranquilizer gun. Its breathing became shallower partway through Lani's careful surgery, and its heartbeat began to slow beneath her hands. He watched her face when he wasn't jumping in to assist, and he marveled at the way she did everything with the same blend of compassion and fierce determination.

"Come on, buddy, stay with us," Lani muttered from behind her mask.

He couldn't help admiring her more and more as the minutes ticked by, her eyes locked on the animal as they had been on that whale, like half of her soul had been poured into it, blended with it. She'd always been like this, he thought, remembering the time she'd cried for an hour over a crushed crab on the beach. It was good to see she hadn't lost her touch, even with everything she'd been through, losing her daughter, losing her friend, Anela's mother. Losing him. The difference was, she'd have been glad to see the back of a man who'd let her and their daughter down so badly.

He could have said so much on that boat this morning, he thought now as his phone pinged in his pocket. It was probably Manu asking when he was free—his brother and everyone else had figured out he was on the island again, no thanks to that reporter and her story on the whale. Or it could be Hayley again, he thought in dismay. He couldn't keep up with her emojis fast enough.

No time to check his phone when Lani needed him. Lani, who he was here to help, but who he also couldn't seem to talk to.

"Oops, sorry," she said now, blushing as she accidentally bumped into him.

"Not a problem," he said, feeling his throat go scratchy.

The tension was always there between them now; it coated their every interaction. Physical, emotional, everything. He'd been wanting to talk to her on the boat, like *really* talk, so why hadn't he? He could at least have spoken their daughter's name, but it had hung like a ghost in the wind, and he'd let it go, telling himself Lani wouldn't *want* to talk about it with him, wouldn't want to face it with him, like Anela wasn't ready to face the water.

They'd grieved alone in the end, after Iolana's death, moving around each other in his parents' place like ships trying and failing to find a port in the darkness. He'd blamed himself for not insisting he stay with Iolana that day, instead of calling the sitter. He'd wanted to go out there with Lani on that boat; he'd wanted to make love to her on the waves like they used to, too. But hearing her *say* she blamed him, too, would have destroyed him, even though he knew he deserved it. So he'd never spoken about any of it, and neither had she. By the time they'd quit on the counselor it had felt a lot like she didn't want him around anymore. And he didn't have any strength left to keep fighting. Leaving here had been the hardest thing he'd ever done.

Finally, after what felt like an eternity, the seal's breathing began to stabilize. Watching Lani press the stethoscope gently to its heart, he knew from the relief on her face that its heartbeat was stronger. The heavy weight of all his thoughts lifted momentarily at the triumph in her smile.

"Close call," she said to the creature, meeting Mika's eyes.

"You're a miracle worker," he heard himself say.

"I don't believe in miracles," she retorted too quickly, her face darkening. "But we got to him just in time. Come on, help me move him. We'll need pain medication and fluids to keep him hydrated—can you get them?"

Maybe it was more skill and compassion than a miracle that had saved the seal's life, he thought, fetching the medication from her meticulously organized cabinet. He wondered what she'd meant, earlier on the boat, when she'd said she didn't trust her heart. She had such a big heart; such good instincts for when animals *and* people were in trouble, even when they weren't saying a word.

Looking up through the door, he saw Lani bustling around the seal, cooing and speaking softly to the petrel on the way past its cage. He knew she'd fixed the bird's wing up, saving it from amputation and a life in a cage just like this.

His jaw started working left to right, tighter by the second. She had put *everything* she'd had left into this place, and taken on fostering, too, *because* her heart was so big. And it all distracted her from having to think about Iolana. Maybe they weren't so different these days after all, he thought. Most of what he'd done every day since leaving here had been in an effort to forget his failures as a husband and father. More work, of course, the same as ever, but what choice did he have?

Suddenly, an idea started forming. Apart from

helping out at the sanctuary in Mahina's absence, maybe there *was* another way he could help around here, while he was temporarily back in Lani's world.

CHAPTER FIVE

"You got the results of the necropsies already?" Lani couldn't believe what she was looking at on the printed papers in front of her.

"Told you I could speed that up," Mika said, tossing another fish at their newest recovering sea lion, who was quite happily swimming in the tank out back with the other one. Anela had nicknamed them Lilo and Stitch.

"So, now we know for sure it's some kind of chemical compound that's reacting adversely with the dolphin's skin, and that it was pretty advanced in your little dead calf, but where's it coming from?"

"That's what we need to find out," she said, watching him hand a fish to Anela, who took it happily and threw it straight into Stitch's mouth.

"Have you seen any suspicious or unregistered boats around lately?" he asked.

She frowned, racking her brains. Surely she'd notice, though; she knew most people who worked out on the waters, and the tourists on their Jet Skis and banana boats couldn't have done anything so drastic as pollute the ocean—could they?

Seeing her look, Mika sighed. "We'll continue with the site analysis and sampling, from the locations where you've spotted irregularities in the dolphins. I'll have everything sent to my lab, too, see if any pathogens, bacteria, parasites or any harmful substances that may contribute to skin diseases match up with anything already discovered."

"I really appreciate your help," she said, realizing her heart was beating harder, just at the way he was looking at her while speaking with such heroic determination.

They locked eyes for what felt like an eternity, and she realized she was waiting again for him to say something about Iolana. Sometimes, she swore she could see all the things he *wasn't* saying building up in him, which was why, whenever her shift had finished this past week, she'd made an excuse to hurry away, and never initiated anything that wasn't related to their cause.

A knock at the door revealed Mr. Benos, her elderly admirer, grinning in his usual uniform of denim cutoffs and Hawaiian shirt.

"Not interrupting, I hope," he said, holding out a basket at her. "Fresh sunflowers, a bag of peaches and some plump kiwis for you, my lady," he said, beaming. "Picked just this morning."

She thanked him and took the basket gratefully. Mika was smiling behind his hand, and she tried not to do the same until Mr. Benos had gone.

"So, he does like you," he teased, and she laughed, admiring the healthy-looking fruit. Bigger than he'd grown them last season.

"No cause for jealousy, I assure you."

"Me? Jealous?" He stepped toward her, grinning that goofy yet manly grin she'd fallen for all those years ago. For a moment it felt like old times.

"Right, I think our boys have had enough fish, Anela. How about we go down to the beach?" he said, busying his hands by wiping them with a towel.

"Why?" Anela's large brown eyes were filled with trepidation, but her curiosity seemed to overpower her fear because she didn't outwardly tell him no.

Lani kept her mouth shut. Anela always needed a valid reason to be on the beach. Usually, she only used it as a path to get to school and back.

"I need some help," Mika told her. "I need to collect some samples of the creatures, and sand and stones, so Lani and I can test them. The trouble is, I've been away from here for so long, I can't remember the names of some of them. Maybe you can help…?"

Lani raised her eyebrows and he winked at her over Anela's head. Of course, he was telling a huge fat lie; he knew every stone and tree and creature that had ever occupied this island. But to her shock, maybe feeling a sense of impending achievement, Anela agreed.

"If Lani comes, too?" she said hopefully.

They spent at least an hour on the beach. Lani couldn't help smiling every time Anela swiped up an object, explained what it was to Mika and gently placed it in her bucket. She stopped, however, the second she thought she was getting too close to the shoreline. To his credit, Mika didn't draw attention to it. He pretended not to notice, and she could tell he was concentrating on building the girl's trust. It warmed her heart, and she realized she'd clean forgotten she had promised to scrub the deck this afternoon.

Oh, well, she could do that tomorrow.

Following along quietly, she watched Mika with Anela, feeling a sense of calm washing over her for the first time since his arrival. This was a little like when they'd brought Iolana to the beach. She could still see her little fingers clutching the handle of the bucket, toddling along with intent. Okay, so they had argued a lot in the past, over him working so much instead of being there with her, but he'd only been doing his best as a young man, trying to support their surprise little family! He'd been such a gentle, encouraging father, she thought, forcing herself to remember how they'd laughed at their delightful daughter discovering shells and starfish on the sand, without letting the later tragedy overshadow what were some of her happiest memories.

She should try harder to remember the good

times more often, she thought to herself. And it wasn't right that so far, she had completely failed to address with Mika the one thing they'd loved more than anything together: Iolana. The dolphins were important, and yes, that was why Mika was here but…maybe they *did* need to talk about more than work.

Ugh. Just the thought of dragging it all up made her shiver.

As they all walked along the shore, Mika showed the sweetest excitement as Anela pointed out various creatures—from crabs scuttling across the sand to a school of silvery fish she said she could see darting through the water just beneath the surface. Though she wouldn't walk to the edge with him to make sure.

"I think I know what fish they are," Mika said, crouching down next to her. "They're called mullet, and they play an important role in keeping our oceans clean. Do you know how?"

Anela looked thoughtful, then told him no.

"By feeding on algae and other underwater plants," he said. "Most fish have a job to do, you know. Every creature in the ocean plays a part in keeping it healthy and balanced. If we don't take care of them, the whole ecosystem could collapse. All of them are equally important. Even the sharks."

"I don't like sharks," she replied straightaway, making Lani's heart leap.

She half expected the girl to stomp away, but instead she adopted a small scowl directed at the ocean. Mika shot Lani a look, and she pulled an apologetic face at him. He was trying; she had to give him that. Thankfully he didn't push it. He looked around, spying a group of seagulls squawking near a tide pool. "Let's check out that pool over there. It's like a tiny underwater world, and I bet we can find some cool stuff in it!"

Soon, the smile returned to Anela's face. Lani stood back as Mika encouraged the child to touch the smooth surface of a sea anemone, explaining how its tentacles captured food.

"Isn't it incredible?" he asked, grinning as Anela's eyes lit up, feeling the anemone's tentacles brushing against her small fingers.

"You said you didn't know about the things on the beach," she accused, and Mika shrugged.

"Maybe you're jogging my memory, because you're such a great sidekick."

"Can I help again sometime?" Anela asked eagerly.

"Of course you can," Mika replied, and Lani's heart swelled with pride.

He was good with her, and even that damn bandanna on his head was growing on her, too, she thought in mild annoyance. His eyes lingered on her face for a moment longer than necessary before he shook his head at some unspoken thought, and she got the distinct impression he was trying to clear his mind of any wandering thoughts regarding her. Not that he could really still find her attractive. Could he?

Of course not, she scorned herself. What about Hayley? He was probably missing her young, lithe body and taut, perfect skin—and her lack of emotional baggage too, no doubt.

But he was in danger of melting her heart like he had when she'd been sixteen, doing all this for Anela. She'd never seen her so engaged in beach activities. Part of her had almost given up suggesting things to do on the sand, but in just a few days, Mika had shown up like foster father of the year and turned the situation around. There was still a long way to go, but something had changed in the girl already, like a light coming on, and Lani was beyond grateful.

If only she could make a habit of enjoying his company like this, she thought, instead of feeling the guilt creep back in every five minutes. She could see it all over again; the smile on his face had been just like this one right now, that day on the boat after their dive when they'd eagerly tugged off each other's wet suits and made love on the waves. They'd had no idea Iolana was being rushed to hospital with suspected meningitis. She'd frequently wondered if he blamed her, for not being more concerned that Iolana was a little sick before they'd left—she was her mother, after all. He'd never brought it up, never doled out any blame, but how could it not have dominated his mind when it was burned into her heart?

Not that it mattered now, she thought wearily. Even if Mika somehow found it in his heart to forgive her, she'd never forgive herself.

The sun had begun to set, casting a warm glow over the shoreline. As they went through the items in Anela's bucket one by one, a growing sense of purpose and connection settled in Mika's chest, taking him by surprise. A purpose, and a connection, not only with the beach and the island, he mused, but also with the little girl by his side. Okay, so he'd failed to convince her the ocean wasn't a writhing mass of unspeakable horrors, but Rome wasn't built in a day.

"Come on, let's head back," he said, standing up and brushing the sand off his shorts. "We have a lot of samples to test for tomorrow, and I think we've collected enough for now, thanks to you, young lady."

Anela looked disappointed, but Mika promised they would come back soon and explore more, and he didn't miss the warm appreciation in Lani's glance as she took the girl's hand.

The setting sun streamed onto them, heating his back with the last of its rays as they made their way back to the sanctuary. These sunsets! There were none like them anywhere else.

He couldn't help thinking back to a thousand

sunsets spent with Lani. She looked pensive now, though, and lost in thought as Anela babbled about the kittens she was going to play with back at the house, and the story she was reading. Was Lani thinking about Iolana? he wondered for the thousandth time. Was having him here too weird for her? Did she feel a sense of longing for what they had lost, watching him interacting with a little girl? Having them *both* be here together, with a little girl? If she was having any of those thoughts, she clearly didn't want to open a can of worms by bringing them up but...maybe *he* should?

Iolana would have been twenty-four by now. She would have been scuba diving with him, and Lani would have had her learning multiple languages, learning how to fix a car, all the things she'd had planned for her. Maybe it would actually help clear some tension if they spoke about it all.

Yes, he decided. They had to talk, he and Lani. Alone. He wasn't letting himself get out of that. Even if she reminded him of his incompetence as an actual father, which he probably deserved to finally hear from her mouth.

Manu called him, just as they were stepping back into the sanctuary's back room by way of the beach. Mika knew what his brother was going to ask before he even asked it. The family's annual beach barbecue, aptly named Mahoe Luau, was coming up soon, and seeing as everyone in the family had RSVP'd except him, it was about time he gave a definitive answer.

He felt Lani's eyes on him the whole time he was on the phone, though when he turned to look at her, she pretended she wasn't looking at all and continued checking on the petrel with Anela. Suppressing a groan, he said he'd be there and hung up, feeling awkward. What had she heard?

"So you're going to go," she said simply, to his chagrin, picking up Anela's schoolbag and turning off the light at the main switch.

He grimaced. Of course she knew when the Mahoe Luau was; it had been held on the same day for over thirty years. She'd been the star of the show for many of those years, with her made-up songs on the ukulele, a performance which had long become part of the annual itinerary.

"I guess I'll *have* to," he said, and she smirked.

"As if they'd let you live it down if you didn't."

"Truer words have never been spoken."

The sun had fully sunk now, and he'd be driving back to the guesthouse in the darkness for another night alone. He followed Lani outside, watched as she locked the doors, and noted how Anela seemed reluctant to leave without checking on Lilo and Stitch one last time—the kid was adorable.

The question hovered on his tongue: *Do you want to come with me to the luau?*

Just ask her!

He should just ask her to the stupid event; it

would be weird not to, seeing as everyone knew he was here, spending time at the sanctuary with her. And it would also be a chance to finally talk, to stop avoiding the important stuff. But she probably wouldn't want to. It would likely just be awkward for her, right?

Mika found he was still making excuses not to ask her by the time he was sitting behind the wheel of his rental car, driving back to the guesthouse, cursing his cowardly self. Why couldn't he just take her aside and talk to her? Why couldn't he so much as even ask her to a party? The woman had been the center of his world once! Until he'd run for the hills. He hadn't wanted to spend one more day knowing his presence did nothing but remind her of Iolana and his failures. He'd gone so she could heal…hoping he might heal, too, but part of him had been broken ever since.

The moon hung like a hammock in the sky as he drove on, till he was digging his nails into the steering wheel in turmoil. Talking to Lani meant leaping down a rabbit hole of misery he'd tried so hard to push deep down and bury out of existence. Only now he couldn't get his mind off it. Any of it.

He could arrange to see a friend, or another family member, and talk to them instead, he reasoned at the moon, but he hadn't done that either yet. He'd buried himself in research and work, work, work. For some reason, he realized now, even as he worked on discovering what was making the dolphins sick, he'd been making himself one hundred percent available for Lani, just in case she needed him. He hadn't even done that for Hayley. That thought only led to another memory: Hayley asking if he'd ever thought about having a child with her. Him having to explain that he hadn't. Her telling him smugly that he'd change his mind. Him assuring her he wouldn't. Her getting emotional and starting a fight. Him resuming his work away from her. So draining. He was literally always running away from emotional conflict.

It was time to stop.

He slammed on the brakes in the middle of the empty street, clenched his fists around the wheel. Then, before he could talk himself out of it, he did a U-turn and sped back toward Lani's house.

CHAPTER SIX

ANELA WAS THE cutest right now, Lani thought, all snuggled up on the couch with three of the snoozing kittens, engrossed in another chapter of *The Lion, the Witch and the Wardrobe*. Folding the last of the laundry into a pile on the back of the couch, she was about to issue a bedtime call when car lights appeared on the driveway. Her heart leaped into her throat. She knew that car.

Mika was standing on the steps already when she opened the door. "Did you forget something?" she asked him. "Do you need the keys to the sanctuary?"

"Er…no," he said, sweeping a big hand through his hair.

He looked worried, she thought as she invited him in. More intense. His eyes seemed to be on fire and Lani felt a tingle in her stomach, a familiar sensation that she hadn't felt in a very long time around anyone else, almost like her body had a totally different set of reactions in reserve, just for him. She'd had a crush on Mika since before she'd even known what a crush was. The first time they'd had sex, she'd actually cried from the intensity of her emotions, and felt like a total idiot for it.

Why are you thinking about all that now? she scolded herself, but she still couldn't keep her eyes off his backside as he walked into the lounge.

Anela looked up. "Mika!" she exclaimed. "Did you come to see the kittens?"

"I sure did," he said, sitting down on the couch next to Anela, who promptly placed one of the kittens on his lap.

Lani sat down opposite him, feeling a little breathless. "What's up?" she asked, trying to keep her voice casual. She'd known the second she saw his face that he had something important to share with her that for whatever reason, he hadn't been able to say earlier. Something beyond the small talk. Was it about Iolana? The thought still made her feel cold. Of course, they'd have to talk about her eventually. But right now?

She would never be ready.

Mika cleared his throat, and she realized she couldn't avoid it any longer. She also got the impression he hadn't expected Anela to still be up. As tactfully as she could, she ushered the girl upstairs, telling Mika to make himself at home. It sounded weird, coming from her mouth. This was not the home they'd always planned to buy together someday, the one on the beach with the yellow doors and shutters—the one Mika had been working so hard to help save up for, should it ever come onto the market. But as she tucked Anela into her bed she felt hot to her core at the thought of him downstairs among her things, in her space.

"What's going on, Mika?" she said when she came back down, resuming her position again on the little chair opposite his. He was stroking the kitten gently, and it purred in his hands just like she used to, she thought, swallowing a golf ball of grief from her throat.

"I just— I had to talk to you." He leaned a little closer, his eyes meeting hers intently. The kitten scampered from his lap down to the floor and chased a shadow. "That whole thing with the family luau felt weird. I should have asked you to come, but I assumed you wouldn't want to. There's so much we've been trying not to say, Lani."

She sucked in her breath and felt her cheeks flush as she looked away. It honestly hadn't crossed her mind that he'd ask her to the luau after all this time.

"We don't have to drag up anything painful if you're not ready," he continued as her heart started to thrum. "I know I hurt you badly..."

"And I hurt you," she said now. "I didn't mean to hurt you," she added, her voice cracking. "I felt dead inside after she died. I wasn't myself. I'm still not, Mika."

"Neither am I, but we have to at least be able to say her name."

"Oh, God." The words came out on a strangled

breath and she stood up quickly, sending the pile of laundry to the floor. She made to pick it up but he was on his feet in a flash, taking her wrist. Lani froze, staring at his hand around the turtle tattoo, feeling her stomach swirl.

He closed the gap between them, his hand coming up to cup her cheek. "It's impossible not to see her everywhere," he said quietly, pressing his lips together a moment, like he was forcing down his own tidal wave of emotion. "I was a coward staying away so long, when you've done so much here, despite your grief, despite all these…memories."

"I had no choice," she whispered, feeling her hand come up to cover his, distracted by the warmth and familiarity and what it was doing to her insides. His impossibly handsome face and intense eyes had always made her heart skip a beat, but now, combined with the current topic, it was almost too much to handle.

She broke the contact, made for the kitchen and pulled the dish of homemade haupia out of the refrigerator. The creamy coconut dessert was her specialty, and she set about cutting it into squares for Anela and her classmates—anything *not* to look at Mika.

"I just wanted to remind you how strong and brave I think you are," he said, following her. "What you've done, for Anela, and at the sanctuary. You've done so much for this whole island, whereas I…" He trailed off and she dared to look at him now over her shoulder. He was pondering the magnets on the fridge like studying a complex code and she could almost see his mind working, his regrets piling up in his head like the dishes in her sink.

"You've done a lot yourself, Mika," she heard herself say, sensing he needed to hear that she recognized his achievements. "Your research and your work has—"

"Exactly. Work," he muttered, cutting her off. "I threw myself into work, like I've always done."

"Your work is important to you. To everyone! And anyway, so did I," she admitted now. She watched his eyes travel around the kitchen. It was painted the same yellow as the shutters on the beach home they'd dreamed about owning together once. Did he even notice?

Mika faced her. "I guess what I'm saying is I can see your *heart* and soul in everything you do here. I'm just following protocol, avoiding…well, you know."

"I know," she admitted, gripping the counter behind her, as if she might fall to the floor without it.

"I'd be lying if I said I don't sometimes think about what we might have done together, if I hadn't left," he said softly.

"You *had* to leave," she told him, realizing she was fighting back tears now. "You told me that. There were too many awful memories here. And yes, like you said, there still are. But that's life,

Mika. *My* life is still here, and yours isn't, but that's what you wanted."

He stepped toward her again, looking like he regretted his last words already. "It's what I *thought* I needed. It's what I thought would be best for *you*."

She gaped at him, her coconut pudding clean forgotten. "You thought leaving the island would be best for me? How?"

"I was just a reminder that I messed up, spending all that time away from you and our daughter… I should have just been a better father. I should have been *there* more."

She looked at him, incredulous. This was the first time she'd heard anything like this from his mouth. They'd barely spoken to each other after the tragedy; she'd been convinced he'd fallen out of love with her and hadn't wanted to give him a chance to actually say it. She'd also assumed that letting him go was the best thing for him—he wouldn't be able to heal with her around, a constant reminder of their failures as parents. Hearing him confirm all that would have broken the final shards of her shattered heart, so she'd gone cold, shut him out. Wallowed in the shame and blame alone. Was it possible he'd felt the same? Had he really assumed she had fallen out of love with *him*?

Lani's throat constricted as she ripped her gaze away from Mika, desperate to conceal the giant swell of emotions that were threatening to engulf her.

"I was her mother, Mika," she uttered through clenched teeth. "I should have seen how sick she really was..."

"Lani." He grasped her hands, looked deep into her eyes with the kind of unwavering conviction that stole her next protest straight from her mouth. "It wasn't your fault."

"Well, maybe we were both to blame," she muttered weakly.

He shook his head slowly, squeezed her hands. "It's not a blame game, and it doesn't help either of us to keep thinking that way. We didn't know her cold was actually meningitis."

They stood there for a moment, their hands intertwined, their eyes locked. "Every day, I wonder what she would be like now, what she would be doing," she told him, feeling her chin wobble. "I can't help but think that if I had just been less focused on that stupid dive..."

"Stop it, Lani. That dive was important for your studies, and you spent more time with Iolana than I ever did," he said.

The warning in his voice told her he wrestled with similar guilt—of course he did. How had they managed to shut each other out so completely after it happened? She should have been there for him.

Lani felt a hot tear streak down her cheek, and she swiped it away, trying to compose herself. Mika was right: they couldn't keep living in the past, blaming themselves. She let herself indulge in the warmth of his touch, the familiar scent of him that still caused a stirring in her belly. He was studying her lips now, like he wanted to kiss her all of a sudden, and just as she found herself leaning in on instinct, she dropped his hands, stepped back to the bench and resumed cutting up her sweets.

No. Nope.

This was all kinds of weird as it was; they had different lives now, not to mention a divorce behind them! A huge, great planet-worth of pain they could still dredge up in each other with so much as a look, just like they were doing now. She would not be crossing *that* line again, not ever. Besides, what about Hayley?

Mika drummed his fingers on the bench. "Maybe we could go to the cemetery. Together," he said, carefully.

"I'll think about it," she told him, handing him a piece of the haupia. He sniffed it, then took a small bite, and she rolled her eyes. "It's good!"

"Has your cooking improved, then?" he teased, and she pretended to swipe at him, thankful the intensity between them had finally subsided, although the thought of going to the cemetery sent her skin to goose bumps. She couldn't stand it there; she avoided it, in fact, which only made her feel even more guilty.

"I'm kidding, this *is* actually good. You should bring some to the luau."

She raised her eyebrows. “Are you serious? You think I should come?”

“Sure, bring Anela.”

“She likes you a lot,” she told him now, wondering if she *should* go to the luau. It would be strange, and probably a little awkward. But if he’d made the first move toward clearing the elephants from the room and finally talking about what happened, she could at least show him the same courtesy and face his wonderful family. She’d been avoiding them for such selfish reasons, she realized with shame—as if they would have judged her in any way. Not that she was about to hurry into telling him she’d attend. The thought of it, and the look on his face just now when she’d almost kissed him, sent butterflies of anxiety take flight inside her.

“I’ll think about that, too,” she said instead, just as the sound of little footsteps behind them made them both turn around. Anela was standing in the doorway, hair ruffled, in her pajamas.

“I had the dream again,” she sniffed, and Lani’s heart sank.

“What dream?” Mika asked.

“About the sharks,” she replied, and he frowned in concern.

“Do you have that a lot?”

“Most nights,” Lani told him on her behalf with a frown, suddenly aware that he was maybe getting a little too invested in Anela’s struggle. She could handle it herself, as her foster mother. In fact, everything had been fine until he showed up…for the most part anyway.

To her relief, Mika seemed to get the message. He backed up, stayed quiet while she and Anela discussed what book they might read to take her mind off the dreams.

Good, she thought. The last thing she wanted was to make him think he had to step in as some kind of temporary foster father for the next few weeks. He had enough on his plate, what with his dolphin research and filling Mahina's shoes, not to mention Hayley. He'd moved on from her, his ex-wife. They were water under a big fat bridge. And anyway, her heart was already a mess around him, changing pace with his every word and action, like it just couldn't figure out how to beat right.

She really shouldn't go to the luau, she thought.

Maybe she should keep on staying away from him, outside of the sanctuary.

"You can see yourself out, right?" she told him, making for the stairs with Anela.

"I know exactly where the door is," he replied coolly.

Five minutes later, she felt the strangest mix of dread and relief when she heard his car pulling out of the driveway.

CHAPTER SEVEN

MIKA STEPPED BACK from the wheel of the boat and let their volunteer driver, Noa, take over. Lani was already halfway into her wet suit, rolled in a neoprene fold up to her waist, and he couldn't help admiring her in her bikini top while she wasn't looking. Maybe it was a little to do with the fact that he couldn't have her, shouldn't touch her, but God, he was still so attracted to her. It went beyond her looks; it was how she carried herself, he thought: her energy and spirit and fire, not in-your-face, or brash or loud, but stoic and quiet and burning under the surface. It was all the things that transcended her physical form and reminded him why he'd married the woman. She was in fact the total opposite of Hayley. He realized now that he'd gone for the opposite of Lani with every woman since their divorce; probably because he didn't *want* to love anyone else that much again, only to lose them.

"Let me get that zip, at the back," he said now as she caught his eye. Damn, she'd caught him looking, and was he imagining it, or did she just get a little redder in the face?

"I can manage," she muttered, wriggling the tight wet suit up faster and over her arms like she couldn't wait to cover herself suddenly. His fingers itched as she fumbled with the zip herself, insisting she was fine.

"I was only trying to help," he said, feeling snubbed.

"I know," she tutted, as if it was the last thing on earth she wanted.

Annoyed, he took over the tanks, checking the compression, attaching the regulators. She'd been distant with him for the last few days, probably because he'd insisted on opening a can of worms in her kitchen. Cute kitchen, he'd thought at the time. She had painted it the same yellow as the finishing on their dream beach house. God, he hadn't thought about that place in years. They'd always planned to buy it someday; they'd driven past so many times, even sneaked onto the private beach out front at night to imagine their lives there, as soon as they could afford it...if indeed it ever came up for sale.

As it happened, they'd never even moved out of his parents' annex. Getting pregnant when Lani was just twenty-two had changed everything. She'd stopped her studies for two years, while he'd worked stints at institutions on and off the island, determined to provide for them, to his detriment in the end; he'd missed so much. After Iolana died, the house might as well have burned down along with all their other dreams.

He cringed to himself, remembering how he'd basically admitted to her that he thought about the what-ifs all the time. She had moved on with her life after *he'd* decided to leave the island; he had no right to openly reflect on how he might regret that decision sometimes. Make that *all* the time.

Okay, so they'd both agreed to the divorce, and obviously both made mistakes in that marriage, clamming up and shutting each other out, instead of talking and sharing, but they'd been so damn young, and while their love had been undeniable, neither of them had been prepared for such intense grief to take its place so abruptly. It had torn in like a beast, and the ripple effects were almost as bad.

It killed him knowing Lani had been blaming herself instead of him all this time, and knowing she might *not* have thought him leaving was the best thing for her after all. Why had he just assumed those things? He'd been so blinded by guilt, nothing anyone could've said would have made a difference back then. Now it was far too late to mend what was broken—but perhaps at least they could try to be friends?

"Almost there," Noa told them now, as Mika pulled on his buoyancy vest, resisting the urge to help Lani with her weight belt when it slipped momentarily from her grasp. Maybe he'd overstepped before, showing up at her house, almost kissing her.

Friends—ha! He couldn't get that almost-kiss out of his head. Obviously she'd thought better of it before he had, but it was built in to him, the attraction to her mouth, even after all these years. Not that anything would happen, he reminded himself, telling her to tighten her weight belt.

She grunted in response, which irked him…but didn't make him want to kiss her any less, even now. He'd have to stop thinking about what used to be, he warned himself. Divorced couples didn't go around locking lips and besides, she couldn't have kicked him out of her kitchen fast enough the other day!

"Here we are. Are you guys ready?" Noa asked, slowing the boat till it bobbed on the surface like a slow spinning top under the sun.

They'd come out to the edge of the reef. Several scuba divers on a tour had reported seeing a white tip reef shark with a fishing hook lodged in its mouth this morning. It was his hope that he and Lani could locate it and help, and he was trying his best to focus on this mission. But it was their first dive together since that terrible day, when they should have been with Iolana. She was thinking about it, too; he could see it in her anguished glances.

Thankfully Anela had been at school when they'd received the call. Poor kid, with those nightmares. He'd offered to talk to her, but Lani had kept the girl away from him these last few days, arranging play dates and other activities to keep her busy elsewhere, even after he'd asked if he could take her to the beach outside the sanctuary again. Even if they had somewhat agreed not to play the blame game over Iolana's death anymore, he got the distinct impression Lani didn't trust him entirely around Anela.

Lani jumped into the water first, holding her regulator to her mouth. The sun was hot in the midday blue sky and the water felt cool against his face as he tumbled backward after her. It was a long shot, looking for this injured shark, but he couldn't help but wonder, too, if his old friend Nala might be around. This had been her hunting ground. Would that beautiful tiger shark even remember him?

The reef looked majestic, almost as beautiful as Lani did swimming in the blue as they made their descent together. Ocean life teemed around them; a blur of tiny silver fish swirled in a vivid tornado, and below them, a turtle eyed them with curiosity. He pulled out his navigation device, signaling to Lani to go left along the reef. She gave him the okay with her fingers, and he let her go ahead. Like him, Lani was an experienced diver.

They floated for ten minutes, maybe fifteen, with no sign of the shark. Usually he could switch his brain off but being down here with Lani, it was racing. Lani *must* still think him somewhat responsible for what happened to Iolana, even if she wasn't saying it.

Maybe she was right to step back from him like this. Part of him didn't trust himself not to mess something up, either, and until meeting Anela, he hadn't even *wanted* to hang out around children.

It always brought back too many painful memories. It still did, because of course he saw Iolana in everything, everywhere, even in the little girl. But he'd done something nice for Anela to help Lani, as much as to help the child, and in doing so something had shifted inside him. A wall was falling away. He'd never be anyone's foster father, or stepfather, or real father… He could never do what Lani did. That would mean living every day in fear of messing up again, and the thought of feeling that kind of pain again was incomprehensible. But while he was here, he wasn't going to give up on his quest to make Anela see the magic in the ocean again, he decided. He'd just have to bide his time and not tread on Lani's toes.

Suddenly, Lani pulled to a stop in front of him, so fast he almost banged into her tank. She motioned ahead of her and clutched for his hand in a cloud of bubbles. Sure enough, they'd found their reef shark. It was swimming slowly, mouthing at the coral in distress as it went round and round in circles.

The shark was around ten feet long and looked

exhausted. The hook in its mouth was obvious. A bright blue nylon fishing line trailed behind it, tangled around its lower jaw. With a nod of agreement, they began to swim slowly toward it together, careful not to startle the shark.

The sight as he drew closer filled him with sadness and anger on behalf of this innocent creature—why did fishermen have to be so careless? He could tell by the look on her face that Lani was thinking the same thing.

Mika flipped his fins till he was floating ahead of Lani. She knew about his special method of calming sharks; they'd discussed it on the way out here, how it had so far never let him down. Lani's eyes were trained on him as he swam ahead, holding out his hands with his palms facing the creature. Just as he expected it would, the shark lunged forward, but Mika's hands came down firmly on its nose, batting it away until it redirected itself and eventually flipped upside down.

Lani clapped her hands in delight and swam to the other side of the shark. He took out his regulator for a second and grinned at her triumphantly, and for a moment the tension that had settled around them since that night at her house seemed to dissipate and float away on the current with their bubbles.

He'd conducted many seminars about sharks; there was nothing better than seeing kids' faces light up when he told them how flipping certain shark species upside down pretty much rendered them immobile for up to fifteen minutes. It was known to induce a trance-like state known as "tonic immobility." In this case, it meant he and Lani could work together to extract the hook from its mouth.

Once they were finished, Lani gathered the fishing line and shoved it into a bag attached to her weight belt. His heart sank for her, knowing she must witness this more and more these days in the waters around Oahu.

They dived deeper, careful to keep their distance as the shark regained its senses, righted itself with a dramatic twirl and darted away into the deep blue beyond.

Lani's smile was unmistakable; not that they weren't attuned to each other under the water already. The two of them had completed thousands of dives together till now, and he'd missed moments like this, just the two of them out here. He met her smile through the bubbles around her face, and instinct took over. He removed his regulator and blew her a kiss. She did the same, laughing now.

It was something they'd always done, a little shared ritual—the under-the-ocean kiss. Usually he pressed his lips to hers before he put his regulator back in, but this time he ignored the urge. There was no way he should be kissing Lani, or even pretending to, underwater, above water, anywhere—things were complicated enough. But he didn't miss the confusion—or was that disappointment?—in her eyes through her mask as he signaled that they should start their ascent. His heart was probably beating harder than he had enough air for.

They were just beginning their slow float upward toward the surface, Lani three feet above him already, when Mika noticed something huge and dark hovering in his periphery. His breath caught as it swam closer, gracefully sweeping through the water toward him.

"Nala?"

Excitedly he motioned to Lani that it *was* her; his tiger shark had returned! But Lani was too close to the surface already. He could tell it was Nala, he thought as he slowed his ascent, and checked his air. The shark had the same beautiful markings around her belly, and a wave of relief washed over him as he noticed she appeared healthy; there were no signs of any fishing line caught in her mouth or fins. A few more scars, yes, but that was to be expected.

He stayed calm and still now, letting her approach his mask. She paused a moment, as if studying him, figuring out if he was indeed her old friend. Thrilled, he held his hands out slowly, and sure enough she bopped her head against his palms several times, eyes rolling in delight the way they always used to do. She recognized him!

Mika laughed as she flipped over, inviting him to rub her belly. "It's so good to see you girl, how've you been?" he mouthed, and he swore she could understand; she'd loved nothing more than getting her belly rubbed, like a giant dog. Sharks loved affection, he thought, bewitched by the creature's grace and beauty.

Mika was so enchanted by this surprise encounter that he clean forgot he was supposed to be back on the boat by now. And when he finally looked up, he realized he couldn't see Lani at all.

CHAPTER EIGHT

LANI SCRAMBLED TO the edge of the boat, searching wildly for Mika. As she peered into the water, her heart started pounding out of her chest, her mind racing with terror as she yanked off her weight belt. Waves lapped around the boat and the sun was glinting on the surface like a spotlight, but she couldn't see Mika anywhere.

"He was right behind me," she told Noa as he took the tank from her back. She barely noticed him doing it. She was paranoid—of course she was—but the panic still rose like a tidal wave in her chest, threatening to overwhelm her. "Where is he?"

"He probably saw something down there. Give him a few minutes," Noa reasoned, and she bit her lip, reminding herself he was an experienced diver. He did this all the time; he was a pro!

Memories of losing Iolana flashed through her mind, and her breathing came in shallow gasps, her chest constricting with dread. It almost felt like the sea was punishing her all over again—they'd been out on a boat like this the day their daughter had died. How could she have ever expected their first dive together after that to go smoothly? It had been on her mind since she'd boarded this boat, even when she'd just been laughing underwater. It was always there.

"Where is he?"

Noa frowned now, peering overboard. His look dried her throat up on the spot.

"I'm going back in," she said, grabbing a snorkel and climbing back up to the ledge. She was just about to leap from the side and dive under when she spotted the bubbles. *Mika.*

Relief flooded her veins as his hands found the rungs of the ladder, and he pulled himself up onto the deck, grinning from ear to ear as he ripped off his mask, dripping glistening salt water all over. Tears flooded her vision as she scrambled back from the edge, but hot on their heels was pure anger, a fire inside her that had probably been smoldering ever since he'd arrived, ever since he'd ripped open old wounds and made her start facing them all over again. The second his tank was on the deck she lunged at him, wiping the grin clean from his face as she pummeled his chest.

"How could you do that to me, Mika?"

"Whoa, Lani, what?" He dodged another thump, tried to take her wrists.

Hot nausea twisted in her stomach, burning up the bile in her throat. "I thought you were gone! I thought I'd lost you, too..."

"Lani, I'm right here!" He grasped her wrists

finally, and she wrestled with him, desperate to drum her fury and pain and bereavement into him, to make him feel what she'd been trying for so long *not* to feel since long before he'd even got here. He held her firmly, calmly and she realized she was sobbing, hurting, physically now, crumpling to the deck.

He sank with her as Noa rushed for towels and water. The second Mika's arms were around her she felt another surge of fury rip inside of her, but this time it seemed to burn away in seconds, leaving only exhaustion and the comfort of his closeness. He was here, and he was very much alive. She was too tired to do anything but accept his embrace and press her cheek against his chest, and cry.

"I'm sorry," he whispered, cupping her face from his place on his haunches, dripping salt water from his hair and wet suit. "I should have come up with you, I'm so sorry. I saw Nala and it distracted me."

"You can never do that to me," she told him through gritted teeth. "Never! Do you hear me?"

She was crying over more than Mika's slipup, and he knew it; she could feel it in the way he was holding her, pressing his mouth to the top of her head. They held each other like that, on the floor, for what felt like forever, until she couldn't cry anymore. She just felt numb.

"I miss her so much."

"So do I," Mika whispered, rocking her gently. Suddenly, there was no point even trying to pretend they hadn't both been bottling this up in their individual corners. But what happened now?

Late that afternoon, as the sun beat down on the porch, Lani could hardly concentrate on anything. The quick rice dinner she'd assembled for Anela was so burnt she'd wound up ordering them a pizza, and felt a little guilty at how relieved she was when it came time to drive Anela to her friend's house for a sleepover.

She drove back toward home slowly, finally pulling into the little parking lot that led to the hiking trails instead. Leaving her car beside a scuffed red bike, she set off absentmindedly toward the waterfall, sucking in lungfuls of the calming, tropical air. The birds sang a high, sweet song, their colors flashes of iridescent reds and blues in the trees, and she let her mind run over it all.

She'd left Mika after the dive, at his insistence that she rest. But now it was just mortifying, knowing she'd embarrassed herself, and him, too, probably. She'd totally overreacted! And now she just couldn't stop thinking about it. Things hadn't exactly been great since their talk the other night; she'd pushed him away, scared he might think she expected him to slip back into his old roles around her: protector, caregiver...father. Scared she might come to rely on him to be there for her again, only to have him go straight back to California, and to Hayley.

But it was more than knowing he was going back to Hayley, whom somehow he never mentioned and…urgh…as if she was going to torture herself by asking about her.

If she let him get too close again, become involved in her life, she would only disappoint him *again* somehow. She still worked as hard as ever—although admittedly, she was understaffed. If she stopped being a control freak with zero social life and hired more staff, maybe she'd free up a little more time. It wasn't like she couldn't afford it these days.

Hmmm. But she'd had her chance with Mika anyway; there would never be another one. She couldn't put her heart through losing him again—this afternoon had proved that. She'd only live in fear of him disappearing one way or another. And no matter what he said, about how she shouldn't feel so guilty for not knowing Iolana was so sick, she always would.

As she walked down the path, the grass tickled her ankles until she heard the crash of the waterfall up ahead. The air was warm and thick and she was sweating, grateful she'd kept her bikini on as she stepped across the rocks. A swim in the cool, refreshing pool at the base of the falls would be heavenly right now.

Only, she wasn't alone. Someone else was standing at the water's edge, stripping off his shirt. She gasped as she recognized the wide, broad shoulders, the tattoo on his upper arm—Mika. Her Honu! Well, ex-Honu, she reminded herself, running a finger absently across her turtle tattoo while looking at his. Trust him to come here now, at the same time. But then, this had always been their spot.

Clasping her hand over her mouth, she froze in place as he discarded his bandanna and sunglasses, watched the muscles flex in his back as he undid his belt and threw his shorts on top of the pile. Then, there he was. Naked.

Suddenly, she was even hotter. Mika was butt naked, and oh, what a butt. It hadn't changed a bit. She watched him dive gracefully from the rocks like an arrow, cutting the water as he started to swim, one arm over the other, in a direct line to the falls. Creeping closer, she shook off her flip-flops, took his place on the rocks, straining her eyes for him. The mist from the raging falls was like a cool breath against her skin and she wanted to get in so badly. But he still had no idea she was here.

Suddenly, out of nowhere, a wide grin took her mouth hostage. The carefree teenager inside her was awake and inspired now, and in that moment she knew exactly what she was going to do.

The cool waters of the waterfall were a balm to Mika's skin as he made for the rocks behind the cascade. It seemed like just yesterday that he and Lani had swum here together, chasing each other in the warm shallows, then later, when they were older, making out behind the falls.

She used to tease him about not being able to dive off the rocks like she could, how he never made a neat splash as he entered the water, not like she did. She'd cut it so clean you could barely tell she'd dived in. Lani had always been so fearless and daring, whereas he'd been, and maybe still was, more of a thinker than a doer. Holding her today, though, on the boat, she hadn't seemed so fearless.

He pressed his back to the cool rocky wall, blinded by the blur of the falls in front of him. God, his heart had shattered right there on that deck, seeing her like that, knowing what he'd put her through. It must have put her on edge, the same it had him, being out there, knowing it was a dive trip that had taken them both away from Iolana for the last time, and then he'd gone and done that to her. He'd regret it forever; no wonder she'd freaked out so badly.

She was still as feisty as ever; he had to give her that. If only he could hear more of her laughter, he thought. He'd have to stop doing such stupid things around her if that was ever going to happen.

His hands were getting wrinkled, he realized after a while. He made his way back to the shore, pondering whether to go check up on Lani after this. He probably should. Unless she didn't want to see him. He had to make up for frightening her, though; there was no question about that.

Shaking off the water from his hair, he looked around for his shirt. Frowning to himself, he spun around, searched the rocks. He'd left his clothes here…hadn't he?

There was no one else in sight, so where the hell did his shirt go? His shorts? He couldn't even see his shoes.

Perplexed he walked around the pool, turning over stones, sweeping foliage aside.

Damn, he was butt naked, a mile from the bike he'd ridden here on, and his clothes were nowhere to be seen. Then he saw it. Tucked away in the rocks, beneath a cluster of ferns, a corner of a small wooden box protruded from the sand. Its tiny hinges creaked as he lifted it out carefully and wrestled it open, hardly believing his eyes. Lani and he had buried this container here years ago, when he'd been twelve or thirteen. He'd almost forgotten about it, but here it was, right in front of him, and the items inside, while weathered, sent the memories racing back in. Inside lay two shells they'd collected together from a beach on the other side of the island, a piece of pink glass shaped like a heart that she must have given him at some point, some old coins they'd found with his uncle's metal detector and a badly written treasure map. It showed where all their adventures had taken place over the years. So many memories wrapped up in one little box!

He was just spilling the items onto the rocks for closer inspection of the map when an arm snaked around his neck from behind, making him gasp. Before he could react he was being pulled back against a body, and a pair of lips were pressed to his ear. "Say you're sorry, or you'll never see your clothes again."

Spinning around, he scrambled to his feet, meeting Lani's grinning face. She was on her feet now, holding out his shirt, dangling his shorts just out of his reach. Remembering his nakedness, he covered himself with both hands quickly, standing there like a fool, and her laughter echoed through the jungle all around them.

"I've seen it all before, remember," she laughed.

"Really? We're doing this?" he said drily, making another grab for his shorts. "What are you, *eleven years old*?"

Lani tutted and tossed him his shorts finally, and he hurried to pull them on, just as she seemed to notice the box, its contents now spilled across the rocks. Her eyes grew wide as she dropped to her knees.

"No way… I forgot about this—where did you find it?" She took the pink glass onto her palm and inspected it from all angles, while he retrieved his sunglasses, setting them atop his head.

"I was looking for my clothes," he said, crouching next to her, and she rolled her eyes, biting back another laugh. It *was* good to hear her laugh, he thought. He wasn't really mad at her for her prank—how could he be? He'd deserved it. "This isn't the first time you've stolen my clothes," he said with a pretend scowl.

"And it probably won't be the last," she retorted. Then she pulled her eyes away, as if realizing there might not be many chances, seeing as he didn't even live here anymore. He took the glass heart from her hands, determined not to make things more awkward.

"Where did you get this?" he asked her.

"The beach outside our dream house… Remember how we'd cycle past it and promise each other we'd buy it someday?"

"I do," he said quietly.

She sighed softly, turning the glass over. "I loved that house."

"So did I. Look, Lani…" He took the glass from her palm and held her hand. "I was such an idiot today, forgive me. I know why you got so angry, and scared, and I deserved to feel your wrath."

She shook her head and chewed on her lip. "I

overreacted. You saw your shark—of course you had to go meet her."

"But not when I was supposed to be ascending with you. I was your dive buddy, and I broke all the rules."

"I forgive you," she said simply.

Mika tilted her chin up, searching her eyes. There were so many things he wanted to say but suddenly he was lost for words. All he could do was kiss her.

He pressed his lips to hers tenderly, asking her without words if this was okay. Lani responded in kind, wrapping her arms around his neck, deepening their kiss till she was straddling him on the ground, her shirt open, the warmth of her flesh tight against his chest. God, he'd missed her kisses, the way she just fit with him. It was like they'd sped right back to day one of their teenage love affair, like he could feel and taste her craving all over again. Back then, she'd been wanting him for years by then, maybe more, she'd always thought, than he'd been wanting her. But she had nothing to worry about; he'd always want her.

After just a few moments, though, she pulled away breathless, covering her mouth in shock.

"I'm sorry," she said, with her back to him. "We shouldn't..."

He nodded silently in agreement, cursing himself, not wanting to ruin this moment any more than he already had. Why had he kissed her? As if things between them weren't muddied enough!

"I know that was purely muscle memory," she said now, facing him again. "Because I know you're not a cheater. It's just because of our history, we both got carried away..."

"Cheater?" He frowned, shoving his bandanna into his pocket. He could still taste her.

Lani snorted, putting her hands to her hips. "Hello, have you forgotten Hayley?"

"Oh." Mika grimaced. Of course, Lani had no idea they'd broken up. He'd been so distracted by everything since he got here, he hadn't even mentioned it, or her, probably. "About that. We...um... we ended things before I came here."

Lani fixed her eyes on his, then ran a finger over her lips. He could almost see her mind whirring. "You never said anything."

"You never asked."

She pursed her lips. "Okay..." she started. "So, you're *not* a cheater."

"I was never a cheater, Lani," he retorted, irritated now. "I never had reason to even *think* about anyone else when I was with you, and Hayley and I, we just..."

He shut his mouth as she looked to the floor. It wasn't fair to talk about Hayley, for so many reasons. Besides, he didn't want to hear himself admit he didn't want her kids, or that he had never wanted kids with anyone but Lani; they'd both moved on. Lani had a different role now, parental duties that he would never have.

He picked up the box and all its trinkets, and they walked in silence back to the parking lot, where she took it from him, to take home in the car. Neither of them said one word. Watching her drive away into the sunset, Mika couldn't help thinking he'd just solved one problem and leaped headfirst into another.

CHAPTER NINE

THIS MUST BE the sanctuary's busiest morning in a long time, Lani thought as she closed the door after Mr. Benos and yet another generous basket of fruit, only to find it opening three seconds later. Her heart lodged in her throat. Mika was here, for which she was more than grateful, even though he might just as well have injected her stomach with a set of hatching butterflies.

"Hi," he said, giving her a lingering look over the top of his sunglasses, as if waiting for her to kick him out.

"Hi," she replied, shutting the door after him, wishing she *could* just kick him out. Maybe she would if she wasn't so damn busy.

Lani couldn't get that kiss at the falls the other day out of her head. It had been her fault as much as his, a spontaneous outpouring of emotion, as was becoming her norm around him, annoyingly. But she'd made things even more complicated than they'd been before. Still, she would have to try to act like it wasn't such a big deal. It wasn't really. They used to kiss all the time, and he wasn't seeing Hayley anymore…whatever had happened there.

Considering Hayley's age, she wondered if Hayley had wanted children and for some reason Mika had been scared off. Maybe he still wanted to play the field. And why should she care if he did?

Mika's desires, or his single status, should not affect anything at all in her life right now, she reminded herself.

He looked very handsome today, she had to admit, as she tidied some papers up and he wandered over to the petrel in its cage. She studied his muscular backside in the same shorts he'd worn to the waterfall. His crisp linen shirt showed off his strong forearms; she could still feel his arms around her when she closed her eyes. The three days since she'd kissed him had felt like an eternity, but she'd have to get used to the fact that it wouldn't happen again. They were exes, they only brought up the worst kind of memories together and the past was the past, she reminded herself quickly. It was all far too complicated.

Well, okay, she reasoned, so not all the memories they shared were bad. There was the treasure box, for example. That had been fun to uncover. A nice reminder that they'd had some good times before everything fell apart. Anela had made the glass heart her own and was very invested in visiting all the places on the treasure map.

Mika turned from one of the birds and caught her looking at him, chewing the lid of her pen.

"Something on your mind?" he asked, probing her with his stare.

"No. Nope."

She panicked suddenly. Was he daring her to bring up their kiss? They'd gone on as usual ever since, casually sweeping it under the carpet. He must know she'd been thinking about it, though; damn it, was it written all over her face?

"I have the results from the samples we took from the beach," he said now, walking past her to the desk in the corner and flicking on the small light. "I cross-checked the results against the others we collected off the coast last year and it turns out I was right—we've encountered this before."

He looked around for Anela.

"She's not here," she told him, self-consciously tightening her hair in its clasp on top of her head. "They're on a school trip until tomorrow, at Rainbow Bay. So, what exactly did you find?"

He put the file down in front of her and opened it, pointing to a list of numbers, and she watched in surprise as he pulled out a pair of glasses.

"Since when do you wear glasses?" she asked, resisting the urge to tell him he looked sexy as hell in them.

"Since I got old," he deadpanned, and she smirked. "We identified the *exact* cadmium chemical compound that's causing the dolphins' skin irritation. It's a highly toxic metal that can enter water bodies through various ways. The next step is to narrow down who's using the compound around the island and run on-site tests."

"You don't think it's an illegal operation, do you?" she asked in horror.

Mika lowered his voice and leaned in so close her stomach dissolved into knots. In a flash she was reflecting on their kiss once again, that stupid mistake of a kiss. But, oh God, it was such a nice kiss.

"I really hope not," he said, making her ear tingle.

He stepped away quickly as the door opened again and a young woman appeared holding a box. Clearing her throat, Lani forced a smile to her face. Her latest sea turtle patient needed their attention; another one had been caught in fishing nets. It was still the most common cause of injury around here, even after all those campaigns by the island activists to make the fishermen well aware of the implications.

"I found him on the beach this morning. His flipper is hurt," the woman explained as Mika took it gently from her hands. "Oh, hi Mika. I heard you were back."

Lani felt her blood start to race as she noticed how this slender, blond-haired, young lady was looking at him through her fluttering eyelashes, both of their hands still on the box between them. Wasn't she the niece of one of Manu's colleagues, or something? Why did it even matter? She frowned, rolling up her sleeves.

"Let's have a look at this, shall we?" she said quickly, marching up to them and taking the box firmly. She didn't miss Mika's cocked eyebrow before he told the woman they'd take care of it and escorted her back outside. Lani kept one eye on the door as they spoke in a hushed whisper for a moment. What were they talking about? Why was she so…jealous?

No. She grimaced to herself, lifting the poor turtle from its back and putting it on the table to examine it. She was not jealous. How ridiculous—she was just busy. And Mika was supposed to be here, with her, not standing outside for like…ten whole seconds.

"Sorry," he said when he came back in.

She forced another smile to her face. "No worries."

"She was just asking me what to bring on Friday."

"Friday?"

"To the luau," he added, as if she should already know. Of course she *did* know; she just hadn't brought it up again.

Mika pulled on a pair of latex gloves and rolled the light over quickly. His face dropped when he saw the turtle's injuries.

"Don't worry, little one, we'll help fix you up,"

he said with confidence, reaching immediately for the medications in her carefully ordered cabinet. He knew where everything was, as if he'd always worked here at her side.

Lani clamped her mouth shut, kept her talk about the turtle. There was no point talking about the luau, because she wasn't going. Absolutely not. It would be too weird, for so many reasons, she thought, glancing at his lips. Kissing him was a silly move, so why was she even imagining doing it again?

Somehow, though, working with Mika was easy. They had a kind of rapport and instinct as to each other's methods that meant they conducted each examination and procedure like a well-oiled machine. He was warm and welcoming to every client who came in, too. Maybe they would have been running this place together if he hadn't left, if they'd stayed married…if they'd fought for it.

Maybe she should just let that water stay under its bridge. It wasn't like she didn't have enough to deal with. There was still a stack of emails to answer from the wildlife rescue organization taking Lilo and Stitch, and she had to prepare their postoperative-care instructions and…so much. As if she even had *time* to think about her husband's regrets, and how they seemed to match her own, or how the women around here reacted to him when they walked through the door. He could have anyone he wanted, she mused, wondering for the thousandth time what had happened with Hayley.

Should she have asked him? He probably thought her selfish for asking nothing at all, but why would she want to hear about her perfect size-two replacement? Or the one before that, or the one before that. No, thanks.

She was jealous, Mika realized in shock as he wheeled the little turtle into recovery. He could read her like the children's book he'd started but hadn't finished writing. She was also clearly harboring all kinds of questions about what had happened with Hayley, but after that kiss, she'd decided not to get personal.

It was probably for the best, he concluded. Whatever happened, he would always just bring up a bundle of bad memories for her in the end. And one kiss didn't exactly mean they were paving a path to a new future together. How could they? Lani was an amazing foster mother who was juggling those duties with her work like a pro. He still worked as hard as he had done back then, though, with little time for much else.

Well, okay, so he could *make* time; it wasn't like he couldn't afford more time off these days. But no. He'd been a terrible father back then and he'd be a terrible one now, too. That was just the way it was.

Out in the back, Lilo and Stitch were splashing about in their tank, like they'd become close friends, and he placed the new turtle into a separate tank, where they could monitor it. Lani was cleaning up inside, so he went about the feeding rounds, tossing small fish to the sea lions, preparing a fruit mush for their recovering petrel, who was almost ready to be released. It was so peaceful out here, just doing his thing for the animals, swinging in the hammock at night. Totally different vibe to California.

As he stood on the deck, he felt a tug of nostalgia for all the times he'd spent making plans out *here*. Funny but he didn't miss California, he thought to himself now, watching the way the sunlight danced in the palm trees over the deck. It was strange how quickly that part of his life had started to feel like a distant dream, as though the whispering palm fronds had woken him up from a deep sleep, and reminded him where…or to whom… his heart belonged.

He caught a glimpse of Lani through the doors, and she looked away quickly. Hah! She'd been watching him, as usual. Not that he could do anything about their obvious attraction, not when their lives were on completely different trajectories. He was back to being a teenager again, trying to ignore her crush on him until she grew up a little more, knowing his infatuation was probably obvious to everyone. But if she wasn't bringing that kiss up, *he* wasn't going to, either.

When Lani stepped onto the deck, looking tired, she joined him in the feeding rounds, and they moved around each other in silence. He should ask her about the luau, he thought, because this was stupid. If she didn't go, it would make things even weirder—everyone knew they were working together, and he'd never avoid all the questions… Besides, he really wanted to hear her play her funny songs on the ukulele after all this time, if she even remembered them.

"Lani, did you think any more about—"

"Oh, no!"

The look on her face sent a bolt of dread to his core. She was staring over his shoulder at the beach. He followed her gaze, heart pounding till he saw the leaping dolphins. One…two…five of them? His mouth fell open.

"What are they doing?"

"They're calling us to help them," she told him, and raced down the steps just ahead of him. Sure enough, he could see the closest dolphin now, floundering in the shallows. He tore off his shirt and shoes and waded straight into the ocean, Lani by his side now as the water crashed around their waists. The dolphin's eyes were piercing black and shining into his, but he knew it was fighting for its life.

"Look at his skin," Lani said in dismay. "It's the same infection. Not as advanced but…"

"Help me," he said to her over the roar of the surf. "Let's get him closer to shore."

"I can do it," she said, so he raced to fetch the specially designed stretcher while she guided the creature slowly toward the shore. Hurrying back, he found Lani crouched on the wet sand, inspecting the dolphin's eyes. Her wet shirt was open, her red spotty bikini top now soaked. In the distance, the rest of the pod were still leaping and arching in the waves, as if encouraging them to help their friend. The dolphin was breathing heavily, his eyes drooping. It wasn't good—they needed to move fast if he was going to make it.

Once they had the dolphin inside the sanctuary, they could breathe a little easier. "He's showing signs of extreme weakness and dehydration," Lani said, as he gathered what they'd need to administer the intravenous fluids and stabilize the mammal.

Mika prepared the IV fluids and equipment and helped steady the dolphin, so that Lani could locate a suitable vein. As she readied the IV catheter for insertion, her face was a picture of determination, but he could almost hear her heartbeat. This was everything to her. It used to be everything to him, too, which left a bitter taste in his mouth now. Could he have done something about this sooner, if he'd been here?

"How many times have you done this procedure already, Lani?"

"Too many," she said, touching a finger to the

skin around the dolphin's eyes. The white patches were the same as on the other dolphins. Whatever was in the water wasn't going away. If anything, it was getting worse. Mika found his jaw pulsing—this wasn't right.

"We'll keep an eye on his heart rate and respiration. I'll run some more tests..." He paused. "If that's okay with you?"

"Yes, please," she said, pressing a hand to his arm. A moment passed between them when helplessness flooded her eyes. It tore at his heart just seeing it. "You've done so much already, to help me. Us."

Yet it still wasn't enough, he thought grimly, though her appreciation was welcome. "We'll gather volunteers for on-site inspections. We can't handle this alone, not as quickly as we need to. Conservationists, rescue and rehabilitation organizations up the coast and beyond, we all need to be on the same page."

He had to find out what was going on before this happened again, he thought, just as Lani spoke his exact thoughts out loud. Without thinking he took her fingers and pressed his lips to her knuckles.

"We will save them," he told her resolutely. "Whatever it takes."

Lani nodded. On this matter at least, they were unwavering allies.

"Lani, come to the luau," he said next, squeezing her fingers. She studied his gaze and for a second, he saw the conflict in her eyes. "It wouldn't be the same without you there," he admitted. What a relief it was to actually admit his real feelings for once!

Finally, Lani bobbed her head, a soft smile spreading across her lips.

"Okay, Mika," she sighed. "I'll be there."

CHAPTER TEN

THE LUAU WAS in full swing when she arrived, little Anela close behind in her pink T-shirt and red flowery skirt. Lani breathed in the smoky-sweet fragrance of the kalua pig, slow-roasting away in its underground oven, but her stomach was so full of butterflies that she couldn't even feel hungry. Mika was already here.

Draped in a lei in an open floral shirt, he was bent backward under the limbo pole. His brother, Manu, cheered as Mika managed it easily. The two high-fived, then Manu said something she couldn't hear and Mika laughed, slapping his back good-naturedly before lowering the pole a notch. They'd often played limbo together, and Mika had always been better at it. Not as good as her, though.

Under the shaded palms, surrounded by twinkling fairy lights that would turn on at sunset, was the coconut bowling arena. A few kids were playing already, tossing the wiry brown coconuts across the sand with gusto. Anela watched them in interest, till Lani walked her over.

"I hope you both brought your coconut bowling skills?" came a voice from behind them before Anela could speak.

"Mika!"

Lani watched in shock as Anela wrapped her arms around his middle, like embracing an old friend. Mika looked just as surprised, like he really didn't know what to do with the child's affection, and Lani felt the strangest mix of love and nostalgia that almost made her hug them both, before she managed to rein it back. She had once loved nothing more than those little group hugs: her, Mika and Iolana. Their flawed yet untouchable unit.

"Come play with us!"

Anela was being called away now by one of the kids, and Lani leaned on the shabby palm frond fence with Mika as the girls gave Anela a coconut to roll toward a set of pins.

"I'm glad you came," he told her after a moment, nudging her shoulder. Lani swallowed her nerves. People were watching; she could literally feel their eyes on them. Adjusting the strap of her striped sundress self-consciously, she wished she didn't have to wonder what people thought about her being here.

Mika took the dish she realized she was still holding from her hands.

"She'll be fine here," he said, bobbing his head Anela's way. She was already giggling as another kid pretended to high-five her with a coconut. "Let's go put this where it belongs."

At the long trestle tables standing under the palm trees, the ocean glistened behind him as he placed her coconut haupia between a pineapple shaped like a hedgehog with sausages for spikes, and a delicious-looking salmon *lomi-lomi*. Everything looked incredible. The tables were laden with tasty Hawaiian dishes of all kinds; as usual everyone had brought something. The pineapple-and-macaroni salad used to be her favorite, and as for the poi...

"Mmmm, your mom always did make the best poi," she enthused.

"She still does!" Mika grabbed a spoon and took a scoop of the thick, purple-colored paste made from taro root. He brought it to her mouth, smiling into her eyes, and she let the tangy coolness of it run over her tongue. He watched her closely as she licked her lips and her heartbeat pulsed through to her fingers.

"It's exactly the same," she affirmed, swiping at her mouth.

She couldn't help staring at his exposed chest inches from her face, and now her mind's eye wouldn't stop showing a replay of his firm naked butt at the waterfall. She'd joked that she'd seen it all before, brushed it off like him standing there naked before her was nothing, but her heated dreams at night ever since told her it wasn't.

Manu wandered over, interrupting their small talk about the food, and promptly engulfed her in the biggest hug known to man.

"Lani, Lani, Lani, where have you been? We've missed you, lady!"

She pretended to slap him away like she'd always done, realizing she was laughing now, bundled against his huge chest. Eventually Mika stepped in. "Okay, okay, leave it, Manu. Haven't you got to start shredding?"

"Do you mean the pig, or my chest?" He puffed up his chest like a peacock in a too-big Hawaiian shirt, and Mika prodded his exposed, slightly podgy belly with the spoon.

"Hey!" Manu grabbed the utensil and pretended to stab him with it.

"Get shredding the pig, big boy," Mika cajoled, but the two continued play-fighting in front of her just like old times, and she shook her head, hiding her laugh in her shoulder.

She had almost turned down the invitation to come here again, but opening up to him a little, finally, and having him around these last few days especially—racing between the sanctuary and various other places to meet with conservationists, every marine biologist on his books and experienced divers from around the island, all in an effort to speed up their investigation—had boosted her confidence. Besides, all of these good people had lost Iolana, too—she'd been pretty selfish, she realized, shutting them out of her life for fear they'd judge her. No one had ever judged her, she mused now as Mika stopped his play-fight and dragged a hand through his hair, glancing at her as if embarrassed that he'd just been reduced to a little boy in front of her.

God, she'd missed Mika, the boy and the man; he was, as ever, a mix of both, still. All the little things, like the way his laughter carried on the breeze and tickled everyone in its reach, the camaraderie he had with his family, so different from hers.

He led her over to where another group had already started the hula competition, and Mika's sister, Betty, sought her out, followed by his uncle, his nephew—everyone seemed nothing short of delighted to see her all afternoon.

"We've missed you. All you have to do is reach out. We're always here," was the general theme. Even the woman who'd flirted with Mika the other day came up to thank Lani for what they'd done for the injured turtle. She'd brought her boyfriend, too. A nice guy with big nerdy glasses. Lani felt a little silly now, for being so paranoid back at the sanctuary.

"I'm starting to think your family might still like me," she whispered to Mika at one point, her eyes on Anela, who was now very much in competition with another child, swaying her hips to keep the hula hoop high.

Mika took her elbow, led her to the side, where no one else could hear. He stepped up closer, his expression now deadly serious.

"They love you. They consider you family. They always did and always will."

"Even if *you* don't," she interjected, no thanks to her nerves. His eyes were bright, brimming with all kinds of emotions she couldn't read suddenly, and the beach and everyone on it seemed to fall away.

"What do you want me to say, Lani?" His breath tickled her face before he shoved his hands into his pockets and threw his eyes up to the trees. "I thought you couldn't stand to be around me."

"When?"

"After I failed you. I should have helped with the baby more in the first place, let you go back to your studies sooner. You delayed your dream of becoming a vet to stay at home with her. I didn't have to work so hard the whole time. I should have stayed with her that day, too."

Her breath hitched. "I wanted you on the boat with me. Anyway, I thought we weren't doing regrets or guilt anymore."

He shrugged and she took his arm with a sigh. "Mika, we loved her, but we didn't know *how* to be parents—we were always making it up as we went along. We both had big plans for our careers before I got pregnant. And do you know how guilty I've felt about *that* over the years? Maybe that's a part of why I took on Anela, you know? So I could finally have both, and make it work out this time."

Her words hung in the salty air as he scanned her eyes, and she hugged her arms around herself. People were looking again now, and she watched him force a grin to his face and straighten up as someone waved him back over. He threw her a look that was half apology, half regret over his shoulder as he walked away. Unnerved, she sat on the sand, listening to the party all around her, watching the water. That last conversation wasn't over, and they both knew it.

Anela was having the time of her life, but all Lani wanted to do now was get out of here. They'd built so many walls around themselves back then that he'd actually left thinking she'd *wanted* him to go. And then, she'd pushed his family away, too. They might not be saying it, but they would always know it.

"Lani, come try this!" His mother was calling her suddenly, and she got to her feet, determined to put on a brave face.

She did love his mother, Alula, and always had. The big comforting bulk of her, the bright-patterned clothing that hung from her round frame, the easy laughing lilt to her voice, the way she somehow always smelled of baking.

Mika was watching her from the coconut bowling lane as they chatted, and she realized that some part of her was aware of where he was at all times, even when she couldn't see him. He did know how important his family had always been to her.

As the sun began to sink it came time for the tug-of-war, and Lani realized she was actually laughing more than she had in a while, watching Mika on the other end of the rope from Anela and the kids. The big Mahoes were letting the kids win, of course, pretending it was some tough, enduring battle. Then he called her over.

"Lani, we need you! Anela and her pals are smashing us!"

Breathing in the salty air, she let it fill her lungs, and gave in. She got behind him, clutched the rope and felt his shirt caress her cheeks whenever she was forced into his back in the battle. Eventually the crowd roared as they fell to the sand in stitches, the kids triumphant.

"We won, we won, we won!"

She'd never heard Anela so happy, and it made her heart swell, even as a wave of remorse flooded in. This had been here for her all this time—all this love, all around her, and she'd pushed it all away, feeling like it shouldn't be hers for the taking, like it was something she just didn't deserve. It might be too late for her and Mika, but she could start making more of an effort with the people who'd always been there for her, she decided.

* * *

Later, with the sun sinking slowly into the ocean, they sat around the campfire, listening to the comforting, crackling undercurrent as the waves lapped the shore beyond. Mika had pulled a cushion up for her, and he sat close, so close she felt forced to keep her hands in her lap while his brother and their friends roasted hot dogs and s'mores on command. What if that stupid muscle memory took over again, and she held his hand or something?

Anela giggled with a little girl, elbows in the sand, playing a game with shells and cards, and Lani watched her with a smile. This was the first time the little girl hadn't seemed cautious about being on the beach. She told Mika so.

"Okay, so she didn't paddle earlier, when the others did, but she is loving this. Look, she's not worried at all."

"Good," he said, smiling warmly, first at Anela, then at her. His eyes glowed in the firelight, so familiar, but still, he looked like a stranger, more handsome now than he had ever been. She found herself so lost in his eyes that she barely noticed when someone waved a ukulele at her.

"Come on, Lani, it's your turn."

Lani groaned and looked around. Shadows danced on their faces as they egged her on; she should have known this was coming. Even Anela stood up to clap in encouragement.

"All right, all right!"

Drawing the ukulele onto her lap, she shot one bashful glance at Mika, who just shrugged, a huge smile on his face. Her fingers worked the strings on autopilot, a Hawaiian folk tune that everyone knew the words to. Sure enough, soon their voices lit up the dusk and the sparks rose to the sky and burst there, scattering red stars above them. One song wasn't enough, it seemed.

"Play one of yours," Mika encouraged.

"One of mine?"

"You know the one I like best," he teased, and she almost refused. Except everyone was cheering for it now. Reluctantly at first, she started to play, and as Mika sung along, like he always had done to this tune, she found she had tears in her eyes suddenly, which she couldn't quite wipe away fast enough at the end.

Mika took the ukulele from her and held it high.

"Ladies and gentlemen, Lani Kekoa Mahoe!" he roared to rapturous applause.

Lani's smile faded on the spot. Lani Kekoa *Mahoe*? She wasn't a Mahoe, not anymore. Why did he say that?

He caught her look, and shrugged again, slightly apologetically after seeing her face. She got to her feet as a couple of others did the same; it was bedtime for the kids. Time for her go.

"I should take Anela home," she said as Mika stood with her.

He frowned, searching her eyes. Already someone else was playing ukulele, but she felt more than a little uncomfortable now if she was honest…maybe because he'd called her a Mahoe. Maybe because she'd been starting to feel a little too relaxed. This was too nice, too familiar, but soon Mika would be gone again, back to his high-flying Cali-career, and she didn't really know how to go about having all of this without him. She'd worked so hard for her dream job, she couldn't be anywhere else. And Mika had worked just as hard over there. She couldn't exactly ask him to give up his whole life and move back to Oahu.

"I shouldn't still be here," she told him, calling Anela. The girl was engrossed in a card game, ignoring her.

"Yes, you should," he said firmly.

"I don't even have nightclothes for…"

"I made a bed for Anela in the red tepee. There are spare pajamas on the pillow."

They had tents set up close by for the children, same as every year. It was the annual tradition to camp on the beach on the night of the luau. Long after the kids went to bed, tucked up in their little tepees with their friends, the adults stayed up talking and playing music around the campfire. They'd slept in those tents themselves as kids and she still remembered the first time they'd been allowed to stay up and join in around the fire. It was such a great vibe, but…no.

"I can't."

"Why not? You can't drag her away now. You just said she's starting to feel okay about being by the ocean—maybe this is just what she needs."

"How do you know what she needs?" she retorted, annoyed at being put on the spot.

Mika's face fell, then grew dark as thunder.

"I'm sorry. I didn't mean it to come out like that," she said quickly, but he dug his toes into the sand and shifted on his feet, his mouth a thin line.

"Maybe I don't," he said, and his voice carried a gravitas that turned her stomach. "But you and I still need to talk about some things, don't you think?"

CHAPTER ELEVEN

MAHINA FOUND HIM as he took his place by the fire again. Lani was still putting Anela to bed. The kid had insisted on sleeping in a different teepee with her new friend Kiki, the little red-haired girl who'd taught her the coconut bowling game. He'd stopped himself from getting involved.

"So, you and Lani looked serious back there," Mahina ventured, resting her leg out on the sand in front of her.

Mika bristled, dragging a stick through the sand. His brother was making up some song on the ukulele now, which should be making him laugh but all he could think about now was how Lani had reacted just then, how he knew *nothing* about what a child might need. She was right but it had stung.

"You okay?" Mahina nudged him and he grunted.

"Sorry," he said, glancing at the tents again. He could hear giggling, a couple of kids singing, a pair of feet he guessed were Anela's sticking out of an awning. It was weird, how much he wanted to walk over there and check things were all right—none of them were his children. It was just that

Lani was bustling around, scolding Anela laughingly for lying down with her shoes on…acting just like a mother. In another world, one where they hadn't lost Iolana, he'd be doing those kinds of things, too. He'd be a pro at it by now. Instead, he was pretty much redundant.

"How are your injuries now?" he heard himself say.

"Better." She nodded. "I'm more concerned about you and Lani. How is it going, working at the sanctuary…um…together?"

Mika told her about the petrel, the sea lions and the turtles, and how they were still gathering data and intel on what could be affecting the dolphins. Mahina tried to seem interested, despite the disappointment on her face. She wanted to know all the things he would not be telling her, of course.

"We're going to be fine," he said on a sigh, as if that should cover it. She pressed an empathetic hand to his arm, just as Lani appeared again.

"What's going to be fine?" she asked, adjusting the straps on her dress. She looked just as good in sundresses as she always had, better even than she had with her long lean legs on display in her Daisy Dukes.

"Everything is going to be fine," Mahina enthused with a smirk in her direction.

Mika got to his feet, and motioned for Lani to walk with him.

"What did you tell her? Did you tell her we

kissed?" she said quickly, stopping him on the shoreline.

He almost laughed. "What? No, why would I do that?"

Lani shrugged, flushing. "It looked like you were talking about something… Why did she say everything is going to be fine?"

"Maybe because she picked up on…" He wiggled his finger between them. "I don't know—this! But I didn't tell her anything. That kiss was between *us*."

"Us," Lani whispered, her gaze firmly fixed on the ocean.

His heart felt heavy and his stomach churned with apprehension. Letting himself kiss her, unwrapping all those emotions they'd both tried so hard to suppress, had been a mistake. But it didn't mean he wasn't constantly thinking about it every time he saw her. In fact, the more he thought about it now, it felt kind of *good* to unwrap some of it with her, after all this time. He'd started it, back in her kitchen. Fake confidence was carrying him through.

"You were right before. Neither of us knew how to be parents back then. We didn't even really know how to be married. There was so much we could have said, but we didn't and…"

"Yet here we are now," she finished. "Saying it."

"Exactly."

Lani kept her eyes on the sea, and he reached for her hand.

"I might not know what Anela needs—you were right about that, too—but it doesn't escape my attention that you're a great mother figure, Lani. In case you ever had any doubts about that. I've said it before, but I could never do what you do, and I think we both know that."

Lani looked at him, her expression furrowed. "But you were an amazing father."

The look in her eyes made his throat contract—was she serious?

"What?" she pressed.

Conflicted, Mika dropped her hand, and continued walking along the sand. He'd openly told her not to play the blame game, but it didn't mean he didn't berate himself daily for putting his career before his family so many times.

"Mika, what?"

"I was a terrible dad. I was hardly there," he said, his voice strained.

"You did what you had to do. You were trying to provide for us, and protect me, too. I always knew you loved me."

The stars were out now, twinkling above the sparks from the fire. They said nothing for a moment as he processed her words. She always knew he loved her. It didn't mean she'd always loved him back.

"What happened with Hayley?" she asked, stopping to face him again.

He felt the folds of her sundress flit about his own ankles in the breeze as he fought for the right words. He should have known she would ask eventually.

"I thought you were happy together," she continued. "Two years, wasn't it?"

He shrugged again, frowning.

Lani sighed. "She wanted your babies, didn't she?" she said, eyeing him closely. He pulled his gaze away, then crouched to his haunches, where a tiny ghost crab was scuttling for the shoreline.

"How did you know?" he asked gruffly.

"Mika, she's only what, twenty-eight, twenty-nine…?"

"Thirty-five next week, but why does it matter?"

"I'm right, aren't I?" she said softly. "And… you said no?"

"What do you *think* I said?" He stood and this time, Lani caught his hands. "You don't even want me around Anela after what I…after what happened to our child, and I can't say I blame you."

Lani's eyes widened. "Is that what you think?"

He screwed up his nose. "It doesn't matter. I don't want *any more* kids in my life, Lani."

Lani shut her mouth, and Mika kicked himself. What he really wanted to say was that he didn't want, and had never wanted, children with anyone *except* her, and he never would, and not just because he wouldn't be able to trust himself with the responsibility a second time. She'd been the love of his life, and he'd totally screwed it all up. He wasn't there when Iolana needed him, and then he'd walked out on their marriage, scuppering the chance for them to have another baby together. How could he even think about having someone else's child after everything *they'd* been through?

Lani was talking again. "I just meant I don't want you thinking Anela's your responsibility. I know she needs a lot of energy and time, and you're busy..."

Mika barely heard the words coming from her mouth; all he heard was that he'd never really been, and never would be, a father. Not the kind Lani needed to have around for her foster kid, if she needed anyone now at all. She was filling two parental roles all by herself and she was doing just fine. More than fine.

"Mika?" she said. "Are you listening?"

He was about to respond when a scream cut through the silence like glass. They turned to each other. *Anela?*

They both rushed as fast as their feet could carry them, back to the tepee. Lani tore at the zip and stuck her head inside, and he pulled it farther open. Inside, Anela was clearly having a terrible nightmare and shouting in her sleep, her face contorted with fear and confusion, tears streaming down her cheeks. Lani shot straight to her side, stroking her hair and murmuring softly, while Mika looked on, his heart aching for them both. He wanted to go to Lani and wrap his arms around her—around both of them. It had become instinctive again now, whether it was right or not, but he held back as Lani leaned over Anela's small body and scooped her up into a hug.

"It's okay, darling," she whispered soothingly into the little girl's ear, rocking her back and forth in the darkness. "It was just a dream."

Kiki, the other child in the tent, was stirring now, sitting up in confusion. Mika turned around, ran back to the trestle tables and grabbed up his backpack, digging out the tissues as he hurried back and handed Lani the small pack. His heart went out to Anela as Lani mopped her tears, but what had him in a stranglehold now was the love emanating from Lani. He hadn't seen such love since she'd held Iolana for the first time. Without thinking, he reached into the bag again and brought out some sheets of paper. He hadn't shown anyone yet, but this was as good a time as any.

"Does anyone want to hear a little story?" he asked.

Lani looked up, still wiping away Anela's tears. Mika cleared his throat and began reading from the papers he was holding, and she could hardly believe what was coming from his mouth, or the fact that far from showing fear now, Anela's eyes had started to shine with excitement and wonder.

> "The dolphin swam in circles, crying out 'Help me!'
> She was stuck on a hook, and she couldn't break free.
> This was no fun, and her face hurt so bad.
> But with no hands to help, it just made her sad."

At that part Anela and Kiki both giggled. "Dolphins should have hands," Anela exclaimed, wiggling her fingers. Mika carried on.

> "The creatures crept closer, a crab with big claws
> Started pulling and tugging, and yanking her jaws.
> The octopus, even with eight gentle limbs,
> Could do nothing to stop the big hook digging in.
> The dolphin was trembling. Was this her fate?
> To be hooked like a fish, maybe served on a plate?"

"No! The poor dolphin," Kiki cried now, inching closer so she could see what was written as Mika was reading it. He shot a look at Lani and she encouraged him on. Okay, so it wasn't exactly

Wordsworth or Keats, but he'd tried his best and she could almost imagine the illustrations already.

> "Two divers approached her with four helpful hands.
> They got to work quickly, disentangling the bands.
> With steady resolve, they worked with great care,
> To ease the big hook and relieve its cruel snare.
> The dolphin was grateful, she stayed really still.
> These humans were helping her, humans had skill!
> Through their patience and smartness, they figured it out.
> 'Thank you, oh, thank you,' she wanted to shout.
> Released from her torment, the dolphin swam free,
> And went back to roaming the beautiful sea."

Mika put the notebook down. "I need another new verse. Something about how she became friends with those humans and told all the other creatures not to be afraid of them anymore." He looked tentatively at Anela, and Lani followed his eyes, realizing she'd been staring only at him the whole time, thinking what a shame it would be if they couldn't find someone to illustrate it.

"She also needs to prove that even the scariest creatures in the ocean are all just trying to live in peace," she suggested.

"Even sharks?" Kiki piped up. She was still watching and listening intently, propped up on one elbow. "My mom says you swim with sharks, Mr. Mika, and that you're friends with one."

Oh, no. Lani held her breath.

Anela shook her head and creased her forehead in disagreement, but her voice was soft as she pulled away from Lani to lie back down on the pillow. "People can't be friends with sharks."

"They can, when they understand them," Lani said tactfully, and she knew Mika could tell she was seizing the moment to make their case. How bad she felt now, knowing he'd assumed she'd been keeping him away from Anela because she didn't trust him around children.

"I know sometimes it's hard to believe, but sharks make mistakes, too," he tried, looking at her for reassurance. "Most of the time, they're trying to figure things out, just like we are," he added.

"I guess…everyone just wants to keep the ocean a safe place," Anela mumbled eventually through a yawn. "We all need to care for it, and everything in it," she added, as her eyes fluttered closed again. "My mom loved sharks."

Carefully, when both girls were silent again, Lani crept out of the teepee, Mika close behind. Halfway back to the campfire she stopped him.

"Your children's story…" she started, and he stifled a groan.

"I know, it needs work. It was just a few notes really."

"But I get what you're trying to do, Mika. This is exactly what you always said you wanted to do—educate kids about the ocean, in a way they can relate to, that connects them emotionally… Anela never told me her mother loved sharks before."

"A love that killed her," he added grimly, and she nodded, looking away.

"Probably nothing will come of the book," he said, walking on with her. At the fire, a few people without kids were getting up to leave already, including Mahina, but Lani stopped again. She felt rooted to the spot, her feet digging deeper into the sand, the moonlight dimming the color of her toenails.

"I'm happy you told them your story," she said sincerely, and he frowned into the distance.

"You don't think I was butting in?"

"Why would I think you were butting in?" She studied his face, the reflections of the firelight in his eyes, the shadows playing on his face, and her heart went out to him, remembering what he'd said earlier. He didn't think he could do what she was doing, and she knew the reasons why. She pressed a palm to his cheek without thinking, forced him to look at her.

"You were an amazing father to Iolana," she reaffirmed, in case he hadn't heard her earlier. "I was the one who..."

No. She forced her mouth shut. What was the point of blaming herself yet again? They'd covered this already, and it had gotten them nowhere. They were finally in a place where they could at least talk about the mistakes they'd both made, even if it seemed to be bringing other things back to the surface, too. Things she had no place revisiting—because his life wasn't even on the island anymore!

His hand came up over hers, and the heat made the pulsing start deep inside her, like a kettle flipped to boil.

"You might have started her thinking differently about the ocean, you know," she said, trying to keep her voice steady. "Thank you. I mean, I wouldn't give up your day job to write poetry, but at least you know your audience."

Mika huffed a laugh. His broad chest rumbled with the sound as he pulled her closer and pressed the back of her hand to his heart.

"Woman, you'll be the death of me," he growled, and for a moment the party fell away again.

Time stopped. Lani held her breath as she saw her entire childhood and young adult life flash before her eyes, a thousand memories all at once, all the nights they'd made love on the sand, and in one of those very tepees more times than once. Her cheeks turned hot as he looked at her, and her blood raced to places it hadn't been to in ages. A wild intensity shone in his eyes as he urged her hips against his and focused on her mouth, leaning closer…and closer…

"Mika! Lani! Come here!"

They sprang apart. Lani's heart beat wildly in her chest and throat, half from the urgency in Mahina's voice as they started to run and half from what just happened. What was she thinking? She'd got swept up in the memories again, in the way he'd opened up to her and then helped Anela after her nightmare. That could not happen again, no way, and anyway, he was probably just missing Hayley. Yes, that was it; he was missing the company and the attention, someone, God forbid, making love to him at night… Of course, why wouldn't he?

Well, she was not going to be sucked right back into that, only to miss him all over again when he left. He didn't want kids in his life—he'd said as much—and part of her plan had always been to have children, to foster them, nurture them, watch them grow, the way she'd never been able to witness Iolana doing. She'd even been thinking seriously about adopting Anela.

As for her, from now on, outside of work she

was going to be a Mika-free zone, she decided firmly. But her heart was a wild bird in her chest as she followed him and Mahina to the parking lot.

CHAPTER TWELVE

"THAT BIKE," MAHINA SAID, pointing to a motorbike on the gravel path by the parked cars at the top end of the beach. "That's the one that forced me off the road!"

"How do you know?" Mika asked, walking over to inspect it.

"I recognize that yellow thing on the side."

He listened as Mahina explained to a few onlookers how the accident happened again, how she'd caught a glimpse of this very bike before it had torn right past her. Lani was at his side now, inspecting the yellow sticker, and he found himself stepping back, crossing his arms over himself. It was a lucky thing that Mahina had interrupted that…whatever that had been back there. A moment? He and Lani seemed to be having too many moments like that lately.

Okay, so most were probably in his head, but either way, it wasn't wise. He should not be hitting on his ex-wife! What was wrong with him? As if stirring up the past and how he'd failed her wasn't uncomfortable enough, now he was on track for rejection, too—she didn't need him anymore.

"Kalama Tours," Lani said, touching a finger to the logo on the bike. "I know of Kai Kalama. He's pretty new in town. He runs the motorized kayak company here, came over from Maui."

"Are you sure it was this bike?" she asked Mahina.

Mahina was adamant.

"I'll go around there tomorrow," Mika stated.

Lani looked as horrified as Mahina. "And say what?"

"Can I help you?" The voice, coming from behind them, made them all turn around to see a bulky guy approaching. He was tall with wild hair and the kind of wide, gym-honed chest and shoulders like spoke of hours lifting weights… or people?

It was Lani who stepped forward.

"Kai Kalama," she said, eyeing him warily.

He was wearing a wet suit, carrying a surfboard, like he'd ridden the last sunset waves and stayed out under the moon, maybe watching their party.

Mika's instincts were primed. Something about this guy set him on edge.

"We think you ran my friend here off the road," Lani said, pointing to Mahina's leg.

Kai looked down his nose at her, which annoyed Mika further, and went about strapping his board to the side of the bike.

"If I did, I'm sorry but I don't remember." He

had the sort of slight half smile now that said he was both amused by and undaunted by them, which put Mika's back up more, though he said nothing. It wouldn't do to step on their toes.

"You did. It was you," Mahina insisted.

"I said I don't remember," he replied tightly.

"The least you can do is apologize," Lani said now.

Kai's jaw moved from side to side as he looked between them. "You run the Mermaid Cove Marine Sanctuary, right?" he said.

"Yes, we've met, briefly," Lani replied.

Another long silence, before Kai frowned darkly. "Someone called me about coming to collect some kind of sample tomorrow, from the beach outside my kayak warehouse. Looking for a chemical match?"

Mika explained it was probably one of his people, looking into what was harming the dolphins in the area.

Kai looked even more infuriated, and straddled his bike seat. "Tell them not to bother, I don't have time tomorrow. And I don't have anything to do with any dolphins."

Before Mika could even reply that the site checks of local businesses like Kai's were mandatory in the eyes of the marine conservation department, Kai revved up the bike and sped off without so much as a glance behind him.

"Charming," Mahina muttered, brushing the sand from her arms and clothes.

She and Lani went back to talking, and Mika watched the road after Kai, noting how he'd sped away so fast. Something told him Kai Kalama was definitely the kind of guy who'd run a woman off the road, and if he could do that unashamedly and deny it, what else was he capable of doing?

The sanctuary was strangely quiet the next afternoon when Mika walked in, trying and failing to stifle a yawn. Most of the party had stayed up till sunrise talking and playing songs, and he'd had a good time; apart from the obvious tension in the air between himself and Lani. They'd danced around the fact that they'd almost kissed again, managed to talk to everyone but each other till she'd extracted Anela from the tepee at six o'clock and taken her home with barely a wave in his direction. Awkward.

Still, he wouldn't dwell on it. He had more important things to think about, like what made Kalama Tours so special that Kai felt it should be excluded from the site checks. Every establishment in the bay had given them the okay. He had every intention of going around there himself if Kai didn't comply today. He'd also had a call from his colleague Megan back in California. They were due at a stakeholders' briefing for the Safe-Coast Guardian Project, part of a global study to help track whether shark behavior was being influenced by sea surface temperatures, and he was starting to feel guilty for taking so much time out. His role was a pivotal one; there were things only he could implement and manage.

"Mika, how did you sleep after you got back?" Lani asked when he walked in, but her voice was muffled somewhat by the huge albatross she was leaning over.

"I got a few hours," he replied. "How is Anela today?" He couldn't shake the look on her face after that nightmare; his heart had broken for her.

"She's fine. She's reading the book you gave her out on the deck," she said, distractedly.

"My shark book?"

Lani shrugged. "She said she slept really well after your story last night, and then she picked your book back up."

"Wow." Mika felt the tiniest jolt of pride, which was quickly stamped out when he saw the expression on Lani's face. She'd put a wall up between them last night and she was keeping it there. He knew that look.

"I've just done the preoperative assessment," Lani told him, all business as he approached the albatross, looking for any clear signs of illness or injury. It looked a little lopsided and he suspected a wing injury. She threw him some gloves.

"It looks like he's healthy overall, but the X-rays show he does have a fractured wing. It's a clean break, but we'll need to stabilize it," she said, confirming his suspicions.

Mika set about carefully administering the anesthetic while Lani finished the surgical prep, and neither of them uttered a word as she made the incision. This one would be mostly Lani, who had mastered the specialized avian surgical techniques he himself had little experience with. The whole time he moved around her, he felt that almost-kiss hovering in the air, like the spirit of the sedated bird. She was thinking about it, too, he could tell. But she wasn't going to bring it up, which meant she wished it hadn't happened. As did he.

Didn't he? This was all messing with his head; too many emotions came tangled up in Lani.

"Right. We'll want antibiotics to prevent infection, analgesics for pain relief, and could you set up the anti-inflammatories," she said as she readied the bird for the recovery room. By the time the meds from her well-organized cabinet were administered, and the cage door was locked behind them, he couldn't stand it any longer.

"What's going on, Lani?"

"Nothing," she said too quickly, turning her back to him and checking on a couple of other patients in the cages.

Mika pressed his lips together. He couldn't read her at all. One minute she was open and warm and the Lani he used to know, and the next she was an island he couldn't reach. He watched her check on the turtle and three birds, then followed her out back to check on Lilo and Stitch, who were now coming on in leaps and bounds and were due to leave them soon, but she was refusing to look at him. Anela looked up from her place on the egg-shaped chair hanging from a chain on the ceiling. She was indeed reading his book.

"Hi," she said, looking over the pages with a frown. "Mika, was she right?"

"Who?" he asked.

"My friend Kiki, when she said you swim with sharks and that you're friends with one?"

He felt his eyebrows shoot up to his bandanna. "Er…yes? That is kind of true."

Anela looked at him a moment in interest, then promptly went back to reading. It registered suddenly that she was *still* reading a book about sharks, and asking him about them, too.

But the thought was fleeting; Lani was putting him on edge. Eventually, back inside, he caught her arm, forcing her to stop in her tracks.

"It keeps happening," he said, his words heavier than he'd intended, his mouth brushing her ear and making her freeze. "This need to kiss you."

She released the breath she'd been holding in, and her answer came out small, guarded. "I know, but it's just because it *used* to happen…and you miss Hayley."

Mika almost laughed as he released her; he hadn't been thinking about Hayley at all.

Lani tutted and walked back inside. She went about filling in some paperwork, putting the desk between them. "I don't blame you if you miss her. She's younger, she's beautiful, she's…"

"She's not in my life anymore," he interrupted, taking a stand in front of the desk. "And she has *nothing* to do with what's going on here," he said, flattening his hands on the table so hard the lamp on it shook.

"There's nothing going on here, Mika," she said carefully, still unable to meet his eyes. "You're a good man, and I appreciate what you're doing for Anela, but please…let's not confuse the situation."

Mika moved the lamp across and leaned over the desk, trying not to feel the jellyfish sting of her brush-off. "The situation, Lani, is that we are both trying to figure out how to be around each other after all this time, and it doesn't help when you shut me out."

Lani stood taller, the glint in her eyes a warning sign. "Oh, really? Well, it didn't help me much when you shut me out, either, after Iolana died, back when I *needed* you."

"We needed each other, Lani, we failed each *other*, we've been over this."

Lani shook her head vehemently now. "You were the love of my life, Mika. But I struggled so much, thinking I was a bad mother, and I was so worried that with your work and my studies, nothing would change. Even if we'd stayed together and had another baby..."

Mika stepped closer, swept her chin up and forced her to face him. "You wanted another baby, with me?"

Lani stuttered in his stare, and her eyes filled with tears. "I don't know...maybe. Eventually. It doesn't matter now, though, does it? We live different lives, in different states."

"I should have fought harder for us," he said quickly, as his heart raced. "I will regret not fighting for our marriage for the rest of my life."

Lani sank back down into the chair, her head in her hands.

"I want to go to the cemetery," he said next, watching the sun fall over her bowed head. "I think I need to, Lani." The words were out before he could even think. Just the thought of seeing that tiny gravestone, the glossy marble covered in flowers from every single member of his family who'd made a continuous effort to keep it a living shrine... "Did you make up your mind yet, to come with me?" he added hopefully.

She sniffed and shook her head. "I still don't know. It would be too hard...both of us there. It's hard enough going on my own."

Mika shut his mouth before he could tell her it might help. It wouldn't help his case, though. Forcing her to confront it all, dredging up the past, was everything he'd sworn he wouldn't do; she had to want to do it herself.

He turned his head to the window, expecting to see the little girl still sitting on the egg chair, reading his book. But she wasn't there.

"Oh," he exclaimed now, making Lani follow his eyes.

"She's on the beach on her own," Lani said, eyes wide as she stepped back outside.

The sky was darker now, a hint of the storm they'd been warned about on the news this morning seemed to be gathering on the horizon, but the clouds weren't what Lani was looking at as she made her way down to the sand.

Anela was inches from the shoreline. Mika sat on the bottom step, watching Lani shake off her sandals and step into the frothy surf, her shapely legs still the same…maybe not quite as firm as they had been once, wrapped around him on the sand, seventeen, hungry for him.

She still looked so good like this, he mused with a sigh. They'd always said they'd grow old and gray and let it all hang out, and fill that big house out by the beach with animals and laughter. Now look at them. Worlds apart. Which reminded him, he should probably let the institute know he might need another week or two off. Had he really been out here almost three weeks already?

"Come, Mika," Anela called, and he stood as

the little girl jumped up and down. "Look, Lani found a starfish!"

He stood beside her and shook off his shoes, striding out into the water next to Lani. They crouched down to where the starfish was shimmering below the surface at their feet.

"It's beautiful," Lani gushed.

"You can't see it properly from over there," he said now, feeling Lani's eyes on his face and letting the warm water wash over his calves. Thunder rumbled ominously in the distance behind the gray clouds, but the sun was still glinting off the water and Anela peered closer, her bare feet barely skimming the shoreline. A wave threatened to wash over her toes and she stepped back, but her body arched over the water and he knew she badly wanted to see what they were looking at.

"One more step, and you'll be able to see it," he encouraged. "You don't want to miss this. The tide will take it away again in a minute."

Lani touched his arm a second and he met her eyes. Was he pushing her too hard?

"Come, Anela, quick," she encouraged next, and he could hardly believe it when Anela gave a huge, exaggerated sigh and stepped across the shoreline into the surf. He took her hand quickly, as Lani reached for the other.

"It's okay," he said as Anela studied the water swishing around her feet, as if it might re-form into a sea beast and swallow her up—who could blame her mind for taking her there?

Lani squeezed her other hand, encouraging her closer, till they were crouching in the shallows, studying the starfish together. Anela's eyes grew wide with delight as he lifted the creature gently and placed it in her hand; she seemed so fascinated by what she was looking at that she was barely registering the fact that she was standing almost knee-high in the water now.

"Thank you," Lani mouthed at him, and Mika bobbed his head. The moment of understanding between them swelled in his chest and made his heart beat faster and seemed to blow all their own problems clean away.

The wind was picking up now, though. The smell of rain hung heavily in the atmosphere as a few drops began to fall, stinging his skin like tiny needles.

"We should go," he said, and they put the starfish back in its watery world, just as the sound of a car horn honked from the front of the sanctuary. Kiki and her mom were here to collect Anela for a play date, and he and Lani still had work to do. Hopefully this storm would blow over quick enough, he thought, as another crash of thunder made them all run faster, laughing as they sped toward the steps.

CHAPTER THIRTEEN

LANI GRIMACED, YANKING another window closed as the guy on the radio announced the latest weather report. "They've upgraded the storm to a hurricane!" she called out to Mika. He was dashing between moving the outdoor cages inside and bringing the cushions in from the deck. The humidity was intense at the best of times, but now it was stifling outside.

"Quick, we need to get everything in," she told him, and he wasted no time in his duties as the rain started pelting the windows so hard she thought they might break.

At one point they crashed into each other and a box of animal feed almost went flying before he caught it, and a loud rumble, followed by a bolt of lightning, made him rush to the window.

"It doesn't look good," he announced, adjusting his crooked bandanna as they watched a deck chair tumble down the steps and dance across the beach.

Pressed to his shoulder at the glass, she became acutely aware of his breathing, his closeness, every steady inch of him at her side as they watched the storm whipping the ocean into a fury of churning whitecaps and salty foam. The deck chair disappeared from view and she pictured the poor starfish. Hadn't it been through enough, getting picked up by curious humans, then placed back into an ocean resembling a washing machine?

Still, she would never forget that moment, watching Anela walk into the water for the first time. It would never have happened without Mika.

I will regret not fighting for our marriage for the rest of my life.

His words had struck her deeply. They'd caused each other so much turmoil, and she felt the same way exactly. But he was here now, and sometimes, she caught herself imagining him staying here.

Of course, he wasn't going to give up the life he'd cultivated over the last two decades without her, and if he didn't want kids in his life, there was no point even going down that path. But it didn't mean she wasn't thinking of a whole new bunch of what-ifs, despite their frequent blowups. He always had challenged her, and she him, and she'd missed that a lot; everything with Mika had always felt like an adventure. Much of her life had seemed pretty stagnant when he'd stopped being in it.

They went about moving what they could from the rain-lashed deck into the storeroom, but Lilo and Stitch would have to stay where they were. She kept stealing looks at Mika in his rain-soaked shirt, getting increasingly wetter. That almost-kiss the other night had thrown her. Her heart was all over the place, wanting to make up for lost time. She should at least go with him to the cemetery, she thought now, catching his eyes on her from across the room before he bolted another window behind the petrel closed. The thought of it was agonizing. She hadn't been in a long time. Too long.

"Mika, about what you said before," she started. "Maybe we *should* go..."

"Hell!" he yelled over her as the lights above them flickered and abruptly went off. "The power's out!"

Lani's heart began to race as the darkness enveloped them, accentuated by the howl of the wind and the whiplash of rain on the deck and windows. The birds were all squawking and flapping their wings and she worried about them exacerbating their injuries, never mind overheating without the air-conditioning.

"They just said this could last all night," she said, pressing her hands to her head, trying to think. "The birds and smaller animals, we need to get them out of here. The animals in the larger tanks will be fine."

She turned to Mika, who'd taken the stressed-out petrel from its cage and was cradling it, and for a moment she was stunned into silence at the way it quietened in his gentle arms.

"We could take them to the house?" he suggested.

"Should we drive in this?" Lani gestured to the door which was all but bending inwards from the force of the wind and rain.

Mika shrugged. "Four-wheel drive," he said simply, and she bit back a laugh. "It's not far, we can manage," he assured her.

Oh, he was serious, then?

The two of them got to work, quick as they could. The storm seemed to be intensifying, and every time she raced outside with a cage and placed it carefully into the vehicle, Lani felt her heartbeat in her throat. Finally, after what felt like far too long, Mika started to drive carefully through the storm, winding up the hill to her house.

By now it was pouring heavier than ever and lightning split the sky open overhead. She gripped the dash with both hands as the birds cried out. Thunder roared above them like a stampede of wild horses. Branches snapped from trees and streetlamps seemed to sway eerily, although it was probably just her eyes, she reasoned, adjusting to the chaos. Mika was calm, and she appreciated his strength, how it calmed her. Her heart swelled with the knowledge that he was willing to do this for her, for the birds and the other animals, despite the tension that clogged the air whenever they were alone. She'd never got to actually tell him she would go to the cemetery with him back there, and now she'd chickened out again. It would be too hard.

Gosh, what was this? One minute she felt able to face their past and their mistakes together, and the next she was drowning in a well of confusion and pain and panic; there was no set way to feel around Mika, she thought now. He was the storm. No, *they* were the storm, blowing around in a thousand directions except for the one that might just offer them the safety and comfort they needed.

Why would she not go with him to see Iolana's grave? It was all for her own selfish fears of being sucked right back into that well of grief alongside him! She owed him this much. She would tell him she would go with him…later, she decided.

When they arrived at Lani's home, thankfully the power was on and the air-conditioner was working just fine. They unloaded the cages as fast as they could, piling them into the kitchen until the counters were overloaded with birds and turtles and the place looked more like a zoo than a place for prepping Anela's dinner.

"Poor little buddy," she heard Mika say as he opened the cage to the petrel again. The bird had been healing so well that they were almost at re-release stage but now it looked sorrowful and its wing was hanging limply again.

"She got scared, I heard her flapping about whenever the thunder struck," Mika told her, holding it still in his arms again, checking the rest of it carefully for obvious signs of injury. Outside on the porch, the hammock was swaying wildly and the door to the shed slammed the wooden wall again and again. In the distance, at the bottom of the hill, a siren wailed ominously.

"We need to stabilize her wing," Mika said, crossing to the kitchen table. Giving low hums of reassurance, they checked along the bones of its wing. The petrel was clearly in shock and Lani was moved, noting the extra care Mika took, even as the windows shook, as if trying to distract him from the task. Lani had packed supplies, so it didn't take long before a minute dose of anesthetic had stilled the bird further and she'd resecured the wing with a tiny splint.

She was just carrying it back to its cage when another sound found her ears—the tiniest meow, coming from somewhere outside.

"Did you hear that?" Mika was at the door in seconds, and she fastened the petrel's cage shut, following him outside.

Chairs were strewed all over the place and as if she wasn't wet enough already, the rain came at her in a soggy assault that almost threw her to her knees. Mika put an arm out, stepping in front of her.

"Get back inside," he instructed.

"No, I think one of the kittens is trapped somewhere," she said, grabbing his arm as another gust of wind almost lifted her off the floor. A tiny, harrowed meow came at them again, louder this time.

"She's close, Mika."

Mika's hand clamped over hers and held it tight. "I think she's under the shed!"

They followed the sound, despite every instinct in her body telling her to get back into the house. No animal would suffer, not on her watch!

Eventually, they located the kitten, but they couldn't see it. Getting to her knees, Lani peered under the shed, but the path of fallen branches and blinding rain meant she couldn't see where it was exactly in order to reach it. Mika started heaving the debris away, his clothing stuck to his skin. Her hair plastered like glue to her own face as she helped, praying no more branches would fall on them. The kitten was now meowing constantly in terror and panic.

"Hold on, little one," she urged, as they discussed how best to get it out. Then Lani spotted an old tarp that usually covered the barbecue, on the other side of the deck. "Help me," she said, but she didn't need to. Mika was already on it.

Together they draped it over the area, creating a makeshift shelter that would protect them while they focused on moving the rest of the branches away from the shed.

"We need to move faster," she urged, panting and soaked, and Mika tugged at heavy pieces of timber while she tried coaxing the kitten out with food and gentle words. It was too scared to even try.

With one last tug of effort from Mika, enough of a gap opened up for Lani to squeeze through. She was about to dive under the shed, but Mika caught her elbow.

"Be careful," he said, and his eyes blazed with caution and reluctance to let her go, so much so that a powerful surge of an emotion she couldn't define caught her completely off guard.

Before she could hold herself back, she pressed her lips to his, breathing him in and letting his warmth flood right though her, right before turning back and crawling into the tiny, suffocating space.

Her lips burned from the wind and the kiss but she kept on crawling. A tiny yelp rose in a desperate plea from the kitten. Lani scrambled closer and sorted through what remained, moving twigs and leaves with her hands, digging deeper into the mud until she could see it; a little ball of fur shaking in fear.

"Can you see it?" Mika called out behind her.

"Yes!"

The nearest branch was still trapping it beneath its weight. Carefully, Lani moved around it and scooped up the kitten in her arms. It was wet and trembling, tiny meows escaping from its mouth as it clung desperately on to her shirt for reassurance. She scrambled backward with it, putting all her weight on her knees and one arm so as not to drop it, and Mika hurried to move the last of the debris away from the entrance. When she was finally back on her knees outside, he huddled in close, wrapping them both in his arms for a moment under the tarp.

"Is she okay? Are you?"

"Everyone's good," she said with a nervous laugh, kissing the top of the kitten's damp head as Mika pressed his own lips to the top of hers.

Lani's heart raced as she turned her face to him. He scanned her eyes and for a moment she thought he was going to kiss her, but instead he urged her up to her feet and used the tarp as a sheltering cloak as he hurried them back to the house.

The other kittens pattered over playfully to check out their thankfully unharmed sibling, giving it affectionate licks before scampering away into the sitting room, and Lani shot her eyes to Mika, who was already hurrying back from the bathroom carrying towels. Just as she put her arm out to take one, she realized she was bleeding.

"What happened?" Mika was beside her in a second.

"I must have scraped it on the branches or something..." she said, trailing off as he sat her at the table on a chair and went about inspecting her arm.

The closeness of his face and his care made her blood pulse harder; the only sounds were the wind and rain and the distant sirens, and her breath, she realized as he drew her arm closer. Lifting his eyes to hers, he pressed his mouth to her arm, just above the cut, as if kissing it better, like he used to. Warmth and love seemed to fill the room and she watched in silence as he trailed more kisses up her arm. A groan rose up in her throat, the flood of desire tingled its way around her navel, the heat spread downward to between her legs… It was all too much.

"Mika…"

"I'll get you a Band-Aid," he said, breaking away and dragging his hands through his hair.

Her heart pounded with anticipation as she heard the sound of his footsteps retreating down the hall again, and back into the bathroom. She'd only kissed him outside on an impulse, ignited by pure excitement in the midst of a storm and a kitten rescue mission, but she knew better than to let her desires get ahead of her. Of course, pursuing this was a bad idea; she already knew what the outcome would be, but, oh, *look at him.*

He'd unbuttoned his wet shirt. The damp folds of it were still stuck to his skin as he crouched at her feet on the floor and went about cleaning her scrape. She said nothing as he pressed the Band-Aid gently over her skin. He was so gentle. Like he'd always been with her, as if she were the most precious treasure, something meant to cherish. Unless she'd begged him to be rougher, she remembered with another stifled groan.

"Mika," she said again, daring to touch a hand to his hair. His gaze rose from her arm to her eyes, and he brushed away a strand of her hair that had come undone from her clip.

"Are you all right?" He frowned.

She nodded, not trusting her voice to say anything else as her heart hammered in her chest. He reached out his other hand and gently cupped hers, his fingers caressing hers lightly. And then with a deep sigh that told her this was getting too much for him to handle, he got up off the floor and stood in front of her.

"I should really get going," he said, with a faint air of reluctance. She swallowed.

"You can't go yet. Look at it out there."

"But I can't stay here, Lani." The pain in his eyes seemed to scald her as his eyes roved across her face. "You know what will happen if I do."

"We said it wouldn't," she managed, closing her eyes.

"We shouldn't," he said, but his voice was strangled.

The fire in her chest made her heart ache as he rose to his feet again and a bird let out a cry from one of the cages as the thunder cracked outside. Lani panicked. It was more than not wanting him to head out into a hurricane; she didn't want him to go yet. Far from it, she realized. Instead she wanted him even closer—for him to kiss her properly this time, like he used to—but she knew she couldn't ask for that, or expect it.

He was walking across the kitchen already, heading toward the door.

"No," she called out, as logic flew out the window. "Please stay." Her voice was trembling. "It's too dangerous for you out there."

The shrill seagulls, screaming in fury at the storm outside, seemed to highlight her words. Mika stopped frozen on the spot, before he slowly turned around to face her. She saw the way his breath had caught in his chest, the way his eyes were still heavy with so many questions, and it almost broke her not to have any answers. She would never have any answers as to why she felt this way for Mika.

The room seemed to throb with tension before she stepped forward and somehow—she would never quite know how—she was pushing him up against the door with a strength and passion she never knew still existed inside her. In seconds they were melting into one another, Mika capturing her lips in a hungry kiss. Their tongues danced and explored eagerly, and Mika's hands ran feverishly all over her body. There was no going back now.

CHAPTER FOURTEEN

THE STORM HOWLED OUTSIDE like a treacherous army trying to break inside. Lani's trembling fingers brushed against Mika's cheek, tracing the contours of his face with a delicate touch as she pulled away, staring into his eyes, asking without saying a word if they should stop yet.

No, they should not stop yet, he told her in another powerful kiss, and her hands started fumbling at his shorts.

His back was pressed against the door and he locked his mouth back to hers, cupped her backside, lifted her up, feeling her legs wrap like a vise around his middle. Sending the fruit bowl, overflowing with Mr. Benos's generous offerings, flying, he swept her onto the dining table, shooting peaches and kiwis across the tiles as she breathed hot and heavy against him, half laughing, half gasping, tearing at his shirt.

Lani's breath hitched as Mika hovered over her, his head barely missing the low-hanging wicker light. He spread her arms above her head, let his lips trail down her neck, leaving heated kisses in his wake that had her tugging her hands back and fumbling to get him out of the rest of his wet clothes as fast as possible.

Seeing him naked again, a softness fell across her features and she slowed her kisses, moaning his name and other indecipherable things that made him hot, despite the fan over the table sending cold rushes of air across his bare backside.

"I told you, you'll be the death of me," he murmured and their lips crashed back together in an urgent heat that melted away the rest of his reservations.

"Ditto."

The room was alive with electricity, and neither one of them seemed able to control it, or the intense passion now melding them together like glue. How could he have forgotten this: the taste of her skin, the silky heat of her mouth, the erotic dances her tongue could perform with his.

Mika's heart raced as Lani's fingertips slid across his skin, feeling her warmth and the gentle strokes of her palm, like she was reverently retracing her steps after all this time. Her obvious desire sent shivers down his spine. He had never felt this kind of intensity with Hayley, or anyone else, and now he'd tasted it again…well, how could he ever get enough?

His head spun, then emptied altogether as she urged him inside her and waves of pleasure swept through him with every thrust until he had to stop or it would be over too soon. She barely wanted to let him.

Lani kissed him with desperate need, hands roaming down his torso, through his hair and across his jaw as if she was wanting to take away every ounce of the pain and loneliness he'd felt since he'd left her. He'd been so bereft without her, he realized now, despite Hayley. Just his ex-wife's closeness and her touch had ignited a fire that was coursing ever hotter through his veins. He knew this could all go badly wrong; they'd built two entirely different worlds by now and he'd be left missing her while she was busy mothering Anela but…let it go wrong, he thought. To hell with it.

The melody of raindrops on the windows almost drowned out her moans. Her breath caught as he held her hips and he thought how they still fit perfectly together like they always had, as if no time had passed at all. Slowing down, he let his hands wander freely along Lani's curves, and she closed her eyes, surrendering as he rediscovered the secrets of her body.

She was perfect, he thought. With each kiss, thrust, caress, the memories cascaded through his mind, all the times they'd done this, all the places they'd done this. She was thinking the same things right now, he could tell, and it only intensified their connection as he lifted her from the table and carried her easily to the couch.

The kittens scattered and Lani gasped as he resumed his place inside her, his hand behind her head, and her back to the soft cushions. The way she clasped him again with her legs took his breath away and he realized he could watch her all day; he could find new ways to pleasure her all night. It was as if their cells were singing the exact same song… Maybe they always would, whatever came to pass between them.

Their bodies moved in sync, a dance of what felt like rekindled love and longing, and he wouldn't be able to say, later, how long they stayed there, making love. But when the storm had subsided, and he could no longer tell how many times she'd shuddered to a climax in his arms, he let her hair fall through his fingers like silk and admitted to himself that his life going forward would never be the same.

Lani almost didn't want to move when she found her eyes fluttering open on the couch. She was naked, and Mika's fingers brushed against her cheek with a tenderness that made her heart ache. If she moved, the spell would be broken. Right now, time was still frozen, and they were both still in a world where only their connection mattered, where their past wasn't ready to jump out and bite them at any moment.

The kittens were snoozing in their basket on the floor, and she sighed as Mika cupped her face and kissed her softly.

"The storm is over. You fell asleep," he murmured, and as he moved his leg over hers the electric current fizzed back into her belly and started flowing between them all over again.

Everything he did had reignited that heady, potent mix of desire and longing that had been brewing for far too long inside her, sending shivers down her spine. Clearly her body and soul wanted more. Mika's arms felt like home. Making love to him had felt like home! Her body had moved so instinctively with his she could have cried at the connection, like she had that very first time. She hadn't realized she'd missed him so much till now, but it was almost 8:00 p.m. and she had to check on Anela, and there was probably no end of damage to contend with outside.

They might have well found some kind of solace in each other's arms, but what had happened.... should *not* have happened. Now she was just getting attached again when their lives were going in opposite directions. He didn't want kids, which meant he didn't want the responsibility of raising Anela with her, and she was in this for good, for as long as she was needed, she thought, picturing the adoption papers right where she'd left them.

Begrudgingly she forced herself to move, rubbing her eyes and grabbing a blanket to cover what was left of her modesty. He didn't seem to mind what she looked like now, she thought vaguely as she excused herself for the bathroom, feeling his eyes on her as she crossed the room. And she certainly did not mind what he looked like. If anything, he looked better naked now than he had before.

"Oh," she said, turning around in the doorway.

He was already walking toward her, looking for his clothes, and he held up his hands, revealing his full naked self again and grinning.

"What?" he asked as she threw him his shorts and located his shirt from the kitchen floor.

Lani drew a deep breath. It felt like every creature they'd relocated to her kitchen was staring at them, waiting to see what happened next. A kiwi rolled across the floor when he knocked it with his foot, and she watched a kitten dart for it as he pulled on his shirt. She'd been meaning to say it, so why couldn't she say it? Chewing her lip, she almost chickened out. It would be awful, and hard, but she owed him, really, especially after they'd just connected like…that. Maybe it would help them both, if they went together.

"The cemetery. I'll go with you, Mika," she forced herself to say.

He sank to the kitchen chair, dashing his hands through his tousled hair, no bandanna in sight. Where that had gone she could only guess—she'd probably find it stuck between the sofa cushions later.

"Okay," he said after a moment, eyeing her warily. "Are you sure?"

"Maybe in a few days. I don't know what kind of damage this storm's left in its wake..."

"Whenever you want, Lani. As long as we go together, I'll let you decide when that is. But I don't have that long left here, you know that, right? I'm running out of vacation days and there are things I need to get back to... I'll have work on the dolphin case remotely."

"Okay." Lani couldn't look at him suddenly. Too many emotions were flooding her senses. With a thudding heart she closed the bathroom door behind her, and realized her hands were trembling at the thought, both of him leaving already and of going with him to Iolana's grave. She hadn't been to the cemetery in a long time and she hadn't exactly told him that. It was always too painful, always just too hard; it usually set her back on a downward spiral, doubting her abilities as a foster mother, let alone the birth mother of a toddler who'd died when she should have been there with her, watching her.

Clutching the sink, she stared at her reflection. She *would* go...but when that would be, she had no answer yet. She supposed it should be soon, though, if he was leaving them.

The weight of her choices landed like lead bars on her head. He was always going to leave; she knew that, and she'd only gone and fallen back in love with him. If she'd ever really fallen out of it.

Stepping into the shower, her mind whirled. She

could spend the time they had left avoiding all her feelings, she supposed, backing away from situations that made her uncomfortable. Or she could just surrender to every last one of them—at last—and pray she made it out the other side.

"Coffee, bro?" Mika held up the pot he'd just heated on the gas-powered stove at the sanctuary and Manu, in his blue SparkyMan work uniform, offered his cup. One thing he knew about electricians was that just like plumbers and painters and, well, marine veterinarians, they couldn't do a job without coffee. Or maybe it was just in the Mahoe blood.

"We really appreciate you getting things back up and running for us, Manu," Lani said, coming up behind him with her own cup.

Mika filled it for her and then clinked his mug to hers, resisting the urge to wrap a possessive arm around her waist.

"I know half the island lost power," she said as Manu resumed his duties with one of the units on the wall. "But the air-conditioning is vital for the animals."

"I know," Manu told her, sticking his head back out from the contraption. "Mika told me to make this one a priority."

Lani shot Mika a look of gratitude and appreciation that he tried not to overthink. Her animals were everything to her. He watched her stroke the petrel through the bars of its cage. The wing was healing nicely again, thanks to her…thanks to both of them, really. They'd been a team throughout this whole situation.

In the days since the storm, they'd been hard at work getting things back to resembling halfway normal. The sanctuary was starting to look the way it had, save for a few severed trees around the deck, which luckily had not affected Lilo and Stitch in their sea lion rehab unit. Their release had also been delayed, thanks to the storm. Most things were looking normal again…except for him and Lani.

They'd spent every night together since. Him arriving at her house after dinner, spending the night in her bed and leaving before Anela left for school. Neither had spoken much about it, or what this meant, but it had started to feel like maybe some kind of closure, before they both resumed their real lives. Even if she hadn't mentioned their visit to the cemetery since that night. He was starting to wonder if she ever would, but he wasn't about to press her.

When the phone rang, Lani was out front meeting a delivery truck, so he answered, only to find the Environment Agency rep most disgruntled over the fact that several companies on their list had now either refused their people access to their properties, or not been there when they'd called. The site tests were behind schedule anyway, no thanks to the storm and its aftermath. This was not good news.

"Surprise, surprise, your man Kai Kalama still hasn't complied," he told her when he met her in the back room, lifting heavy boxes of medical supplies and animal feed. He took a crate from her, insisting he do it himself, and she stood back, looking somewhat relieved. "How's your cut," he asked her now, motioning to the Band-Aid he'd pressed to the wound.

"Better," she said, putting a hand to it, but she looked distracted. "Why won't he let anyone in? What's he hiding? What if he's the one poisoning the dolphins?"

Mika didn't want to say it out loud, but it definitely seemed like Kai wanted to keep *something* to himself.

"Like I said before, I'm happy to go round there myself," Mika said, only for Lani to shake her head.

"Don't get involved," she said now. "We don't know him—we don't know what he might do."

Mika rolled his eyes. "You think I'm scared of some beefed-up bro in a wet suit who takes tourists out on blow-up bananas?" He flexed his muscles playfully and Lani snatched up a brochure, pretending to slap him with it. Mika laughed and grabbed her around the waist, and she mock-wrestled away from him.

"Never underestimate the power of a blow-up

banana," she laughed, batting at him again, and Mika went to snatch the brochure away.

They play-fought back and forth and Lani squealed in his arms, right until he urged her up against the refrigerator and silenced her with a kiss. She groaned against his mouth, then snatched the brochure back, and it was only then that Mika realized what he was looking at. A real estate magazine. And on the front was a photo of a house he would recognize anywhere.

"What is it?"

Mika felt his stomach drop into his shoes. He stopped wrestling with Lani immediately, standing in stunned silence as he opened the brochure. His heart drummed in silence as he stared at the image of the beach house with its painted canary yellow shutters, hugged by the beach. Lani had gone still beside him, her eyes widening in surprise as she read the accompanying text regarding recent renovation works and land potential.

"It's for sale," Lani said.

Her voice was barely a whisper over his shoulder. He could hardly speak now, either. He was thinking about all the things they planned to do in that house if this should ever happen, all the times they'd sneaked onto the private beach when they knew the owners weren't home, the night they'd snuggled together drinking whisky in the hammock on the deck and wound up so drunk they'd passed out, only to find the owners had come home and were staring at them in confusion through the kitchen window. He reminded her of this now and she reminded him of another time, when she'd set up a picnic for him on the beach under the trees, and they'd been so busy having sex that he'd squished the sandwiches.

"We were terrible," she said now.

Lani seemed to sense that he was reminiscing even more in silence. She grabbed the brochure from him and spun away, walking out front and gazing at it in silence. Mika followed her outside and joined her.

"We weren't so terrible. We loved that house."

"We loved each other in what we could get of that house," she added quietly, and he took her fingers, pressing his mouth to her knuckles. "That's where I fell pregnant."

A breeze stirred up sand from the beach below them, and this time, he did wrap his arm around her, and drew her close.

"Er… Lani, Mika, sorry to interrupt. I think I'm done."

Mika released her quickly. Manu was standing behind them in the doorway, wiping his hands on a towel. His brother raised his eyebrows at them both. Lani pretended to ignore it, smoothing down her hair, thanking him for his work, telling him again how grateful she was.

They hadn't told anyone the extent of their reconnection. At least, *he* hadn't. But something else he knew about electricians, who spent their days in and out of people's homes making small talk, was that they weren't the best at keeping secrets.

CHAPTER FIFTEEN

"EVERYONE'S TALKING ABOUT IT, so what's the deal?" Mele was looking at her expectantly from the passenger seat and Lani kept her face neutral.

"I don't know what you're talking about," she said, focusing on the swaying palms through the windshield, praying for the light to change. Mele scoffed at her over the cage on her lap.

"We all have eyes, Lani."

Anela giggled from the back seat, as if she too knew what Mele was talking about. Who *didn't* know? she thought to herself, cursing the way she'd gotten careless with Mika; too comfortable. This island wasn't his home anymore. He didn't want the life she wanted... He didn't want kids around, and he had his reasons for that, she supposed, although she had to wonder how much guilt had influenced his decision—he'd been such an amazing father. But he'd backed off trying to hang out with Anela lately, too, and she knew he was probably freaking out inside, that because they were sleeping together she might also start loading parental responsibilities on him. She had vowed to have a good time while she could; that was all. That was all he wanted, too...surely?

"Let's just get this bird released, okay," she sighed, taking a left at the sign for the road to the national park. Her mind had a tendency to get all worked up about what this whole Mika thing really meant to her, if she didn't keep it busy on other things.

The albatross was doing much better and she was determined to get it to her contact at the Division of Forestry and Wildlife in the park before sunset. Mele had a keen interest in all the local bird life, something Lani had instilled in her whenever the girl had spent time with her, and now the teen came to every single release day with her. Each experience was filmed and added to her YouTube channel for her however many thousands of followers to comment on. Lani didn't know too much about how all that worked, but Mele was certainly becoming somewhat of a conservation expert in the eyes of all those followers, and pride put a smile on Lani's face whenever she saw the way her neighbor's daughter interacted with the birds.

Just as she was about to make another turn, something caught her eye. Was that... Mika's car? It was parked haphazardly on a verge, just off the road. She pulled her car to stop and told the girls to stay put as she jumped out and sprinted toward it.

It was definitely Mika's car. But why was it here? And why at this particular address?

Then she realized something else. This was Kai Kalama's warehouse. The same yellow logo screamed from the shutters across one window. Of course! She'd only seen it properly from the beach side, never paid much attention from the road.

"Mika?" She hurried up the driveway.

Everything was quiet, no sign of him or Kai, or anyone, but the damage from the storm was evident. The wind had uprooted trees, and broken branches littered the yard. The front was a mess and a downstairs window had been smashed. She stepped over a few shards of glass, still strewed across the ground, and called for Mika again. Where was he? He'd probably come here to confront Kai about dodging the site checks; that would be such a typical Mika thing to do, she thought, a little annoyed. He'd be gone soon enough, and she'd be the one left dealing with the consequences!

Creeping closer to the window, wondering how her world had got so shaken up again and admitting that it was, actually, the most alive she'd felt in years, she peered inside. The vast warehouse was all but empty, save for a few boats and what she assumed were water sports equipment locked up and covered in tarps. A light shone from beneath one of the doors off the main space. It was the only light she could see in the whole place.

Then, was that…a whimpering animal? Maybe another victim of the storm!

Curiosity and fear that there might be an injured animal inside got the better of her. Lani hitched up her dress and prepared herself.

"What do you think you're doing?"

Lani sprang back from her position halfway through the window and accidentally hit her head. "Mika?"

Mika's face was a mixture of amusement and shock, his hair damp and his eyes mischievous and twinkling.

"Were you seriously about to break and enter Kai Kalama's place?" He grinned, folding his arms like a school headmaster who'd just caught a student doing something reckless.

"What are you doing here?" she accused, smoothing out her clothes and hair. "I saw your car!"

"I was on the way back from a dive with Manu and I thought…"

"I know what you thought," she snapped, aware that beneath her annoyance she was actually touched that he wanted to help her so much, and angry at herself that she was letting him in again to the point that it was going to hurt, badly, letting him go.

Mika stepped closer, leaving her breathless. "You were, weren't you? You were one step away from crawling through that window!"

He cupped her face and kissed her, and for a moment she was so thrown she kissed him back, grinning now underneath his mouth. How did he do this; make her forget why she *shouldn't* be doing this? His kiss was salty from the ocean and needy, his lips demanding and hungry. His tongue teased her mouth as if she were the most delicious thing he had ever tasted, and he hadn't eaten in days, even though he'd only left her bed at six thirty this morning, after he'd certainly had his fill.

"You're one sexy burglar," he growled, cupping her backside now and squeezing it with intent, and Lani's laugh became a groan of hot desire, right before the animal's whimpering noises stole the smile from their faces.

In one second Mika was at the window himself, looking in, and Lani was smoothing down her shirt again, flustered. Suddenly, something moved in the shadows.

Lani gasped as she saw what it was. "It's a dog, Mika."

Mika followed her eyes to the sandy-colored golden retriever lying in the shadow of a desk some ten feet away. She could see it clearly now her eyes had adjusted. Whoever's dog it was, it was likely injured, hungry and dehydrated. Lani instructed him to give her a leg up.

Mika didn't look sure. "It's not breaking and entering if we're helping an injured animal," she reasoned. "Lots of animals were displaced after the storm. Someone could be missing this one!"

Mika helped her up somewhat reluctantly, mumbling something about how he was pretty sure this was still breaking and entering, and she was just about to drop through to the other side on her feet when the golden retriever gave a gut-wrenching howl, nearly breaking her heart.

"It's okay, baby," she cooed, "we're coming!"

Mika climbed in expertly after her and the dog limped over to them, relief written all over his goofy face. Lani cradled the fluffy animal in her arms. Sure enough, the dog was injured; his left front paw was bloodied and bruised, and she supposed he'd been struck by something before jumping in here and injuring himself further.

"There's no collar, but he could be chipped. We'll have to check."

Mika offered her his shirt as a makeshift carrier for the animal, and before she could refuse he was unbuttoning it and standing shirtless in the warehouse. She couldn't help the way her eyes kept running over his impressive muscles, or how her lips kept tasting his kisses as together they carried the dog toward the window and made to lift it outside. But no sooner had they managed, than Mika turned back and scrambled in again, and made straight for the door. The one with the light underneath.

"I just have to check," he said, pulling a face and shrugging, even as she begged him not to.

"The kids are in the car!" she called out, suddenly remembering she'd left them there waiting for her, with the albatross. How was this her life now?

Lani didn't know whether to be amused as Mika's shirtless frame yanked the door open and disappeared…or horrified.

Mika still couldn't believe what he'd just discovered in the warehouse. He knew they should probably get away from the warehouse before they could see to the dog, so he'd driven behind Lani to the national park.

Mele and Anela were watching them now, Mele still clutching the albatross's cage as he and Lani carried the injured dog toward the park's medical station and set about fixing up his wounds. Thankfully the dog seemed brighter already, thanks to a generous supply of food and water, and he was chipped, too, it turned out. His owner, a lady in her late sixties, had been looking for him since the storm.

"He'll be fine, soon," he said to Lani now, glancing around the wooden shack that constituted a med facility and a meeting point for Lani and her wildlife rep pals. It was a communal space filled with an assortment of different objects. Half-filled thermoses, net baskets, car parts and a textbook about marine biology all had to be moved before they could put the animal on the table in the corner, but soon, her contact arrived and Mika took a step back, watching her and watching how the kids watched her, like they were in awe of everything she did. Even the teenager.

He went to the window, realizing he hadn't intended to be here for the albatross's release. Lani had mentioned this morning that releases were something she usually did with Mele and Anela, and he'd changed the subject before she could invite him, too.

Sensing he might be getting too close for her comfort, and for his own comfort too, he had taken a step back with Anela the past few days. There was a very high risk he was getting attached as much to the little girl as to Lani, which was ruffling his feathers; where had this come from? He'd been a terrible father once, been so sure he'd never get the chance again, been *afraid* of getting the chance again, perhaps, in case he messed up. But Lani was managing. *She* wasn't messing up, far from it…

"So are you going to tell me what was behind that door?" she said now in a hushed tone, walking with him outside with the albatross.

Behind them Mele was setting up a camera on a tripod. In the distance he could see the lighthouse, a pillar of white on the cliffs that jutted from the park out into the ocean, and the wind blew her hair from its ponytail around her face.

"I'm so curious now!" she continued.

Mika bit back a smile. "Let's just say Kai, or whoever handles that warehouse, has a very nice collection of plants."

Lani frowned at him. Then he saw the penny drop. "No way! You mean…"

"The kind of plants that could land someone in trouble, if they should be accidentally uncovered by the wrong people."

Behind them, Anela was performing a little dance so that Mele could test her camera shots for the bird's release, and he lowered his voice. "I guess we know why he didn't want that site inspection."

Lani wrinkled up her nose. "Yes. But just because he's a keen gardener, so to speak, it doesn't mean he's automatically at fault where the dolphins are concerned."

Mika nodded sagely. "You're right. We still need a sample, though, and he has to agree to it. If we go ahead and get one ourselves, it'll raise too many questions."

"At least we have some leverage," she told him.

"You've been watching too many crime shows," he chuckled, and she rolled her eyes, just as his phone rang in his pocket. He fished it out, expecting Manu to tell him to check his email for the photos he'd just uploaded from their recent dive, but it was Megan.

"Megan?" Lani had read his screen, and now she was trying not to appear too interested in who Megan was, which tickled him more than it should. He told her it was his colleague, and that she was probably checking again on when he'd be back in California.

"Oh," she said, drawing her eyes away even as he was halfway through explaining the Safe-Coast Guardian project. "That sounds important. I thought you were doing something with sharks in Egypt."

"There's a *lot* going on," he explained.

"I see."

He waited, expecting her to ask when exactly he was leaving, but still, she didn't. "I suppose your life is waiting for you to get back to it," she said instead, after a moment. "Just as mine will carry on without you, like it has since we signed the divorce. Don't let us stop you, Mika."

Okay, then.

Mika felt his jaw tick. He was about to say something rather biting when a vision of the house struck him out of nowhere—that house, for sale again out on the beach, the beach they'd had their eyes on since their teenage years. He hadn't even asked her how she'd wound up with that brochure but it had felt like a sign. Was he back on the right track, finally, in a place he felt he belonged, with Lani, who he'd never stopped loving?

Mika rolled his eyes at himself. Lani had turned to Mele already. Soon all of her attention was back on the girls and somehow, the next time he tried to meet Lani's eyes, she seemed so indifferent to his presence that she might not have noticed at all if he'd strapped himself to the bird's feathery wings and flown away to the lighthouse with the albatross.

CHAPTER SIXTEEN

THE HEAVYSET LADY with graying hair and glasses opened the door a crack, as if wary of a sudden attack. Lani smiled warmly.

"Hi, Mrs. Rosenthal," she said, almost bumping into Mika as the golden retriever started yanking on his leash, desperate to get to his owner.

"Lani and Mika, together again." Mrs. Rosenthal beamed, flinging open the door and looking between them as she fussed over the dog and beckoned them inside. "I couldn't believe it when I heard you both found Bones. Come, come inside. It's been a while since I saw you two together."

Mika hadn't seemed too keen on going with her to take the dog home after they'd dropped Mele and Anela off back at the house. But the dog's owner had turned out to be Mrs. Rosenthal, their old church group tutor, and the woman had sounded so excited on the phone at the prospect of seeing him again. Rather begrudgingly he'd joined her.

Soon they were being served cold lemonade and warm, thick, chocolate cookies, as if she'd been expecting the two kids who'd once run away from her church group to play on the beach.

"You were pretty mischievous when you were kids," she teased them now, taking a seat in the chair opposite.

Lani smiled and nibbled a cookie as Mika shifted uncomfortably in the chair. Bones seemed to like him; the dog kept snuffling his shorts, but Lani knew he was only here for the dog and Mrs. Rosenthal. It felt a lot to her like he was backing away from her, one foot off the island already, his head already in his work back in California. What was the point in pretending this hadn't been going to happen? All the spontaneous hot kisses, and early-morning lovemaking in the world wouldn't change that, or the fact that their past still brought up more heartache than she cared to try to handle.

Lani made polite small talk with the older woman, and tried to act like everything with Mika was fine, even though it wasn't. She wasn't about to *present* as if his approaching departure was bothering her, even though it was. Ugh. His kisses were addictive; they'd fired her up and had her thinking things she hadn't dared to think in ages. That house, too…the one for sale. Last night, she'd had a dream that he'd bought it, and told her he wanted her to live in it with him.

So strange!

Mrs. Rosenthal suddenly paused midsentence and reached for a box on the side table. The woman's lined face broke into another broad smile as she passed them both a photo each.

"I dug these out when I knew you were coming. Look at you two, all those years ago!"

Lani felt her pulse start to throb through her smile at the photo of her and Mika. He was around thirteen years old, she no more than eleven, their arms slung around each other's shoulders, sand in their hair from another day spent running wild on the beach when they should have been brushing up on the Bible with Mrs. Rosenthal.

"Wow," she heard herself murmur, as Mika studied his own photo next to her.

His picture had them both side by side in the classroom, seemingly oblivious to everyone else. She was staring at him with a goofy look on her face while he was grinning straight at the camera. Her crush was achingly obvious here. Mika could see it now. She could literally see him processing it.

"You were cute," he said to her without looking away from the photo.

"Yeah, well, everything changes," she muttered, and tried to change the subject.

The older woman shook her head fondly. "I remember thinking you'd go far," she said softly. "When I heard about what happened with your little girl, I was so worried for you both, but here you are now, taking everything in anew with open hearts… I'm not the only one around here who's proud of how far you've come."

Lani swallowed. Who else had been talking about them behind their backs? Everyone, probably.

"It was a long time ago," she said, hearing how choked her voice was coming out.

Mrs. Rosenthal pressed her hand to Mika's arm, then to Lani's over the table. "But you never really heal, do you, from something like that?" she said kindly, before getting up to fetch more lemonade.

"Life has moved on," Mika said carefully. "Lani and I have both managed to keep on moving forward."

"He's going back to California soon," she added, hoping her disappointment didn't show; maybe he'd counter her statement with some kind of new development, she thought, while guilt crashed over her yet again. Mrs. Rosenthal was right: you never could heal from something like that. In more than twenty years she had only been to Iolana's grave maybe three or four god-awful times.

When Mika said nothing, she felt the stone sinking further in her stomach, weighting her shoulders. Mika's eyes roved over her face but she refused to meet his gaze as she put her photo down.

"Shame you're leaving us again, Mika. This place always was better for having you around. You Mahoes," she laughed, before continuing to reminisce about the past with stories about their shenanigans, including when they'd sneaked off to go swimming against her orders one day and come home with an injured red-crested cardinal. "You nursed that bird back to health together," she said and smiled. "It's hardly surprising you went on to make healing animals your profession. Individually, of course. How is life in California, compared to here, Mika?"

Individually, of course.

Lani could barely look at Mika as he talked about his projects. This was excruciating: hearing someone who'd known them bringing up all these happy times, while simultaneously reminding them of everything they no longer had together.

Lani was shocked to feel Mika's hand clasp hers suddenly underneath the table, but as he continued talking about his work in California, the people he'd met and what he was learning about the sharks, Lani couldn't stop the panic rising inside her. There had never been anyone else for her but him, never, and maybe there never would be. She'd grown to be okay with that, but now she'd been reminded what it was like to be loved by him, it was going to be so much harder when he left again.

Think of Anela, she told herself, untangling her fingers from him, remembering the adoption pack at the house.

She hadn't told anyone about it yet, but the

thought of Anela going anywhere else didn't sit right with her at all. She and Anela could have an amazing future together…if only she could forget the way *Mika* had always made—and *would* always make—her feel. Mika, who seemed so dead set on a life without children in it.

The sun was setting as they left Mrs. Rosenthal's. Mika was about to take the road back to Lani's house in his car, but she knew she couldn't escape the part of their past she'd been avoiding for much longer.

"We're so close, from here," she said, realizing her voice was as shaky as her hands had been, holding those photographs just now, reliving all those memories.

Mika glanced at her sideways and slowed the car. She knew he knew what she meant.

"You want to stop at the cemetery now?" he said, softly.

Lani nodded mutely, feeling her heart about to burst. "It's time."

Mika nodded and slowly turned onto a road lined with trees, glancing over at her biting her nails before parking outside the wrought iron gates. She took in the worn expression on his face as they sat there quietly for a moment in the car, listening to the birds. Eventually, Lani broke the silence.

"I guess we should go in."

Opening the gates slowly, she let him take her hand again as they stepped inside, just for a moment, as though they were both drawing strength from the other. She held her breath as they walked the single path together past row after row of tidy gravesites, wildflowers blooming around the headstones. Soon, she saw it. The small marble headstone glinting in the late-evening sun. She heaved a breath, which promptly lodged in her throat.

"It's so hard to imagine her in there," she said to him, her voice strangled even more by the overwhelming emotions.

A single rose lay on the marble slab; from someone in Mika's family, probably. Mika walked up close, taking her with him, and she found herself leaning into him, holding his entire arm for strength now as she took in the shiny headstone. The inscription on the marble read Iolana Mahoe. Forever in our Hearts. Lani felt the tears well up. Inescapable.

She flinched as Mika ran his fingers over the words, then cast his eyes up to the granite angel perched on the top. It had been a gift from the community, a sign that the angels were watching over their daughter. It should have been comforting to Lani, but it wasn't. She looked around at all the other graves nearby; different stories of grief and tragedy were etched into every single headstone, like chapters in an unfinished book. Iolana's was just one of many. There were people in the town who'd never remember she'd so much as existed, and she, Iolana's own mother, hadn't even been here often enough to remind anyone. Where were *her* flowers, even now?

"How are you, little one?" Mika whispered to the marble slab, and his words, so full of remorse, were like knives that slashed what was left of Lani's strength. With a sob, her knees turned to jelly and she stumbled, almost falling to the mossy ground.

Mika caught her, put his arm around her shoulders and held her close as she cried.

"It's okay," he said, pressing a kiss to her temple as if it alone might stop her reeling, but she could feel his chest contracting now, as if her sobs had penetrated his hardened exterior and were threatening to break him, too.

"I never come here," she said now, sniffing, dragging a hand across her eyes. He pulled her closer as the guilt crashed over her. "I haven't been here in forever, Mika. I just… I can't do it. I should be the one putting roses on her grave…"

"It's okay," he said again, turning her to face him. He took her face in her hands and tilted it up to his, wiping away her tears with his thumbs. "We're here now for Iolana. That's all that matters. And you know she's not really *here*, right? She's somewhere else, somewhere better—you know that."

Lani watched as a single tear slipped from his

eye and threatened to travel down the side of his face. She made to wipe it away as he'd done hers, but his fingers stopped her hand. He pulled her against his chest, breathing into her hair.

The sun had dipped low now, casting an orange hue over the cemetery, and the birdsong seemed even louder than before. Lani felt her heart ache as she held him, and felt his heart beating against hers like a drum. Then she felt the warmth of his words through her tears as he sat with her and began to tell her stories about Iolana, like he'd been bottling it all up and only now was able to speak out loud about their daughter's life and all the memories they'd made together. This was just as important to him as it was to her, she realized suddenly with a flicker of shame. She'd been so selfish, refusing to come with him till now.

"What about that time when we were camping out by the lake?" he said, recalling the night they'd all spent under the stars, telling Iolana stories of Hawaiian legends around a small campfire. "She just wanted to stay up all night and watch for shooting stars. We must have seen dozens that night."

"Remember when she saw the deer?" Lani followed, smiling now at the memories and resting her head on his shoulder. "We had to get her a stuffed one, right after that."

It was still so hard to accept that she was gone, but the longer they stayed there talking, letting the grief consume them and wash through them and out of them, the more at peace she started to feel.

Next time, even if she'd be thinking of Mika in California, thousands of miles away again, wishing more than anything that he were here, Lani knew she'd have the strength to come alone.

CHAPTER SEVENTEEN

"WELL, WHAT DO you know? Kai Kalama finally agreed to the site test," Mika said, putting the phone back down. He couldn't help but feel victorious, although Lani, who was perched on the edge of the desk with the bird she was holding, looked like she was biting her tongue.

"What?" he laughed.

She shook her head. "I know you told him we were driving past when we heard that injured dog, and 'accidentally' discovered his secret garden while we were looking for it."

"I did what I had to do." He shrugged, running a gentle hand across the bird's soft head, then pressing his lips to hers over it.

"He's probably clearing up that garden as we speak—the inspectors will be there this afternoon."

She laughed softly as he turned his attention back to the baby seal in its small tank. The poor little thing had been brought to them severely dehydrated after being caught up in some sea trash. It was halfway through a course of fluid therapy. Lani's eyes felt like burning lasers on him as he checked the catheter and tried not to think about what he'd do if they *didn't* locate the source of these chemical nasties before he was due to return to California. Not that he wanted Kai Kalama, or anyone on the island, to be found guilty of intentionally putting marine life in danger, but he'd exhausted almost all sources already and time was ticking.

He couldn't hold off on getting back to the stakeholders about the briefing much longer, but it was more than the dolphins here that was causing him to stall.

"Mika!" Anela came bounding into the sanctuary with Kiki close behind. They'd been inseparable since the luau. "Look what we found in the school library!" she said excitedly, thrusting a book at him. *A Life in the Eye of Nature.*

"That was my favorite," Lani said, peering at the pages over his shoulder, so close he could smell the honeysuckle in her shampoo. "You put your whole heart into that."

For a moment the four of them were silent, admiring the glossy black-and-white and color photos of nature that he'd taken almost three whole decades ago: delicate images with his new zoom lens, focused in on birds with wings spread wide, bumblebees at rest, blossoms in full bloom and wildflowers swaying in the breeze. He'd self-published the book, just to distribute around the community.

"Look, it's for you," Kiki said to Lani, jabbing a finger at the dedication. "'To my Beloved Lani.'"

Anela clapped her hands and prodded them both, reciting "Beloved, beloved, beloved..." But Mika bristled. So did Lani. His throat tightened tenfold at the look on her face: one of pride, but also apprehension. When Anela asked if he would come play ball with her and Kiki out on the beach, he made his excuses and left the sanctuary altogether.

Driving in his car toward the lighthouse he let his thoughts run wild. Anela was starting to want him around, requesting his presence more often, and he found himself wanting it, too...but what kind of a father figure would he be? Not a great one!

Dropping to the rocks outside the towering lighthouse, he let the wind tousle his hair and fixed his eyes on the swirling gulls searching for fish. But he saw only Lani, crying in his arms the other day at the cemetery, breaking down in her grief. Then, miraculously, laughing, reciting long-forgotten stories of things she'd done with Iolana. Things they had both done with their daughter. They had actually laughed, right there, sitting beside her grave together. He didn't think in a million years he'd ever be doing that...or any of this.

Something had changed irrevocably in that cemetery; a load had been lifted from his back, and maybe from hers, too. She'd been right, he supposed, the other week, when she'd reminded him that they hadn't really known how to be parents back then, back when he'd been working so damn hard, thinking it was what they'd all needed, instead of giving his presence and time. Later he'd felt so guilty, thinking maybe she didn't know how much he'd loved her and Iolana. Those precious moments when he hadn't been working had been some of the best of his whole life.

Mika was so lost in thought out on the cliffs that he barely heard his phone. Pulling it from his pocket, he sprang to his feet.

"Meet me at Hook's Bay. As soon as you can," Lani said. Then she promptly hung up.

The little boat sped over the waves with intent and Lani watched Mika's face, etched with determination as he steered it expertly, his eyes scanning the horizon over their heads. His shirt was half-undone again, the sun glinting off the top of his exposed chest, revealing a few inches of sun-kissed skin. Skin she had spent far too much time pressed up against recently, imprinting on...reclaiming.

Ugh. She was getting in far too deep, and neither had brought up what all of this really meant. Coward. She was a coward. She should just ask him to stay, but he'd already left her once, and it would be unbearable hearing him say he was choosing another life a second time. And why wouldn't he, when he didn't want to be a dad, a foster dad or any kind of dad? He'd barely spent three seconds with Anela lately.

"Where is the whale?" Anela said beside her on the back seat now, and Lani tore her eyes away, realizing her heart was acting crazy again.

"We're not there yet," she told her, pulling her arm around her tighter, and double-checking the straps on her lifejacket for the thousandth time.

She still couldn't believe the girl had asked to come out on the boat, but looking at her now, watching Mika at the wheel, she knew the child was entranced by him. She'd go wherever he went at this point. Anela pretty much worshipped the ground he walked on, no thanks to him making her face her fears in a way Lani herself hadn't ever been able to do. If he still thought he wasn't good father material, he was crazy. She'd told him he'd been an amazing father to Iolana, but now... maybe he still didn't believe it. He'd been withdrawing from any group activities as fast as they'd been making progress with Anela and earlier on today, he hadn't been able to get out of the sanctuary fast enough. Her foster daughter would be gutted when he left. She had to protect her—she'd already lost her mother! This reunion, or fling, whatever it was, had been fun but...

But...

God, she should never have started this, even if being at the cemetery with him had changed things for the better somehow. Falling back into bed after that, back at her place, had seemed inevitable. Healing, maybe.

Lani furrowed her brow under her sunglasses. There it was again, the rickety old roller coaster of thoughts about Mika taking her up, down and sideways. It just wouldn't stop!

Suddenly, Anela's excited cries brought her back to the moment. She was pointing out into the distance, past Mika at the wheel. Lani followed her finger. The giant whale's head was sticking out of the water near the fishing boat they were approaching, and the people on board were waving them over urgently. It was just as they'd described on the phone.

"Wow!" Anela stood excitedly, but Lani pulled her down again quickly as Mika powered up their engine. They moved closer cautiously toward it, and the fishermen beckoned them in.

"She's been nudging the boat wherever we've gone for the last hour," one of the burly guys called out to them over the side.

Mika lowered the anchor carefully. Lani didn't let go of Anela's hand. Her heart was in her throat already.

"Stay there, sit still, don't move," Mika told the girl now, and Anela nodded mutely.

By the look on his face, Lani was getting the distinct impression that she probably shouldn't have given in and let the girl come. But it was so momentous that she'd even asked, Lani had felt compelled to encourage her any way she could!

In the water, the whale's head went for the fishing boat again, then turned to them. Lani held her breath and held on to Anela, waiting for impact, but Mika was zipping up his wet suit already, pulling a snorkel over his head. It dangled about his neck as he leaned over the edge. Tentatively, when the whale didn't hit their boat, Lani followed, never letting go of Anela. Together they took in what they could see of the gray pilot whale.

"I think it requires our assistance," she said now.

"I think you're right." Mika frowned.

"How do you know?" Anela asked curiously.

"See those things on its head and back?" she said now, pointing over the side.

"They're called cyamids, or whale lice," Mika followed, motioning to the pale creatures that looked a bit like crabs, which were crawling about on the animal's giant head like strange little white aliens with claws.

Lani listened as he explained how they could be beneficial for the whales by feeding on all the other nasties on their bodies, like healing wounds and algae, but he guessed the whale was uncomfortable, having so many of them clinging on.

"She's probably itchy. We'll have to lend a hand, or the whale will just keep asking humans for help," he said, reaching for a set of fins.

Anela looked fascinated, Lani thought, watching as she stuck a tentative hand out toward the gentle creature. To her surprise, the whale lifted its head to her, and blew air around her face. Mika dived in front of her like lightning, even as Anela squealed in delight.

"It's okay," Anela told him, promptly moving him aside with her little hands. "I think she likes me," she beamed, and Lani couldn't help laughing. Then she noticed the look of apprehension on Mika's face, the way he wrung his hands and turned away. Her stomach churned at his distress, but she wouldn't show it; Anele deserved this moment.

The whale did indeed seem to show a special interest in her. Lani dared to reach out to it, too, and in seconds, she had plucked a cyamid from the creature's head. Quickly, Anela followed, giggling in joy. The whale stayed close and still, as if this grooming session was indeed what it had been begging for, and soon, all three of them were peeling the critters away and dropping them back into the ocean, and there wasn't a hint of the girl who'd been so terrified of the ocean just a few short weeks ago.

Mika however, still looked agitated. He kept glancing at her and Anela, as if he expected a giant octopus to emerge and curl its giant tentacles around them and drag them both to the ocean floor.

"See how far she's come," she whispered proudly

to Mika, just as Anela leaned a little too far and almost toppled overboard.

Lani's grip on the lifejacket was strong, but Mika lunged for the girl again. With one swift move, he grabbed her shoulders and pulled her to safety on the deck, leaving Lani feeling useless. She hovered behind him as he dropped to his knees in front of Anela.

"You have to be more careful," he scolded.

Anela bit her lip. "Sorry, Mika."

"I'm serious, Anela, you shouldn't even be out here!"

Lani covered her mouth. "Mika!"

Anela crossed her arms and looked at him defiantly. "Why not? You wanted me to go in the water."

He turned to Lani now. "She shouldn't be here!"

Silence.

Lani pursed her lips. She wanted to defend the young girl's exuberance, and her own decision for bringing her, but she knew he was reacting this way for the same reason she'd lost her cool that time he'd stayed down in the water with Nala during their dive. He was frightened of losing someone else he cared about.

She stayed quiet as Mika turned away from them both, adjusting his snorkel, preparing to jump into the water. A palpable tension radiated from him like heat from a fire, but she bit her tongue and counted to ten in her head. He was just being protective. She could see what a good father figure he could be to Anela if only that was what he wanted. Judging by his face now, though, he didn't. He wanted to get away from them both again. But when was he leaving?

"Let's keep going—you just have to be more careful," she warned Anela now, determined not to let their own issues ruin the girl's day. This was a breakthrough for her.

Anela continued peeling the critters from the whale, albeit with a bit less excitement than before. Mika was silent for the rest of the mission. And he didn't speak during the whole ride back, either.

Maybe, Lani decided, it was time for a real talk—one that did not just end up back in the bedroom, burying their issues under their prominent sexual attraction. Even if there *were* admittedly moments of healing now, when the shadows seemed fewer and the burden lighter, it seemed he'd never be ready to take on the kind of parental responsibilities she was ready for. All the more ready, perhaps, because of him? He'd helped Anela more than she ever had!

"Dinner tonight?" she braved when they pulled the boat up, looking at him hopefully. Regardless of their relationship, whatever that was, he meant something special to Anela now. She'd make his old favorite, lasagna, maybe with a salad and some wine, and she would tell him about her plans to adopt Anela. He deserved to hear it from her, instead of later down the line, through someone else. She also needed to ask if he'd consider visiting her ever. Anela would like that, too. Maybe he wouldn't be opposed to doing that, once in a while.

"I'm making lasagna. Anela's doing the sauce."

"I can't tonight," he said abruptly. "I said I'd have dinner with my family."

Oh.

Mika was coiling up the ropes now, wet suit down around his waist, and he was not looking at her. Time to try a new tactic—honesty. Lani instructed Anela to go wait by the car, then the words stumbled out.

"Mika… I just thought we could talk."

He sighed heavily, refusing to meet her gaze. "This isn't working, Lani."

Lani balked inside. She opened her mouth to reply but one look at his hardened expression destroyed the words on her lips. He stepped closer.

"This was always going to end badly. I can't seem to ever do the right thing around you or Anela. I completely overreacted in the boat."

She hung her head. "I know why you overreacted, Mika, I know. But—"

"I'm just not cut out for this dad stuff," he interrupted. "It wasn't anything I asked for, Lani. Besides, I have a life somewhere else now. I think we've been getting carried away."

Digging her teeth into her cheeks, she curled her fingers up hard into her palms. They just got carried away? It was true, they had, but there was love here, too. Love that was pointless fighting for if he didn't want to be a father, her internal voice warned her.

Think of Anela. It's your job to protect her now; she's already lost her parents!

"I need you to tell her that you're leaving, Mika," she said, fighting back her tears—no, she would not cry right now. "Tell her now, so the news doesn't come as a shock," she demanded, straightening her back defiantly.

Mika glared directly into her eyes. His face was a mask of anger, and it looked like a hurricane had taken up residence inside his brain.

"Just tell us both *when*," she insisted, before she could chicken out. "So I can make arrangements."

He snorted and tossed the rope back into the boat hard, and her heart pounded at her from the inside… Why was she practically ordering him away when all she wanted to do was beg him never to leave her again?

"I'll let you know as soon as I can," he said with an intensity that could shatter glass. "Then you can make all the arrangements you like, without me messing things up for you. Again."

Lani watched in stunned silence as he grabbed his hat and pulled it down over his face. Each step he took toward his car seemed to rip her heart in two, but somehow she managed to stop herself chasing after him.

CHAPTER EIGHTEEN

ANELA SHOULDN'T HAVE been on the boat; she could have been hurt, or even killed, Mika thought for the thousandth time as he flipped his fins below the surface, trying to make his swirling thoughts slow down to the point that they'd disappear. Today, even diving wasn't helping. Even seeing Nala gliding gracefully toward him, looking as happy as a toothy shark could look, didn't altogether push the thoughts of that last altercation with Lani from his head.

He'd messed up with Anela and it was nothing to be proud of, but he'd acted so defensively…so self-righteously…no wonder he wasn't the most popular person right now.

"What's going on?" Manu asked when they were lying on the deck of the boat drying off in the sun. Trust his brother to bring it up instead of just letting him stew.

Mika told him how he'd overreacted to Anela being on the boat, how awful he'd felt about it for the last two days, how he and Lani had argued and how she'd demanded he tell Anela when he was leaving. Probably because she wanted to know herself and who could blame her? All he'd done was make her life even more complicated.

"You're too hard on yourself, but then you always were," was Manu's reply.

"It's better this way, I guess," he sniffed, ignoring his brother and swigging from his water bottle. "Best that we both know where we stand. She pretty much told me she can't wait for me to leave."

As he said it, he grimaced at the horizon. It wasn't entirely true. He'd twisted it all up inside his head so he could feel angry at Lani instead of himself; so he wouldn't have to feel the sting of her rejection, or even more guilt about how he'd overreacted.

Manu said all the things a brother should say: that Lani obviously cared a lot about him; that she was simply worried that Anela was getting too attached to him; that she probably didn't *really* want him to leave at all. Then, seeing his face, he delivered the real kicker:

"Brother, you do know you were always a great dad to Iolana, right?" The look on his face was almost one of pity. It turned his stomach.

Mika turned away. "Lani said that, too, but I don't think I was," he admitted.

"Because she died? That wasn't your fault. She was sick, and you couldn't have known that, neither of you could. Even if you'd been with her, you couldn't have saved her. But if you use it as an excuse to shut your heart down around this kid, you're going to lose them both. Her and Lani."

Manu's brow creased above his sunglasses now. "Tell Lani you still love her, because I know you do. You can still make this work."

"Yeah right, like divorced guys go around saying they're in love with their ex-wives."

"Like divorced guys go around sleeping with their ex-wives," Manu countered. "Mika, you and Lani have never been ordinary, admit it!"

Mika stewed over it all afternoon, which he'd taken off to catch up on paperwork and prepare for his return trip, meetings with Megan, a call with the temporary tenant living in his apartment in Pasadena. As he tidied his things into piles, without managing to actually pack anything at all, Manu's words kept coming back to bite him. He'd said what a great dad he'd been, just like Lani had insisted. He so desperately wanted to believe them both.

And his brother was right about something else, too: he and Lani had never been ordinary. They had been shaking each other's lives up since the moment they'd locked eyes all those years ago. He'd been irrevocably in love with her since the day he'd carried her up that beach, after her shoes washed away on the tide, since she'd looked deep into his eyes and told him jokingly, in the corniest way possible, "You're my hero!" That day, he'd resolved to always be her hero. His world only had one axis from that point on—Lani—and in his grief he'd given up on her, way too soon.

Later, as dinnertime approached, he was still turning things over in his mind, and he still hadn't packed a damn thing or organized a ticket home, when the phone call about the samples came. He didn't pick up at first. As soon as the guys at the lab confirmed the chemical compounds did indeed match the sample they'd finally managed to get from Kai Kalama, he would officially have no reason to be here any longer. The case would be closed, and he'd be free to leave and never get in Lani's way again.

But when he finally did answer, what they ended up telling him was not what Mika had expected at all. The sample didn't match the compounds after all; instead, it pointed to something beyond what any of them could have imagined. He had to go and tell Lani in person. And maybe he should tell her how much he loved her, too, he thought, a new way of living suddenly panning out in his mind. Maybe they *could* try again. They'd had significant barriers to hurdle but they'd come so far these past few weeks, further than they ever had before, in finally talking about what actually went wrong between them. Maybe Lani and Manu were right, and he had been a pretty good dad once. He'd just forgotten, so caught up in grief and guilt over what had never been his fault—or Lani's, either.

As for Anela… It wasn't what he'd expected at all; he'd pushed it away as far as he could, but the truth kept springing back at him like a persistent palm frond—he loved her too. As much as his Honu. Those matching tattoos stood for a lot more than either of them had been putting into their relationship for a long time, but things could change, he thought, grabbing up his car keys. They *would* change…

Mika could hear Anela singing softly on the porch as he walked up the drive. She was playing with the kittens, so he stood quietly for a moment just listening to her voice. It reminded him of Iolana singing nursery rhymes, a sweet little bird, chirping away without any worries in the world. Funny, he thought, feeling a wide smile cross his lips, how often now he could think of his daughter without the tight knot of dread constricting his mind, body and soul.

"Hi, Mika," she called out happily when he walked up the steps.

An open book was still resting on the hammock and he looked around for Lani. Then he saw her shadow through the window, puttering in the kitchen, and his heart lodged in his throat like a wrecking ball at just the thought of telling her how he really felt about her. And that if she wanted him to, he'd go back to California, quit his job, pack his things up and then come straight back to Oahu so they could run the sanctuary together like they'd always planned, and care for Anela, if only Lani wanted all that with him.

"Hi," he said, squatting down next to Anela and smiling gently at her inquisitive face before handing over a small bag full of treats for the kittens. "Thought they might like these."

The little one they'd rescued in the storm scampered over and he scooped it up. Soon the kittens were clambering over them both and Anela was laughing…and Mika knew he had to say something to her, too.

"Hey, Anela, you know the other day, when you got too close to that whale on the boat?"

Anela cocked her head at him over a kitten's head. "Why didn't you want me on the boat? Don't you like me?" she asked.

"It's *because* I like you so much," he said quickly, drawing a deep breath through his teeth. Where to start? "Anela, Lani and I had a daughter once, did she tell you that?"

Anela grew quiet. Her eyes narrowed as she shook her head. "Where is she?"

Mika ran a hand over the mother cat as she purred around his legs. "She died when she was little," he told her, forcing himself to meet her eyes.

"Like my mom did?" Anela said, sadly.

Lani had appeared in the doorway behind Anela now. Strands of her hair fell from her ponytail and framed her face as she took a step forward and put a hand to Anela's head.

"Yes, sweetie, like your mom did," she added softly, throwing him a look he couldn't read. He hoped it was okay, suddenly telling Anela this. "We loved her very much."

Mika's heart was threatening to explode in his chest as Lani lowered herself to her knees beside him and scooped up a kitten. "So, that's kind of why we both get a little nervous when someone we love is in a potentially dangerous situation, but that doesn't mean we don't think you're very brave, or that you should stop coming out on the boat with..." Lani paused, flashed her eyes to Mika and back to Anela. "With *me*," she finished. "You can come out on the boat with me, anytime."

"And Mika?" Anela asked hopefully.

Both of them fixed their eyes on him, and Mika struggled for the words as his heart sank. What was he supposed to say? Lani had just openly stated she expected him to be leaving, and any future boat trips would most definitely not include him. But then, it wasn't like he could blame her for keeping him at arm's length after their spat the other day.

Lani got to her feet and fetched the book from the hammock, and he squeezed Anela's hand a moment. "I need to talk to Lani for a moment," he told her gently. "Do you want to go play inside, and we'll come find you after?"

* * *

Lani let him lead her past the shed with its neat pile of swept-up branches, remnants of the storm that were perfect for firewood, and through the little gate to the lookout spot. As soon as she'd seen him just now on her porch with Anela, she'd had the distinct gut feeling he had come to tell them both exactly when he was leaving and she had needed a moment to actually process it.

She wrapped her arms around herself now and watched him frown, as the dread built up in her belly. Of course, he was always going to leave. She had to be strong, even if watching him with Anela just now had yet again given her reason to think their love could overcome anything…if only he didn't have such an aversion to being a father again.

"I never had that conversation with her, about Iolana," she said, taking the stone steps up to the circular lookout platform beside him. He cast his eyes out to the twinkling ocean alongside her, ran a hand across his jaw.

"I'm sorry. I just thought I owed her a truthful explanation for the other day—"

"No, you were right," she cut in. "She's old enough to know. I just never knew how to bring it up. To be honest, I never wanted to talk about it before because… You know."

"I know," he said gently.

"She hasn't had a nightmare in a while now."

Lani glanced at him sideways, surprised to feel the love building tenfold inside her. Whenever they'd had an argument before, it had only made her want to cling to him more, and something about him in this light, too, standing here…she wished she could kiss him and make up. The last thing she wanted him to do was fix a one-way trip back to California. Now her mind was spinning with all the what-ifs again. Seeing him with Anela, watching her respond and open up to him over these last few weeks had given her the warm glowing feeling she'd had, watching him hold Iolana. She almost said it now.

Why don't you just stay? Because we both love you, Mika.

But if he didn't want what she did, despite how good he was with Anela, her heart would shatter.

"So, did you come to tell us when you're leaving?" The words were out before she had a chance to rein them back in.

Above them the palms ruffled in the breeze and he averted his gaze again. "I came to tell you we have a development," he said, shoving his hands into his shorts pockets. "The compound matched a sample from a different facility. It wasn't Kai Kalama poisoning the dolphins."

Lani struggled to process what he was telling her. "It wasn't Kai?"

Mika explained that it was actually the run-off from Mr. Benos's greenhouses that had contaminated the ocean—an unfortunate oversight from him, as well as his producers. He'd been using the chemicals quite innocently to boost the growth of his fruit and vegetables, without knowing they were toxic to marine life.

She shook her head, aghast. "Mr. Benos? It can't be… He's…so old! And his peaches…"

Lani was aghast. She could barely believe it when Mika told her the chemicals had probably been seeping into the ocean for months, and it was only now that they, and the government, had been alerted to it.

"The officials have no choice but to shut down Mr. Benos's business," Mika told her.

Lani took a breath, overwhelmed by the news. Poor Mr. Benos, he'd probably had no idea what he was doing; he was probably as devastated as they were. And to think about all those produce parcels she had gratefully accepted…

"Ugh, what a disaster," she groaned, and Mika nodded in sympathy. They stood in silence for a moment, her thoughts whirring.

He hadn't uttered a word about his plans for departure yet, and as they made their way back along the path to the house, the tension between them seemed to rise with each step. Part of her wanted to ask him to stay, while another part of her wished he would just leave already so she wouldn't have to wait any longer to feel the heartache that always came back to bite her somehow, when she put her heart in his hands. Best to just have him go and let her get on with things, she thought.

Unless she was being a total coward.

She stopped him on the porch, her heart thumping. "I'm so sorry for what happened the other day, Mika..." she started, her stomach churning with anticipation as she traced the outline of his mouth with her eyes. So many thoughts were swirling in her head now, she could hardly get any of them to make sense. "The thing is, I'm thinking about Anela and how our future looks. I swore nothing would get in the way of that, and you and I have so much history—"

The scream from inside the house cut her off midsentence.

Anela?

CHAPTER NINETEEN

MIKA'S STOMACH DROPPED as they raced inside, his thoughts of what Lani had been about to tell him clean forgotten.

"She sounds hurt," Lani panted as they rushed upstairs together.

Anela was sprawled on the floor in her bedroom, clutching her wrist, her dress all bunched up around her, the kittens scampering around like nothing had happened.

"What happened?" Lani cried, moving the kittens away.

"I fell off the bunk bed, but I was trying to stop the kitten from falling first!"

Mika took charge of the situation, all while his heart raced. They should have been watching her! Anger at himself boiled up inside him as he gently inspected Anela's arm, reassuring her that it wasn't broken but that she would need some ice on it.

"It's just bruised," he said as Lani gathered the sheets that had tumbled from the top bunk with Anela. He could tell from her face, and by the way she was grabbing at the sheets, that she was mad at herself, too; this had been entirely preventable.

"I should have been watching her," she mumbled to herself when they'd gotten Anela back downstairs.

Mika had carried the girl in his arms, and to be fair, she seemed more shocked than hurt, but from his place on the sofa, he heard Lani's anguished sighs as she fumbled around in the freezer for the ice. She was mumbling again, and he knew she was blaming herself, just as he was.

"What if something worse had happened?" she hissed at him, turning as he entered the kitchen. "I wasn't watching her!"

"Neither was I," he said, as calmly as his voice would allow.

"It's not your *job* to watch her, it's mine!" Her words came out as a strangled sound and it froze him to the spot. She dashed her hands through her hair, and resumed her mission in the freezer, as he stood there, feeling the helplessness mount in his heart.

"Lani..." he started. "I'm here to help you."

"Well, it's too late now, the damage is done."

"She's totally fine," he reasoned.

"But she was hurt on my watch. You distracted me, and I let you."

Mika felt his fists ball, but he wouldn't take the bait and play the blame game again. He wouldn't let her panic override his common sense. She was bound to be mad under the circumstances and blame herself, and so was he, but this couldn't be the case forever.

"You have to forgive yourself, for this, and for what happened to Iolana." He took the ice from her gently and told her to sit at the dining table, but she hugged her arms around herself instead. "Lani, we can't let what happened to Iolana rule everything we do. We were finally doing better, moving on..."

"I will *never* move on," she spit, pressing her palms to her eyes, but her breathing wasn't as labored now and her hands had stopped shaking. He put a hand gently to her shoulder, said nothing. Soon, her fingers came up over his, holding him there, like she was steadying herself. This was how she had to handle it, he thought as she apologized softly, pressing her cheek to his hand. She had to let the fury wash through her, not bottle it up. She'd been teaching him the same thing ever since he got back here.

Lani followed him to the living room and watched as he sat with Anela, pressing the ice to her wrist. Soon, though, Lani took over.

"I want my book," Anela said. "Can Mika read to me?"

"Mika has things to do, honey," Lani said.

"Please!" Anela looked between them hopefully, and Mika stalled, conflicted.

His pride and dignity told him to go, to leave

them both, because they didn't need him. But he'd come here to talk to Lani, to tell her he would stay if she felt anything remotely the same as he did. His cowardice would haunt him forever if he didn't.

"Where's the book?" he asked.

"Upstairs in the study," Lani replied.

Mika climbed the stairs, a million emotions running through him like liquid fire. He knew Lani was feeling guilty and needed time to process it, but he also knew she was tough and resilient and had come further than even she realized over the last few weeks. Still, his heart ached for her as he headed into the study.

He took in the bookshelves full of hardbacks along one wall and an ancient teak desk at the far end near the window. Her mother's desk—he recognized it. He ran his hands over it softly for a second, surprised as the image of that beach house flashed into his head again. Lani had talked about putting this desk in there if they ever bought it, how she'd do her work overlooking the ocean. Sighing, Mika located Anela's book on a chair by the window, but something else caught his eye, right underneath. Anela's full name on the first sheet of a stack of papers—adoption papers.

His stomach lurched as he picked them up and took in their contents—they were one hundred percent adoption papers for Anela. Lani had been planning to adopt her all along, and hadn't said a word to him. Probably because she didn't think he was ready for anything like this.

A sound from downstairs brought him back to the moment, and quickly he put everything back in place before anyone noticed he'd been snooping around. But he couldn't unsee this now. How could he?

Making his way back downstairs with the book, his head reeled. He couldn't help but feel touched. Lani had really bonded with Anela. She loved her like her own child…but then, she hadn't always been so eager to have *him* involved. She'd been protecting her future with Anela so vehemently, which was admirable, but where did that leave him? Them?

Handing the book over, he stood there a moment, watching as Lani scooped the girl closer under one arm. She clearly wasn't over *his* part of what had happened after Iolana died. She never would be. Him walking away from their marriage would always come back to bite them.

"I should go," he said now, inching backward toward the door.

"Stay," Anela demanded, patting the chair at the other side of her.

"You can stay," Lani offered, but he shook his head, trying desperately to process what he had just discovered. It was clearly no concern of his, or she would have mentioned it sooner. She was already planning a life for both of them without him around. Of course she was; he'd been kidding himself, thinking they could ever make something work a second time, with their history! She would be much better off without him.

Telling them both he really had to go, he made for the hallway. Lani followed him outside and shut the door softly behind her. Apprehension was written all over her face.

"Mika—"

"I'll be leaving within the next day or two," he said, cutting her off. "I came here to tell you, now we know what's been going on with the dolphins, that I've got to get back. I'll say goodbye to Anela before I do, but..." he trailed off.

Lani had drawn her lips together, and was seething inwardly, he could tell. Suddenly he regretted the lie.

"I knew it," she said, clicking her tongue.

"Knew what?"

"You can't wait to leave again, can you?"

"Again? Lani, you've made it quite clear you don't want me here," he retaliated, stepping up closer to her. "I just saw the adoption papers. You didn't even tell me you were thinking of adopting Anela, all this time!"

Lani looked stunned. Stepping backward, she stared at the ground. "But you don't want another child in your life," she said eventually, shaking her head. "You've made *that* perfectly clear. So it doesn't affect you, does it?"

Mika stared at her, grappling for words, his brain whirling frantically. He had said that numerous times, yes. He had even believed it. But now…now he didn't know *what* to think. He did love Lani, he wanted to fight for her, but could he ever really trust himself not to let her, or Anela, down again? He had as much work going on now as he had back then. What if he wasn't able to split his time the way she'd need him to? He'd live his whole life worrying about not being enough, and missing things that he should be paying more attention to, like Anela's accident just now.

Lani threw her hands in the air. "You know what, you were right before when you said you were just messing things up," she said now. "Anela and I will be fine, so you can go now, Mika. Go live your life."

"This isn't what I wanted—" he started to say, staring deeply into her eyes as he held her wrists. Her expression had melted into a look of longing and for a moment, he thought she was about to kiss him. But as he spoke, her expression clouded over with grief and sadness till she was shoving at his chest.

"Go!"

Mika staggered backward.

"Get it over with, Mika. If you're going to go, just go. It's what you're good at, after all."

* * *

Everywhere Lani looked over the course of the next few weeks, there were reminders of Mika, absolutely everywhere. He was in the sanctuary, in his books, which Anela had taken to reading relentlessly, and he was in her dreams. Every single night.

On the last night before his departure, she had sent Anela with Mele to say goodbye to him, but she herself had bowed out, citing too much work. Instead, she had listened to another of Mr. Benos's profuse in-person apologies, then driven across town and sat on a bench at the cemetery, talking to Iolana, trying not to think that she was potentially letting her own stubborn streak and fear of a second rejection get in the way of her own happiness.

She could have just asked him to stay; wasn't that what she'd been wishing for, and denying, and finding excuse after excuse not to say in case he refused? Now she'd never know.

She found herself talking about Mika to Iolana again today, on—what was it?—the eighth or ninth time she'd visited their daughter's grave since he'd left.

"I do miss your daddy," she admitted now, placing the small bunch of yellow flowers she'd brought beside the candle. No matter how much she tried not to talk about him, how could she *stop* thinking about the laughter they'd enjoyed, even in *this* very place, and all the love they had made, despite their past, and their differences? How had it happened, that they had actually started to heal together, after all this time, only for her to watch him leave again?

"Okay, so I practically marched him off the island," she said out loud, making a sweet old woman at the next gravesite turn in surprise and start looking around for a person. "That was not my finest hour," she continued, with a wave at her.

She'd been consumed by so much emotion, after Anela was hurt on her watch, then discovering Mika had found the adoption papers. She'd just leaped into self-defense mode, then freak-out mode! All she had been thinking about was protecting Anela, doing the right thing by her. After all, he'd mentioned more than once that he didn't want another kid in his life. He'd had every opportunity to tell her that wasn't the case, or that he'd changed his mind, but he'd said nothing. So clearly, this was for the best.

Yes, she decided, yet again. "It's for the best, Iolana. Not that I won't miss him."

Dejectedly she made her way home alone again. She'd felt more alone than ever since his departure. If this was really for the best, why did she feel even more lost than when he'd left the first time?

CHAPTER TWENTY

MANU FOUND LANI one afternoon in the sanctuary. She'd just finished surgery on another turtle victim, and literally just shooed a still-apologetic Mr. Benos out the door—he just wouldn't stop coming over to say sorry, poor guy. She had vowed to make it clear to everyone that he hadn't been causing intentional harm to the dolphins, but she felt so bad for him.

"Lani, I thought I'd find you here," Manu said, closing the door behind him.

A fully recovered Mahina smiled and played with her hair, and the two said a brief hi that made Lani think there was something going on with them that she'd been too caught up in her own thoughts to notice since Mahina had started back at the sanctuary. Interesting.

Lani tore her gloves off and perched on the desk, giving Manu her full attention. Oh, God, had he come with news of Mika? The thought made her cold suddenly. She hadn't heard from him for weeks, not since he'd left, and she was starting to think she never would again.

"What's up?" she asked him, bracing herself.

"I need you," he said, casting Mahina a surreptitious look that set another spark of intrigue aflame. "I was hoping you could come with me? There's an injured animal of some kind around the bay, by the beach..."

"Okay, what kind of animal?" she asked, wondering how the heck he would have found it all the way around the bay, and then come here without even bringing it with him.

"You should go. I'll be fine handling the checkups and feeding," Mahina said, ushering her out the door before she could even so much as remove her white coat.

"I guess I'm coming with you, then," Lani said distractedly, picking up a cage and a blanket for whatever animal he'd found.

Manu was quiet on the drive, and she resisted the urge to ask about Mika. Had he heard anything? Had Mika mentioned them to him at all? Ugh, she scolded herself for even wondering. She had slammed that door shut and now she just had to deal with the consequences.

Soon enough, Manu slowed the car on the roadside and left the engine running as he opened her door. Lani turned to him in confusion, but he told her to get out. "It's down there, on the beach," he said, pointing through the gap in the trees.

Lani climbed out, realizing now where she was. She was right by the house that she and Mika had always talked about buying. And the For Sale sign was nowhere in sight. What a cruel twist of fate, she thought to herself, that the animal should be found here, in a place that would only serve to rub salt in her wounds.

"I'll wait here," Manu said, keeping the engine idling.

Begrudgingly she made her way through the trees adjacent to the house, craning her neck to try to see through the windows on the side. Whoever had bought this place had something truly special on their hands, and she would not be jealous, she decided.

Oh, who was she kidding? This was her dream house! Jealous didn't cover it.

As she made her way down to the beach, the palms seemed to whisper at her; this was private property. But she had to get to this animal…wherever it was. Turning around, she couldn't see anything.

And then, she spotted something moving inside the house. So, there *was* someone there? Maybe they'd already rescued the animal and taken it inside, she thought. Lani approached the house, its beautiful porch spilling right onto the beach. The hot tub was all covered up, the barbecue draped with a tarp, but the plants blooming in their pots carried the scent of jasmine and orchids straight to her nose. She breathed in, wishing she could bottle it, then to her surprise, noticed a trail of flowers up the steps to the yellow-painted back door. It was a path of petals!

What...?

The door was ajar. "Hello?" she called out, making her way tentatively to the top step.

Then she looked down. More petals. These ones spelled out the words Mika Loves Lani.

Lani held her breath in disbelief. Was this real? Mika had done this years ago, too…

"Mika…" she whispered, the word barely leaving her lips as she felt the tears welling up in her eyes.

She stepped over the flowery message, realizing she was shaking. Then, there he was, standing at the bottom of the stairs, a faint smile playing on his lips as he watched her take it all in. He was dressed in khaki shorts, a crisp white shirt, no sign of the bandanna, which she'd actually grown to quite like. For a moment she just stared at him through the blur. Mika stepped toward her and took her hands.

"I'm sorry, false alarm. There is no injured animal," he told her, just as she heard Manu's car speeding off. They'd set her up.

Lani half laughed. "They were in on this, your brother and Mahina. Mika, what is going on, and why are you in this house?"

"It's my house now," he said, sweeping her hair back and cradling her face. "And yours and Anela's, too. I mean, you can take all the time you need. I know I messed up. But this island is my home, *you* are my home. I did a lot of thinking after I left. My work is not the most important thing to me, Lani, you are. And I know what happened to Iolana shouldn't stop me from at least trying to be the best dad I can for Anela."

Lani could barely believe what she was hearing. Tears streamed down her cheeks, faster than he or she could wipe them away. It felt like that dream she'd had, being here with him, surrounded by all these petals and the sound of the waves crashing on the beach, hearing him say *she* was his home.

"I'm so sorry I pushed you away, Mika. I was just scared in case you did it first. In case you don't want what I want for Anela…"

"I want to look after both of you," he said now. "That's all I want, Lani. I thought I didn't want any more children in my life, but my God, I have missed that little girl. I was thinking…" He glanced at her sheepishly. "We could get married, again, better this time, and we could adopt her. Together."

"Are you serious?" Lani was so stunned she laughed and threw her arms around him impulsively.

"Is that a yes?" Mika picked her up, and he spun her around so many times she was dizzy by the time her feet touched the ground.

"Yes, I want that," she managed, just as Mika got to his knee and kneeled before her, a box suddenly in his hand. Her heart raced as he opened it up, revealing an exquisite diamond ring that caught the sun streaming in over the ocean through the open back door.

"Lani," he said softly, "my Honu, for life. Will you do me the honour of becoming my wife? Again?"

Lani gasped, not quite believing what was happening. First the house of their dreams, which he'd only gone and bought for them, and now this. She nodded fervently, barely able to contain her joy as she told him yes, yes, yes! Mika slipped the ring onto her finger and she stared at it in shock and delight, imagining showing Anela. How on earth was this even happening?

He rose to embrace her and they clung together for what felt like an eternity, kissing passionately, until eventually, Mika stepped back and grinned. "Should we explore our new house? I know you've always had plans for it."

"Oh, I have so many plans," she said now, laughing into her hand and catching sight of the ring again. How did she get so lucky?

As they climbed the stairs and marked out what would be their room, and which would be Anela's room and which would be the study overlooking the ocean, she still felt like she was dreaming, and was possibly going to wake up and find this was all just a cruel act of her own imagination.

But later, when they drove to Mika's parents'

place with the news, they organized an impromptu beach party that same night, and with all the congratulations coming at them, she had no choice but to believe this was her new reality. Her, and the only man she'd ever loved, and the little girl they both loved.

Anela was so happy to have Mika back. Just the look on her face as Mika swung her around on the beach and waded into the surf with her was enough to bring the tears right back to Lani's eyes. Tears of total happiness, she realized, wondering when exactly the cloud of pain and grief had stopped following them around. She couldn't quite put her finger on it, she thought, watching them splashing each other and laughing with the sun sinking into the water on the horizon. All she knew was that somewhere along the line, in ways she'd never dreamed possible, she had found the healing she'd needed in the last place she'd expected to find it. And so had Mika.

One year later

Mika couldn't even hide his grin right now. He wrapped his arms around Lani from behind, resting his chin on her shoulder as they both watched Anela take the microphone on the stage. The children's corner of the library was packed; she'd invited all her friends and even some of her schoolteachers were present.

So was Mr. Benos, he noticed now. The elderly man was sitting right at the front, applauding her already. To his credit, he'd done his best to redeem himself for his negligence regarding the chemicals and was now a fervent marine life ambassador in the community, offering his old greenhouse space for officials to host workshops on caring for wildlife and sustainable fishing practices.

They were nothing compared to the parties he and Lani threw, however. The big new house had become a real home, especially since Anela's adoption papers had been completed, and she was now officially their daughter. Their private beach had seen many a get-together by now, lots of singing, dancing, laughing. Sometimes he wondered why he'd stayed away so long, but it was possible that he and Lani were even closer now because of it. They visited Iolana a lot, told her everything that was happening, told her they missed and loved her. But they didn't let the grief darken their days anymore. And while his work was still important, he'd learned to say no when it mattered, to focus on his family, making more precious memories together.

"I don't know how she finds the confidence," Lani whispered now as Anela, dressed in jeans and her dolphin-patterned shirt, tapped the mic and took the small plastic chair, laying Mika's book out on her lap.

"This is my dad Mika's new book," she explained now, picking it up again and flashing the cartoon-like cover at the audience. "He self-published it, like his last book, only this one's for kids."

Mika smiled, as proud of himself and Lani as Anela went on to explain how the proceeds from the book were going to provide educational resources for local schools, teaching them about the importance of looking after the oceans, sharks, dolphins and other marine life.

Anela had become a real ocean ambassador in the last year. Her story about her mother had given her reason to learn more about shark behavior, and to his relief she had only grown to respect and appreciate them more. Sometimes she talked about becoming a marine scientist. Next month she'd learn to dive, and soon… Well, maybe someday she'd meet Nala.

Sure, his book gave her leverage to make regular visits to libraries, schools and even the other beachside towns along the coast, impressing everyone she met, but the thought of having his daughter at his side, spreading his message for a long time to come, made him happier than he'd ever thought possible. Her bubbly enthusiasm and her fantastic imagination were a joy, and a credit to Lani, too, he thought now, hugging Lani tighter.

"Did I tell you I love you yet today, wife?" he whispered, nuzzling on her ear. She turned in his arms, smiling.

"I don't believe you did."

"Well, I love you," he said, whispering now, so no one else in the audience could hear. "And when we get home, I plan to show you just how much."

"I'll hold you to that," she told him.

Sadly, they would have to wait a few hours, he thought. After Anela finished her reading, they had another bird release planned, then his and Lani's parents were coming over—something that was now a pretty regular occasion. The two families loved being reunited, and they all adored Anela, who was always the center of attention.

Whatever happened next in their much-loved, slightly unconventional family unit, he thought, they would take it in their stride. Somehow he had gotten the family he never thought he deserved. But now he had it, Mika was never going to let it go.

* * * * *